Resounding praise for
New York Times bestselling author
ELIZABETH PETERS
and

THE MUMMY CASE

"Amelia Peabody Emerson, archaeologist
extraordinaire, and arguably the most potent
female force to hit Egypt since Cleopatra, is
digging again!"
Philadelphia Inquirer

"Elizabeth Peters returns triumphantly. . . .
Fascinating. . . . The skillful way she blends
humor and suspense really makes this
an enjoyable tale."
United Press International

"Amelia is rather like Indiana Jones, Sherlock
Holmes, and Miss Marple all rolled into one."
Washington Post Book World

"No one is better at juggling torches while
dancing on a high wire than Elizabeth Peters."
Chicago Tribune

"Fun seems to be guaranteed whenever the
prolific Peters brings Amelia Peabody back for
another 19th-century mix of archaeol
comedy, and murder mystery."
Kirkus Reviews

"Thi

Books by Elizabeth Peters

ELIZABETH PETERS

THE MUMMY CASE

HARPER

An Imprint of HarperCollinsPublishers

HARPER

An Imprint of HarperCollins*Publishers*
195 Broadway
New York, NY 10007

Copyright © 1985 by Elizabeth Peters
ISBN 978-0-06-199920-8

First Harper premium printing: March 2011
First William Morrow hardcover printing: September 2007
First Avon Books paperback printing: May 2006

THE
MUMMY CASE

FOREWORD

After the death of the author of these memoirs (of which this is the third volume to appear), her heirs felt that her animated (if biased) descriptions of the early days of excavation in Egypt should not be kept from historians of that period. Since certain episodes involve matters that might embarrass the descendants of the participants therein (and possibly render publisher and editor subject to legal action), it was agreed that the memoirs should appear in the guise of fiction. A certain amount of judicious editing was done, and many of the names were changed, including that of Mrs. "Emerson." However, in recent years rumors have circulated regarding the accuracy of these works and the identity of their author—originated, we suspect, by disaffected members of Mrs. "Emerson's" family, who resent their exclusion from the financial proceeds (modest though they are) of the works in question. The editor therefore wishes to disclaim all responsibility for, first, the opinions expressed herein, which are those of the late lamented Mrs. "Emerson"; and second, certain minor errors of fact, which are due in part to Mrs. "Emerson's" faulty memory and in even larger part to her personal eccentricities and prejudices.

The editor also wishes to apologize for the stylistic peculiarities of this foreword, which seems to have been unconsciously influenced by the literary style of Mrs. "Emerson." She would no doubt be pleased at such a demonstration of the influence she continues to exert on those who were affected by it during her long and vigorous life.

ONE

I never meant to marry. In my opinion, a woman born in the last half of the nineteenth century of the Christian era suffered from enough disadvantages without willfully embracing another. That is not to say that I did not occasionally indulge in daydreams of romantic encounters; for I was as sensible as any other female of the visible attractions of the opposite sex. But I never expected to meet a man who was my match, and I had no more desire to dominate a spouse than to be ruled by him. Marriage, in my view, should be a balanced stalemate between equal adversaries.

I had resigned myself to a life of spinsterhood when, at a somewhat advanced age, I met Radcliffe Emerson. Our first encounter was *not* romantic. Never will I forget my initial sight of Emerson, as we stood face to face in that dismal hall of the Boulaq Museum—his black beard bristling, his blue eyes blazing, his fists clenched, his deep baritone voice bellowing invectives at me for dusting off the antiquities. Yet even as I answered his criticism in kind, I knew in my heart that our lives would be intertwined.

I had several logical, sensible reasons for accepting Emerson's offer of marriage. Emerson was an Egyptologist; and my first visit to the realm of the pharaohs planted seeds of affection for that antique land that were soon to blossom into luxuriant flower. Emerson's keen intelligence and acerbic tongue—which had won him the title "Father of Curses" from his devoted Egyptian workmen—made him a foeman worthy of my steel. And yet, dear Reader, these were not my real reasons for yielding to Emerson's suit. I deplore clichés, but in this case I must resort to one. Emerson swept me off my feet. I am determined to be completely candid as I pen these pages, for I have made certain they will not be published, at least during my lifetime. They began as a personal Journal, perused only by a Critic whose intimate relationship gave him access to my private thoughts—so he claimed at any rate; as his remarks on style and content of my writing became more critical, I decided to disallow the claim and lock up my Journals. They are therefore mine alone, and unless my heirs decide that the scholarly world should not be deprived of the insights contained therein (which may well occur), no eyes but mine will read these words.

Why, then, the gentle Reader will ask, do I infer his or her existence by addressing her, or him? The answer should be obvious. Art cannot exist in a vacuum. The creative spirit must possess an audience. It is impossible for a writer to do herself justice if she is only talking to herself.

Having established this important point, I return to my narrative.

Not only did Emerson sweep me off my feet, I swept him off his. (I speak figuratively, of course.) By current standards I am not beautiful. Fortunately for me, Emerson's tastes in this area, as in most others, are highly original. My complexion, which others find sallow and dark, he described (on one memorable occasion) as resembling the honey of Hymettus; my coarse, jet-black hair, which refuses to remain confined in braids, buns, or nets, arouses in him a peculiar variety of tactile enjoyment; and his remarks about my figure, which is unfashionably slender in some areas and overly endowed in others, cannot be reproduced, even here.

By any standards Emerson is a remarkably fine-looking man. He stands over six feet tall, and his stalwart frame possesses the elasticity and muscular development of youth, thanks to a vigorous outdoor life. Under the rays of the benevolent Egyptian sun his brawny arms and rugged face turn golden-brown, forming a striking setting for the sapphire brilliance of his eyes. The removal of his beard, at my urgent request, uncovered a particularly attractive dimple in his chin. Emerson prefers to call it a cleft, when he refers to the feature at all; but it is a dimple. His hair is sable, thick and soft, shining with Titian gleams in the sunlight. . . .

But enough of that. Suffice it to say that the wedded state proved highly agreeable, and the first years of our marriage were fully as pleasant as I had expected. We spent the winter in Egypt, excavating by day and sharing the delightful privacy of an (otherwise) unoccupied tomb by night; and the summer in England with Emerson's brother

Walter, a distinguished philologist, and the husband of my dear friend Evelyn. It was a thoroughly satisfactory existence. I cannot imagine why I, who am normally as farsighted and practical as a woman can be, did not realize that the matrimonial state quite often leads to another, related state. I refer, of course, to motherhood.

When the possibility of this interesting condition first manifested itself I was not excessively put out. According to my calculations, the child would be born in the summer, enabling me to finish the season's work and get the business over and done with before returning to the dig in the autumn. This proved to be the case, and we left the infant—a boy, named after his uncle Walter—in the care of that gentleman and his wife when we set out for Egypt in October.

What ensued was not entirely the child's fault. I had not anticipated that Emerson's next view of his son the following spring would induce a doting idiocy that manifested itself in baby talk, and in a reluctance to be parted from the creature. Ramses, as the child came to be called, merited his nickname; he was as imperious in his demands and as pervasive in his presence as that most arrogant of ancient Egyptian god-kings must have been. He was also alarmingly precocious. A lady of my acquaintance used that term to me, after Ramses, aged four, had treated her to a lecture on the proper method of excavating a compost heap—hers, in point of fact. (Her gardener was extremely abusive.) When I replied that in my opinion the adjective was ill-chosen, she believed me to be offended. What I meant was that

the word was inadequate. "Catastrophically precocious" would have been nearer the mark.

Despite his devotion to the child, Emerson pined
in the dreary climate of England. I refer not only to
its meteorological climate, but to the sterile mo-
notony of academic life to which my husband had
been doomed by his decision to forgo his Egyptian
excavations. He would not go to Egypt without
Ramses, and he would not risk the boy's health in
that germ-infested part of the world. Only an appeal
from a lady in distress (who turned out to be, as I
suspected from the first, a thoroughgoing villain-
ess) drew him from Ramses' side; and, seeing him
glow and expand among his beloved antiquities, I
determined that never again would I allow him to
sacrifice himself for family commitments.

We decided to take Ramses with us the following
year, but a series of distressing events allowed me to
postpone that pleasure. My dear friend and sister-
in-law, Evelyn, who had produced four healthy children without apparent effort, suffered two successive
disappointments (as she called them). The second
miscarriage threw her into a state of deep depression. For some reason (possibly related to her confused mental condition) she found Ramses' company
comforting and burst into tears when we proposed
to take him away. Walter added his appeals, claiming that the boy's merry little tricks kept Evelyn
from brooding. I could well believe that, because
it required the concentrated attention of every
adult in the household to restrain Ramses from self-
immolation and a widespread destruction of property. We therefore yielded to the pleas of Ramses'

aunt and uncle, I with gracious forbearance, Emerson with grudging reluctance.

When we returned from Egypt the following spring, Ramses seemed nicely settled at Chalfont, and I saw no reason to alter the arrangement. I knew, however, that this excellent situation (excellent for Evelyn, I mean, of course) could not endure forever. But I decided not to worry about it. "Sufficient unto the day," as the Scripture says.

The day duly arrived. It was during the third week in June. I was at work in the library trying to get Emerson's notes in order before he returned from London with the next installment. Some dark premonition undoubtedly brushed my mind; for though I am not easily distracted, particularly from a subject that enthralls me as much as Eighteenth Dynasty rock-cut tombs, I found myself sitting with idle hands, staring out at the garden. It was at its best that lovely summer afternoon; the roses were in bloom and my perennial borders were looking their loveliest. None of the plants had been trampled or dug up; the blossoms had been culled with tender deliberation by the expert in that trade, not torn out, roots and all, to make bouquets for the servants and the dogs; the smooth green turf was unmarked by small booted feet or the holes of amateur excavation. Never before had I seen it in that pristine condition. Ramses had begun walking a month after we moved into the house. A gentle nostalgia suffused me and I brooded in quietude until my meditation was interrupted by a knock on the door.

Our servants are trained to knock before entering. This custom confirms the suspicions of our county neighbors that we are uncouth eccentrics, but I see no reason why the well-to-do should lack the privacy poor people enjoy. When Emerson and I are working or when we are alone in our bed-chamber we do not appreciate being interrupted. One knock is allowed. If there is no response, the servant goes quietly away.

"Come in," I called.

"It is a telegram, madam," said Wilkins, tottering toward me with a tray. Wilkins is perfectly hale and hearty, but he makes a point of tottering, in order not to be asked to do anything he doesn't want to do. I took the telegram, and again the wings of shadowy foreboding brushed my spirit. Wilkins quavered (he quavers for the same reason he totters), "I hope it is not bad news, madam."

I perused the telegram. "No," I said. "On the contrary, it appears to be good news. We will be leaving for Chalfont tomorrow, Wilkins. Make the arrangements, if you please."

"Yes, madam. I beg your pardon, madam . . ."

"Yes, Wilkins?"

"Will Master Ramses be returning home with you?"

"Possibly."

A shadow of some passionate emotion passed rapidly over Wilkins' face. It did not linger; Wilkins knows what is proper.

"That will be all, Wilkins," I said sympathetically.

"Yes, madam. Thank you, madam." He weaved an erratic path to the door.

With a last wistful look at my beautiful garden I returned to my labors. Emerson found me so engaged when he returned. Instead of giving me the affectionate embrace to which I was accustomed, he mumbled a greeting, flung a handful of papers at me, and seated himself at his desk, next to mine.

An ordinary, selfish spouse might have made a playful comment on his preoccupation and demanded her due in the form of non-verbal greetings. I glanced at the new notes and remarked temperately, "Your date for the pottery checks with Petrie's chart, then? That should save time in the final—"

"Not enough time," Emerson grunted, his pen driving furiously across the page. "We are badly behind schedule, Peabody. From now on we work day and night. No more strolls in the garden, no more social engagements until the manuscript is completed."

I hesitated to break the news that in all probability we would soon have with us a distraction far more time-consuming than social engagements or strolls. And, since most archaeologists consider themselves prompt if they publish the results of their work within ten years, if at all, I knew something must have happened to inspire this fiend-ridden haste. It was not difficult to surmise what that something was.

"You saw Mr. Petrie today?" I asked.

"Mmmp," said Emerson, writing.

"I suppose he is preparing his own publication."

Emerson threw his pen across the room. His eyes blazed. "He has finished it! It goes to the printer this week. Can you imagine such a thing?"

Petrie, the brilliant young excavator, was Emerson's bête noire. They had a great deal in common—their insistence on order and method in archaeology, their contempt for the lack of order and method displayed by all other archaeologists, and their habit of expressing that contempt publicly. Instead of making them friends, this unanimity had made them rivals. The custom of publishing within a year was unique to the two of them, and it had developed into an absurd competition—a demonstration of masculine superiority on an intellectual level. It was not only absurd, it was inefficient, resulting, at least in Petrie's case, in rather slipshod work.

I said as much, hoping this would comfort my afflicted husband. "He can't have done a good job in such a short time, Emerson. What is more important, the quality of the work or the date on which it is published?"

This reasonable attitude unaccountably failed to console Emerson. "They are equally important," he bellowed. "Where the devil is my pen? I must not waste an instant."

"You threw it against the wall. I doubt that we will be able to get the ink off that bust. Socrates looks as if he has measles."

"Your humor—if it can be called that—is singularly misplaced, Peabody. There is nothing funny about the situation."

I abandoned my attempts to cheer him. The news might as well be told.

"I had a telegram from Evelyn this afternoon," I said. "We must go to Chalfont at once."

The flush of temper drained from Emerson's face, leaving it white to the lips. Remorsefully I realized the effect of my ill-considered speech on a man who is the most affectionate of brothers and uncles and the most fatuous of fathers. "All is well," I cried. "It is good news, not bad. That is what Evelyn says." I picked up the telegram and read it aloud. "'Wonderful news. Come and share it with us. We have not seen you for too long.' There, you see?"

Emerson's lips writhed as he struggled to find words in which to express his relief. Finally he shouted, "Amelia, you are the most tactless woman in the universe. What the devil ails you? You did that deliberately."

I pointed out the injustice of the charge, and we had a refreshing little discussion. Then Emerson mopped his brow, gave himself a shake, and remarked calmly, "Good news, eh? An honorary degree for Walter, perhaps. Or someone has endowed a chair of Egyptology for him."

"Foolish man," I said with a smile. "You are off the mark. My guess is that Evelyn is expecting again."

"Now that is ridiculous, Peabody. I have no strong objection to my brother and his wife continuing to produce offspring, but to call it wonderful news—"

"My sentiments are in accord with yours, Emerson. But neither of us wrote this telegram. You know Evelyn's feelings about children."

"True." Emerson reflected, pensively, on the peculiar opinions of Evelyn. Then his face became radiant. "Peabody! Do you realize what this means? If Evelyn has recovered from her melancholia, she will no longer require Ramses to keep her company. We can bring our boy home!"

"I had arrived at the same conclusion."

Emerson leaped up. I rose to meet him; he caught me in his arms and spun me around, laughing exultantly. "How I have missed the sound of his voice, the patter of his little feet! Reading to him from my *History of Ancient Egypt*, admiring the bones he digs up from the rose garden. . . . I have not complained, Peabody—you know I never complain—but I have been lonely for Ramses. This year we will take him with us. Won't it be wonderful, Peabody—we three, working together in Egypt?"

"Kiss, me, Emerson," I said faintly.

II

Our neighbors are not interesting people. We have little to do with them. Emerson has antagonized most of the gentlemen, who consider him a radical of the most pernicious sort, and I have not cultivated their ladies. They talk of nothing but their children, their husbands' success, and the faults of their servants. One of the favorite sub-topics under the last head is the rapidity with which the servants' hall becomes acquainted with the private affairs of the master and mistress. As Lady Bassington once declared, in my presence, "They are frightful gossips, you know. I suppose they have nothing better to do. By the by, my dear, have you heard the latest about Miss Harris and the groom?"

Our servants unquestionably knew more about our affairs than I would have liked, but I attributed this to Emerson's habit of shouting those affairs aloud, without regard for who might be listening. One of the footmen may have overheard his cries of rapture at the prospect of being reunited with his child, or perhaps Wilkins had allowed himself to theorize. In any event, the word spread quickly. When I went up to change for dinner, Rose knew all about it.

Rose is the housemaid, but since I do not employ a personal servant, she acts in that capacity when I require assistance with my toilette. I had not called her that evening; yet I found her in my room, ostensibly mending a skirt I could not recall having ripped. After asking what she should pack for the journey to Chalfont, she said, "And while you are away, ma'am, shall I see that Master Ramses' room is got in order?"

"His room is in order," I replied. "I see no reason to do anything more, since it won't remain in order for five minutes after he occupies it."

"Then Master Ramses will be coming home, ma'am?" Rose asked with a smile.

Rose's fondness for Ramses is absolutely unaccountable. I cannot calculate how many cubic feet of mud she has scraped off carpets and walls and furniture as a result of his activities, and mud is the least disgusting of the effluvia Ramses trails in his wake. I replied, rather shortly, that the day and hour of Ramses' return was as yet mere speculation, and that if any action on her part was necessary, she would be informed as soon as I knew myself.

Ramses had no nanny. We had naturally employed one when we took the house; she left after a week, and her successors passed in and out of the place so rapidly, Emerson complained that he never got to know what they looked like. (He had once taken the Honorable Miss Worth, whose religious beliefs demanded a puritanical simplicity of dress, for the new nanny, and before this assumption could be corrected, he had insulted the lady to such a degree that she never called on me again.) At the age of three Ramses had informed us that he did not need a nanny and would not have one. Emerson agreed with him. I did not agree with him. He needed something—a stout healthy woman who had trained as a prison wardress, perhaps—but it had become more and more difficult to find nannies for Ramses. Presumably the word had spread.

When we went in to dinner I saw that Ramses' imminent return had been accepted as fact. Wilkins' face bore the look of supercilious resignation that constitutes his version of sulking, and John, the footman, was beaming broadly. Like Rose, he is unaccountably devoted to Ramses.

I had long since resigned myself to the impossibility of teaching Emerson the proper subjects of conversation before the servants. Wilkins is not resigned; but there is nothing he can do about it. Not only does Emerson rant on and on about personal matters at the dinner table, but he often consults Wilkins and John. Wilkins has a single reply to all questions: "I really could not say, sir." John, who had never been in service before he came to us, had adapted very comfortably to Emerson's habits.

That evening, however, Emerson sipped his soup and made banal remarks about the weather and the beauty of the roses. I suspected he was up to something; and sure enough, as soon as John had retired to fetch the next course, he said casually, "We must make plans for our winter campaign, Peabody. Will you be taking your maid?"

Neither of us has ever taken a personal attendant on our expeditions. The very idea of Rose, in her neat black frock and ruffled cap, crawling in and out of a tent or pitching a camp cot in an abandoned tomb, was preposterous. I reminded Emerson of this, which he knew as well as I did.

"You may do as you like, of course," he replied. "But I believe that this year I may require the services of a valet. John—" for the young man had returned with the roast beef, "how would you like to go with us to Egypt this year?"

Wilkins rescued the platter before much of the juice had dripped onto the floor. John clasped his hands. "What, sir? Me, sir? Oh, sir, I would like it above all things. D'you really mean it, sir?"

"I never say anything I don't mean," Emerson shouted indignantly.

"Have you taken leave of your senses?" I demanded.

"Now, now, Mrs. Emerson—*pas devant les domestiques.*" Emerson grinned in a vulgar manner.

Naturally I paid no attention to this remark, which was only meant to annoy me. Emerson had introduced the subject; I was determined to thrash it out then and there.

"You, with a valet? You don't employ one here; what possible use could you have for an attendant in Luxor?"

"I had in mind—" Emerson began.

He was interrupted by John. "Oh, please, sir and madam—I'd be of use, truly I would. I could keep them tombs clean, and polish your boots—I'm sure they take a deal of polishing, with all that sand there—"

"Splendid, splendid," Emerson said. "That's settled, then. What the devil are you doing, Wilkins? Why don't you serve the food? I am ravenous."

There was no response from Wilkins, not even a blink. "Put the platter on the table, John," I said resignedly. "Then take Mr. Wilkins away."

"Yes, madam. Thank you, madam. Oh, madam—"

"That will do, John."

Though John is an extremely large person, he is only a boy, and his fair complexion reflects every shade of emotion. It had run the gamut from the flush of excitement to the pallor of apprehension; he was now a delicate shell-pink with pleasure as he led his unfortunate superior away.

Emerson attacked the beef with knife and fork. He avoided my eye, but the quirk at the corner of his mouth betokened a smug satisfaction I found maddening.

"If you believe the subject is closed, you are in error," I said. "Really, Emerson, you ought to be ashamed of yourself. Will you never learn? Your inconsiderate behavior has shocked Wilkins into a stupor and raised hopes in John that cannot be realized. It is too bad of you."

"I'll be cursed if I will apologize to Wilkins," Emerson mumbled. "Whose house is this, anyway? If I can't behave naturally in my own house—"

"He will recover; he is accustomed to your ways. It is John I am thinking of. He will be so disappointed—"

"I am surprised at you, Amelia," Emerson interrupted. "Do you suppose I really want John to act as my valet? I have another function in mind."

"Ramses," I said.

"Naturally. Devoted as I am to that adorable child, I know his ways. I cannot concentrate on my work if I must worry about him."

"I had, of course, planned to employ a woman to look after the boy when we arrive in Cairo—"

"A woman!" Emerson dropped the knife and planted both elbows on the table. "No native servant can deal with Ramses; Egyptians spoil their own children badly, and those who work for English people have been taught to indulge all members of the so-called superior race. Superior! It makes my blood boil when I hear such—"

"You are changing the subject," I warned, knowing his propensity to lecture on this topic. "We will find a man, then. A strong, healthy young man—"

"Like John. Do use your head, Amelia. Even if we could find a suitable person in Cairo—what about the journey out?"

"Oh," I said.

"It turns me cold with terror to think of Ramses running loose aboard ship," Emerson said—and indeed, his bronzed countenance paled visibly as he spoke. "Aside from the possibility that he might tumble overboard, there are the other passengers, the crew, and the ship's engines to be considered. We could go down with all hands, never to be heard of again. Only a life preserver, floating on the surface. . . ."

With an effort I shook off the dreadful vision. "That seems an exaggeration," I assured him.

"Perhaps." Emerson gave me a look I knew well. "But there are other difficulties, Amelia. If Ramses has no attendant, he will have to share our cabin. Curse it, my dear, the trip lasts two weeks! If you expect me to forgo—"

I raised a hand to silence him, for John had returned, carrying a bowl of brussels sprouts and beaming like the sun over the pyramids of Giza. "You have made your point, Emerson. I confess that problem had not occurred to me."

"Had it not?" The intensity of Emerson's gaze increased. "Perhaps I had better remind you, then."

And he did, later that evening, in a most effective manner.

III

We reached Chalfont on the next afternoon and were greeted by Evelyn herself. One look at her radiant face assured me of the correctness of my surmise, and as I gave her a sisterly embrace I murmured, "I am so happy for you, Evelyn."

Emerson's acknowledgment of the news was less conventional. "Amelia informs me you are at it again, Evelyn. I had hoped you were finished; you promised to come out with us once you had got this business of children over and done with; we haven't had a satisfactory artist on a dig since you abandoned the profession, and it does seem to me—"

Laughing, Walter interrupted him. "Now, Radcliffe, you ought to know that in these matters Evelyn is not solely responsible. Leave off abusing my wife, if you please, and come see my latest acquisition."

"The demotic papyrus?" Emerson can be distracted from almost any subject by an antiquity. He released his affectionate grasp of Evelyn and followed his brother.

Evelyn gave me an amused smile. The years had dealt kindly with her; her fair beauty was as serene as it had been when I first met her, and motherhood had scarcely enlarged her slim figure. Her blooming looks reassured me, but I could not help but feel a certain anxiety; as soon as the gentlemen were out of earshot, I inquired, "You are certain this time that all is well? Perhaps I ought to stay with you for the remainder of the summer. If I had been here last time—"

I had believed Emerson could not overhear, but his ears are abnormally keen on occasion. He turned. "Are you at it again, Amelia? The Egyptians may call you Sitt Hakim, but that does not qualify you to practice medicine. Evelyn will do much better without your dosing her."

Having made this pronouncement, he vanished into the corridor that led to the library.

"Ha," I exclaimed. "Now you know, Evelyn—"

"I know." Her arm stole round my waist. "I will never forget the day you restored me to life when I fainted in the Roman Forum. Your husband cannot spare you to nurse me, Amelia, and I assure you, there is no need. I am past the point where . . . That is, the dangerous period has . . ."

Evelyn is absurdly modest about these things. Since I consider motherhood a natural and interesting event, I see no reason for reticence. I said briskly, "Yes, the first three months were, for you, the period of risk. I conclude then that you will bear the child in December or January. Speaking of children . . ."

"Yes, of course. You will be eager to see Ramses."

She spoke in a hesitating manner, avoiding my eyes. I said coolly, "Has something happened to him?"

"No, no, of course not. At least . . . The truth is, he is missing."

Before I could pursue my inquiries, Emerson came bursting into the hallway where we stood. "Missing!" he bellowed. "Peabody—Ramses has disappeared! He has not been seen since breakfast. Curse it, why are you standing there? We must search for him immediately."

I caught hold of a marble pillar and managed to resist Emerson's efforts to drag me toward the door.

"Calm yourself, Emerson. I have no doubt a search is under way. You can do nothing that is not already being done. In fact, you would probably lose your way, and then everyone would have to look for you. It is not unheard of for Ramses to take himself off for long periods of time; he will return when he is ready."

The last part of this calm and reasonable speech was lost on Emerson. Finding himself unable to budge me, he released his hold and rushed out the door, leaving it open.

"There is no cause for concern," Evelyn assured me. "As you said, Ramses has done this before."

"Ra-a-amses!" Emerson's voice is notable for its carrying quality. "Papa is here, Ramses—where are you? Ram-ses . . ."

I said to Evelyn, "I believe I could fancy a cup of tea."

Tea is regarded, in these islands and elsewhere, as a restorative. It was in this light that Evelyn offered it, as she continued to reassure me as to Ramses' safety. I was glad of the tea, for the long train ride had made me thirsty. If I had wanted a restorative, I would have asked for whiskey and soda.

As I could have predicted, it was only a few minutes later that Emerson returned, with Ramses cradled in his arms. I studied the touching tableau with disfavor. Ramses was, as usual, incredibly dirty, and Emerson's suit had just been sponged and pressed.

Trotting behind them came the large brindled cat we had brought from Egypt on our last expedition but one. She was Ramses' constant companion, but unfortunately few of the admirable habits of the feline species had rubbed off onto her young owner. She threw herself down on the carpet and began cleaning herself. Ramses freed himself from his father's hold and rushed at me without so much as wiping his feet.

His small and sticky person was redolent of dog, chocolate, straw (used straw, from the stables) and stagnant water. Having embraced me, and left liberal traces of his presence on the skirt of my frock, he stood back and smiled. "Good afternoon, Mama."

Ramses has a rather prepossessing smile. He is not otherwise a handsome child. His features are too large for his juvenile countenance, especially his nose, which promises to be as commanding as that of his ancient Egyptian namesake. His chin, which is almost as oversized in proportion to the rest of his face, has the same cleft as his father's. I must confess that Ramses' chin softens me. I returned his smile. "Where have you been, you naughty boy?"

"Letting de animals out of de traps," Ramses replied. "I t'ought your train was not coming till later."

"What is this?" I frowned. "You are lisping again, Ramses. I told you—"

"It is not a lisp, Amelia." Evelyn hastened to defend the miscreant, who had turned to the tea table and was devouring sandwiches. "He pronounced his s's perfectly."

"Some other speech defect, then," I replied. "He does it deliberately. He knows how it annoys me."

Leaning against his father's knee, Ramses stuffed an entire watercress sandwich into his mouth and regarded me enigmatically. I would have continued the lecture but for the arrival of Walter, breathless and perspiring. He let out a sigh of relief when he saw the boy.

"So there you are, you young rascal. How could you wander off when you knew your mama and papa would be here?"

"I t'ought . . ." Ramses glanced at me. Slowly and deliberately he repeated, "I t'ought de train would be later dan was de case. You must swear out a warrant against Will Baker, Uncle Walter. He is setting traps again. It was necessary for me to free de unfortunate captives dis afternoon."

"Indeed? I will see to it at once," said Walter.

"Good Gad," I exclaimed loudly. Walter had once spanked Ramses (for tearing pages out of his dictionary), and now he too had succumbed to the imperious dictates of the miniature tyrant.

"Language, Amelia, language," Emerson exclaimed. "Remember that young, innocent, impressionable ears are listening."

At my suggestion Ramses retired to bathe and change. When he returned after a short interval he was accompanied by his cousins. It would have been difficult to deduce the relationship. Ramses' cheeks of tan and mop of curly black hair resembled the coloring of residents of the eastern Mediterranean regions, while his cousins had inherited their mother's fair hair and the sweet regularity of countenance of both parents. They are handsome children, especially Emerson's namesake, young Radcliffe. Raddie, as we called him, was then nine years of age, but looked older. (A few months of Ramses' companionship has that effect on sensitive individuals.) The twins, Johnny and Willy, appeared to have suffered less, perhaps because there were two of them to share the tempestuous effect of Ramses' personality. They greeted us with identical gap-toothed smiles and shook hands like little gentlemen. Then Ramses came forward with the fourth and (as yet) youngest of Evelyn's children—a dear little cherub of four, with golden curls and wide blue eyes. The curls were somewhat disheveled and the eyes were bulging, since Ramses had her firmly about the neck. Thrusting her at me, he announced, "Here is Melia, Mama."

I freed the unoffending infant from his stranglehold. "I know my namesake well, Ramses. Give Aunt Amelia, a kiss, my dear."

The child obeyed with the grace all Evelyn's offspring possess, but when I suggested she sit beside me she shook her head shyly. "T'ank you, Auntie, but if I may I will sit wit' Ramses."

I sighed as I beheld the look she turned on my son. I have seen the same expression on the face of a mouse about to be devoured by a cobra.

Evelyn fussed over the children, stuffing them with cakes and encouraging them to chatter about their activities; but I joined in the discussion between the men, which had to do with our plans for the autumn campaign.

"You won't be returning to Thebes, then?" Walter asked.

This was news to me, and I was about to say so when Emerson exclaimed in exasperation, "Curse you, Walter, it was to be a surprise for Amelia."

"I don't like surprises," I replied. "Not in matters concerning our work, at any rate."

"You will like this one, my dear Peabody. Guess where we are to excavate this winter."

The beloved name halted the reproof hovering on my lips. Its use goes back to the early days of our acquaintance, when Emerson used my surname in an attempt to annoy me. Now hallowed by tender memories, it is a symbol of our uniquely satisfying relationship. Emerson prefers me to use his last name for the same touching reason.

So I said, humoring him, "I cannot possibly guess, my dear Emerson. There are dozens of sites in Egypt I am dying to dig up."

"But what do you yearn for most? What is your Egyptological passion, hitherto unsatisfied? What is it you crave?"

"Oh, Emerson!" I clasped my hands. In my enthusiasm I overlooked the fact that I was holding a tomato sandwich. Wiping the fragments from my hands, I went on in mounting rapture, "Pyramids! Have you found us a pyramid?"

"Not one, but five," Emerson replied, his sapphire orbs reflecting my delight. "Dahshoor, Peabody— the pyramid field of Dahshoor—that is where I mean to dig. I intended it as a treat for you, my dear."

"You mean to dig," I repeated, my first enthusiasm fading. "Do you have the firman for Dahshoor?"

"You know I never apply to the Department of Antiquities beforehand, my love. If certain other archaeologists learned where I wanted to excavate they would also apply, out of pure spite. I don't mention names, but you know whom I mean."

I waved this unwarranted slur upon Mr. Petrie aside. "But, Emerson, M. de Morgan dug at Dahshoor last spring. As head of the Department of Antiquities he has first choice; what makes you suppose he will yield the site to you?"

"I understand that M. de Morgan is more reasonable than his predecessor," said Walter, the peacemaker. "Grebaut was an unfortunate choice for the position."

"Grebaut was an idiot," Emerson agreed. "But he never interfered with ME."

"He was terrified of you," I exclaimed. "I recall at least one occasion upon which you threatened to murder him. De Morgan may not be so timid."

"I cannot imagine where you get such ideas," Emerson said in mild surprise. "I am a particularly even-tempered man, and to suggest that I would threaten the Director General of the Department of Antiquities with physical violence—even if he was the most consummate fool in the entire universe—really, Amelia, you astonish me."

"Never mind," said Walter, his eyes twinkling with amusement. "Let us hope there will be no violence of any kind this season. Especially murder!"

"I certainly hope not," said Emerson. "These distractions interfere with one's work. Amelia suffers from the delusion, derived I know not whence, that she has talents as a criminal investigator—"

"I, at least, have cause to thank her for those talents," said my dear Evelyn quietly. "You cannot blame Amelia, Radcliffe; I was the unwitting cause of your first encounter with crime."

"And," Walter added, "on the second occasion you were the guilty party, Radcliffe—taking on the direction of an expedition plagued with mysterious disappearances and ancient curses."

"She tricked me into it," Emerson grumbled, glancing at me.

"I don't know what you are complaining about," I retorted. "It was a most interesting experience, and we made some valuable discoveries that season in the Valley of the Kings."

"But you were wrong about de identification of de tomb," said Ramses, turning to his father. "I am of de opinion dat Tutankhamon's sepulcher is yet to be discovered."

Seeing that an argument was about to ensue—for Emerson brooks criticism of his Egyptological expertise from no one, not even his son—Walter hastened to change the subject.

"Radcliffe, have you heard anything more about the recent flood of illegal antiquities? Rumor has it that some remarkably fine objects have appeared on the market, including jewelry. Can it be that the tomb robbers of Thebes have found another cache of royal mummies?"

"Your uncle is referring to the cave at Deir el Bahri," Emerson explained to Ramses. "It contained mummies of royal persons hidden by devout priests after the original tombs had been robbed."

"T'ank you, Papa, but I am fully acquainted wit' de details of dat remarkable discovery. De cache was found by de tomb robbers of Gurneh near Thebes, who marketed de objects found on de mummies, enabling de den Head of de Antiquities Department, M. Maspero, to track dem down and locate de cleft in de cliffs where de—"

"Enough, Ramses," I said.

"Hmph," said Emerson. "To answer your question, Walter—it is possible that the objects you refer to come from such a collection of royal mummies. However, from what I have heard, they range widely in date; the most remarkable is a Twelfth Dynasty pectoral ornament in gold, lapis lazuli and turquoise, with the cartouche of Senusret the Second. It seems to me more likely that a new and more efficient gang of tomb robbers has taken up the trade, plundering a variety of sites. What vultures these wretches are! If I could lay my hands on them—"

"You have just now declared you will not play detective," said Walter with a smile. "No murders for Amelia and no burglaries for you, Radcliffe. Only an innocent excavation. Don't forget you promised to look out for papyri—demotic papyri, if you please. I need more examples of that form of the language if I am to succeed with my dictionary."

"And I," said Ramses, feeding the last of the sandwiches to the cat, "wish to dig up dead people. Human remains are de indicators of de racial affiliations of de ancient Egyptians. Furdermore, I feel a useful study might be made of techniques of mummification down de ages."

Emerson bent a tender look upon his son and heir. "Very well, Ramses; Papa will find you all the dead bodies you want."

TWO

The voyage from Brindisi to Alexandria was without incident. (I do not consider the halting of the ship, at Emerson's frenzied insistence, as truly an incident in Ramses' career; as I told Emerson at the time, there was almost no possibility that the boy could have fallen overboard. Indeed he was soon found, in the hold, examining the cargo—for reasons which I did not care then, or at a later time, to inquire into.)

Except for this single error—for which John could not be blamed, since Ramses had locked him in their cabin—the young man performed well. He followed Ramses' every step and scarcely took his eyes off the boy. He attended to the needs of Bastet, such as they were; the cat required far less attendance than a human child. (Which is one of the reasons why spinster ladies prefer felines to babies.) Ramses had not insisted on bringing the cat; he had simply taken it for granted that she would accompany him. The few occasions on which they had been parted had proved so horrendous for all concerned that I gave in with scarcely a struggle.

But to return to John. He proved to be one of Emerson's more brilliant inspirations, and with my characteristic graciousness I admitted as much to my husband.

"John," I said, "was one of your more brilliant inspirations, Emerson."

It was the night before we were to dock at Alexandria, and we reclined in harmonious marital accord on the narrow bunk in our stateroom. John and Ramses occupied the adjoining cabin. Knowing that the porthole had been nailed shut and the key to the locked cabin door was in Emerson's possession, I was at ease about Ramses' present location and therefore able to enjoy my own, in the embrace of my husband. His muscular arms tightened about me as he replied sleepily, "I told you so."

In my opinion this comment should be avoided, particularly by married persons. I refrained from replying, however. The night was balmy with the breezes of the Orient; moonlight made a silver path across the floor; and the close proximity of Emerson, necessitated by the narrowness of the couch on which we reclined, induced a mood of amiable forbearance.

"He has not succumbed to mal de mer," I continued. "He is learning Arabic with remarkable facility; he gets on well with the cat Bastet."

Emerson's reply had nothing to do with the subject under discussion, and succeeded in distracting me, accompanied as it was by certain non-verbal demonstrations. When I was able to speak, I went on, "I am beginning to believe I have underestimated the lad's intelligence. He may be of use to us on the dig: keeping the records of pay for the men, or even—"

"I cannot conceive," said Emerson, "why you insist on talking about the footman at such a moment as this."

I was forced to concede that once again Emerson was quite correct. It was not the time to be talking about the footman.

II

John proved a weak vessel after all. He was snuffling next morning, and by the time we reached Cairo he had a fully developed case of catarrh, with all the attendant internal unpleasantnesses. Upon being questioned he weakly admitted he had left off the flannel belt with which I had provided him, cautioning him to wear it day and night in order to prevent a chill.

"Madness!" I exclaimed, as I tucked him into bed and laid out the appropriate medications. "Absolute madness, young man! You disregarded my instructions and now you see the consequences. Why didn't you wear your belt? Where is it?"

John's face was crimson from the base of his sturdy throat to the roots of his hair, whether from remorse or the exertion of attempting to prevent me from putting him to bed I cannot say. Pouring out a dessert spoonful of the gentle aperient I commonly employ for this ailment, I seized him by the nose and, as his mouth opened in a quest for oxygen, I poured the medicine down his throat. A dose of bismuth succeeded the aperient, and then I repeated my question. "Where is your belt, John? You must wear it every instant."

John was incapable of speech. However, the briefest flicker of his eyes in the direction of Ramses gave the answer I expected. The boy stood at the foot of the bed, watching with a look of cool curiosity, and as I turned in his direction he answered readily, "It is my fault, Mama. I needed de flannel to make a lead for de cat Bastet."

The animal in question was perched on the footboard, studying the mosquito netting draped high above the couch with an expression that aroused my deepest suspicions. I had noted with approval the braided rope with which Bastet had been provided. It was one item I had not thought to bring, since the cat usually followed Ramses' steps as closely as a devoted dog; but in a strange city, under strange circumstances, it was certainly a sensible precaution. Not until that moment, however, had I recognized the rope as the remains of a flannel belt.

Addressing the most pressing problem first, I said sternly, "Bastet, you are not to climb the mosquito netting. It is too fragile to bear your weight and will collapse if you attempt the feat." The cat glanced at me and murmured low in its throat, and I went on, now addressing my son, "Why did you not use your own flannel belt?"

"Because you would have seen it was gone," said Ramses, with the candor that is one of his more admirable characteristics.

"Who needs the cursed belts anyway?" demanded Emerson, who had been ranging the room like a caged tiger. "I never wear one. See here, Amelia, you have wasted enough time playing physician. This is a temporary affliction; most tourists suffer from it, and John will get on better if you leave him alone. Come; we have a great deal to do, and I need your assistance."

So adjured, I could only acquiesce. We retired to our own room, which adjoined that of the sufferer, taking Ramses (and of course the cat) with us. But when I would have turned toward the trunk that contained our books and notes, Emerson grasped my arm and drew me to the window.

Our room was on the third floor of the hotel, with a small iron-railed balcony overlooking the gardens of Ezbekieh Square. The mimosa trees were in bloom; chrysanthemums and poinsettias mingled in riotous profusion; the famous roses formed velvety masses of crimson and gold and snowy white. But for once the flowers (of which I am exceedingly fond) did not hold my gaze. My eyes sought the upper air, where roofs and domes, minarets and spires swam in a misty splendor of light.

Emerson's broad breast swelled in a deep sigh, and a contented smile illumined his face. He drew Ramses into his other arm. I knew—I shared—the joy that filled his heart as for the first time he introduced his son to the life that was all in all to him. It was a moment fraught with emotion—or it would have been, had not Ramses, in an effort to get a better look, swarmed up onto the railing, whence he was plucked by the paternal arm as he teetered perilously.

"Don't do that, my boy," said Emerson. "It is not safe. Papa will hold you."

With a visible sneer of contempt for human frailty the cat Bastet took Ramses' place on the rail. The noises from the street below rose in pitch as travelers returning from the day's excursions dismounted from donkeys or carriages. Conjurers and snake charmers sought to attract the attention, and the baksheesh, of the hotel guests; vendors of flowers and trinkets raised their voices in discordant appeal. A military band marched down the street, preceded by a water carrier running backward as he poured from a huge jar in order to lay the dust. Ramses' juvenile countenance displayed little emotion. It seldom did. Only a gentle flush warmed his tanned cheek, which was, for Ramses, a display of great excitement and interest.

The cat Bastet attacked her sleek flank with bared teeth.

"She cannot have picked up a flea already," I exclaimed, carrying the animal to a chair.

But she had. I dealt with the offender, made certain it had been a solitary explorer, and then remarked, "Your notion of a lead was a good idea, Ramses, but this dirty rag will not do. Tomorrow we will purchase a proper leather collar and lead in the bazaar."

My husband and son remained at the window. Emerson was pointing out the sights of the city. I did not disturb them. Let Emerson enjoy the moment; disillusionment would come soon enough when he realized he was destined to enjoy several days—and nights—of his son's companionship. Ramses could not share the infected chamber where John reposed, and John was in no state to provide the proper degree of supervision. He was barely up to the job even when he was in the full bloom of health.

The burden would rest principally on me, of course. I was resigned. Clapping my hands to summon the hotel safragi, I directed him to help me unpack.

III

We were to dine that evening with an old friend, Sheikh Mohammed Bahsoor. He was of pure Bedouin stock, with the acquiline features and manly bearing of that splendid race. We had decided to take Ramses with us—to leave him in the hotel with only the feeble John to watch over him was not to be thought of for a moment—but my misgivings as to his behavior were happily unfulfilled. The good old man welcomed him with the gracious courtesy of a true son of the desert; and Ramses, uncharacteristically, sat still and spoke scarcely a word all evening.

I was the only female present. The sheikh's wives, of course, never left the harim, and although he always received European ladies courteously, he did not invite them to his intimate dinner parties, when the conversation dwelled upon subjects of political and scientific interest. "Women," he insisted, "cannot discuss serious matters." Needless to say, I was flattered that he did not include me in that denunciation, and I believe he enjoyed my spirited defense of the sex of which I have the honor to be a member.

The gathering was cosmopolitan. In addition to the Egyptians and Bedouins present, there was M. Naville, the Swiss archaeologist, Insinger, who was Dutch, and M. Naville's assistant, a pleasant young fellow named Howard Carter. Another gentleman was conspicuous by the magnificence of his dress. Diamonds blazed from his shirt front and his cuffs, and the broad crimson ribbon of some foreign order cut a swath across his breast. He was of medium height, but looked taller because of his extraordinary leanness of frame. He wore his black hair shorter than was the fashion; it glistened with pomade, as did his sleek little mustache. A monocle in his right eye enlarged that optic with sinister effect, giving his entire face a curiously lopsided appearance.

When he caught sight of this person, Emerson scowled and muttered something under his breath; but he was too fond of Sheikh Mohammed to make a scene. When the sheikh presented "Prince Kalenischeff," my husband forced an unconvincing smile and said only, "I have met the—er—hem—gentleman."

I had not met him, but I knew of him. As he bowed over my hand, holding it pressed to his lips longer than convention decreed, I remembered Emerson's critical comments. "He worked at Abydos with Amelineau; between them, they made a pretty mess of the place. He calls himself an archaeologist, but that designation is as inaccurate as his title is apocryphal. If he is a Russian prince, I am the Empress of China."

Since Emerson was critical of all archaeologists, I had taken this with a grain of salt; but I must admit the prince's bold dark eyes and sneering smile made a poor impression on me.

The conversation was largely confined that evening to archaeological subjects. I remember the main topic concerned the proposed dam at Philae, which in its original design would have drowned the Ptolemaic temples on the island. Emerson, who despises the monuments of this degenerate period, annoyed a number of his colleagues by saying the cursed temples were not worth preserving, even if they did retain their original coloring. In the end, of course, he added his name to the petition sent to the Foreign Office, and I do not doubt that the name of Emerson carried considerable weight in the final decision to lower the height of the dam and spare the temples.

His eyes twinkling merrily, the sheikh made his usual provocative remarks about the female sex. I countered, as usual, and treated the gentlemen to a lecture on women's rights. Only once did a ripple of potential strife disturb the calm of the evening, when Naville asked Emerson where he would be digging that season. The question was asked in all innocence, but Emerson replied with a dark scowl and a firm refusal to discuss his plans. It might have passed off had not Kalenischeff said, in a lazy drawl, "The most promising sites have been allocated, you know. You ought not delay so long in applying, Professor."

Emerson's response would certainly have been rude. I managed to prevent it by popping a chunk of lamb into his open mouth. We were eating Arab-style, sitting cross-legged around the low table and feeding one another choice bits, a manner of dining that proved particularly useful on this occasion.

Throughout the meal Ramses sat like a little statue, speaking only when spoken to and eating as neatly as was possible under the circumstances. When we were ready to take our departure he made an impeccable salaam and thanked the sheikh in flawless Arabic. The ingenuous old gentleman was delighted. Folding Ramses to the bosom of his spot-less robes, he addressed him as "son" and proclaimed him an honorary member of his tribe.

When we were at last in the carriage, Emerson subsided with a groan and clasped his hands over his midsection. "The only fault I have to find with Arab hospitality is its extravagance. I have eaten too much, Amelia. I know I shan't sleep a wink tonight."

Since the main course had consisted of a whole roasted sheep stuffed with chickens, which were in turn stuffed with quail, I shared Emerson's senti-ments. But of course it would have been the height of discourtesy to refuse a dish. Suppressing an un-seemly sound of repletion, I said, "Ramses, you be-haved very well. Mama was proud of you."

"I was testing my knowledge of de language," said Ramses. "It was reassuring to discover dat de purely academic training I have received from Uncle Walter was adequate for de purpose. I com-prehended virtually everyt'ing dat was said."

"Did you indeed?" I said, somewhat uneasily.

Ramses had been so subdued I had almost forgotten he was present, and I had expressed myself forcibly on certain of the sexual and marital customs that keep Egyptian women virtually slaves in their own homes. While I was trying to remember what I had said, Ramses went on, "Yes, I have no complaints regarding Uncle Walter's tuition. I am somewhat weak wit' regard to current slang and colloquialisms, but dat is only to be expected; one can best acquire dem from personal experience."

I murmured an abstracted agreement. I had certainly used some expressions I would have preferred Ramses not to hear. I consoled myself by hoping that Walter had not taught him words like "adultery" and "puberty."

When we reached the hotel Ramses flew to embrace the cat and Emerson flung open the shutters. The room was stifling, but we had been afraid to leave the windows open for fear Bastet would escape. She had resented her imprisonment, and told Ramses so, in hoarse complaint, but I was pleased to see that she had taken my warning about the mosquito netting to heart. It hung in filmy, unmarred folds about our bed, and another netting enclosed the smaller cot which had been moved in from the next room.

Leaving Emerson to prepare Ramses for bed, I went to see how John was getting on. He assured me he was better and expressed himself as prepared to resume his duties at once; but my questioning brought out the fact that the internal disturbances were not yet reduced to a normal number (an interrogation that rendered John incoherent with embarrassment). So I told him to stay in bed, administered his medicine (he told me he had already taken it, but naturally I paid no attention), checked to make sure the new flannel belt I had given him was in place, and bade him good night.

Returning to my own chamber, I found Emerson, Ramses, and the cat lying in a tangled heap atop our bed, all sound asleep and, in Emerson's case, snoring. Contrary to his opinion, repletion does not affect Emerson's ability to sleep; it only makes him snore. I placed Ramses in his cot without waking him and tucked the netting securely in place. The cat wanted to get in with him—she always slept with Ramses at home—but after I had pointed out the problem of the netting and the hindrance it presented to her nocturnal prowling, she settled down on the foot of the bed. They made a picture to touch any mother's heart. The filmy fabric softened my son's rather large features, and in his little white nightgown, with his mop of sable curls, he resembled a small Semitic saint with a lion at his feet.

It may have been the charm of this sight that relaxed my internal guards, or it may have been that I was exhausted after a long tiring day. Whatever the cause of my negligence, I awoke after daylight to find Ramses' cot empty and the miscreant flown.

I was not surprised, but I was put out. Emerson was still snoring in blissful ignorance. I dressed quickly, not because I was alarmed about Ramses' safety but because I preferred to deal with the matter without my husband's agitated and vociferous assistance. Remembering one of Ramses' statements the previous night, to which I had not paid the attention it deserved, I was able to locate him almost immediately.

The street in front of the hotel teemed with the usual motley array of beggars, guides, donkeys and donkey boys, lying in wait for the tourists. Sure enough, Ramses was among them. Though I had expected to find him there, it took me several moments to recognize him. Barefoot and bareheaded, his white nightgown similar in design (and, by now, in filthiness) to the robes worn by the donkey boys, he blended admirably with the others, even to his tanned complexion and tousled black curls. I admit it gave me something of a shock. I was unable to move for an instant; and during that instant one of the bigger boys, finding Ramses blocking his path, addressed him in a flood of gutter slang. The shock I had experienced earlier paled by comparison to the sensation that seized me when I heard my offspring respond with a phrase of whose meaning even I was uncertain, though the general reference, to certain animals and their habits, was unfortunately only too clear.

I was not the only European standing on the terrace. Several other early birds had emerged, ready for touring. Though I am ordinarily unmoved by the uninformed opinions of others, I was not keen to admit an acquaintance with the dusty child in the dirty white robe; but, seeing that Ramses was about to be knocked unconscious by the infuriated young person he had just addressed as a misbegotten offspring of an Englishman and a camel, I thought I had better intervene.

"Ramses!" I shouted.

Everyone within earshot stopped and stared. I

suppose it must have been startling to hear an aris-
tocratic English person shout the name of an ancient Egyptian pharaoh at dawn on the terrace of
Shepheard's Hotel.

Ramses, who had ducked behind a morose little
donkey, started to his feet. His assailant halted, fist
raised; and the cat Bastet, appearing out of nowhere,
landed on the latter's back. The cat Bastet is a
large cat, weighing approximately twelve pounds.
The unlucky donkey boy fell flat upon the ground
with a sound like that of a cannonball hitting a
wall, this effect being further strengthened by the
cloud of dust that billowed up. Emerging from the
cloud, Bastet sneezed and fell in behind Ramses,
who advanced toward me. I seized him by the collar. In silence we retreated into the hotel.

We found Emerson placidly drinking tea. "Good
morning, my dears," he said, with a smile. "What
have you been doing so bright and early?"

Bastet sat down and began to wash herself. This
struck me as an excellent idea. I thrust Ramses into
his father's arms. "Wash him," I said briefly.

As they went out I heard Ramses explain, "I was
improving my command of de colloquial form of de
language, Papa," to which Emerson replied, "Splendid, my boy, splendid."

IV

After breakfast we set out on our errands, Emerson
to call on M. de Morgan, in order to obtain his
firman for excavating at Dahshoor, I to do some

necessary shopping. Normally I would have accompanied Emerson, but that would have meant taking Ramses along, and after hearing the latest additions to his Arabic vocabulary I felt it would be unwise to expose de Morgan to my linguistically unpredictable child—not to mention the cat, for Ramses refused to stir a step without her. I gave in to this request, since one of my errands was to buy a proper collar for Bastet.

The Muski, which is the main thoroughfare of old Cairo, had quite lost its former quaint oriental character; modern shops and buildings lined its broad expanse. We left our hired carriage at the entrance to the bazaars, for the narrow alleyways do not permit vehicular traffic. At my suggestion Ramses took the cat up lest she be stepped on. She assumed her favorite position, her head on one of Ramses' shoulders and her hindquarters on the other, with her tail hanging down in front.

We went first to the bazaar of the leathermakers, where we purchased not one but two collars for Bastet. One was plain and well constructed (my selection); the other was bright-red, adorned with fake scarabs and imitation turquoise. I was surprised to see Ramses exhibit such tawdry taste, but decided the issue was not worth arguing about. Ramses immediately decorated Bastet with the bejeweled collar and attached the matching crimson lead. They made a singular pair, Ramses in the tweed jacket and trousers his father had ordered to be made in imitation of his own working costume and the great feline, looking exactly like the hunting cats depicted in Egyptian tomb paintings. I was only relieved that Ramses had not suggested putting a gold earring in her ear, as had been done by the ancient pet owners.

I proceeded methodically with my shopping—medications, tools, ropes and other professional needs. The morning was well advanced by the time I finished, for even the simplest transaction cannot be completed without bargaining, coffee drinking and an exchange of florid compliments. There was one other inquiry I wanted to pursue before returning to the hotel; turning to ask if Ramses was hungry, I saw the question was unnecessary. He had just stuffed into his mouth a piece of pastry dripping with honey and bristling with nuts. The honey had trickled down his chin and onto his jacket. Each spot was already black with flies.

"Where did you get that?" I demanded.

"De man gave it to me." Ramses indicated a vendor of sweetmeats who stood nearby, his large wooden tray balanced expertly on his head. Through the swarm of insects that surrounded him the vendor gave me a gap-toothed smile and a respectful salutation.

"Did I not tell you you were not to eat anything unless I gave you permission?" I asked.

"No," said Ramses.

"Oh. Well, I am telling you now."

"Very well," said Ramses. He wiped his sticky hands on his trousers. A wave of flies dived upon the new spots.

We proceeded in single file through a covered passageway into a small square with a public fountain. Women in ragged black robes clustered around the marble structure, filling their jars. The appearance of Ramses and Bastet distracted them; they pointed and giggled, and one boldly lifted her veil in order to see better.

"Where are we going?" Ramses asked.

"To the shop of an antiquities dealer. I promised your Uncle Walter I would look for papyri."

Ramses began, "Papa says antiquities dealers are cursed rascals who—"

"I know your papa's opinions concerning antiquities dealers. However, it is sometimes necessary to resort to these persons. You are not to repeat your papa's comments to the man we are about to meet. You are not to speak at all unless you are asked a direct question. Do not leave the shop. Do not touch anything in the shop. Do not allow the cat to wander off. And," I added, "do not eat anything unless I tell you you may."

"Yes, Mama," said Ramses.

The Khan el Khaleel, the bazaar of the metalworkers, is, if possible, even more crowded than the others. We threaded our way past the cupboard-sized shops and the narrow stone benches called mastabas in front of them. Many of the mastabas were occupied by customers; the merchant, just inside the shop, produced his glittering wares from the locked drawers within.

Abd el Atti's place of business was on the edge of the Khan el Khaleel. The small shop in front was only a blind; preferred customers were invited into a larger room at the rear of the shop, where the old rascal's collection of antiquities was displayed.

Ever since the days of M. Mariette, the distinguished founder of the Department of Antiquities, excavation in Egypt has been—in theory at least— strictly controlled. Firmans are awarded only to trained scholars. The results of their labors are studied by an official of the Department, who selects the choicest objects for the Museum. The excavator is allowed to keep the remainder. Anyone wishing to export antiquities must have a permit, but this is not hard to obtain when the object in question has no particular monetary or historical value.

The system would work well enough if the law were obeyed. Unfortunately it is impossible to supervise every square acre of the country, and illegal excavation is common. Working in haste and in fear of discovery, untrained diggers demolish the sites at which they work and of course keep no records of where the objects were found. The fellahin of Egypt have a keen nose for treasure; they have often located tombs unknown to archaeologists. The famous cache of royal mummies that Emerson had mentioned is a conspicuous example. But the peasants are not the only offenders. Wallis Budge of the British Museum took a positive delight in outwitting the antiquities officials. The Amarna tablets, the papyrus of Ani, and the great Greek manuscript of the *Odes* of Bacchylides are among the valuables smuggled out of Egypt by this so-called scholar.

In this ambiguous moral ambience the antiquities dealers flourished. Some were more unscrupulous than others, but scarcely any of them operated wholly within the law. The honest merchant had no chance against his dishonest colleagues, for the best wares were obtained from illegal excavations. Abd el Atti's reputation was middle-of-the-road—worse than some merchants, not so bad as others—which meant he might have the kind of papyrus I wanted for Walter.

The mastaba before the shop was unoccupied. I looked within. The room was dimly lit and crowded with merchandise. Most of the remaining space was filled by Abd el Atti himself. He was almost as short as I and almost as wide as he was tall. Before affluence got the better of his figure he must have been a handsome fellow, with soft brown eyes and regular features. He was still something of a dandy. His outer robe was of salmon-pink cashmere and he wore a huge green turban, perhaps in order to increase his stature. From behind, which was how I saw him, the effect was that of a large orange balloon surmounted by a cabbage.

His body very nearly concealed the other man, who stood just inside the curtained doorway at the rear of the shop. I saw only the latter's face, and a most sinister countenance it was—almost as dark as a Nubian's, shaped into lines and pouches of sagging flesh that suggested dissipation rather than age. When he saw me, his lips drew back in a snarl under his ragged black mustaches, and he interrupted Abd el Atti with a harsh warning. "*Gaft— ha'at iggaft . . .*"—followed by another comment of which I caught only a few words.

Turning with a serpentine swiftness surprising in a man of his bulk, Abd el Atti cut the other short with a peremptory gesture. His brown face shone greasily with perspiration. "It is the Sitt Hakim," he said. "Wife to Emerson. You honor my house, Sitt."

Since *I* knew who I was, and Abd el Atti knew who I was, I could only assume that the identifying statement was aimed at the other man. It was not an introduction, for upon hearing it the creature vanished, so suddenly and smoothly that the curtain scarcely swayed. A warning, then? I had no doubt of it. When he greeted me, Abd el Atti had spoken ordinary Arabic. The whispered remarks I had overheard had been in another kind of speech.

Abd el Atti bowed, or tried to; he did not bend easily. "Be welcome, honored lady. And this young nobleman—who can he be but the son of the great Emerson! How handsome he is, and how great the intelligence that shines in his eyes."

This was a deadly insult, for one does not praise a child for fear of attracting the envy of malicious demons. I knew Abd el Atti must be badly rattled to make such a mistake.

Ramses said not a word, only bowed in response. The cat—I observed with a touch of uneasiness— was nowhere to be seen.

"But come," Abd el Atti went on, "sit on the mastaba; we will drink coffee; you will tell me how I may serve you."

I let him nudge me out of the shop. He squatted beside me on the mastaba and clapped his hands to summon a servant. Under his salmon robe he wore a long vest of striped Syrian silk, bound with a sash stiff with pearls and gold thread. He paid no attention to Ramses, who remained inside the shop. Hands clasped ostentatiously behind his back in compliance with my instructions, Ramses appeared to be studying the merchandise on display. I decided to let him remain where he was. Even if he broke something, it would not matter; most of the objects were forgeries.

Abd el Atti and I drank coffee and exchanged insincere compliments for a while. Then he said, apropos of nothing in particular, "I hope the speech of that vile beggar did not offend you. He was trying to sell me some antiquities. However, I suspected they were stolen, and as you and my great good friend Emerson know, I do not deal with dishonest people."

I nodded agreeably. I knew he was lying and he knew I knew; we were playing the time-honored game of mercantile duplicity, in which both parties profess the most noble sentiments while each plans to cheat the other as thoroughly as possible.

Abd el Atti smiled. His countenance was trained in imperturbability, but I knew the old wretch well; his remark was not an apology, but an implicit question. He was desperately anxious to learn whether I had understood those whispered words.

Many trades and professions, especially criminal trades, develop private languages in order that the members may speak among themselves without being understood by outsiders. The thieves' cant of seventeenth-century London is one example of such an argot, as it is called. Abd el Atti and his companion had employed the *siim issaagha*, the argot of the gold- and silver-sellers of Cairo. It is based on ancient Hebrew, a language I had studied with my late father. In fact, they had spoken so rapidly and so softly, I had only comprehended a few words.

Abd el Atti had said, "The Master will eat our

hearts if . . ." Then the other man had warned him to watch what he said, since a stranger had entered.

I had no intention of admitting that I was familiar with the *siim issaagha*. Let the old man wonder and worry.

He was worried. Instead of *fahddling* (gossiping) for the prescribed length of time, he abruptly got down to business, asking what I wanted.

"It is for the brother of Emerson that I come," I explained. "He studies the ancient language of Egypt, and I promised I would bring him papyri."

Abd el Atti sat like a glittering statue, his hands rock-steady; but a strange livid hue overspread his face. The harmless word "papyri" had wrought that remarkable change; could it be, I wondered, that a cache of these objects had been found? I saw myself exposing the criminal ring, arresting the criminals, carrying back basketfuls of papyri to Walter.

Abd el Atti cleared his throat. "It grieves me that I cannot assist one whom I would wish to honor. Alas, alas, I have no papyri."

Well, I had expected that. Abd el Atti never had the object one wanted, and if my suspicions were correct (as I felt sure they were) he had pressing reasons for refusing to admit that he possessed those particular objects. I did not doubt, however, that cupidity would eventually overcome his caution. He had to market his loot to someone; why not to me?

So I proceeded to the next stage of the negotiations, which usually ended with Abd el Atti suddenly remembering that he had heard of such a thing—not that he made a habit of dealing with thieves, but as a favor to an old friend he might be willing to act as middleman. . . . But to my surprise Abd el Atti remained firm. He offered me other antiquities, but not papyri.

Finally I said, "It is a pity, my friend. I will have to go to another dealer. I regret this; I would rather have bought from you." And I made as if to rise.

This was the last stage in the maneuvering and usually brought the desired result. An expression of agony crossed Abd el Atti's rotund face, but he shook his head. "I also regret, honored Sitt. But I have no papyri."

His fat body filled the narrow doorway of the shop. Over his shoulder there appeared a strange appendage, like a third arm—a small, thin arm clothed in brown tweed. Ramses' voice piped, "Mama, may I speak now?"

Abd el Atti made a frantic grab for the object Ramses was holding. He missed. Before he could try again, a heavy weight landed on his shoulder, tipping him backward. He let out a shriek and began beating the air with ringed brown hands. Bastet leaped again, onto the mastaba next to me, and Ramses squeezed through the space the cat had cleared for him. He was still holding the scrap of papyrus.

I took it from him. "Where did you find this?" I asked, in English.

"In de room behind de curtain," said Ramses. He squatted beside me, crossing his legs in Egyptian style. Gesturing at Bastet, he added, "I was looking for de cat Bastet. You told me not to let her wander off."

Abd el Atti levered himself to an upright position.

I expected he would be angry—and indeed he had some reason to be—but the look he gave the great brindled cat and the small boy held a touch of superstitious terror. I saw his hand move in a quick gesture—the old charm against the evil eye and the forces of darkness. "I know nothing of it," he said heavily. "I have never seen it before."

The scrap had been broken off a larger manuscript. It was roughly rectangular and about six inches by four in size. The papyrus was brown with age, but less brittle than such relics usually are, and the writing stood out black and firm.

"It is not hieratic or demotic," I said. "These are Greek letters."

"It is as I said," Abd el Atti babbled. "You asked for Egyptian papyri, Sitt; this is not what you desire."

"I t'ink dat de writing is Coptic," said Ramses, legs crossed, arms folded. "It *is* Egyptian—de latest form of de language."

"I believe you are correct," I said, examining the fragment again. "I will take it, Abd el Atti, since you have nothing better. How much?"

The dealer made an odd, jerky gesture of resignation. "I ask nothing. But I warn you, Sitt—"

"Are you threatening me, Abd el Atti?"

"Allah forbid!" For once the dealer sounded wholly sincere. Again he glanced nervously at the cat, at Ramses, who contemplated him in unblinking silence, and at me. And behind me, I knew, he saw the shadow of Emerson, whom the Egyptians called Father of Curses. The combination would have daunted a braver man than poor, fat Abd el Atti. He swallowed. "I do not threaten, I warn. Give it to me. If you do, no harm will follow, I swear it."

As Emerson might have said, this was the wrong approach to take to me. (In fact, Emerson would have put it more emphatically, using terms like "red flag to a bull.") I tucked the fragment carefully into my bag. "Thank you for your warning, Abd el Atti. Now hear mine. If the possession of this scrap is dangerous to me, it is also dangerous to you. I suspect you are in over your turbaned head, old friend. Do you want help? Tell me the truth. Emerson and I will protect you—word of an Englishman."

Abd el Atti hesitated. At that moment Bastet rose upon her hind legs and planted her forefeet on Ramses' shoulder, butting her head against his. It was a habit of hers when she was restless and desirous of moving on, and it was sheer coincidence that she should have chosen that precise moment to move; but the sight seemed to strike terror into Abd el Atti's devious soul.

"It is the will of Allah," he whispered. "Come tonight, with Emerson—when the muezzin calls from the minaret at midnight."

He would say no more. As we retraced our steps I glanced over my shoulder and saw him squatting on the mastaba, still as a glittering life-sized statue. He was staring straight ahead.

We pressed against the wall to let a donkey squeeze by. Ramses said, "De old gentleman was lying, wasn't he, Mama?"

"What about, my boy?" I inquired absently.

"About everyt'ing, Mama."

"I rather think you are correct, Ramses."

V

I was afire with impatience to tell Emerson we had been given an opportunity to expose the ring of antiquities thieves. When we reached Shepheard's I was surprised to find he had not yet returned. He was not so fond of de Morgan that he would have lingered, chatting. However, he had many friends in Cairo, and I supposed he had stopped to see one of them and, as he often did, lost track of the time.

After looking in on John and finding him sweetly sleeping, I ordered water to be brought. Ramses needed a bath. He needed a bath three or four times a day under normal circumstances, and the dust of the bazaars, not to mention the honey, had had dire effects. Ramses obediently retired behind the plaited screen that concealed the implements of ablution. For a time he splashed and sputtered in silence; then he began to hum, another annoying habit he had picked up while staying with his aunt and uncle. Like his father, Ramses is completely tone-deaf. The flat insistent drone of his voice was extremely trying to sensitive ears like mine, and it seemed now to have acquired a certain oriental quality—a quavering rise and fall, reminiscent of the Cairo street singers. I listened until I could bear it no longer and then requested that he desist.

He had finished bathing and was almost dressed

before my senses, straining for the longed-for harbingers of his father's return, became aware of a sound like distant thunder. Ever louder and more furious the noise became as it neared our door. I looked at Ramses. He looked at me. The cat Bastet rose from the mat and retreated, with dignity but in haste, under the bed. The door quivered, shuddered, and flew open, striking the wall with a crash. Loosened plaster dribbled floorward.

Emerson stood in the opening. His face was brickred. The veins in his throat stood out like ropes. He strove to speak, and failed; only a low growling noise emerged from his writhing lips. The growl rose to a roar and from the roar words finally took shape.

I covered my ears with my hands, then removed one hand to gesture imperatively at Ramses. Emerson was cursing in Arabic, and I felt sure the boy was making mental notes of "de colloquial speech."

Emerson's rolling eyes focused on his son's fascinated face. With a mighty effort he controlled his wrath. He allowed himself the final solace of kicking the door closed. A stream of plaster added itself to the heap already on the floor. Emerson took a long breath, his chest expanding to such an extent, I feared the buttons would pop off his shirt. "Er— hem," he said. "Hello, my boy. Amelia. Did you have a pleasant morning?"

"Let us eschew the amenities on this occasion," I exclaimed. "Get it off your chest, Emerson, before you explode. Only avoid profanity, if at all possible."

"It is not possible," Emerson cried in an anguished voice. "I cannot speak without expletives concerning that villain—that vile—that . . . that—de Morgan!"

"He has refused you the firman for Dahshoor."

Emerson kicked a stool, sending it flying across the room. The head of Bastet, which had cautiously protruded from under the bed, vanished again.

"He means to work at Dahshoor himself this season," said Emerson in a strangled voice. "He had the effrontery to tell me I was too late in applying."

My lips parted. Before I could speak, Emerson turned a hideous glare upon me. "If you say 'I told you so,' Peabody, I will—I will—kick the bed to splinters!"

"By all means do so, if it will relieve your feelings, Emerson. I am deeply wounded by your accusation, which I feel sure you would never have made had you been in control of your emotions. You know I abhor the phrase you mentioned and that I never in all the years of our marriage—"

"The devil you haven't," Emerson snarled.

"De devil you haven't," echoed Ramses. "Don't you remember, Mama, yesterday on de train from Alexandria, and de day before dat, when Papa forgot—"

"Ramses!" Emerson turned, more in sorrow than in wrath, to his offending heir. "You must not use such language, particularly to your dear mama. Apologize at once."

"I apologize," Ramses said. "I meant no offense, Mama, but I do not see what is wrong wit' dat expression. It has a quality of colorful emphasis dat appeals strongly—"

"Enough, my son."

"Yes, Papa."

The silence that ensued was like the hush after

a tempest, when the leaves hang limp in the quiet air and nature seems to catch her breath. Emerson sat down on the bed and mopped his streaming brow. His complexion subsided to the handsome walnut shade that is its normal color in Egypt, and a tender, affectionate smile transformed his face. "Were you waiting for me before lunching? That was kind, my dears. Let us go down at once."

"We must discuss this, Emerson," I said.

"Certainly, Amelia. We will discuss it over luncheon."

"Not if you are going to lose your temper. Shepheard's is a respectable hotel. Guests who shout obscenities and throw china across the dining salon—"

"I cannot imagine where you get such notions, Amelia," Emerson said in a hurt voice. "I never lose my temper. Ah—there is Bastet. That is a very handsome collar she is wearing. What is she doing under the bed?"

Bastet declined Ramses' invitation to lunch—an invitation made, I hardly need say, without reference to me—so the three of us went down. I was not deceived by Emerson's apparent calm; the blow had been cruel, the disappointment grievous, and I felt it hardly less than he. Of course it was Emerson's fault for not doing as I had suggested, but I would not for all the world have reminded him of that. After we had taken our places and the waiters had been dispatched in quest of the sustenance we had ordered, I said, "Perhaps I might have a little chat with M. de Morgan. He is a Frenchman, after all, and young; his reputation for gallantry—"

"Is only too well deserved," Emerson growled.

"You are not to go near him, Amelia. Do you suppose I have forgotten the abominable way he behaved the last time we met?"

M. de Morgan's abominable behavior had consisted of kissing my hand and paying me a few flowery French compliments. However, I was touched by Emerson's assumption that every man I met had amorous designs on me. It was a delusion of his, but a pleasant delusion.

"What did he do?" Ramses asked interestedly.

"Never mind, my boy," Emerson said. "He is a Frenchman, and Frenchmen are all alike. They are not to be trusted with ladies or with antiquities. I don't know a single Frenchman who has the slightest notion of how to conduct an excavation."

Knowing that Emerson was capable of lecturing on this subject interminably and that Ramses was about to request more specific information about the untrustworthiness of Frenchmen with ladies, I turned the conversation back to the subject that concerned me.

"Very well, Emerson, if you would prefer I did not talk with him I will not. But what are we going to do? I assume he offered you another site?"

Emerson's cheeks darkened. "Control yourself," I implored. "Speak slowly and breathe deeply, Emerson. It cannot be as bad as that."

"It is worse, Peabody. Do you know what site that bas—that wretch had the effrontery to offer me? 'You desire pyramids,' he said, with that French smirk of his, 'I give you pyramids, my dear cabbage. Mazghunah. What do you say to Mazghunah?'"

He gave the guttural a rolling sound that made

the word resemble an oath in some exotic language. "Mazghunah," I echoed. "Emerson, I confess the name is wholly unfamiliar. Where is it?"

My admission of ignorance had the desired effect of soothing Emerson's wounded dignity. He seldom gets the chance to lecture me on Egyptology. However, in this case I was not just being tactful. I did not recognize the name, and when Emerson had explained, I knew why it meant nothing to me—and why my poor spouse had been so wroth.

Mazghunah is only a few kilometers south of Dahshoor, the site we had wanted. Dahshoor, Sakkara, Giza and Mazghunah itself are the ancient cemeteries of Memphis, the once-great capital of ancient Egypt, of which only a few mounds of ruins now remain. All are close to Cairo and all boast pyramid tombs; but the two "pyramids" of Mazghunah exist only as limestone chips on the level desert floor. No one had bothered to investigate them because there was hardly anything left to investigate.

"There are also late cemeteries," said Emerson with a sneer. "De Morgan made a point of that, as if it were an added inducement instead of a handicap."

He pronounced the word "late" as if it were an insult, which to Emerson it was. Emerson's interest in Egypt began about 4000 B.C. and stopped 2500 years later. Nothing after 1500 B.C. had the slightest attraction for him, and the late cemeteries were dated to Roman and Ptolemaic times—trash, so far as Emerson was concerned.

Though my own spirits were low, I sought to cheer my afflicted husband. "There may be papyri,"

I said brightly. "Remember the papyri Mr. Petrie found at Hawara."

Too late I realized that the name of Mr. Petrie was not designed to improve Emerson's mood. Scowling, he attacked the fish the waiter had set in front of him, as if his fork were a spear and the fish were Mr. Petrie, boiled, flayed and at his mercy.

"He lied to me," he grunted. "His publication was not ready. It was late this year. Did you know that, Amelia?"

I did know. He had told me approximately fifteen times. Emerson brooded darkly on the iniquities of Petrie and de Morgan. "He did it deliberately, Amelia. Mazghunah is close to Dahshoor; he will make sure I receive daily reports of his discoveries while I dig up Roman mummies and degenerate pottery."

"Then don't take Mazghunah. Demand another site."

Emerson ate in silence for a time. Gradually his countenance lightened and a smile curved his well-shaped lips. I knew that smile. It boded ill for someone—and I thought I knew for whom.

At last my husband said slowly, "I will accept Mazghunah. You don't mind, do you, Peabody? When I visited the site some years ago I determined to my own satisfaction that the remains were those of pyramids. The superstructures have entirely disappeared, but there are surely passageways and chambers underground. There is not a chance of anything better; Firth has Sakkara, and the Giza pyramids are so popular with tourists, one can't work there."

"I don't mind. 'Whither thou goest,' you know, Emerson; but I do hope you are not planning any ill-advised assaults on M. de Morgan."

"I cannot imagine what you mean," said Emerson. "Naturally I will offer the gentleman the benefit of my experience and superior knowledge whenever the opportunity presents itself. I am determined to turn the other cheek, and render good where . . ."

He broke off, catching my skeptical eye upon him; and after a moment his great hearty laugh boomed out across the dining salon, stopping conversation and making the crystal chime. Emerson's laugh is irresistible. I joined him, while Ramses watched with a faint smile, like an elderly philosopher tolerant of the antics of the young. It was not until after we had returned to our room that I discovered Ramses had taken advantage of our distraction to conceal his fish under his blouse as a present for Bastet. She enjoyed it very much.

THREE

Though I attempted to conceal my feelings, I was exceedingly put out. It seemed hard indeed that I should have to suffer from Emerson's blunder, for it was nothing less. De Morgan had dug at Dahshoor the year before. It would have required considerable tact and persuasion to convince him to yield the site to another excavator, and Emerson's methods of persuasion were not calculated to win over an opponent. Though I had not been present, I knew only too well what had transpired. Emerson had marched into de Morgan's office, unannounced and uninvited; rested his fists on the director's desk; and proclaimed his intent. "Good morning, monsieur. I will be working at Dahshoor this season."

De Morgan had stroked his luxuriant mustache. *"Mais, mon cher collègue, c'est impossible.* I will be working at Dahshoor this season."

Emerson's response would have been an indignant shout and a crash of his fist on the table; de Morgan would have continued to stroke his mustache and shake his head until Emerson stamped out of the door, annihilating small tables and miscellaneous chairs as he went.

I looked through the reference books we had brought with us in a vain attempt to find something about Mazghunah. Few of the authorities so much as mentioned it, and if there were pyramids at the site, that fact was not widely known. If Emerson had not confirmed their existence, I would have suspected de Morgan of inventing them, to taunt Emerson.

Emerson exaggerates, in his humorous fashion, when he says I have a passion for pyramids. However, I admit to a particular affection for these structures. On my first visit to Egypt as a tourist I had fallen victim to the charm of their dark, stifling passageways, carpeted with rubble and bat droppings. Yet, since taking up the practice of archaeology I had never been able to investigate a pyramid professionally. Our interests had taken us elsewhere. I had not realized how I yearned to explore a pyramid until I found I could not.

"Abusir," I said. "Emerson, what about Abusir? The pyramids there are much decayed, but they *are* pyramids."

"We will dig at Mazghunah," said Emerson. He said it very quietly, but his chin protruded in a manner I knew well. Emerson's chin is one of his most seductive features. When it jutted out in that particular fashion, however, I had to repress a desire to strike it smartly with my clenched fist.

"The remains of the pyramid at Zawaiet el 'Aryân," I persisted. "Maspero failed to enter it ten years ago. We might find the entrance he missed."

Emerson was visibly tempted. He would love to

do Maspero or any other archaeologist one better. But after a moment he shook his head. "We will dig at Mazghunah," he repeated. "I have my reasons, Amelia."

"And I know what they are. They do you no credit, Emerson. If you intend—"

Crossing the room in a few long strides, he stopped my mouth with his. "I will make it up to you, Peabody," he murmured. "I promised you pyramids, and pyramids you will have. In the meantime, perhaps this . . ."

Being unable to articulate, I gestured wordlessly at the door connecting our room to the next. Ramses had retired thither, purportedly to give John an Arabic lesson. The murmur of their voices, broken now and again by a chuckle from John, bore out the claim.

With a hunted look at the door, my husband released me. "When will this torment end?" he cried, clutching his hair with both hands.

Ramses' voice broke off for a moment and then continued.

"John should be able to resume his duties tomorrow," I said.

"Why not tonight?" Emerson smiled meaningfully.

"Well . . . Good heavens," I exclaimed. "I had forgotten. We have a rendezvous this night, Emerson. The distressing news quite shook it out of my head."

Emerson sat down on the bed. "Not again," he said. "You promised me, Amelia . . . What are you up to now?"

I told him what had transpired at the bazaar.

Little gasps and cries escaped his lips as I proceeded, but I raised my voice and went on, determined to present him with a connected narrative. At the end I produced the scrap of papyrus.

"Obviously Abd el Atti was lying when he claimed he had no papyri," I said. "To be sure, this is Coptic, but—"

Emerson pushed the fragment aside. "Precisely. Walter is not interested in Coptic; that is the language of Christian Egypt."

"I am well aware of that, Emerson. This fragment proves—"

"You had no business going to that fat scoundrel. You know what I think of—"

"And you know that the dealers are likely to have the best manuscripts. I promised Walter—"

"But this is not—"

"Where there is one scrap there must be a papyrus. I—"

"I told you—"

"I am convinced—"

"You—"

"You—"

By this time we were both on our feet and our voices had risen considerably. I make no apologies for my exasperation. Emerson would try the patience of a saint. He loses his temper on the slightest provocation.

We broke off speaking at the same time, and Emerson began pacing rapidly up and down the room. In the silence the rise and fall of Ramses' voice went placidly on.

Finally Emerson left off pacing. Rapid movement

generally calms him, and I will do him the justice to admit that although he is quick to explode, he is equally quick to regain his temper. I smoothed his ruffled locks. "I told Abd el Atti we would come to the shop tonight."

"So you said. What you failed to explain is why the devil I should put myself out for the old rascal. There are other things I would rather do tonight."

His eyes sparkled significantly as he looked at me, but I resisted the appeal. "He is desperately afraid of something or someone, Emerson. I believe he is involved in the illicit antiquities business."

"Well, of course he is, Peabody. All of them are."

"I am referring, Emerson, to the recent, unprecedented flood of stolen objects you and Walter were discussing. You yourself said that some new player must have entered the game—some unknown genius of crime, who has organized the independent thieves into one great conspiracy."

"I said no such thing! I only suggested—"

"Abd el Atti is a member of the gang. His reference to the Master eating his heart—"

"Picturesque, but hardly convincing," said Emerson. His tone was less vehement, however, and I saw that my arguments had made an impression. He went on, "Are you certain you understood correctly? I cannot believe he would make a damaging admission in your presence."

"He didn't know I was present. Besides—weren't you listening, Emerson?—he was speaking the *siim issaagha*."

"Very well," Emerson said. "I agree that Abd el Atti may well be involved in something deeper and darker than his usual shady activities. But your notion that he is a member of some imaginary gang is pure surmise. You have an absolutely unique ability to construct a towering structure of theory on one single fact. Foundationless towers totter, my dear Peabody. Control your rampageous imagination and spare your afflicted spouse, I beg."

He was working himself into another fit of temper, so I only said mildly, "But supposing I am right, Emerson? We may have an opportunity to stop this vile traffic in antiquities, which we both abhor. Is not the chance of that, however remote, worth the trifling inconvenience I propose?"

"Humph," said Emerson.

I knew the grunt was as close to a concession as I was likely to get, so I did not pursue the discussion, which would have been ended in any case by the advent of our son, announcing that the Arabic lesson was over. I did not want Ramses to get wind of our plan. He would have insisted on accompanying us, and his father might have been foolish enough to agree.

I was about to put my scrap of papyrus away when Ramses asked if he might look at it. I handed it over, cautioning him to be careful, an admonition to which he replied with a look of mingled scorn and reproach.

"I know you will," I said. "But I don't see what you want with it. Your Uncle Walter has not taught you Coptic along with hieroglyphs, has he?"

"Uncle Walter does not know de Coptic," replied Ramses loftily. "I am only curious to see what I can make of dis from my acquaintance wit' de ancient language; for, as you may be aware, de Coptic language is a development of de Egyptian, t'ough written in Greek script."

I waved him away. Bad enough to be lectured on Egyptology by one's husband; the smug and dogmatic pronouncements of my juvenile son were sometimes extremely trying to my nerves. He settled down at the table with Bastet beside him. Both bent their attention upon the text, the cat appearing to be as interested as the boy.

The door of the adjoining room now responded to a series of blows—John's version of a knock. He has extremely large hands and no idea of his own strength. It was a pleasure to hear the sound, however, after the long silence from that direction, and I bade him enter. Emerson took one look at him and burst out laughing.

He wore the uniform of a footman, which he had presumably brought with him from England—knee breeches, brass buttons and all—and I must confess that he looked rather ridiculous in that setting. Emerson's mirth brought a faint blush to his boyish face, though it was apparent he had no idea what his master found so funny. "I am at your service, sir and madam," he announced. "With apologies for failing to carry out me duties in the past days and respectful thanks for the kind attentions received from madam."

"Very well, very well," Emerson said. "Sure you are fit, my boy?"

"Quite fit," I assured him. "Now, John, be sure never to leave off your flannel, and take care what you eat and drink."

I glanced at Ramses as I concluded my advice,

remembering the sweetmeat he had consumed—an incident I had not thought worth mentioning to his father. He seemed quite all right. I had been sure he would. Poisonous leaves and berries, india rubbers, ink and quantities of sweets that would have felled an ox had all passed through Ramses' digestive tract without the slightest disturbance of that region.

Standing stiffly at attention, John asked for orders. I said, "There is nothing to do at present; why don't you go out for a bit? You have seen nothing of the city, or even the hotel."

"I will go wit' him," said Ramses, pushing his chair back.

"I don't know," I began.

"What of your work, my son?" inquired Emerson. This attempt, more subtle than my own, was equally fruitless. Ramses picked up his hat and started for the door. "De manuscript appears to have belonged to a person called Didymus Thomas," he said coolly. "Dat is all I can make out at present, but I will have anodder go at it after I have procured a Coptic dictionary. Come along, John."

"Stay in the hotel," I said quickly. "Or on the terrace. Do not eat anything. Do not speak to the donkey boys. Do not repeat to anyone the words you learned from the donkey boys. Do not go in the kitchen, or the bathrooms, or any of the bedrooms. Stay with John. If you mean to take Bastet with you, put her on the lead. Do not let her off the lead. Do not let her chase mice, dogs, other cats or ladies' skirts."

I paused for breath. Ramses pretended to take this

for the end of the lecture. With an angelic smile he slipped out the door.

"Hurry," I implored John. "Don't let him out of your sight."

"You may count on me, madam," said John, squaring his shoulders. "I am ready and equal to the task. I—"

"Hurry!" I pushed him out the door. Then I turned to Emerson. "Did I cover all the contingencies?"

"Probably not," said my husband. He drew me into the room and closed the door.

"There is no way of locking it," I said, after an interval.

"Mmmm," said Emerson agreeably.

"They will not be gone long. . . ."

"Then we must make the best use of the time at our disposal," said Emerson.

II

I had neglected to forbid Ramses to climb the palm trees in the courtyard. He explained in an injured tone that he had only wanted to get a better look at the dates, of which he had heard; but he had not eaten a single one. In proof of this he presented me with a handful, removing them with some difficulty from the pocket of his little shirt.

I sent him off to be bathed by John and began laying out Emerson's evening clothes. He studied them with loathing.

"I told you, Amelia, I have no intention of wearing those garments. What torture have you planned now?"

"I have invited guests to dine with us tonight," I said, removing my wrapper. "Help me with my dress, will you please?"

Emerson is so easily distracted. He moved with alacrity to drop the gown over my head, and then bent his attention upon the buttons. "Who is it? Not Petrie; he never accepts invitations to dine. Sensible man. . . . Naville? Carter? Not . . ." The hands fumbling along my spine stopped, and Emerson's face loomed up over my shoulder, glaring like a gargoyle. "Not de Morgan! Peabody, if you have some underhanded scheme in mind—"

"Would I do such a thing?" De Morgan had refused the invitation, with polite regrets; he was engaged elsewhere. "No," I continued, as Emerson returned to the buttons—the frock had dozens of them, each about the size of a pea. "I was happy to learn the *Istar* and the *Seven Hathors* are in port."

"Oh. Sayce and Wilberforce." Emerson breathed heavily on the back of my neck. "I cannot imagine what you see in those two. A dilettante clergyman and a renegade politician—"

"They are excellent scholars. The Reverend Sayce has just been appointed to the new chair of Assyriology at Oxford."

"Dilettantes," Emerson repeated. "Sailing up and down the Nile on their dahabeeyahs instead of working like honest men."

A wistful sigh escaped me and Emerson, the most sensitive of men, again interrupted his labors to look inquiringly over my shoulder. "Do you miss your dahabeeyah, Peabody? If it would please you—"

"No, no, my dear Emerson. I confess that season of sailing was utter bliss; but I would not exchange it for the pleasure of our work together."

This admission resulted in a longer interruption of the buttoning, but I finally persuaded Emerson to complete the task. Turning, I demanded his comment.

"I like that dress, Peabody. Crimson becomes you. It reminds me of the gown you wore the night you proposed marriage to me."

"You will have your little joke, Emerson." I inspected myself in the mirror. "Not too bright a shade for a matron and the mother of a growing boy? No? Well, I accept your judgment as always, my dear Emerson."

I too had fond memories of the gown to which he referred. I had worn it on the night *he* proposed to *me*, and I took care always to have in my wardrobe a frock of similar cut and color. One abomination of the past was gone, however—the bustle. I could have wished that some fashion arbiter would also do away with corsets. Mine were never as tight as fashion decreed, for I had grave suspicions about the effect of tight lacing on the internal organs. I did not wear them at all under my working clothes, but some concession was necessary with evening dress in order to attain the smooth flowing line then in style.

I clasped about my neck a gold chain bearing a scarab of Thutmose III—my husband's gift—and, my toilette completed, went to assist Emerson with his. John and Ramses returned in time to contribute their assistance, which was not unwelcome, for Emerson carried on in his usual fashion, losing collar buttons, studs and links because of the vehemence with which he attacked these accessories. Ramses had become particularly good at locating collar buttons; he was small enough to crawl under beds and other furniture.

Emerson looked so handsome in evening dress that the effort was all worthwhile. His heightened color and the brilliant blue of his eyes, flaming with rage, only added to his splendid appearance. Unlike most of the men of my acquaintance, he remained clean-shaven. I preferred him without hirsute adornment, but I suspected it was only another example of Emersonian perversity. If beards had gone out of style, Emerson would have grown one.

"You are very handsome, Papa," said Ramses admiringly. "But I would not like a suit like dat. It is too hard to keep clean."

Emerson brushed absently at the cat hairs adhering to his sleeve, and I sent Ramses off for another bath. It was apparent that no one ever dusted under the bed. We ordered supper to be sent up for John and Ramses and went downstairs to meet our guests.

Dinner was not wholly a success. But then dinner never was when Emerson was in a surly mood, and he was almost always in a surly mood when he was forced to dine out in public and in formal attire. I have seen him behave worse. He had a grudging respect for Mr. Wilberforce, but the Reverend Sayce brought out all his baser instincts. There could not have been a greater contrast between two men—Emerson, tall, broad-shouldered and hearty, Sayce small and spare, with sunken eyes behind his steel-rimmed spectacles. He wore clerical garb even when on an excavation, and looked like a magnified beetle in his long-tailed black coat and reversed collar.

Wilberforce, whom the Arabs called "Father of a Beard," was a more phlegmatic character, and Emerson had given up teasing him, since he only responded by smiling and stroking his magnificent white beard. They greeted us with their customary affability and expressed regret that they would not have the pleasure of meeting Ramses that evening.

"As usual you are au courant with all the news," I said in a spritely manner. "We only arrived yesterday, yet you are aware that our son is with us this season."

"The community of scholars and Egyptologists is small," said Wilberforce with a smile. "It is only natural we should take an interest in one another's activities."

"I don't see why," said Emerson, with the air of a man who has determined to be disagreeable. "The personal activities of others, scholars or not, are exceedingly dull. And the professional activities of most of the archaeologists of my acquaintance are not worth talking about."

I tried to turn the conversation by a courteous inquiry after Mrs. Wilberforce. I had, of course, included that lady in my invitation, but she had been forced to decline. She was always forced to decline. She appears to have been a rather sickly person.

My tactful efforts were unavailing, however. The

Reverend Sayce, who had been needled by Emerson on only too many occasions, was not Christian enough to forgo a chance at revenge. "Speaking of professional activities," he said, "I understand our friend de Morgan has great hopes for his excavations at Dahshoor. Where is it that you will be working this season, Professor?"

Seeing by Emerson's expression that he was about to launch into a diatribe against de Morgan, I kicked him under the table. His expression changed to one of extreme anguish and he let out a cry of pain. "Mazghunah," I said, before Emerson could collect himself. "We are excavating at Mazghunah this season. The pyramids, you know."

"Pyramids?" Wilberforce was too courteous to contradict a lady, but he looked doubtful. "I confess I don't know the site, but I did think I was familiar with all the known pyramids."

"These," I said, "are unknown pyramids."

Conversation then became general. It was not until we had retired to the lounge for brandy and cigars (in the case of the gentlemen) that I produced my scrap of papyrus and handed it to the reverend.

"I procured this today from one of the antiquities dealers. Since you are the biblical authority among us, I thought you might make more of it than I have been able to do."

The reverend's deep-set eyes lit with the flame of inquiry. Adjusting his spectacles, he examined the writing, saying as he did so, "I am no authority on Coptic, Mrs. Emerson. I expect this is probably . . ." His voice trailed off as he bent his full attention to the text, and Wilberforce remarked, smiling, "I am surprised at you, Mrs. Amelia. I thought you and your husband refused to buy from dealers."

"I do refuse," said Emerson, his nose in the air. "Unfortunately, my wife's principles are more elastic than mine."

"We are looking for papyri for Walter," I explained.

"Ah, yes—Professor Emerson the younger. One of the finest students of the language. But I'm afraid you will find the competition keen, Mrs. Amelia. With so many of the younger men studying Egyptian, everyone wants new texts."

"Including yourself?" I asked, with a keen look at Mr. Wilberforce.

"To be sure. But," the American said, his eyes twinkling, "I'll play fair and square, ma'am. If you find something worthwhile, I won't try to steal it."

"Which is more than can be said for some of our associates," grumbled Emerson. "If you happen to meet Wallis Budge, tell him I carry a stout stick and will use it on anyone who tries to make off with my property."

I did not hear Mr. Wilberforce's reply. My attention was caught by two people who had just entered the lounge.

The young man had turned his head to address his companion. The profile thus displayed was pure Greek, with the spare and exquisite modeling of a fifth-century Apollo or Hermes. His hair, brushed back from his high, classical brow, shone like electrum, the blend of silver and gold used by the Egyptians in their most priceless ornaments. The extreme pallor of his skin—which led me to deduce that he had not been long in the sunny clime of Egypt—added to the impression of a carving in alabaster. Then he smiled, in response to some comment of his companion, and a remarkable transformation took place. Benevolence beamed from every aspect of his countenance. The marble statue came alive.

The lady with him . . . was no lady. Her gown of deep-purple satin in the latest and most extravagant style suggested not the world of fashion but the demi-monde. It was trimmed with sable and beads, ruffles and lace, bows, puffs and plumes, yet it managed to bare an improper amount of plump white bosom. Gems blazed from every part of her portly person, and cosmetics covered every square centimeter of her face. If the gentleman was a classic marble carving, his companion was a blowsy, painted carnival statue.

Emerson jogged my elbow. "What are you gaping at, Amelia? Mr. Wilberforce asked you a question."

"I beg your pardon," I said. "I confess I was staring at that extremely handsome young man."

"You and every other lady in the room," said Mr. Wilberforce. "It is a remarkable face, is it not? I was reminded when I first met him of the young horsemen on the Parthenon frieze."

The pair came toward us, the female clinging to her companion's arm, and I saw with a shock that the Greek hero wore a clerical collar. "A clergyman," I exclaimed.

"That accounts for the fascination of the ladies," said Emerson with a curling lip. "All weak-minded females dote on weedy curates. One of your colleagues, Sayce?"

The reverend looked up. A frown wrinkled his brow. "No," he said, rather curtly.

"He is an American," Wilberforce explained. "A member of one of those curious sects that proliferate in my great country. I believe they call themselves the Brethren of the Holy Jerusalem."

"And the—er—lady?" I inquired.

"I cannot imagine why you are interested in these persons," Emerson grumbled. "If there is anything more tedious than a pious hypocrite of a preacher, it is an empty-headed fashionable woman. I am thankful I have nothing to do with such people."

It was Mr. Wilberforce to whom I had addressed my inquiry, and as I expected he was able to satisfy my curiosity. "She is the Baroness von Hohensteinbauergrunewald. A Bavarian family, related to the Wittelsbachs, and almost as wealthy as that royal house."

"Ha," Emerson cried. "The young man is a fortune hunter. I knew it. A weedy, sanctimonious fortune hunter."

"Oh, do be quiet, Emerson," I said. "Are they engaged? She seems very friendly with the young man."

"I hardly think so," said Wilberforce, smothering a smile. "The baroness is a widow, but the disparity of their ages, to mention only one incongruity . . . And to call the young man a fortune hunter is unjust. All who know him speak of him with the greatest respect."

"I don't want to know him, or talk about him,"

said Emerson. "Well, Sayce, what do you make of Mrs. Emerson's fragment?"

"It is a difficult text," Sayce said slowly. "I can read the proper names—they are Greek—"

"Didymus Thomas," I said.

"I congratulate you on your understanding, Mrs. Emerson. I am sure you also noted this ligature, which is the abbreviation for the name of Jesus."

I smiled modestly. Emerson snorted. "A biblical text? That's all the Copts ever wrote, curse them—copies of Scripture and boring lies about the saints. Who was Didymus Thomas?"

"The apostle, one presumes," said the reverend.

"Doubting Thomas?" Emerson grinned. "The only apostle with an ounce of sense. I always liked old Thomas."

Sayce frowned. " 'Blessed are they who have not seen and who have believed,' " he quoted.

"Well, what else could the man say?" Emerson demanded. "I admit he knew how to turn a phrase—if he ever existed, which is questionable."

Sayce's wispy goatee quivered with outrage. "If that is your view, Professor, this scrap can be of little interest to you."

"Not at all." Emerson plucked it from the reverend's hand. "I shall keep it as a memento of my favorite apostle. Really, Sayce, you are no better than the other bandits in my profession, trying to steal my discoveries."

Mr. Wilberforce loudly announced that it was time to go. Emerson continued to talk, expressing a series of opinions calculated to infuriate the Reverend Sayce. They ranged from his doubts as to the historicity of Christ to his poor opinion of Christian missionaries. "The effrontery of the villains," he exclaimed, referring to the latter. "What business have they forcing their narrow-minded prejudices on Muslims? In its pure form the faith of Islam is as good as any other religion—which is to say, not very good, but . . ."

Wilberforce finally drew his affronted friend away, but not before the reverend got off a final shot. "I wish you luck with your 'pyramids,' Professor. And I am sure you will enjoy your neighbors at Mazghunah."

"What do you suppose he meant by that?" Emerson demanded as the two walked off, Wilberforce's tall form towering over that of his slighter friend.

"We will find out in due course, I suppose."

Those were my precise words. I recall them well. Had I but known under what hideous circumstances they would recur to me, like the slow tolling of a funeral bell, a premonitory shudder would have rippled through my limbs. But it did not.

After looking in on Ramses and finding him wrapped in innocent slumber, with the cat asleep at his feet, Emerson proposed that we seek our own couch.

"Have you forgotten our assignation?" I inquired.

"I hoped that you had," Emerson replied. "Abd el Atti is not expecting us, Amelia. He only said that to get rid of you."

"Nonsense, Emerson. When the muezzin calls from the minaret at midnight—"

"He will do no such thing. You ought to know better, Amelia. There is no midnight call to prayer.

Daybreak, midday, mid-afternoon, sunset and nightfall—those are the prescribed times of *salah* for faithful Muslims."

He was quite correct. I cannot imagine why the fact had slipped my mind. Rallying from my momentary chagrin, I said, "But surely I have sometimes heard a muezzin call in the night."

"Oh yes, sometimes. Religious fervor is apt to seize the devout at odd times. But one cannot predict such occasions. Depend on it, Amelia, the old scoundrel won't be at his shop."

"We can't be certain of that."

Emerson stamped his foot. "Curse it, Amelia, you are the most stubborn woman of my acquaintance. Let us compromise—if that word is in your vocabulary."

I folded my arms. "Propose your compromise."

"We'll sit on the terrace for another hour or so. If we hear a call to prayer, from any mosque within earshot, we will go to the Khan el Khaleel. If by half past twelve we have heard nothing, we will go to bed."

Emerson had come up with a sensible suggestion. The plan was precisely what I had been about to propose, for after all, we could not start out for the shop until we had heard the signal.

"That is a very reasonable compromise," I said. "As always, Emerson, I submit to your judgment."

There are worse ways of passing an hour than on Shepheard's terrace. We sat at a table near the railing, sipping our coffee and watching the passerby, for people keep late hours in the balmy clime of Egypt. The stars, thickly clustered, hung so low they appeared to be tangled in the branches of the trees, and they gave a light almost as bright as day. Flower sellers offered their wares—necklaces of jasmine, bouquets of rosebuds tied with bright ribbons. The scent of the flowers hung heavy and intoxicating in the warm night air. Emerson presented me with a nosegay and squeezed my hand. With the warm pressure of his fingers on mine, and his eyes speaking sentiments that required no words of ordinary speech; with the seductive breeze caressing my cheek and the scent of roses perfuming the night—I almost forgot my purpose.

But hark—what was that? High and clear above the moonlit cupolas, rising and falling in musical appeal—the cry of the muezzin! *"Allâhu akbar, allâhu akbar—lâilâha illa'llâh!"* God is great, God is great; there is no God but God.

I sprang to my feet. "I knew it! Quickly, Emerson, let us be off."

"Curse it," said Emerson. "Very well, Amelia. But when I get my hands on that fat villain he will be sorry he suggested this."

We had, of course, changed into our working attire before coming down to the terrace. Emerson changed because he hated evening dress; I changed because I had been certain all along we would be going to the Khan el Khaleel. And, as events proved, I was right. Emerson insists to this day that Abd el Atti never meant us to come, and that the spontaneous exclamation of the muezzin that night was pure coincidence. The absurdity of this should be readily apparent.

Be that as it may, we were on our way before the last testimonial of the religious person had faded into silence. We went on foot; it would have been inapropos to take a carriage to a secret rendezvous, and, in any case, no wheeled vehicle could have entered the narrow alleys of the Khan el Khaleel. Emerson set a rapid pace. He was eager to have the business over and done with. I was eager to reach the shop and learn what deadly secret threatened my old friend. For I had a certain fondness for Abd el Atti. He might be a scoundrel, but he was an engaging scoundrel.

After we had turned from the Muski into the narrower ways of the bazaar, the starlight was cut off by the houses looming high on either hand, and the farther we penetrated into the heart of the maze, the darker it became. The protruding balconies with their latticed wooden shutters jutted into the street, almost meeting overhead. Occasionally a lighted window spilled a golden glimmer onto the pathway, but most of the windows were dark. Parallel slits of light marked closed shutters. The darkness teemed with foul movement; rats glided behind heaps of refuse; lean, vicious stray dogs slunk into even narrower passageways as we approached. The rank stench of rotting fruit, human waste and infected air filled the tunnel-like street like a palpable liquid, clogging the nostrils and the lungs.

Emerson plunged on, splashing through puddles of unspeakable stuff and sometimes slipping on a melon rind or rotten orange. I stayed close behind him. This was the first time I had been in the old city at night without a servant carrying a torch. I am not easily daunted. Danger I can face unafraid, enemies I have confronted without losing my calm; but the stealthy, stinking silence began to overpower my mind. I was glad Emerson was with me, and even happier that he had not suggested I remain behind. In this, as in all our adventures, we were equal partners. Few men could have accepted that arrangement. Emerson is a remarkable man. But then, if he had not been a remarkable man, I would not have married him.

Except for the soft, sinister movements of the predators of the night, the silence was complete. In the modern street, where the tourists and those who catered to their whims still sought pleasure, there were lights and laughter, music and loud voices. The dwellers of the Khan el Khaleel were asleep or engaged in occupations that demanded dim lights and barred doors. As we proceeded I caught a whiff of sickening sweetness and saw a pallid streak of light through a shuttered window. A voice, muted by the thick mud-plaster walls, rose in a thin shriek of pain or ecstasy. The house was a *ghurza*, an opium den, where the *hashshahiin* lay wrapped in stuporous dreams. I bit back a cry as a dark form rushed through an opening ahead and vanished into a doorway, blending with the blackness there. Emerson chuckled. "The *nadurgiyya* was dozing. He ought to have heard us approaching before this."

He spoke softly; but oh, how wonderfully, blessedly comforting was that calm English voice! "*Nadurgiyya?*" I repeated.

"The lookout. He took us for police spies. The ghurza will close down until the supposed danger is past. Are you sorry you came, Peabody?"

The street was so narrow we could not walk side by side and so dark I could scarcely make out the vague outline of his form. I sensed, rather than saw, the hand stretched toward me. Clasping it, I replied truthfully, "Not at all, my dear Emerson. It is a most interesting and unusual experience. But I confess that if you were not with me I would be conscious of a certain trepidation."

"We are almost there," Emerson said. "If this is a wild-goose chase, Peabody, I will hold it over you for the rest of your life."

Like all the others, Abd el Atti's shop was dark and seemingly deserted. "What did I tell you?" Emerson said.

"We must go round to the back," I said.

"The back, Peabody? Do you take this for an English village, with lanes and kitchen doors?"

"Don't play games, Emerson. I am quite confident you know where the back entrance is located. There must be another entrance; some of Abd el Atti's clients would hardly choose to walk in the front door with their goods."

Emerson grunted. Holding my hand, he proceeded along the street for a distance and then drew me toward what appeared to be a blank wall. There was an opening, however, so narrow and opaque that it looked like a line drawn with the blackest of ink. My shoulders brushed the walls on the other side. Emerson had to sidle along sideways.

"Here it is," he said, after a moment.

"Where? I can't see a thing."

He directed my hand toward an invisible surface. I felt wood under my fingers. "There is no knocker," I said, groping.

"Nor a doorbell," Emerson said sarcastically. He tapped lightly.

There was no response. Emerson, never the most patient of men, let out an oath and struck his fist against the door.

The panel yielded. A scant inch, no more, and in utter silence it moved; and through the slit came a pallid light, so dim it did not penetrate the darkness where we stood.

"The devil," Emerson muttered.

I shared his sentiments. There was something strange and sinister about the movement of the door. From within came not the slightest whisper of sound. It was as if a pall of horror lay over the region, silencing even breath. More prosaically, the yielding of the portal held ominous implications. Either the person who had opened it was concealed behind it, or the door had not been latched in the first place. It was inconceivable that a merchant in that quarter would leave his shop unlocked at night, unless . . .

"Stand back, Peabody," Emerson ordered. He reinforced the command with an outthrust arm that flung me back against the wall with rather more force than was necessary. Before I could protest, he raised his foot and kicked the door.

If he had intended to pin a would-be assassin between door and inner wall he failed. The portal was

so heavy it responded sluggishly to his attack, opening only halfway. Emerson cursed and clutched his
foot.

I went to his side and looked in. A single lamp,
one of the crude clay bowls that have been used
since ancient times, lit the room; the flickering,
smoking flame created an eerie illusion of surrepti-
tious movement in the shadows. The place was in
the wildest disorder. Abd el Atti was not noted for
neatness, but something more alarming than sloth
was responsible for the confusion that prevailed. A
rickety wooden table had been overturned. The bits
of pottery and glass littering the floor must have
fallen from its surface, or from the shelves on the
righthand wall, which were empty. Mingled with
the broken pieces were scarabs and ushabtis, scraps
of papyrus and linen, stone vessels, carvings, and
even a wrapped mummy, half-hidden by a wooden
packing case.

Emerson repeated his adjuration to the Prince of
Evil and stepped boldly forward. I caught his arm.
"Emerson, take care. I hypothesize that a struggle
has ensued here."

"Either that or Abd el Atti has suffered a seizure
at long last."

"Were that the case, his prostrate body would be
visible."

"True." Emerson fondled the cleft in his chin,
his invariable habit when deep in thought. "Your
hypothesis seems more likely."

He tried to shake off my hold, but I persisted.
"Presumably one of the combatants was our old

friend. But the other—Emerson, he may be lying in wait, ready to attack."

"He would be a fool if he stayed," Emerson replied. "Even if he had been on the premises when we arrived, he had ample time to make good his escape through the front of the shop while we stood here debating. Besides, where would he hide? The only possible place . . ." He peered behind the door. "No, there is no one here. Come in and close the door. I don't like the look of this."

I followed his instructions. I felt more secure with the heavy door closed against the dangers of the night. Yet a sinking feeling had seized me; I could not shake off the impression that something dreadful lurked in that quiet, shadowy place.

"Perhaps Abd el Atti was not here after all," I said. "Two thieves fell out—or down—"

Emerson continued to worry his chin. "Impossible to tell if anything is missing. What a clutter! Good Gad, Amelia—look there, on the shelf. That fragment of painted relief—I saw it only two years ago in one of the tombs at El Bersheh. Confound the old rascal, he has no more morals than a jackal, robbing his own ancestors!"

"Emerson," I remonstrated, "this is not the time—"

"And there . . ." Emerson pounced on an object half-concealed by pottery shards. "A portrait panel—torn from the mummy—encaustic on wood . . ."

Only one thing can distract Emerson from his passion for antiquities. It did not seem appropriate to apply this distraction. I left him muttering and scrabbling in the debris; slowly, with dread impeding my every step, I approached the curtained doorway that led to the front room of the shop. I knew what I would find and was prepared, as I thought, for the worst; yet the sight that met my eyes when I drew the curtain aside froze my limbs and my vocal apparatus.

At first it was only a dark, shapeless mass that almost filled the tiny room. The dark thing moved, gently swaying like a monster of the deep sluggishly responding to the slow movements of watery currents. A shimmer of gold, a flash of scarlet—my eyes, adjusting to the gloom, began to make out details—a hand, glittering with rings . . . A face. Unrecognizable as human, much less familiar. Black and bloated, the dark tongue protruding in ghastly mockery, the wide eyes suffused with blood . . .

A shriek of horror burst from my lips. Emerson was instantly at my side. His hands closed painfully over my shoulders. "Peabody, come away. Don't look."

But I had looked, and I knew the sight would haunt my dreams: Abd el Atti, hanging from the roofbeam of his own shop, swaying to and fro like some winged monster of the night.

FOUR

Clearing my throat, I reassured my husband. "I am quite myself again, Emerson. I apologize for startling you."

"No apologies are necessary, my dear Peabody. What a horrible sight! He was grotesque enough in life, but this . . ."

"Should we not cut him down?"

"Impractical and unnecessary," Emerson said. "There is not a spark of life left of him. We will leave that unpleasant task to the authorities." I tried to put his hands away, and he went on, in mounting indignation, "You don't mean to play physician? I assure you, Peabody—"

"My dear Emerson, I have never pretended I could restore life to the dead. But before we summon the police I want to examine the situation."

Accustomed as I am to violent death, it cost me some effort to touch the poor flaccid hand. It was still warm. Impossible to calculate the time of death; the temperature in the closed room was stiflingly hot. But I deduced he had not been dead long. I struck several matches and examined the floor, averting my eyes from Abd el Atti's dreadful face.

"What the devil are you doing?" Emerson demanded, arms akimbo. "Let's get out of this hellish place. We will have to return to the hotel to call the police; people in this neighborhood don't respond to knocks on the door at night."

"Certainly." I had seen what I needed to know. I followed Emerson into the back room and let the curtain fall into place, concealing the horror within.

"Looking for clues?" Emerson inquired ironically, as I inspected the litter on the floor. The mummy portrait was not there. I made no comment; the piece had been stolen anyway, and it could not be in better hands than those of my husband.

"I don't know what I'm looking for," I replied. "It is hopeless, I suppose; there is no chance of finding a clear footprint in this debris. Ah! Emerson, look here. Isn't this a spot of blood?"

"The poor fellow died of strangulation, Peabody," Emerson exclaimed.

"Obviously, Emerson. But I am sure this blood—"

"It is probably paint."

". . . that this blood is that of the thief who . . ."

"What thief?"

". . . who cut himself during the fight," I continued, being accustomed to Emerson's rude habit of interrupting. "His foot, I expect. He trampled on a bit of broken pottery while struggling with Abd el Atti—"

Emerson seized me firmly by the hand. "Enough, Peabody. If you don't come with me, I will throw you over my shoulder and carry you."

"The passageway outside is too narrow," I pointed out. "Just one minute, Emerson."

He tugged me to my feet as my fingers closed over the object that had caught my attention. "It is a scrap of papyrus," I exclaimed.

Emerson led me from the room.

We had reached the broad stretch of the Muski before either of us spoke again. Even that popular thoroughfare was quiet, for the hour was exceedingly late; but the beneficent glow of starlight lifted our spirits as it illumined the scene. I drew a long breath. "Wait a minute, Emerson. I can't walk so fast. I am tired."

"I should think so, after such a night." But Emerson immediately slowed his pace and offered me his arm. We walked on side-by-side, and I did not scruple to lean on him. He likes me to lean on him. In a much milder tone he remarked, "You were right after all, Peabody. The poor old wretch did have something on his mind. A pity he decided to end it all before he talked to us."

"What are you saying?" I exclaimed. "Abd el Atti did not commit suicide. He was murdered."

"Amelia, that is the merest surmise. I confess I had expected you would concoct some wild theory. Sensationalism is your meat and drink. But you cannot—"

"Oh, Emerson, don't be ridiculous. You saw the murder room. Was there anything near the body—a table, a chair, a stool—on which Abd el Atti might have stood while he tied the noose around his neck?"

"Damnation," said Emerson.

"No doubt. He was murdered, Emerson—our

old friend was foully slain. And after he had appealed to us to save him."

"Pray do not insult my intelligence by attempting to move me with such sentimental tosh," Emerson exclaimed furiously. "If Abd el Atti was murdered, the killer was one of his criminal associates. It has nothing to do with us. Only an unhappy coincidence—or, more accurately, your incurable habit of meddling in other people's business—put us on the spot at the wrong time. We will notify the police, as is our duty, and that will be the end of it. I have enough on my mind this year. I will not allow my professional activities to be interrupted. . . ."

I let him grumble on. Time would prove me right; the inexorable pressure of events would force our involvement. So why argue?

II

A few hours' sleep restored me to my usual vigor and spirits. When I awoke the sun was high in the heavens. My first act, even before drinking the tea the safragi brought me, was to open the door to the adjoining room. It was empty. A note, placed prominently on the table, explained that John and Ramses, not wishing to waken us, had gone out to explore the city. "Do not worry, sir and madam," John had written. "I will watch over Master Ramses."

Emerson was not reassured by the message. "You see what happens when you go off on your absurd adventures," he grumbled. "We overslept and now our helpless young son is wandering the streets of this wicked city, unprotected and vulnerable."

"I too am deeply concerned," I assured him. "I dare not imagine what Ramses can do to Cairo in the space of a few hours. No doubt we will soon be receiving delegations of outraged citizens, with bills for damages."

I spoke half in jest. I did expect a confrontation, not with Ramses' victims, but with the police; for though Emerson resolutely refused to discuss the murder of Abd el Atti, I felt sure our involvement with that affair was not over. And indeed the message came as we were finishing breakfast, which had been brought to our room. The white-robed safragi bowed almost to the floor as he delivered it. Would we, in our infinite condescension, come to the manager's office, where an agent of the police wished to consult us?

Emerson flung down his napkin. "There, you see? More delay, more vexation. It is all your fault, Amelia. Come along, let's get this over and done with."

Mr. Baehler, the manager of Shepheard's, rose to greet us as we entered his office. He was Swiss—a tall, handsome man with a mane of graying hair and an ingratiating smile.

My answering smile turned to a grimace when I saw the other persons who were present. I had expected to find a police official. I had not expected that the official would have in his custody the small and incredibly filthy person of my son.

Emerson was equally affected. He brushed past Mr. Baehler, ignoring the latter's outstretched hand,

and snatched Ramses up in his arms. "Ramses! My dear boy! What are you doing here? Are you injured?"

Crushed to his father's bosom, Ramses was incapable of replying. Emerson turned an infuriated look upon the policeman. "How dare you, sir?"

"Control yourself, Emerson," I exclaimed. "You ought rather to thank this gentleman for escorting the boy home."

The police officer gave me a grateful look. He was a grizzled, heavyset man, with a complexion of beautiful coffee-brown. His excellent English and tidy uniform displayed the unmistakable British discipline that has transformed Egypt since her Majesty's government assumed beneficent control over that formerly benighted land.

"Thank you, ma'am," he said, touching his cap. "The young master is not hurt, I promise."

"So I see. I had anticipated, Inspector—is that the proper mode of address?—I had anticipated that you had come to question us concerning the murder last night."

"But I have, ma'am," was the respectful reply. "We found the young master at the shop of the dead man."

I sank into the chair Mr. Baehler held for me. Ramses said breathlessly, "Mama, dere is a matter I would prefer to discuss wit' you in private—"

"Silence!" I shouted.

"But, Mama, de cat Bastet—"

"Silence, I say!"

Silence ensued. Even Mr. Baehler, whose reputation for equanimity and social pose was unequaled, appeared at a loss. Slowly and deliberately I turned to focus my gaze on John, who stood flattened against the wall between a table and a tall carved chair. It was not possible for a person of John's size to be inconspicuous. But he was trying his best. When my eye fell upon him he stammered, "Ow, madam, Oi tried me best, indeed Oi did, but Oi didn't 'ave the least idear where we was until—"

"Watch your vowels," I said sternly. "You are reverting to the unacceptable verbal customs of the ambience from which Professor Emerson rescued you. Five years of my training ought to have eradicated all traces of your past."

John swallowed. His Adam's apple quivered violently. "I," he said slowly, "did not know where we was—where we were—until—"

"Dat is right, Mama," Ramses piped up. "It was not John's fault. He t'ought we were only exploring de bazaars."

Everyone spoke at once. Mr. Baehler implored we would settle our family disputes in private, since he was a busy man; the inspector remarked that he had work to do elsewhere; Emerson bellowed at John; John tried to defend himself, his vowels suffering dreadfully in the process; Ramses defended John. I silenced the uproar by rising impetuously to my feet.

"Enough! Inspector, I presume you have no further need of Ramses?"

"I do not," said the gentleman, with heartfelt sincerity.

"John, take Ramses upstairs and wash him. Remain in your room—both of you—until we come. No, Emerson, not a word."

I was, of course, obeyed to the letter. After the miscreants had departed, I resumed my chair. "Now," I said. "To business."

It was soon dispatched. To my exceeding annoyance I found that the policeman's view of the case coincided with that of Emerson. He could hardly refuse to listen to my interpretation, but from the glances that passed among the gentlemen, not to mention Emerson's constant interruptions, I knew my views would be disregarded. "A falling-out between thieves," was the inspector's summary. "Thank you, Professor and Mrs. Emerson, for your assistance."

"When you have located the suspect, I will come to the police station to identify him," I said.

"Suspect?" The inspector stared at me.

"The man I saw yesterday talking to Abd el Atti. You noted down the description I gave you?"

"Oh. Yes, ma'am, I did."

"That description would fit half the male population of Cairo," Emerson said disparagingly. "What you really require, Inspector, is an expert to evaluate the contents of the shop. Most of it is stolen property; it belongs by rights to the Department of Antiquities. Though heaven knows there is no one in that dusty barn of a museum who has the slightest notion of how to care for the exhibits."

"My friends," Mr. Baehler said piteously. "Forgive me—"

"Yes, of course," I said. "Emerson, Mr. Baehler is

a busy man; I cannot imagine why you continue to take up his time. We will continue our discussion of the case elsewhere."

However, the inspector unaccountably refused to do this. He did not even accept Emerson's offer of assistance in cataloging the contents of the shop. Emerson would have followed him, arguing, had I not detained him.

"You can't go out on the street looking like that. Ramses has rubbed off on you. What is that blackish, sticky substance, do you suppose?"

Emerson glanced at the front of his coat. "It appears to be tar," he said in mild surprise. "Speaking of Ramses—"

"Yes," I said grimly. "Let us speak of, and to, that young man."

We found John and Ramses sitting side by side on the bed, like criminals awaiting sentence—though there was little sign of guilt on Ramses' freshly scrubbed countenance. "Mama," he began, "de cat Bastet—"

"Where is the cat?" I asked.

Ramses became quite purple in the face with frustration. "But dat is what I am endeavoring to explain, Mama. De cat Bastet has been mislaid. When de policeman took hold of me, radder more roughly dan de circumstances required, in my opinion—"

"Roughly, did you say?" Emerson's countenance reflected the same angry shade as that of his son. "Curse it, I knew I should have punched the villain in the jaw. Remain here, I will return as soon as I—"

"Wait, Emerson, wait!" I caught hold of his arm

with both hands and dug my heels into the mat. As we struggled, I to hold on and Emerson to free himself, Ramses remarked thoughtfully, "I would not have kicked him in de shin if he had been more courteous. To refer to me as a meddlesome imp of Satan was uncalled for."

Emerson stopped struggling. "Hmmm," he said.

"Forget the policeman," I cried. "Forget the cat. She will return of her own accord, Ramses; she is, after all, a native of the country."

"De reputed ability of animals to cross great stretches of unknown country is exaggerated, in my opinion," said Ramses.

"You have too many opinions," I retorted severely. "What were you doing at Abd el Atti's establishment?"

I find myself incapable of reproducing Ramses' explanation. His style of speech was extremely prolix, and he appeared deliberately to select as many words as possible beginning with the diphthong "th." Nor was it a convincing explanation. Ramses said he had been curious to examine further several objects he had seen in the back room of the shop during his unauthorized visit the day before. When directly questioned, he admitted he had overheard us discussing our intention of visiting Abd el Atti that night. "I meant to go wit' you," he added accusingly, "but I could not stay awake, and you, Mama, did not waken me."

"I had no intention of taking you, Ramses."

"I suspected dat," said Ramses.

"What objects were you curious about?" his father asked.

"Never mind," I said. "Do you realize that the day is half gone? I have never known any group of people to waste so much time over inconsequential matters."

Emerson shot me a look that said, plain as speech, "And whose fault is it that we have wasted half the day?" He did not speak aloud, however, since we try not to criticize one another before Ramses. A united front is absolutely essential for survival in that quarter. Instead he groaned, "I cannot shake the dust of this abominable city off my shoes too soon. I had hoped to leave by the end of the week, but . . ."

"We can leave tomorrow if we get to work at once," I replied. "What remains to be done?"

There was not really a great deal. I agreed to take care of our travel arrangements and the dispatch of the supplies I had purchased. Emerson was to go to Aziyeh, the nearby village from which we recruited our skilled workers, to make the final plans for their travel to Mazghunah.

"Take him with you," I said, indicating Ramses.

"Certainly," said Emerson. "I had intended to do that. What about John?"

John had lumbered to his feet when I entered the room. He remained standing, stiff as a statue, throughout the discussion, without venturing to speak. His eyes, fixed unblinkingly on my face, held the same expression of mingled shame and hope I had often seen on the countenances of the dogs after they had misbehaved.

"Madam," he began, with the most meticulous attention to his vowels, "I wish to say—"

"Too much has been said already," I interrupted. "I don't blame you, John. You are off your native turf, so to speak. In future I will define the perimeters of your wanderings more carefully."

"Yes, madam. Thank you, madam." John beamed. "Am I to go with Master Ramses and the professor, madam?"

"No. I need you. Is that all right with you, Emerson?"

Emerson, in his consummate innocence, said that it was quite all right with him.

And so, after a hasty meal, we separated to complete our assigned tasks. I was soon finished with mine. Europeans constantly complain about the dilatory habits of the East, but I fancy that is only an excuse for their own incompetence. I have never had the least difficulty getting people to do what I want them to do. It only requires a firm manner and a determination not to be distracted from the matter at hand. That is Emerson's trouble, and, in fact, the trouble with most men. They are easily distracted. I knew, for instance, that Emerson would spend the rest of the day on a project that could have been completed in three hours, travel time included. He would loll around smoking and *fahddling* (gossiping) with Abdullah, our old foreman; Ramses would come home with his stomach stuffed with insanitary sweeties and his precocious brain stuffed with new words, most of them indelicate. I was resigned to this. The alternative would have been to take Ramses with me.

John followed me with mute and meticulous devotion while I carried out my tasks. The faintest

shade of apprehension crossed his ingenuous countenance when I directed the driver of the carriage to
let us out near the entrance to the Khan el Khaleel,
but he held his tongue until we were almost at our
destination.

"Ow, madam," he began. "Oi promised the
master—"

"Vowels, John," I said. "Mind your vowels."

John fell in behind me as I passed under the arch-
way leading from the square. "Yes, madam. Madam,
are we going to that there—to that place?"

"Quite right."

"But, madam—"

"If you promised Professor Emerson you would
prevent me from going there, you ought to have
known better. And he ought not to have extracted
from you a promise you could not possibly keep."
John let out a faint moan and I condescended to
explain—something I seldom do. "The cat, John—
Ramses' cat. The least we can do is search for the
animal. It would break the boy's heart to leave it
behind."

A scene of utter pandemonium met our eyes when
we turned into the street before the shop. The narrow way was completely blocked by bodies, including those of several donkeys. Most of the people
were men, though there were a few women, all of the
humblest class, and all seemed intent on some spectacle ahead. They were laughing and talking, their
bodies swaying as they tried to see over the heads of
those in the front rank. Children wriggled through
the crowd.

A few polite Arabic phrases, and the judicious

application of my useful parasol to backs, shoulders and heads soon captured the attention of those nearest me. Obligingly they parted to let me pass.

Abd el Atti's shop was the focus of the crowd's interest. I had expected to find it locked and shuttered, with a constable on duty. Instead the place stood wide open, with not a policeman in sight. The small front room of the shop was filled with workmen wearing the cheap blue-and-white-striped robes of their class, and raglike turbans upon their heads. As soon as I saw what was going on I understood the amusement of the spectators. One workman would rush forward with a bundle in his arms, which he would load on the nearest donkey. Another workman would remove it. The process appeared to have all the futility of Penelope's weaving and unpicking of her tapestry, and at first I could not imagine what it all meant. Then I saw two people who stood nose to nose in the center of the room, shouting contradictory orders. One was a man, wearing a proper European suit and a bright red tarboosh. The other was a woman clad in dusty black from head to foot. In her agitation she had let fall her veil, disclosing a face as wrinkled as a currant and as malevolent as that of a witch in a German fairy tale. Her mouth gaped, showing toothless gums, as she alternatively shouted orders at the workmen and insults at her opponent.

It appeared to be the sort of situation that demanded the assistance of a sensible person. I applied the ferrule of my parasol briskly but impartially to the people blocking my way, and proceeded to the door of the shop. The old lady was the first to catch sight of me. She stopped in midword—a most improper word for anyone, much less a woman, to employ—and stared at me. The workmen dropped their bundles and gaped; the crowd murmured and swayed, watching expectantly; and the man in the tarboosh turned to face me.

"What is going on here?" I demanded. "This is the shop of Abd el Atti. Who are these people who are stealing his property?"

I had spoken in Arabic, but the man, identifying my nationality by my dress, replied in accented but fluent English. "I am no thief, missus. I am the son of the late Abd el Atti. May I ask your honored name?"

The last question was pronounced with a decided sneer, which vanished as soon as I gave my name. The old woman let out a high-pitched cackle of laughter. "It is the woman of the Father of Curses," she exclaimed. "The one they call Sitt Hakim. I have heard of you, Sitt. You will not let an old woman be robbed—an honorable wife be cheated of her inheritance?"

"You are the wife of Abd el Atti?" I asked in disbelief. This hideous old harridan? Abd el Atti, who was wealthy enough to purchase any number of young wives, and who had a keen appreciation of beauty?

"His chief wife," said the beldam. Belatedly recalling her bereaved state, she let out a sharp, unconvincing yelp of woe and stooped to scrape up a handful of dust, which she poured haphazardly over her head.

"Your mother?" I asked the man.

"Allah forbid," was the pious reply. "But I am the eldest living son, missus. I am taking the merchandise to my own shop; it is a fine shop, missus, on the Muski, a modern shop. Many English come to me; if you come, I will sell you beautiful things, very cheap—"

"Yes, yes; but that is not the question," I said, absently accepting the card he handed me. "You cannot take these things away now. The police are investigating your father's death. Didn't they tell you to leave the scene of the crime undisturbed?"

"Crime?" A singularly cynical smile transformed the man's face. His eyes narrowed to slits and his lips barely parted. "My unfortunate father has gone to make his peace with Allah. He had the wrong friends, missus. I knew that sooner or later one of them would remove him."

"And you don't call that a crime?"

The man only shrugged and rolled his eyes, in the ineffable and unanswerable fatalism of the East.

"In any case," I said, "you cannot remove anything from the shop. Replace all the objects, if you please, and lock the door."

The old woman's cacodemonic laughter broke out again. She began to shuffle her feet in a grotesque dance of triumph. "I knew the honored sitt would not let an old woman be robbed. The wisdom of the Prophet is yours, great lady. Accept an old woman's blessing. May you have many sons—many, many sons. . . ."

The idea was so appalling I think I turned pale. The man mistook my reaction for fear. He said in a grating voice, "You cannot make me do that, missus. You are not the police."

"Don't you talk that way to my lady," John said indignantly. "Madam, shall I punch him in the nose?"

A cheer, half-ironic, half-enthusiastic, broke out from those in the crowd who understood English. Evidently the son of Abd el Atti was not popular with the latter's neighbors.

"Certainly not," I said. "What is this talk of punching people? You must not attempt to imitate all your master's habits, John. Mr."—I glanced at the card I held—"Mr. Aslimi will be reasonable, I am sure."

Mr. Aslimi had very little choice in the matter. The donkeys departed unencumbered, and although it is difficult to read the countenance of a donkey, they appeared pleased to be relieved of their burdens. The workmen left, cursing the paltriness of their pay, the crowd dispersed. I dismissed the dear old lady before she could repeat her ominous blessing. She went hopping off, cackling like a large black raven. Then I turned to Mr. Aslimi. He was an unpleasant individual, but I could not help feeling some sympathy for anyone who had to deal with such a stepmother.

"If you will cooperate, Mr. Aslimi, I will do my best to plead your case with the authorities."

"How cooperate?" Aslimi asked cautiously.

"By answering my questions. How much do you know about your father's business?"

Well, of course he swore he knew nothing about

any criminal connections. I expected him to say that, but my intuition (which is scarcely ever at fault) told me he was not directly involved with the antiquities gang—probably to his regret. He also denied any acquaintance with the suspicious character I had seen with Abd el Atti. This time my intuition assured me he was lying. If he did not know the man's identity, he had a good idea as to who it might have been.

I then asked to be allowed to search the shop. There were some fine and obviously illegal antiquities in various locked cupboards, but they were not my concern, and Aslimi's dour expression lightened perceptibly when I passed them by without comment. I found nothing that gave me a clue to the identity of Abd el Atti's murderer. The place had been trampled by many feet and thoroughly ransacked—and besides, I had no idea what I was looking for.

Nor was there any trace of the missing Bastet. Mr. Aslimi denied having seen her. This time I felt sure he was telling the truth.

We parted with protestations of goodwill that were false on both sides. I felt sure he would not venture to reopen the shop, since I had assured him I would notify the police of his activities.

As John and I retraced our steps through the crooked, shady streets, I kept on the lookout for a lithe, tawny form, but to no avail. There was no answer to my repeated cries, except for curious glances from passersby. I heard one say, in response to a question from his companion, "It is the name of one of the old gods. They are magicians of great power, she and her husband; no doubt she is pronouncing a curse on that—Aslimi."

Reaching the Muski we took a carriage at the entrance to the bazaar. John sat uneasily on the very edge of the seat. "Madam," he said.

"Yes?"

"Oi—I won't be mentioning this to the master, if you like."

"There is no reason why you should bring up the subject, John. But if you are asked a direct question, naturally you will tell the truth."

"I will?"

"Certainly. We were looking for the cat. Unfortunately we found no trace of her."

But when I entered my room the first thing I saw was the familiar feline shape, curled up at the foot of my bed. As I had predicted, Bastet had found her way home.

III

The sun was setting the gilded spires and minarets of Cairo ablaze when the wanderers returned, in precisely the state I had expected. Ramses rushed, as usual, to embrace me. I was wearing my oldest dressing gown in anticipation of this. I was the only person, aside from his Aunt Evelyn, with whom Ramses was so physically demonstrative. Sometimes I suspected him of doing it out of malice, for he was almost always covered with some noxious substance or other. On this occasion, however, he veered off at the last moment and flung himself on the cat.

"Where did you find her, Mama?"

I was flattered by his assumption that I was responsible, but truth compelled me to reply, "I did not find her, Ramses—though I did look for her. She found her own way back."

"That is a relief," said Emerson, smiling wanly. "Ramses was quite cut up about her. Keep her on the lead from now on, my boy."

"And put her down until after you have bathed," I added. "I spent an hour combing and cleaning her. You will get her dirty again."

Clutching the cat to his bosom, in flagrant disregard of this order, Ramses retired, with John in attendance. He (Ramses) smelled very peculiar. Goat, I believe.

Emerson also smelled of goat, and of the strong tobacco favored by the men of Aziyeh. He looked tired, and admitted as much when I questioned him. When I questioned him further, he admitted that Ramses' "boyish joie de vivre," as he put it, was responsible for his fatigue. Ramses had fallen out of a palm tree and into the river; he had been attacked and slightly trampled by a goat after attempting to loosen the rope around its neck, which he felt was too tight (the animal had either mistaken his motives or yielded to the irascibility of temper to which billy goats are traditionally prone); and had concluded the afternoon by consuming several pints of date wine, forbidden to devout Muslims, but brewed on the sly by some of the villagers.

"Strange," I said. "He did not appear to be inebriated."

"He rid himself of the wine almost immediately," said Emerson. "On the floor of Abdullah's house."

At my suggestion Emerson retired behind the screen to freshen up, while I called the safragi and ordered whiskey and soda for both of us.

As we sipped this refreshing beverage, we compared notes on the day's activities. The results were most satisfactory. All the necessary arrangements had been completed and we were ready to leave at dawn. I had spent the remainder of the afternoon packing and sealing up our boxes—or rather, supervising the hotel servants in that endeavor—so we could spend the evening in quiet enjoyment. It would be the last evening for many weeks that we would enjoy civilized amenities, and although I yield to no one in my appreciation of desert life, I intended to take advantage of wine and good food, hot baths and soft beds while they were available.

We took Ramses with us to dinner, though he was reluctant to part with Bastet. "Someone has hurt her," he said, looking accusingly at me. "Dere is a cut on her back, Mama—a sharp cut, like dat made by a knife."

"I saw it, and have attended to it, Ramses."

"But, Mama—"

"It is a wonder she has no more scars than that to show for her adventure. I only hope she has not . . ."

"Has not what, Mama?"

"Never mind." I stared at the cat, who stared back at me with enigmatic golden eyes. She did not appear to be in a state of amatory excitement. . . . Time, and only time, would tell.

For once Emerson did not grumble about being forced to dine out. Puffed with fatherly pride, he presented, "my son, Walter Peabody Emerson," to everyone he knew and several he did not know. I was rather proud of the boy myself. He was wearing Scottish dress, with a little kilt in the Emerson tartan. (Designed by myself, it is a tasteful blend of scarlet, forest-green and blue, with narrow yellow and purple stripes.)

All in all, it was a most pleasant evening, and when we retired to our rooms we sought our couch in serene contemplation of a day well spent and of useful work ahead.

The moon had set, and silvery starlight was the only illumination when I woke in the small hours of the morning. I was instantly alert. I never wake unless there is cause, and I soon identified the cause that had roused me on this occasion—a soft, stealthy sound in the corner of the room where our bags and boxes were piled, ready to be removed in the morning.

For an interval I lay perfectly still, allowing my eyes to adjust to the faint light, and straining to hear. Emerson's stertorous breathing interfered with this latter activity, but in the lulls between inspiration and expiration I could hear the thief scrabbling among our luggage.

I am accustomed to nocturnal alarms. For some reason they occur frequently with me. I hardly need say that I was not in the least afraid. The only question in my mind was how to apprehend the thief. There was no lock on our door. The presence of the safragi in the hallway was supposed to be sufficient to deter casual thieves, few of whom would have had the temerity to enter a place like Shepheard's. I felt certain that this unusual event was the result of my investigation into Abd el Atti's murder. It was a thrilling prospect. Here at last, in my very room, was a possible clue. It did not occur to me to awaken Emerson. He wakens noisily, with cries and gasps and thrashing about.

On several previous occasions I had fallen into the error of tangling myself up in the mosquito netting, thus giving a midnight invader a chance to escape. I was determined not to commit the same mistake. The filmy folds of the netting were tucked firmly under the mattress on all sides of the bed. I began tugging gently at the portion nearest my head, pulling it free an inch at a time. Emerson continued to snore. The thief continued to explore.

When the netting was loose as far down as I could reach without moving more than my arm, the crucial moment was upon me. Mentally I reviewed my plans. My parasol stood ready as always, propped against the head of the bed. The thief was in the corner farthest from the door. Speed rather than silence was now my aim. Gathering a handful of the netting, I gave it a sharp tug.

The whole cursed apparatus came tumbling down on me. Evidently the nails holding it to the ceiling had become weakened. As I struggled in vain to free myself, I heard, mingled with Emerson's bewildered curses, the sound of feet thudding across the floor. The door opened and closed.

"Curse it," I cried, forgetting myself in my frustration.

"Curse it," Emerson shouted. "What the devil . . ." And other even more forceful expressions of alarm.

My efforts to extricate myself were foiled by Emerson's frantic thrashing, which only succeeded in winding the netting more tightly about our limbs. When the sleepers in the next room rushed to the scene we were lying side by side, wrapped like a pair of matched mummies and incapable of movement of any kind. Emerson was still roaring out curses; and the look on John's face as he stood staring, his nightcap standing up in a peak and his bare shanks showing under the hem of his gown, moved me to a peal of hysterical laughter.

Emerson's breath finally gave out—he had inhaled a portion of the netting, which was wound around his face. In the blessed silence that followed I instructed John to put down the lamp before he dropped it and set the place on fire. The cat lowered her head and began sniffing about the room. The hair on her back stood up in a stiff ridge.

Ramses had taken in the situation with a look of mild inquiry. Now he disappeared into his own room and returned carrying some object that glittered in the light. Not until he approached close to the bed did I identify it. I let out a shriek.

"No, Ramses! Drop it. Drop it at once, do you hear?"

When I speak in that tone, Ramses does not argue. He dropped the knife. It was at least eight inches long, and polished to a wicked shine. "My intention," he began, "was to free you and Papa from de incumbrance dat in some wholly unaccountable manner seems to have—"

"I have no quarrel with your intentions, only with your methods." I managed to free one arm. It was not long before I had kicked off the netting, and I turned at once, with some anxiety, to Emerson. As I feared, his open mouth was stuffed with netting. His eyes bulged and his face had turned a portentous shade of mauve.

It took some little time to restore order. I resuscitated my wheezing spouse, confiscated the knife—a gift from Abdullah, which Ramses had not thought it expedient to mention—and ordered my son, my servant and my cat to return to their beds. Then, at last, I was able to turn my attention to the crime— for attempted burglary, I venture to assert, must be called a crime.

It was no use pursuing the thief. He had had time to cross half of Cairo by then. One look at the scene of his inquiries assured me he was a master at his illegal craft, for he had managed to create considerable havoc with a minimum of sound. He had not ventured to open any of the packing cases, for they had been nailed shut, but all our personal baggage had been searched. The contents lay in untidy heaps on the floor. A bottle of ink had lost its stopper, with disastrous consequences to my best shirtwaist.

Emerson, now fully restored but breathing loudly through his nose, pulled himself to a sitting position. Arms crossed, face engorged, he watched in grim silence for a time and then inquired gently, "Amelia, why are you crawling on all fours?"

"I am looking for clues, of course."

"Ah, yes. A calling card, perhaps. A fragment of

cloth torn from our visitor's robe—a robe identical with those worn by half the population of Egypt. A lock of hair, courteously torn from his scalp in order to assist—"

"Sarcasm does not become you, Emerson," I said, continuing to crawl. And a tedious process it is, I might add, when the folds of one's nightgown keep bunching up under one's knees. Then I let out a cry of triumph. "Aha!"

"A photograph of the burglar's wife and children," Emerson went on, warming to his theme. "A letter, bearing his name and address—though there are no pockets in these robes, and few of the wearers can read and write—"

"A footprint," I said.

"A footprint," Emerson repeated. "Hobnailed boots, perhaps? Of an unusual pattern, made by only one bootmaker in all Cairo, who keeps records of his customers—"

"Correct," I said. "At least as to the boots. I doubt, however, that the pattern will prove to be unique. I will make inquiries, of course."

"What?" Emerson bounded from the bed. "Booted feet, did you say?"

"See for yourself. There is a clear print. He must have trod in the spilled ink. I am glad of the accident on that account, though I do not understand why there should have been a bottle of ink in my bag. I suppose Ramses put it there."

Now on all fours like myself, Emerson inspected the print. "There is no reason why a common sneak thief should not wear boots. If he were dressed in European clothing—or if he were European—he would find it easier to gain entry to the hotel. . . ." His voice trailed off in an indecisive manner.

"A common sneak thief would not dare enter the hotel, Emerson. Even if the safragi is asleep most of the time."

Emerson sat back on his haunches. "I know what you are thinking," he cried accusingly. "You will insist on some connection with the death of Abd el Atti."

"It would be a strange coincidence if the two events were not connected."

"Stranger coincidences have happened. What could he have been after?"

"The mummy portrait," I suggested.

Emerson looked uncomfortable. "I intend to hand it over to the Museum, Amelia."

"Of course."

"It is a handsome piece of work, but not valuable," Emerson mused, rubbing his chin. "Did you—er—rescue anything from the shop?"

"Only a scrap of papyrus, which appeared to be from the same manuscript as the one I obtained from Abd el Atti."

"Both together would not be worth the risk taken by the thief." Emerson seated himself. Elbow on his knee, chin on his hand, he might have sat as the model for M. Rodin's splendid statue, even to his costume—or, to put it as delicately as possible, the absence thereof. Emerson refuses to wear a nightshirt, and the new fad of pajamas has prompted a number of rude jests from him.

"The papyrus from which the fragments came might conceivably be of value," he said after a time.

"Sayce was intrigued, though he tried to hide it—the devious fellow. We do not have the papyrus, though. Do we?"

"Emerson, you cut me to the quick. When have I ever deceived you about something of importance?"

"Quite often, Amelia. However, in this case I will take your word. You agree that we possess nothing that would explain a visit from an emissary of your imaginary Master Criminal?"

"Not to my knowledge. However—"

Emerson rose majestically to his feet. "The invasion was that of a common ordinary thief," he proclaimed, in orotund tones. "That is the end of it. Come to bed, Amelia."

FIVE

Mazghunah.
Mazghunah! Mazghunah . . .

No, there is no magic in the name, punctuate it as one will. Not even a row of exclamation points can lend charm to such an uncouth collection of syllables. Giza, Sakkara, Dahshoor are no more euphonious, perhaps, but they evoke the lure of antiquity and exploration. Mazghunah has nothing whatever to recommend it.

It does possess a railway station, and we descended from the train to find that we were eagerly awaited. Towering above the spectators who had gathered on the platform was the stately form of our *reis*, Abdullah, who had gone on ahead to arrange for transport and accommodations. He is the most dignified of men, almost as tall as Emerson—that is to say, above the average Egyptian height—with a sweeping array of facial hair that turns a shade lighter every year, so that it will soon rival the snowy whiteness of his robe. Yet he has the energy of a young man, and when he saw us a broad

smile lightened the solemnity of his bronzed countenance.

After our luggage had been loaded onto the donkeys Abdullah had selected, we mounted our own
steeds. "Forward, Peabody," Emerson cried. "Forward, I say!"

Cheeks flushed and eyes glowing, he urged his
donkey into a trot. It is impossible for a tall man to
look heroic when mounted on one of these little
beasts; but as I watched Emerson jog away, his elbows out and his knees well up, the smile that curved
my lips was not one of derision. Emerson was in his
element, happy as a man can be only when he has
found his proper niche in life. Not even the disappointment of de Morgan's decision could crush that
noble spirit.

The inundation was receding, but sheets of water
still lay on the fields. Following the dikes of the
primitive irrigation system, we rode on until suddenly the green of the trees and young crops gave
way to the barren soil of the desert, in a line so
sharp it appeared to have been drawn by a celestial
hand. Ahead lay the scene of our winter's work.

Never will I forget the profound depression
that seized me when I first beheld the site of Mazghunah. Beyond the low and barren hills border-
ing the cultivation, a vast expanse of rubble-strewn
sand stretched westward as far as the eye could
see. To the north, outlined bravely against the sky,
were the two stone pyramids of Dahshoor, one regular in outline, the other marked by the curious
change in the angle of the slope that has given it
the name of the "Bent Pyramid." The contrast

between these two magnificent monuments and the undulating sterility of our site was almost too painful to be endured. Emerson had halted; when I drew up beside him I saw that his eyes were fixed on the distant silhouettes and that a grimace of fury distorted his lips.

"Monster," he growled. "Villain! I will have my revenge; the day of reckoning cannot be far off!"

"Emerson," I said, putting my hand on his arm.

He turned to me with a smile of artificial sweetness.

"Yes, my dear. A charming spot, is it not?"

"Charming," I murmured.

"I believe I will just ride north and say good morning to our neighbor," Emerson said casually. "If you, my dear Peabody, will set up camp—"

"Set up camp?" I repeated. "Where? How? With what?"

To call the terrain in this part of Egypt desert is misleading, for it is not the sort of desert the reader may picture in his mind—vast sand dunes, rolling smoothly on to infinity without so much as a shrub or ridge of rock. This area was barren enough; but the ground was uneven, broken by pits and ridges and hollows, and every foot of the surface was strewn with debris—fragments of broken pottery, scraps of wood and other, less palatable evidences of occupation. My experienced eye at once identified it as a cemetery site. Beneath the rock surface lay hundreds of graves. All had been robbed in ancient times, for the scraps littering the ground were the remains of the goods buried with the dead—and the remains of the dead themselves.

Ramses got off his donkey. Squatting, he began sifting through the debris.

"Here, Master Ramses, leave that nasty rubbish alone," John exclaimed.

Ramses held up an object that looked like a broken branch. "It is a femuw," he said in a trembling voice. "Excuse me, Mama—a femur, I meant to say."

John let out a cry of disgust and tried to take the bone away from Ramses. I understood the emotion that had affected the child, and I said tolerantly, "Never mind, John. You cannot keep Ramses from digging here."

"That nasty rubbish is the object of our present quest," Emerson added. "Leave it, my son; you know the rule of excavation—never move anything until its location has been recorded."

Ramses rose obediently. The warm breeze of the desert ruffled his hair. His eyes glowed with the fervor of a pilgrim who has finally reached the Holy City.

II

Having persuaded Ramses to abandon his bones for the nonce, we rode on toward the northwest. Near a ridge of rock we found our men, who had come down the day before to select a campsite. There were ten of them in all, including Abdullah—old friends and experienced excavators, who would supervise the unskilled laborers we expected to hire locally. I returned their enthusiastic salutations, noting as I did so that the camp consisted of a fire pit and two tents. Questioning elicited the bland response, "But, Sitt, there is no other place."

On several of my expeditions I had set up housekeeping in an empty tomb. I recalled with particular pleasure the rock-cut tombs of El Amarna; I always say, there is nothing more commodious or convenient than a tomb, particularly that of a well-to-do person. Obviously no such amenity was available here.

I climbed to the top of the ridge. As I scrambled among the stones I gave thanks for one blessing at least—that I was no longer encumbered by the voluminous skirts and tight corsets that had been de rigueur when I first took up the study of Egyptology. My present working costume had been developed and refined by myself, and was wholly satisfactory, aesthetically and practically. It consisted of a broad-brimmed man's straw hat, a shirtwaist with long sleeves and a soft collar, and flowing Turkish trousers to the knee with stout boots and gaiters below the trousers. The uniform, if I may so designate it, was completed by an important accessory—a broad leather belt to which was attached a modification of the old-fashioned chatelaine. Instead of the scissors and keys housewives once attached to this device, my collection of useful tools included a hunting knife and a pistol, notepaper and pencil, matches and candles, a folding rule, a small flask of water, a pocket compass, and a sewing kit. Emerson claimed I jangled like a chained prisoner when I walked. He also objected to being jabbed in the ribs by knife, pistol, et cetera, when he embraced me. Yet I am certain the usefulness of each item will be readily apparent to the astute reader.

Abdullah followed me onto the hill. His face had the remote, meditative expression it wore when he was expecting a reprimand.

We were not far from the cultivation. A cluster of palms some half-mile distant betokened the presence of water, and among the palms I could see the low roofs of a village. Nearer at hand was the object I sought. I had caught a glimpse of it as we rode—the ruinous remains of a building of some sort. I pointed. "What is that, Abdullah?"

"It is a building, Sitt," said Abdullah, in tones of amazement. One would suppose he had never noticed the place before.

"Is it occupied, Abdullah?"

"I do not think it is, Sitt."

"Who owns it, Abdullah?"

Abdullah replied with an ineffable Arabic shrug. As I prepared to descend the far side of the ridge, he said quickly, "That is not a good place, Sitt Hakim."

"It has walls and part of a roof," I replied. "That is good enough for me."

"But, Sitt—"

"Abdullah, you know how your Muslim reticence annoys me. Speak out. What is wrong with the place?"

"It is filled with devils," said Abdullah.

"I see. Well, don't concern yourself about that. Emerson will cast the devils out."

I hailed the others and directed them to follow

me. The closer we approached, the more pleased I was with my discovery, and the more puzzled by it. It was not an ordinary house; the extent of the walls, some tumbled, some still intact, suggested a structure of considerable size and complexity. There were no signs of recent habitation. The barren waste stretched all around, with never a tree or blade of grass.

The building materials were an odd mixture. Some of the walls were of mud brick, some of stone. A few blocks were as large as packing cases. "Stolen from our pyramids," Emerson grumbled. He pushed through a gap in the nearest wall. I need not say I was close behind.

The area within had been a courtyard, with rooms on three sides and a stout wall on the fourth. The wall and the southern range of rooms had fallen into ruin, but the remaining sections had survived, though most gaped open to the sky. A few pillars supported a roofed walkway along one side.

Emerson snapped his fingers. "It was a monastery, Peabody. Those were the monks' cells, and that ruin in the far corner must have been the church."

"How curious," I exclaimed.

"Not at all. There are many such abandoned sanctuaries in Egypt. This country was the home of monasticism, after all, and religious communities existed as early as the second century A.D. The nearest village, Dronkeh, is a Coptic settlement."

"You never told me that, Emerson."

"You never asked me, Peabody."

As we continued our tour of inspection I became conscious of a strange feeling of uneasiness. It was wholly unaccountable; the sun beamed down from a cloudless sky and, except for the occasional agitated rustle when we disturbed a lizard or scorpion from its peaceful nest, there was no sign of danger. Yet an air of brooding desolation lay over the place. Abdullah sensed it; he stayed close on Emerson's heels and his eyes kept darting from side to side.

"Why do you suppose it was abandoned?" I asked.

Emerson stroked his chin. Even his iron nerves seemed affected by the atmosphere; his brow was slightly furrowed as he replied, "It may be that the water supply failed. This structure is old, Peabody—a thousand years, perhaps more. Long enough for the river to change its course, and for a deserted building to fall into ruin. Yet I think some of the destruction was deliberate. The church was solidly built, yet hardly one stone remains on another."

"There was fighting, I believe, between Muslims and Christians?"

"Pagan and Christian, Muslim and Christian, Christian and Christian. It is curious how religion arouses the most ferocious violence of which mankind is capable. The Copts destroyed the heathen temples and persecuted the worshipers of the old gods, they also slaughtered co-religionists who disagreed over subtle differences of dogma. After the Muslim conquest, the Copts were treated leniently at first, but their own intolerance finally tried the patience of the conquerors and they endured the same persecution they had inflicted on others."

"Well, it does not matter. This will make an admirable expedition house. For once we will have enough storage space."

"There is no water."

"It can be carried from the village." I took my pencil and began making a list. "Repair the roof; mend the walls; insert new doors and window frames; sweep—"

Abdullah coughed. "Cast out the afreets," he suggested.

"Yes, to be sure." I made another note.

"Afreets?" Emerson repeated. "Peabody, what the devil—"

I drew him aside and explained. "I see," he replied. "Well, I will perform any necessary rituals, but first perhaps we ought to go to the village and carry out the legal formalities."

I was happy to acquiesce to this most sensible suggestion. "We should not have any difficulty obtaining a lease," I said, as we walked side by side. "Since the place has been so long abandoned, it cannot be of importance to the villagers."

"I only hope the local priest does not believe in demons," said Emerson. "I don't mind putting on a show for Abdullah and the men, but one exorcism per day is my limit."

As soon as we were seen the villagers came pouring out of their houses. The usual cries of "Baksheesh!" were mingled with another adjuration—*Ana Christian, Oh Hawadji*—I am a Christian, noble sir!"

"And therefore entitled to additional baksheesh," said Emerson, his lip curling. "Bah."

Most of the houses were clustered around the well. The church, with its modest little dome, was not much larger than the house next to it. "The parsonage," said Emerson, indicating this residence. "And there, if I am not mistaken, is the parson."

He stood in the doorway of his house—a tall, muscular man wearing the dark-blue turban that distinguishes Egyptian Christians. Once a prescribed article of dress for a despised minority, it is now worn as a matter of pride.

Instead of coming to greet us, the priest folded his arms and stood with head held high like a king waiting to receive petitioners. His figure was splendid. His face was all but invisible, adorned by the most remarkable assemblage of facial hair I had ever seen. It began at ear level, swept in an ebon wave across cheeks and upper lip, and flowed like a sable waterfall almost to his waist. His eyebrows were equally remarkable for their hirsute extravagance. They were the only feature that gave any indication of the owner's emotions, and at the moment their configuration was not encouraging, for a scowl darkened the pastoral brow.

At the priest's appearance most of the other villagers faded quietly away. Half a dozen men remained, loitering near the priest. They wore the same indigo turbans and the same suspicious scowls as their spiritual leader.

"The deacons," said Emerson with a grin.

He then launched into a speech of greeting in his most impeccable Arabic. I added a few well-chosen words. A long silence ensued. Then the priest's bearded lips parted and a voice growled a curt *"Sabakhum bil-kheir*—good morning."

In every Muslim household I had visited, the formal greeting was followed by an invitation to enter, for hospitality to strangers is enjoined by the Koran. We waited in vain for this courtesy from our co-religionist, if I may use that term loosely, and after an even longer silence the priest asked what we wanted.

This outraged Abdullah, who, though an admirable person in many ways, was not devoid of the Mussulman's prejudice against his Christian fellow-countrymen. Ever since he entered the village he had looked as if he smelled something bad. Now he exclaimed, "Unclean eaters of swine's flesh, how dare you treat a great lord in this way? Do you not know that this is Emerson, Father of Curses, and his chief wife, the learned and dangerous Lady Doctor? They honor your filthy village by entering it. Come away, Emerson; we do not need these low people to help with our work."

One of the "deacons" edged up to his leader and whispered in his ear. The priest's turban bobbed in acknowledgment. "The Father of Curses," he repeated, and then, slowly and deliberately, "I know you. I know your name."

A chill ran through my limbs. The phrase meant nothing to the priest, but all unknowingly he had repeated an ominous formula used by the priest-magicians of ancient Egypt. To know the name of a man or a god was to have power over him.

Abdullah found the comment offensive, though probably for other reasons. "Know his name? Who is there who does not know that great name? From the cataracts of the south to the swamps of the Delta—"

"Enough," Emerson said. His lips were twitching,

but he kept a grave face, for laughter would have hurt Abdullah and offended the priest. "You know my name, Father? It is well. But I do not know yours."

"Father Girgis, priest of the church of Sitt Miriam in Dronkeh. Are you truly Emerson, the digger-up of dead man's bones? You are not a man of God?"

It was my turn to repress a smile. Emerson chose to ignore the second question. "I am that Emerson. I come here to dig, and I will hire men from the village. But if they do not want to work for me, I will go elsewhere."

The villagers had begun edging out into the open as the conversation proceeded. A low murmur arose from them when they heard the offer to work. All the fellahin, Muslim and Copt alike, are pitifully poor. The chance to earn what they considered munificent wages was not an offer to be missed.

"Wait," the priest said, as Emerson turned away. "If that is why you have come, we will talk."

So at last we were invited into the "manse," as Emerson called it. It was like all the other Egyptian houses we had seen, except that it was a trifle larger and slightly cleaner. The long divan that was the chief piece of furniture in the main room was covered with cheap, faded chintz, and the only ornament was a crucifix with a horribly lifelike image of Christ, smeared with red paint in lieu of blood.

At the priest's suggestion we were joined by a timid little walnut-colored gentleman who was introduced as the *sheikh el beled*—the mayor of the village. It was obvious that he was a mere figurehead, for he only squeaked acquiescence to everything the priest said until, the matter of employment having been settled, Emerson mentioned that we wanted to occupy the abandoned monastery. Then the mayor turned as pale as a man of his complexion can turn and blurted, "But, effendi, that is not possible."

"We will not profane the church," Emerson assured him. "We only want to use the rooms that were once storerooms and cells."

"But, great Lord, no one goes there," the mayor insisted. "It is accursed—a place of evil, haunted by afreets and devils."

"Accursed?" Emerson repeated incredulously. "The home of the holy monks?"

The mayor rolled his eyes. "Long ago all the holy men were foully murdered, O Father of Curses. Their spirits still haunt their house, hungry for revenge."

"We do not fear devils or vengeful ghosts," Emerson said courageously. "If that is your only objection, effendi, we will take possession immediately."

The mayor shook his head but did not protest further. The priest had listened with a sardonic smile. Now he said, "The house is yours, Father of Curses. May the restless spirits of the holy men requite you as you deserve."

III

Abdullah followed us along the village street, radiating disapproval as only Abdullah can. It felt like a chilly breeze on the back of my neck.

"We are going the wrong way," I said to Emerson. "We entered the village at the other end."

"I want to see the rest of the place," was the reply. "There is something strange going on here, Amelia. I am surprised your vaunted intuition did not catch the undercurrents."

"They would have been hard to miss," I replied haughtily. "The priest is patently hostile to outsiders. I hope he won't undermine our authority."

"Oh, I pay no attention to such persons." Emerson stepped over a mangy dog sprawled in the middle of the path. It growled at him and he said absently, "Good dog, then; nice fellow," before continuing, "it is not concern but curiosity that makes me wonder why the reverend gentleman should demonstrate such antagonism. I always have trouble with religious persons; they are so confoundedly superstitious, curse them. Yet the priest was rude to us even before he learned who we were. I wonder . . ."

His voice trailed off and he stood staring.

Half hidden by a splendid group of stately palms and partially removed from the rest of the village stood several houses. In contrast to the other hovels in that wretched place, these were in impeccable repair and freshly whitewashed. Even the dust before the doors looked as if it had been swept. Three of the houses were the usual small two- and three-room affairs. The fourth was somewhat larger and had undergone reconstruction. A stubby steeple graced the flat roof, and above the door was a sign in gilt letters on black. It read, "Chapel of the Holy Jerusalem."

As we stood in silent wonderment, the door of one of the smaller houses opened. An explosion of small boys burst out into the open, shouting and laughing with the joy of youths escaping from studies. As soon as they caught sight of us they darted at us, shouting for baksheesh. One minuscule cherub caught at my trousers and stared up at me with eyes like melting chocolate. "Baksheesh, Sitt," he lisped. "*Ana Christian—ana Brotestant!*"

"Good Gad," I said weakly.

Emerson put a hand to his head. "No," he cried passionately. "No. It is a delusion—it cannot be real. After all the other cruel blows of fate I have endured . . . Missionaries! Missionaries, Amelia!"

"Courage," I implored, as the swarthy infant continued to tug at my trousers. "Courage, Emerson. It could be worse."

Other children emerged from the door of the school—little girls, too timid to emulate the joie de vivre of their male counterparts. They were followed by another, taller form. For a moment he stood in the doorway blinking into the sunlight, and the rays of the noon-high orb set his silver-gilt hair to blazing like a halo. Then he saw us. A smile of ineffable sweetness spread over his handsome face and he raised a hand in greeting or in blessing.

Emerson collapsed onto a block of stone, like a man in the last throes of a fatal disease. "It is worse," he said in a sepulchral voice.

IV

"Boys, boys." The beautiful young man strode toward us, waving his arms. He spoke in Arabic, perfectly pronounced but slow and simple. "Stop it, boys. Go home now. Go to your mothers. Do not ask for baksheesh, it is not pleasing to God."

The youthful villains dispersed and their mentor turned his attention to us. At close range he was absolutely dazzling. His hair gleamed, his white teeth shone, and his face beamed with goodwill. Emerson continued to stare dazedly at him, so I felt it incumbent upon myself to address the amenities.

"I fear we must apologize for intruding on private property, sir. Allow me to introduce myself. I am Amelia Peabody Emerson—Mrs. Radcliffe Emerson—and this . . ."

"This block of wood" might have been an appropriate description, for all the response Emerson made, but the beautiful young man did not allow me to proceed. "You need no introduction, Mrs. Emerson; you and your distinguished husband are well known to all visitors in Cairo. It is an honor to welcome you. I was informed only yesterday that you would be coming."

The monolithic indifference or catatonia of Emerson was shattered. "Who informed you, pray?" he demanded.

"Why, it was M. de Morgan," said the young man innocently. "The director of the Antiquities Department. As you may know, he is working at Dahshoor, not far from—"

"I know the location of Dahshoor, young man," snapped Emerson. "But I don't know you. Who the devil are you?"

"Emerson!" I exclaimed. "Such language to a man of the cloth!"

"Pray don't apologize," said the young gentleman. "It is my fault, for not mentioning my name earlier. I am David Cabot—of the Boston Cabots."

This formula seemed to have some significance to him, but it meant nothing to me—nor, I hardly need add, to Emerson, who continued to glare at young Mr. Cabot, of the Boston Cabots.

"But I am forgetting my manners," the latter went on. "I am keeping you standing in the sun. Will you enter and meet my family?"

Knowing him to be unmarried, I assumed he was referring to his parents, but when I inquired he laughed and shook his head. "I refer to my spiritual family, Mrs. Emerson. My father in the Lord, the Reverend Ezekiel Jones, is the head of our little mission. His sister also labors in the vineyards of the Lord. It is almost time for our midday repast; will you honor our humble abode?"

I politely declined the invitation, explaining that the other members of our expedition were waiting for us, and we took our leave. Before we were quite out of earshot, Emerson said loudly, "You were confoundedly polite, Amelia."

"You make it sound like a crime! I felt it necessary to be overly cordial to compensate for your rudeness."

"Rude? I, rude?"

"Very."

"Well, I call it rude to walk into a man's house and order him to leave off worshiping his chosen god. What effrontery! Mr. Cabot and his 'father in the Lord' had better not try their tricks on ME."

"I hardly think even Mr. Cabot would try to

convert you," I said, taking his arm. "Hurry, Emerson, we have been too long away. Goodness knows what mischief Ramses has got into by now."

But for once Ramses was innocent of wrongdoing. We found him squatting in the sand near the monastery, digging. Already a small pile of potsherds had rewarded his efforts. At the sight of his dedicated labors Emerson's expression lightened, and I hoped the irritation produced by the presence of the missionaries had been alleviated.

V

Shortly thereafter the arrival of a contingent of men from the village assured us that the priest did mean to cooperate with our endeavors. This first levy consisted of craftsmen—masons and brickmakers, carpenters and plasterers. Emerson beamed when he saw his augmented audience; he may and does deny it, but he loves putting on a theatrical performance. His exorcism that day was one of his best, despite the fact that he turned his ankle while capering around the house chanting poetry and prayers. The audience applauded enthusiastically and declared themselves relieved of all apprehension concerning evil spirits. Before long the place was swarming with activity, and I had high hopes that by nightfall we would have a roof over our heads and a cleared floor on which to place our camp cots, tables and chairs.

The men from Aziyeh did not fraternize with the villagers. Their professional skills and the parochi-

alism of the peasant mentality, which regards a man
from a village two miles off as a foreigner—not to
mention the religious differences—made them view
the "heretics" with haughty contempt. I knew there
would be no trouble, however, for Abdullah was an
excellent foreman and his men were guided by
him. No less than four of them were his sons. They
ranged in age from Feisal, a grizzled man with
grown children of his own, to young Selim, a handsome lad of fourteen. He was obviously the apple of
his father's eye and the adored Benjamin of the family. Indeed, his infectious boyish laughter and pleasant ways made him a favorite with all of us. In
Egyptian terms he was already a man, and would
soon take a wife, but since he was closer in age to
Ramses than any of the others, the two soon struck
up a friendship.

After I had watched the lad for a while and assured myself that my initial impression of his
character was correct, I decided to appoint him as
Ramses' official guide, servant and guard. John's un-
suitability for the role was becoming only too apparent. He was always trying to prevent Ramses from
doing harmless things—such as digging, which was,
after all, our reason for being there—and allowing
him to do other things, such as drinking unboiled
water, that were not at all harmless. Besides, John
was proving useful in other ways. He had picked up
Arabic with surprising quickness and mingled readily with the men, displaying none of the insular
prejudices that afflict many English persons, including some who ought to know better. As I swept sand
from the large room, once the refectory of the

monastery, that we had selected for our parlor, I could hear John chatting away in his ungrammatical but effective Arabic, and the other men laughing good-naturedly at his mistakes.

Late in the afternoon, when I emerged from the house to inspect the repairs on the roof, I saw a small procession advancing toward me. Leading it were two gentlemen mounted on donkeyback. The tall, graceful figure of Mr. Cabot was immediately recognizable. Beside him was another man wearing the same dark clerical garb and a straw boater. It was not until the caravan had come closer that I realized the third person was female.

My heart went out to the poor creature. She wore a high-necked, long-sleeved gown of dark calico, with skirts so full they almost hid the donkey. Only its head and tail protruded, with bizarre effect. One of the old-fashioned shovel bonnets—a style I had not seen in years—completely hid her face, and so enveloping was her attire it was impossible to tell whether she was dark or fair, young or old.

Mr. Cabot was the first to dismount. "We are here," he exclaimed.

"So I see," I replied, thanking heaven I had sent Emerson and Ramses out to survey the site.

"I have the honor," Mr. Cabot continued, "to present my revered mentor, the Reverend Ezekiel Jones."

There was nothing in the appearance of this person to justify the reverence and pride in Mr. Cabot's voice. He was of middle height, with the heavy shoulders and thick body of a workingman, and his coarse features would have been better hidden by a beard. His forehead was crossed by lowering dark brows as thick as my finger. His movements were awkward; he climbed awkwardly off his mount and awkwardly removed his hat. When he spoke I had some inkling as to why he commanded the admiration of his young acolyte. His voice was a mellow baritone, marred by an unfortunate American accent, but resonant and musical as a cello.

"How do, ma'am. We figured as how you could use some help. This here's my sister, Charity."

The woman had dismounted. Her brother grasped her by the shoulder and shoved her at me, like a merchant hawking his wares. "She's a hard worker and a handmaiden of the Lord," he went on. "You tell her what you want done."

A thrill of indignation passed through me. I offered the girl my hand. "How do you do, Miss Jones."

"We don't use worldly titles," her brother said. "Brother David here tends to forget that. Oh, it's all right, my friend, I know it's respect that prompts you—"

"It is indeed, sir," said "Brother David" earnestly.

"But I don't deserve respect, Brother. I'm just a miserable sinner like the rest of you. A few steps farther up the road that leads to salvation, maybe, but a miserable sinner just the same."

The self-satisfied smile with which he proclaimed his humility made me want to shake him, but the young man gazed at him with melting admiration. "Sister Charity" stood with her hands folded at her waist and her head bowed. She looked like a silhouette cut out of black paper, lifeless and featureless.

I had been undecided as to whether to invite the visitors to enter the house; the decision was taken out of my hands by Brother Ezekiel. He walked in. I followed, to find that he had seated himself in the most comfortable chair the room contained.

"You've got quite a bit done," he said in obvious surprise. "Soon as you paint over that heathen image on the wall—"

"Heathen?" I exclaimed. "It is a Christian image, sir; a pair of matched saints, if I am not mistaken."

"'Ye shall make unto yourselves no heathen images,'" Ezekiel intoned. His sonorous voice echoed hollowly.

"I am sorry I cannot offer you refreshment," I said. "As you see, we are not yet settled in."

This was an act of rudeness worthy of Emerson himself, for the portable stove was alight and the kettle was coming to the boil. As I was to learn, rudeness was no defense against Brother Ezekiel. "As a rule I don't hold with stimulants," he remarked coolly. "But I'll take a cup of tea with you. When in Rome, eh? I know you Britishers can't get on without it. You set down, ma'am. Charity'll tend to the tea. Well, go on, girl, where are your manners? Take off your bonnet. It ain't overly bright in here and I don't want you spilling nothing."

The room was bright enough for me to get a good look at the face displayed by the removal of the absurd bonnet. It was not a fashionable style of beauty. Her skin was extremely pale—not surprising, if she went about in that stovepipe of a bonnet—and the delicacy of her features, combined with her diminutive size, made her look like a child some years away from the bloom of womanhood. But when she glanced shyly at me, as if asking my permission to proceed, I was struck by the sweetness of her expression. Her eyes were her best feature, soft and dark, half veiled by extraordinarily long, curling lashes. Her abundant brown hair was strained back from her face into an ugly bun, but a few curls had escaped to caress her rounded cheeks.

I smiled at her before turning a less amiable look on her brother. "My servant will prepare the tea," I said. "John?"

I knew he had been listening. The new door into the courtyard had been hung, and it stood a trifle ajar. The door promptly opened, and I felt an almost maternal pride when he appeared. He was such a splendid specimen of young British manhood! The sleeves of his shirt were rolled high, displaying the muscular arms of a Hercules. He stood with stiff dignity, ready to receive my orders, and I felt sure that when he spoke his vowels would be in perfect order.

The response to my summons was never uttered. Vowels and consonants alike died in his throat. He had seen the girl.

A phrase of Mr. Tennyson's struck into my mind with the accuracy of an arrow thudding into the center of the target. "The curse is come upon me," cried the Lady of Shalott (a poor specimen of womanhood) when she first beheld Sir Launcelot. So might John have cried, had he been poetically inclined, when his eyes first beheld Charity Jones.

The girl was not unaware of his interest. It could not have been more apparent if he had shouted aloud. A faint, wild-rose flush warmed her cheeks and she lowered her eyes.

The lashes and the blush completed John's demoralization. How he managed to make and serve the tea I am sure I do not know, since he never took his eyes off the girl. I expected Brother Ezekiel to resent John's interest. Instead he watched the pair with a curious absence of expression, and spoke scarcely a word. Brother David's gentlemanly manners had never shown to better advantage. He carried on an animated conversation, describing with considerable humor some of the problems he and his colleague had encountered with the villagers.

I thought I would have to take John by the shoulders and turn him out of the room when he was finished, but on the third repetition of my dismissal he stumbled out. The door remained slightly ajar, however.

Mr. Jones finally rose. "We'll be getting back," he announced. "I'll come for Charity at sundown."

"No, you'll take her with you," I said. "I appreciate your offer of assistance, but I do not need it. My people have matters well in hand." The reverend started to object. I raised my voice and continued, "If I require domestic help I will hire it. I certainly will not permit this young lady to act as my scullery maid."

Ezekiel's face turned puce. Before he could speak, David said, "My dear Mrs. Emerson, your delicacy does you credit, but you do not understand our views. Honest labor is no disgrace. I myself would willingly roll up my sleeves and wield brush or broom. I know Charity feels the same."

"Oh, yes, gladly." It was the first time the girl had ventured to speak. Her voice was as soft as a breeze sighing through the leaves. And the look she gave young David spoke louder than words.

"No," I said.

"No?" Ezekiel repeated.

"No."

When I employ a certain tone and accompany it with a certain look, it is a brave man who dares contradict me. Brother Ezekiel was not a brave man. If he had been, his companion's sense of fitness would have intervened.

"We will take our leave then," he said with a graceful bow. "I hope our offer has not been misinterpreted."

"Not at all. It has only been declined. With thanks, of course."

"Humph," said Brother Ezekiel. "All right, then, if that's how you want it. Good-bye. I will see you in church on Sunday."

It was a statement, not a question, so I did not reply. "And your servant too," Ezekiel continued, glancing in a meaningful way at the partially open door. "We make nothing of the social distinctions you Britishers believe in. To us all men are brothers in the eyes of the Lord. The young man will be heartily welcome."

I took Brother Ezekiel by the arm and escorted him out of the house.

As I watched them ride away, the girl a modest distance behind the two men, such indignation flooded my being that I stamped my foot—a frustrating gesture in that region, since the sand muffled the sound. The wretched pastor was not only a religious bigot and a crude boor, he was no better than a panderer for his god. Seeing John's interest in Charity, he meant to make use of it in winning a convert. I almost wished Emerson had been there, to take the wretch by the collar and throw him out the door.

I described the encounter later to my husband as we sat before the door enjoying the magnificent display of sunset colors across the amber desert sands. Ramses was some distance away, still digging. He had amassed quite a sizable heap of potsherds and bones. The cat Bastet lay beside him. From time to time her whiskers quivered as the scent of roasting chicken from the kitchen reached her nostrils.

To my annoyance Emerson gave me scant sympathy. "It serves you right, Amelia. I told you you were too polite to that fellow."

"Nonsense. If you had met the Reverend Ezekiel Jones, you would realize that neither courtesy nor rudeness affects him in the slightest."

"Then," said Emerson coolly, "you should have drawn your pistol and ordered him to leave."

I adjusted the weapon in question. "You don't understand the situation, Emerson. I foresee trouble ahead. The girl is infatuated with young David, and John—our John—has taken a fancy to her. It is a classic triangle, Emerson."

"Hardly a triangle," said Emerson, with one of those coarse masculine snickers. "Unless the pretty young man takes a fancy to—"

"Emerson!"

"To someone else," Emerson concluded, with a guilty look at Ramses. "Amelia, as usual you are letting your rampageous imagination run away with you. Now that your detectival instincts have been frustrated, by my removing you from the scene of Abd el Atti's death, you are inventing romantic intrigues. Why can't you confine your energies to the work that awaits us here? Forgo your fantasies, I beg. They are all in your own head."

Ramses glanced up from his digging. "John," he remarked, "is in de house reading de Bible."

VI

Alas, Ramses was correct. John *was* reading the Bible, and he continued to spend a great deal of his spare time in this depressing pursuit. The rest of his spare time was employed in mooning around the village (the expression is Emerson's) in hopes of catching a glimpse of his love. When he came back with a light step and an idiotic smile on his face I knew he had seen Charity; when he tramped heavily, looking as if his dog had died, I knew his vigil had been unrewarded.

The morning after the visit of the missionaries we completed our preliminary survey of the site. Its total length was about four miles, from the village of Bernasht to a line approximately half a mile south of the Bent Pyramid of Dahshoor. We found traces of many small cemeteries, from the Old Kingdom to Roman times. Almost all had been thoroughly ransacked. Two sunken areas, one approximately three miles south of the Bent Pyramid, the other a quarter of a mile north of the first, were thickly covered with limestone chips. These, Emerson announced, were the remains of the pyramids of Mazghunah.

I repeated the word in a hollow voice. "Pyramids?"

"Pyramids," Emerson said firmly. Clear on the horizon the monuments of Dahshoor rose in ironic commentary.

After luncheon Emerson declared his intention of paying a call on M. de Morgan. "We cannot begin work for another day or two," he explained glibly. "And Ramses ought to see Dahshoor. I had intended to take him to Giza and Sakkara, but we left Cairo in such haste the poor lad was not even allowed to visit the Museum."

"There will be ample time for sightseeing after the season," I replied, neatly folding my napkin.

"It is only courteous to call on our neighbor, Peabody."

"No doubt; but this is the first time I have ever seen you so conscious of propriety. Oh, very well," I added quickly. "If you insist, Emerson, we will go."

We took Selim with us, leaving John to superintend the renovation of our living quarters and Abdullah to conclude the survey. He knew Emerson's methods and was competent to carry them out; but it was a departure for Emerson to leave anyone else in charge. I knew it testified to the anguish of his spirit.

Despite the equanimity of temper for which I am well known, the closer we approached the noble monuments of Dahshoor, the more bitter was the emotion that choked me. With what indescribable yearning did I view the objects with which I had hoped to become intimately acquainted!

The two large pyramids of Dahshoor date from the same period of time as the Giza pyramids, and they are almost as large. They are built of white limestone, and this snowy covering exhibits bewitching changes of tint, according to the quality of the light—a mazy gold at sunset, a ghostly translucent pallor under the glow of the moon. Now, at a little past noon, the towering structures shone dazzlingly white against the deep blue of the sky.

There are three smaller pyramids at the site, built at a later period, when building skills had deteriorated. Constructed not of solid stone but of mud brick faced with stone, they lost their original pyramidal shape when the casing blocks were removed by their successors or by local peasants desirous of obtaining pre-cut building materials. Despite its ruined state, one of these brick pyramids—the southernmost—dominates the terrain, and from some aspects it appears to loom even larger than its stone neighbors. Stark and almost menacing it rose up as we approached, as dark as the great pyramids were pale. My eyes were increasingly drawn to it and finally I exclaimed, "What a strange and indeed sinister appearance that structure has, Emerson. Can it be a pyramid?"

Emerson had become increasingly morose as we neared Dahshoor. Now he replied grumpily, "You know perfectly well that it is, Peabody. I beg you will not humor me by pretending ignorance."

He was correct; I knew the monuments of Dahshoor as well as I knew the rooms of my own house. I felt I could have traversed the area blindfolded. Emerson's bad humor was due in no small part to the fact that he was aware of my poignant yearning and felt guilty—as well he might.

The Arabs called the dark structure the "Black Pyramid," and it merited the name, even though it more resembled a massive truncated tower. As we approached, signs of activity could be seen near the eastern side, where M. de Morgan was excavating. There was no sign of de Morgan, however, until Emerson's hail brought him out of the tent where he had been napping.

M. de Morgan was in his thirties. He had been a mining engineer before being appointed to head the Department of Antiquities, a position traditionally held by a citizen of France. He was a good-looking man, with regular features and a pair of luxuriant mustaches. Even though he had been roused suddenly from sleep his trousers were neatly creased, his Norfolk jacket buttoned, and his pith helmet in place—though of course he removed this latter object of dress when he saw me. Emerson's lip curled at the sight of this "foppishness"; he refused to wear a hat and usually went about with his sleeves rolled to the elbows and his shirt collar open.

I apologized for disturbing de Morgan. "Not at

all, madame," he replied, yawning. "I was about to arise."

"High time, too," said my husband. "You will never get on if you follow this eastern custom of sleeping in the afternoon. Nor will you locate the burial chamber in that amateurish way—digging tunnels at random, instead of searching for the original opening to the substructure—"

With a forced laugh, de Morgan broke in. "*Mon vieux*, I refuse to discuss professional matters until I have greeted your charming lady. And this must be young Master Emerson—how do you do, my lad?"

"Very well, thank you," said Ramses. "May I go and look at de pyramid?"

"A true archaeologist already," said the Frenchman. "*Mais certainement, mon petit.*"

I gestured at Selim, who had maintained a respectful distance, and he followed Ramses. De Morgan offered us chairs and something to drink. We were sipping wine when one of the tent flaps opened and another man appeared, yawning and stretching.

"By the Almighty," said Emerson in surprise. "It is that rascal Kalenischeff. What the devil is he doing here?"

De Morgan's eyebrows rose, but he said only, "He offered his services. One can always use an extra pair of hands, you know."

"He knows less about excavation than Ramses," said Emerson.

"I will be glad of Master Ramses' expertise," said de Morgan, smiling but clearly annoyed. "Ah, your highness—you have met Professor and Mrs. Emerson?"

Kalenischeff shook Emerson's hand, kissed mine, apologized for his disarray, asked after Ramses, commented on the heat and hoped that we were pleased with Mazghunah. Neither of us felt inclined to reply to this last remark. Kalenischeff put his monocle in his eye and ogled me in a familiar fashion. "At any rate, Madame lends beauty to an otherwise dismal site," he said. "What a fetching costume!"

"I did not come here to talk about women's clothing," said Emerson, scowling fiercely as the Russian studied my booted calves.

"Of course not," Kalenischeff said smoothly. "Any advice or assistance we can offer you—"

That is only a sample of the unsatisfactory tenor of the conversation. Every time Emerson tried to introduce a sensible subject, de Morgan talked about the weather or the Russian made some slighting suggestion. Needless to say, I burned with indignation at seeing my husband, so infinitely superior in all ways, insulted by these two, and finally I decided to suffer it no longer. I can, when necessary, raise my voice to a pitch and volume very trying to the ears, and impossible to ignore.

"I wish to talk to you about the illegal antiquities trade," I said.

Kalenischeff's monocle fell from his eye, de Morgan choked in mid-swallow, the servants jumped, and one dropped the glass he was holding. Having achieved my immediate goal of capturing the gentlemen's attention, I continued in a more moderate tone. "As director of Antiquities, monsieur, you are of course fully informed about the situation. What steps are you taking to halt this nefarious trade and imprison the practitioners?"

De Morgan cleared his throat. "The usual steps, madame."

"Now, monsieur, that will not suffice." I shook my finger playfully and raised my voice a notch or two. "You are not addressing an empty-headed lady tourist; you are talking to ME. I know more than you suppose. I know, for instance, that the extent of the trade has increased disastrously; that an unknown Master Criminal has entered the game—"

"The devil!" Kalenischeff cried. His monocle, which he had replaced, again fell from its place. "Er—your pardon, Madame Emerson . . ."

"You appear surprised," I said. "Is this information new to you, your highness?"

"There has always been illicit digging. But your talk of a Master Criminal . . ." He shrugged.

"His highness is correct," de Morgan said. "Admittedly there has been a slight increase in the illegal trade of late, but—forgive me, madame—the Master Criminal exists only in sensational fiction, and I have seen no evidence of a gang at work."

His denials proved to me that he was quite unfit for his responsible position. Kalenischeff was obviously hiding something. I felt I was on the verge of great discoveries, and was about to pursue my inquiries more forcibly when a shout arose. It held such a note of terror and alarm that we all started to our feet and ran in the direction from which it had come.

Selim lay flat on the ground, his arms flailing,

his cries for help rising to a frenzied pitch. Such a cloud of sand surrounded him that we were quite close before I realized what the trouble was. The terrain, west of the pyramid base, was very uneven, covered with sunken hollows and raised ridges—certain evidence of ancient structures buried beneath the sand. From one such hollow an arm protruded, stiff as a tree branch. Around it Selim was digging furiously, and it required very little intelligence to deduce that *(A)*, the arm belonged to Ramses, and *(B)*, the rest of Ramses was under the sand.

Bellowing in horror, Emerson flung Selim aside. Instead of wasting time digging, he seized Ramses' wrist and gave a mighty heave. Ramses rose up out of the *souterrain* like a trout rising to a fly.

I stood leaning on my parasol while Emerson brushed the sand off his son, assisted halfheartedly by the others. When the worst of it was removed I uncorked my flask of water and offered it to Emerson, together with a clean white handkerchief.

"Pour the water over his face, Emerson. I observe he has had the sense to keep his eyes and mouth tightly shut, so the damage should not be extensive."

And so it proved. Emerson decided we had better take Ramses home. I agreed to the suggestion; the interruption had shattered the web I had been weaving around the villainous Russian, and there was no point in continuing. De Morgan did not attempt to detain us.

As we bade a reluctant farewell to Dahshoor,

Selim tugged at my sleeve. "Sitt, I have failed you. Beat me, curse me!"

"Not at all, my boy," I replied. "It is quite impossible to prevent Ramses from falling into, or out of, objects. Your task is to rescue him or summon assistance, and you performed quite well. Without you, he might have smothered."

Selim's face cleared. Gratefully he kissed my hand.

Emerson, with Ramses, had drawn a short distance ahead. Overhearing what I had said, he stopped and waited for us.

"Quite right, Peabody. You have summed up the situation nicely. I have already cautioned Ramses to be more careful and—er—no more need be said on the subject."

"Humph," I said.

"All's well that ends well," Emerson insisted. "By the way, Peabody, what was the purpose of your quizzing de Morgan about antiquities thieves? The man is a perfect fool, you know. He is as ineffectual as his predecessor in office."

"I was about to question Kalenischeff about Abd el Atti's death when Ramses interrupted, Emerson."

"Interrupted? Interrupted! I suppose that is one way of putting it."

"Kalenischeff is a most suspicious character. Did you observe his reaction when I spoke of the Master Criminal?"

"If I had been wearing a monocle—"

"A most unlikely supposition, Emerson. I cannot imagine you wearing such an absurd accoutrement."

"If," Emerson repeated doggedly, "I had been wearing a monocle, I would have let it fall on hearing such a preposterous suggestion. I beg you will leave off playing detective, Amelia. That is all behind us now."

VII

Emerson was, of course, engaging in wishful thinking when he said our criminal investigations were ended. If he had stopped to consider the matter, he would have realized, as I did, that removal from Cairo did not mean we were removed from the case. The thief who had entered our hotel room had been led thither as a result of our involvement in Abd el Atti's death. I was as certain of that as I was of my own name. The thief had not found the object he was looking for. It must be something of considerable importance to him or he would not have risked entering a place as well guarded as Shepheard's. The conclusion? It should be obvious to any reasonable person. The thief would continue to search for the missing object. Sooner or later we would hear from him—another attempt at burglary, or an assault on one of us, or some other interesting attention. Since this had not occurred to Emerson, I did not feel obliged to point it out to him. He would only have fussed.

On the following day we were ready to begin work. Emerson had decided to start with a late cemetery. I tried to dissuade him, for I have no patience with martyrs.

"Emerson, you know quite well from the visible remains that this cemetery probably dates from Roman times. You hate late cemeteries. Why don't we work at the—er—pyramids? You may find subsidiary tombs, temples, a substructure—"

"No, Amelia. I agreed to excavate this site and I will excavate it, with a thoroughness and attention to detail that will set new standards for archaeological methodology. Never let it be said that an Emerson shirked his duty."

And off he marched, his shoulders squared and his eyes lifted to the horizon. He looked so splendid I didn't have the heart to point out the disadvantages of this posture; when one is striding bravely into the future one cannot watch one's footing. Sure enough, he stumbled into Ramses' pile of potsherds and went sprawling.

Ramses, who had been about to go after him, prudently retired behind my trousers. After a malignant glance in our direction Emerson got up and limped away.

"What is Papa going to do?" Ramses inquired.

"He is going to hire the workers. See, they are coming now."

A group of men had gathered around the table where Emerson now seated himself, with John at his side. We had decided to put John in charge of the work records, listing the names of the men as they were taken on, and keeping track of the hours they worked, plus additional money earned for important finds. Applicants continued to trickle in from the direction of the village. They were a somber group in their dark robes and blue turbans. Only the children lent some merriment to the scene. We would hire a number of the latter, both boys and girls, to carry away the baskets of sand the men filled as they dug.

Ramses studied the group and decided, correctly, that it promised to be a dull procedure. "I will help you, Mama," he announced.

"That is kind of you, Ramses. Wouldn't you rather finish your own excavation?"

Ramses gave the potsherds a disparaging glance. "I have finished it, to my own satisfaction. I was desirous of carrying out a sample dig, for, after all, I have had no experience at excavation, t'ough I am naturally conversant wit' de basic principles. However, it is apparent dat de site is devoid of interest. I believe I will turn my attention now—"

"For pity's sake, Ramses, don't lecture! I cannot imagine whence you derive your unfortunate habit of loquacity. There is no need to go on and on when someone asks you a simple question. Brevity, my boy, is not only the soul of wit, it is the essence of literary and verbal efficiency. Model yourself on my example, I beg, and from now on—"

I was interrupted, not by Ramses, who was listening intently, but by Bastet. She let out a long plaintive howl and bit me on the ankle. Fortunately my thick boots prevented her teeth from penetrating the skin.

In the pages of this private journal I will admit I made a mistake. I should not have interrupted Ramses when he spoke of his future plans.

I was fully occupied all that morning with do-

mestic arrangements. Not until after the men resumed work after the midday break did I have time
to look them over.

The first trench had been started. We had fifty
men at work with picks and shovels, and as many
children carrying away the detritus. The scene was
familiar to me from previous seasons, and despite
the fact that I expected nothing of interest to turn
up, my spirits lifted at the well-loved scene—the
picks of the men rising and falling rhythmically,
the children scampering off with the loaded baskets, singing as they worked. I walked along the
line, hoping someone would stop me to announce a
find—a coffin or a cache of jewelry or a tomb. Not
until I reached the end of the trench did I make the
discovery.

One frequently hears, from English and European tourists, that all Egyptians look alike. This is
nonsense, of course; Emerson calls it prejudice, and
he is probably correct. I will admit, however, that
the omnipresent, shapeless robes and turbans create an impression of uniformity. The facial hair to
which our workers were addicted also added to the
impression that they were all closely related to
one another. Despite these handicaps, it was not
five minutes before I had seen one particular face
that made an electrifying impression on me.

I sped back to Emerson. "He is here," I exclaimed.
"In section A-twenty-four. Come at once, Emerson."

Emerson, with a singularly sour expression on
his face, was inspecting the first find of the day—a

crude pottery lamp. He glowered. "Who is here, Amelia?"

I paused a moment for effect. "The man who was talking to Abd el Atti."

Emerson flung the lamp onto the ground. "What the devil are you talking about? What man?"

"You must remember. I described him to you. He spoke the gold sellers' argot, and when he saw me, he—"

"Are you out of your senses?" Emerson bellowed.

I seized his arm. "Come quickly, Emerson."

As we went, I explained. "He was a very ill-favored fellow, Emerson. I will never forget his face. Only ask yourself why he should turn up here, unless he is following us with some nefarious purpose in mind."

"Where is this villain?" Emerson inquired, with deceptive mildness.

"There." I pointed.

"You, there," Emerson called.

The man straightened. His eyes widened in simulated surprise. "You speak to me, effendi?"

"Yes, to you. What is your name?"

"Hamid, effendi."

"Ah, yes, I remember. You are not a local man."

"I come from Manawat, effendi, as I told you. We heard there was work here."

The answer came readily. The fellow's eyes never left Emerson's face. I considered this highly suspicious.

"Proceed discreetly, Emerson," I said in a low voice. "If accused, he may strike at you with his pick."

"Bah," said Emerson. "When were you last in Cairo, Hamid?"

"Cairo? I have never been there, effendi."

"Do you know Abd el Atti, the dealer in antiquities?"

"No, effendi."

Emerson gestured him to return to his work and drew me aside. "There, you see? You are imagining things again, Amelia."

"Of course he will deny everything, Emerson. You did not carry out a proper interrogation. But never mind; I didn't suppose we would wring a confession from the villain. I only wanted to draw your attention to him."

"Do me a favor," Emerson said. "Don't draw my attention to anyone, or anything, unless it has been dead at least a thousand years. This work is tedious enough. I do not need further aggravation." And off he marched, grumbling.

To be honest, I was beginning to regret I had acted so precipitately. I might have known Emerson would question my identification, and now I had let my suspect know I was suspicious of him. It would have been better to let him believe his disguise (of an indigo turban) had not been penetrated.

The damage was done. Perhaps, knowing my eyes were upon him. Hamid might be moved to rash action, such as a direct attack on one of us. Cheered by this reasoning, I returned to my work.

Yet I found it difficult to concentrate on what I was supposed to be doing. My gaze kept returning to the northern horizon, where the Dahshoor pyramids rose like mocking reminders of a forbidden paradise. Gazing upon them I knew how Eve must have felt when she looked back at the flowers and lush foliage of Eden, from which she was forever barred. (Another example of masculine duplicity, I might add. Adam was under no compulsion to eat of the fruit, and his attempt to shift the blame onto his trusting spouse was, to say the least, unmanly.)

Because of this distraction I was the first to see the approaching rider. Mounted on a spirited Arab stallion, he presented a handsome spectacle as he galloped across the waste. He drew up before me with a tug on the reins that made the horse rear, and removed his hat. The full effect of this performance was spoiled, for me, by the sight of the object de Morgan held before him on his saddle. The object was my son, sandy, sunburned, and sardonic. His look of bland innocence as he gazed down at me would have driven most mothers to mayhem.

Tenderly de Morgan lowered Ramses into my arms. I dropped him immediately and dusted off my hands. "Where did you find him?" I inquired.

"Midway between this place and my own excavations. In the middle of nowhere, to be precise. When I inquired of him where he thought he was going, he replied he had decided to pay me a visit. *C'est un enfant formidable!* Truly the son of my dear *collègue*—a splinter off the old English block of wood, *n'est pas?*"

Emerson came trotting up in time to hear the final compliment. The look he gave de Morgan would have withered a more sensitive man. De Morgan only smiled and twirled his mustaches. Then he began to congratulate Emerson on the intelligence, daring, and excellent French of his son.

"Humph, yes, no doubt," Emerson said. "Ramses, what the devil—that is to say, you must not wander off in this careless fashion."

"I was not wandering," Ramses protested. "I was aware at all times of my precise location. I confess I had underestimated de distance between dis place and Dahshoor. What I require, Papa, is a horse. Like dat one."

De Morgan laughed. "You would find it hard to control a steed like Mazeppa," he said, stroking the stallion's neck. "But a mount of some kind—yes, yes, that is reasonable."

"I beg you will not support my son in his ridiculous demands, monsieur," I said, giving Ramses a hard stare. "Ramses, where is Selim?"

"He accompanied me, of course," said Ramses. "But M. de Morgan would not let him come on de horse wit' us."

De Morgan continued to plead Ramses' case, probably because he saw how much his partisanship annoyed Emerson. "What harm can come to the lad, after all? He has only to follow the line of the cultivation. A little horse, madame—Professor—a pony, perhaps. The boy is welcome to visit me at any time. I do not doubt we will have more interesting— we will have interesting things to show him."

Emerson made a sound like a bull about to charge, but controlled himself. "Have you found the burial chamber yet?"

"We have only just begun our search," said de

Morgan haughtily. "But since the burial chambers are generally located directly under the exact center of the pyramid square, it is only a matter of time."

"Not that it will matter," Emerson grunted. "Like all the others, it will have been robbed and you will find nothing."

"Who knows, *mon cher*? I have a feeling—here—" De Morgan thumped the breast of his well-tailored jacket—"that we will find great things this season. And you—what luck have you had?"

"Like you, we have only begun," I said, before Emerson could explode. "Will you come to the house, monsieur, and join us in a cup of tea?"

De Morgan declined, explaining that he had a dinner engagement. "As you know, Dahshoor is a popular stop for tourists. The dahabeeyah of the Countess of Westmoreland is there presently, and I am dining with her tonight."

This boast failed to wound Emerson; he was not at all impressed by titles, and considered dining out a painful chore, to be avoided whenever possible. But the Frenchman's other digs had hit the mark, and his final speech was designed to twist the knife in the wound. He wished us luck, told us to visit his excavations at any time, and repeated his invitation to Ramses. "You will come and learn how to conduct an excavation, *n'est pas, mon petit*?"

Ramses gazed worshipfully at the handsome figure on the great stallion. "T'ank you, monsieur, I would like dat."

With a bow to me and a mocking smile at Emerson, de Morgan wheeled the horse and rode off into the sunset. It was the wrong direction entirely, and I had to agree with Emerson when he muttered, "These cursed Frenchmen—anything for a grand gesture!"

SIX

In the end Ramses got his way. After considering the matter, I decided it would be advisable for us to have some form of transport at hand, for the site was isolated and extensive. So we hired several donkeys, on a long-term lease, so to speak, and had the men build a shed for them near the ruins of the church. My first act upon coming into possession of the donkeys was, as usual, to strip off their filthy saddlecloths and wash them. It was not an easy task, since water had to be carried from the village, and the donkeys did not at all like being washed.

I will say for Ramses that he tried to be of use. However, he was more hindrance than help, falling over the water jars, getting more liquid on his own person than on the donkeys, and narrowly avoiding losing a finger to one irritated equine whose teeth he was trying to brush. The moment the animals were ready for locomotion he demanded the use of one.

"Certainly, my boy," his naive father replied.

"Where do you mean to go?" his more suspicious mother demanded.

"To Dahshoor, to visit M. de Morgan," said Ramses.

Emerson's face fell. He had been deeply wounded by Ramses' admiration for the dashing Frenchman. "I would rather you did not call on M. de Morgan, Ramses. Not alone, at any rate. Papa will take you with him another time."

Instead of debating the matter, Ramses clasped his hands and raised imploring eyes to his father's troubled face. "Den, Papa, may I make a widdle excavation of my own? Just a widdle one, Papa?"

I cannot fully express in words the dark suspicion that filled my mind at this patent demonstration of duplicity. It had been months since Ramses had mispronounced the letter *l*. His father had been absurdly charmed by this speech defect; indeed, I am convinced that it originated with Emerson's addressing the infant Ramses in "baby-talk," as it is called. Before I could express my misgivings, Emerson beamed fondly at the innocent face turned up to his and said, "My dear boy, certainly you may. What a splendid idea! It will be excellent experience for you."

"And may I take one or two of de men to help me, Papa?"

"I was about to suggest it myself, Ramses. Let me see whom I can spare—besides Selim, of course."

They went off arm in arm, leaving me to wonder what Ramses was up to this time. Even my excellent imagination failed to provide an answer.

II

The cemetery *was* of Roman date. Need I say more?
We found small rock-cut tombs, most of which
had been robbed in ancient times. Our labors
were rewarded (I use the word ironically) by a
motley collection of rubbish the tomb robbers had
scorned—cheap pottery jars, fragments of wooden
boxes, and a few beads. Emerson recorded the
scraps with dangerous calm and I filed them away
in the storeroom. The unrobbed tombs did contain
coffins, some of wood, some molded out of cartonnage (a variety of papier-mâché) and heavily
varnished. We opened three of these coffins, but
Emerson was forced to refuse Ramses' request that
he be allowed to unwrap the mummies, since we
had no facilities for that particular enterprise. Two
of the mummies had painted portraits affixed to
the head wrappings. These paintings, done in col-
ored wax on thin panels of wood, were used in late
times in lieu of the sculptured masks common earlier. Petrie had found a number of them, some exceedingly handsome, when he dug at Hawara, but
our examples were crude and injured by damp. I
hope I need not say that I treated these wretched
specimens with the meticulous care I always employ, covering them with a fresh coating of beeswax
to fix the colors and storing them in boxes padded
with cotton wool, in the same manner I had employed with the portrait painting Emerson had rescued from Abd el Atti's shop. They compared
poorly with the latter, which was that of a woman
wearing elaborate earrings and a golden fillet. Her

large dark eyes and expressive lips were drawn and shaded with an almost modern realism of technique.

On Sunday, which was our day of rest, John appeared in full regalia, knee breeches and all. His buttons had been polished to dazzling brightness. Respectfully he asked my permission to attend church services.

"But neither of the churches here are yours, John," I said, blinking at the buttons.

This rational observation had no effect on John, who continued to regard me with mute appeal, so I gave in. "Very well, John."

"I will go too," said Ramses. "I want to see de young lady dat John is—"

"That will do, Ramses."

"I also wish to observe de Coptic service," continued Ramses. "It is, I have been informed, an interesting survival of certain antique—"

"Yes, I know, Ramses. That is certainly an idea. We will all go."

Emerson looked up from his notes. "You are not including me, I hope."

"Not if you don't wish to go. But as Ramses has pointed out, the Coptic service—"

"Don't be a hypocrite, Peabody. It is not scholarly fervor that moves you; you also want to see John with the young lady he is—"

"That will do, Emerson," I said. John gave me a grateful look. He was bright red from the collar of his jacket to the curls on his brow.

Services at the Coptic church had already begun when we reached the village, though you would not have supposed it to be so from the babble of voices that could be heard within. From the grove of trees where the American mission was situated the tinny tolling of the bell called worshipers to the competing service. There was a peremptory note in its persistent summons, or so it seemed to me; it reminded me of the reverend's voice, and the half-formed idea that had come to me as we proceeded crystallized into a determination not to accede, even in appearance, to his demand that I attend his church.

"I am going to the Coptic service," I said. "Ramses, will you come with me or go with John?"

Somewhat to my surprise, Ramses indicated he would go with John. I had not believed vulgar curiosity would win over scholarly instincts. However, the decision suited me quite well. I informed the pair that we would meet at the well, and saw them proceed toward the chapel.

The interior of the Coptic church of Sitt Miriam (the Virgin, in our terms) was adorned with faded paintings of that lady and various saints. There were no seats or pews; the worshipers walked about chatting freely and appearing to pay no attention to the priest, who stood at the altar reciting prayers. The congregation was not large—twenty or thirty people, perhaps. I recognized several of the rough-looking men who had appeared to form the priest's entourage sanctimoniously saluting the pictures of the saints, but the face I had half-hoped to see was not among them. However, it did not surprise me to learn that Hamid was not a regular churchgoer.

I took up my position toward the back, near but not within the enclosure where the women were segregated. My advent had not gone unnoticed. Conversations halted for a moment and then broke out louder than before. The priest's glowing black eyes fixed themselves on me. He was too experienced a performer to interrupt his praying, but his voice rose in stronger accents. It sounded like a denunciation of something—possibly me—but I could not understand the words. Clearly this part of the service was in the ancient Coptic tongue, and I doubted that the priest and the congregation understood much more of it than I did. The prayers were memorized and repeated by rote.

Before long the priest switched to Arabic and I recognized that he was reading from one of the gospels. This went on for an interminable time. Finally he turned from the *heikal*, or altar, swinging a censer from which wafted the sickening smell of incense. He began to make his way through the congregation, blessing each individual by placing a hand upon his head and threatening him with the censer. I stood alone, the other worshipers having prudently edged away, and I wondered whether I would be ignored altogether or whether some particularly insulting snub was in train. Conceive of my surprise, therefore, when, having attended to every *man* present, the priest made his way rapidly toward me. Placing his hand heavily upon my head, he blessed me in the name of the Trinity, the Mother of God, and assorted saints. I thanked him, and was rewarded by a ripple of black beard that I took to betoken a smile.

When the priest had returned to the *heikal* I

decided I had done my duty and could retire. The interior of the small edifice was foggy with cheap incense and I feared I was about to sneeze.

The sun was high in the heavens. I drew deep satisfying breaths of the warm but salubrious air and managed to conquer the sneeze. I then took off my hat and was distressed to find that my forebodings had been correct. Of fine yellow straw, to match my frock, the hat was draped with white lace and trimmed with a cluster of yellow roses, loops of yellow ribbon and two *choux* of white velvet. Clusters of artificial violets and leaves completed the modest decorations, and the entire ensemble was daintily draped with tulle. It was my favorite hat; it had been very expensive; and it had required a long search to find a hat that was not trimmed with dead birds or ostrich plumes. (I deplore the massacre of animals to feed female vanity.)

As the priest's hand pressed on my head I had heard a crunching sound. Now I saw the bows were crushed, the roses hung drunkenly from bent stems, and that the mark of a large, dirty hand was printed on the mashed tulle. The only consolation I could derive was that there was also a spot of blood on the tulle. Apparently one of my hat pins had pricked the ecclesiastical palm.

There was nothing to be done about the hat, so I replaced it on my head and looked about. The small square was deserted except for a pair of lean dogs and some chickens who had not been inspired to attend the service. As John and Ramses were nowhere to be seen, I walked toward the mission.

The church door stood open. From it came

music—not the mellifluous strains of the organ or the sweet harmony of a trained choir, but motley voices bellowing out what I had to assume must be a hymn. I thought I recognized Ramses' piercing, offkey treble, but I could not make out any of the words. I sat down on the same rock Emerson had once used as a seat, and waited.

The sun rose higher and perspiration trickled down my back. The singing went on and on, the same monotonous tune repeated interminably. It was finally succeeded by the voice of Brother Ezekiel. I could hear him quite well. He prayed for the elect and for those still in the darkness of false belief (every inhabitant of the globe except the members of the Church of the Holy Jerusalem). I thought he would never stop praying. Eventually he did, and the congregation began to emerge.

The "Brotestants" appeared to be succeeding in their efforts at conversion, for Brother Ezekiel's audience was somewhat larger than that of the priest. Most, if not all, of the converts wore the dark Coptic turban. Christian missionaries had had little success in winning over Muslims, perhaps for ideological reasons and perhaps because the Egyptian government disapproved (in a number of effective and unpleasant ways) of apostates from the faith of Islam. No one cared what the Copts did; hence the higher conversion rate and the resentment of the Coptic hierarchy against missionaries. This resentment had, on several occasions, resulted in physical violence. When Emerson told me of these cases I exclaimed in disbelief, but my cynical husband only smiled contemptuously. "No one slaughters a coreligionist with quite as much enthusiasm as a Christian, my dear. Look at their history." I made no comment on this, for in fact I could think of nothing to say.

Among the worshipers wearing the blue turban was one I recognized. So Hamid was a convert! When he saw me he had the effrontery to salute me.

Eventually John came out of the church. His face was pink with pleasure—and probably with heat, for the temperature in the chapel must have been over one hundred degrees. He came running to me, babbling apologies: "It was a long service, madam."

"So I observed. Where is Ramses?"

"He was here," said John vaguely. "Madam, they have done me the honor to ask me to stay for dinner. May I, madam?"

I was about to reply with a decided negative when I saw the group coming toward me and forgot what I was going to say. Brother David, looking like a young saint, had given his arm to a lady—the same lady I had seen with him at Shepheard's. Her gown that morning was of bright violet silk in a broché design; the short coat had a cutaway front displaying an enormous white chiffon cravat that protruded a good twelve inches in front of her. The matching hat had not only ribbons and flowers, but an egret plume and a dead bird mounted with wings and tail uppermost, as if in flight.

Completing the trio was Ramses, his hand in that of the lady. He was looking as pious as only Ramses can look when he was contemplating some reprehensible action, and he was smeared with dust from his once-white collar to his buttoned boots. Ramses is the only person of my acquaintance who can get dirty sitting perfectly still in a church.

The group bore down on me. They all spoke at once. Ramses greeted me, Brother David reproached me for not coming into the chapel, and the lady cried, in a voice as shrill as that of a magpie, "*Ach du lieber Gott*, what a pleasure it is! The famous Frau Emerson, is it you? I have often of you heard and intended on you to call and now you are here, in the flesh!"

"I fear you have the advantage of me," I replied.

"Allow me to present the Baroness Hohensteinbauergrunewald," said Brother David. "She is—"

"A great admirer of the famous Frau Emerson and her so-distinguished husband," shrieked the baroness, seizing my hand and crushing it in hers. "And now the mother of the *liebe Kind* I find you are—it is too much of happiness! You must me visit. I insist that you are coming. My dahabeeyah is at Dahshoor; I inspect the pyramids, I entertain the distinguished archaeologists, I gather the antiquities. This evening come you and the famous Professor Doctor Emerson to dine, *nicht*?"

"*Nicht*," I said. "That is, I thank you, Baroness, but I am afraid—"

"You have another engagement?" The baroness's small muddy-brown eyes twinkled. She nudged me familiarly. "No, you have not another engagement. What could you do in this desert? You will come. A dinner party I will have for the famous archaeologists. Brother David, he will come also." The young man nodded, smiling, and the baroness continued, "I stay only three days at Dahshoor. I make the Nile cruise. So you come tonight. To the famous Professor Doctor Emerson I show my collection of antiquities. I have mummies, scarabs, papyrus—"

"Papyrus?" I exclaimed.

"Yes, many. So now you come, eh? I will the young Ramses with me take, he wishes to see my dahabeeyah. Then at night you will come and fetch him. Good!"

I gave Ramses a searching look. He clasped his hands. "Oh, Mama, may I go wit' de lady?"

"You are too untidy—" I began.

The baroness guffawed. "So a small boy should be, *nicht*? I will take good care of him. I am a mama, I know a mama's heart." She rumpled his ebony curls. Ramses' face took on the fixed look that usually preceded a rude remark. He loathed having his curls rumpled. But he remained silent, and my suspicions as to his ulterior motives, whatever they might be, were strengthened.

Before I could frame further objections the baroness started, and said in what is vulgarly called a pig's whisper, "*Ach*, he comes, *der Pfarrer*. Too much he talks already. I escape. I come only to see Brother David, because he is so beautiful, but *der Pfarrer* I do not like. Come, *Bübchen*, we run away."

She suited the action to the words, dragging Ramses with her.

Brother Ezekiel had emerged from the chapel. Behind him was Charity, hands clasped and face obscured by the bonnet. At the sight of her John jumped as if a bee had stung him. "Madam," he groaned piteously, "may I—"

"Very well," I said.

The baroness was certainly one of the most vulgar women I had ever met, but her instincts were basically sound. I also wished to run away from Brother Ezekiel. As I beat a hasty retreat I felt as if I had tossed John to him like a bone to a lion, in order to make good my escape. At least John was a willing martyr.

So the baroness had papyri. In my opinion that fact justified a visit. Emerson would not be pleased, though. I had lost John to the missionaries and Ramses to the baroness, and I had committed my husband to a social call of the sort he particularly abominated. However, there was one mitigating circumstance. We would be alone in the house that afternoon, and I had no doubt I could persuade Emerson to do his duty.

III

Emerson was duly persuaded. He refused to wear proper evening dress, and I did not insist, for I had discovered that my red velvet gown was not suited to riding donkey-back. I put on my best Turkish trousers and we set off, accompanied by Selim and Daoud.

Bastet had been even more annoyed than Emerson to learn I had not brought Ramses back with me. We had shut her in one of the empty storerooms to prevent her from attending church with us; when I let her out she addressed me in raucous complaint and bolted out of the house. She had not returned by the time we left, nor had John.

"Something must be done about this nonsense, Amelia," Emerson declared, as we jogged northward. "I won't have John turning into a Brother of Jerusalem. I thought he had more intelligence. I am disappointed in him."

"He has not been converted by Brother Ezekiel, you booby," I said affectionately. "He is in love, and as you ought to know, intelligence is no defense against that perilous condition."

Instead of responding to this tender remark, Emerson only grunted.

It was another of those perfect desert evenings. A cool breeze swept away the heat of the day. The western sky was awash with crimson and gold, while the heavens above our heads had the clear translucence of a deep-blue china bowl. Golden in the rays of the setting sun, the slopes of the great pyramids of Dahshoor rose like stairways to heaven. Yet the somber tower of the Black Pyramid dominated the scene. Because of its position it appeared as high or higher than the nearby southern stone pyramid.

We passed close by its base on our way to the riverbank. The ground was littered with chips of white limestone, the remains of the casing blocks that had once covered the brick core. The previous season de Morgan had uncovered the ruins of the enclosure wall and the funerary chapel next to the pyramid. A few fallen columns and fragments of bas-relief were all that remained above the surface of the ground. So much for futile human vanity; in a few years the relentless sand would swallow up the signs of de Morgan's work as it had covered the structures designed to ensure the immortality of the pharaoh. The site was deserted. De Morgan was staying at Menyat Dahshoor, the nearest village.

We rode on, following the lengthening shadow of the pyramid toward the river. Several dahabeeyahs rocked gently at anchor, but it was easy to distinguish that of the baroness, since the German flag flew at the bow. A freshly painted plaque displayed the vessel's name: *Cleopatra*. It was precisely the sort of trite, obvious name I would have expected the baroness to select.

A gentle nostalgia suffused me when I set foot on the deck. There is no more delightful means of travel than these houseboats; the Nile steamers of Mr. Cook, which have almost replaced them, cannot compare in comfort and charm.

The main salon was in the front of the boat, with a row of wide windows following the curve of the bow. The baroness's dragoman threw open the door and announced us, and we stepped into a chamber swimming with sunset light and furnished with garish elegance. A wide divan covered with cushions filled one end of the room, and upon it, in more than oriental splendor, reclined the baroness. Golden chains twined the dusky masses of her unbound hair, and golden bracelets chimed when she raised a hand in greeting. Her snowy robes were of the finest chiffon; a heavy necklace or collar, of carnelian and turquoise set in gold, covered her breast. I assumed that the absurd costume was meant to conjure up the fabulous queen after whom the boat was named, but I could not help being reminded of the late and not much lamented Madame Berengeria, who had also affected ancient Egyptian costume, laboring as she did under the impression that she was the reincarnation of several long-dead queens. Poor Berengeria would have turned green with envy at the magnificence of the baroness's garb, for her bracelets were of pure gold and the collar around her neck appeared to be a genuine antiquity.

From Emerson, behind me, came sounds of imminent strangulation. I turned to find that his apoplectic gaze was fixed, not on the lady's ample charms, but upon another object. It was a handsome mummy case, gleaming with varnish, that stood carelessly propped against the grand piano like some outré parlor ornament. A table was covered with an equally casual display of antiquities—scarabs, ushebtis, vessels of pottery and stone. On another table were several papyrus scrolls.

The baroness began to writhe. After a moment I realized her movements were not those of a peculiar, recumbent dance, but merely an attempt to rise from the couch, which was low and soft. Succeeding in this, she swept forward to welcome us. Since Emerson made no move to take the hand she held under his nose, she snatched his. The vigorous shaking she gave it seemed to wake him from his stupor. His eyes focused in a malignant glare upon her conspicuous bosom, and he inquired, "Madam, do you realize the object you have slung across your chest is a priceless antiquity?"

The baroness rolled her eyes and covered the

collar with ringed hands. "*Ach*, the monster! Would you tear it from my helpless body?"

"Not at all," Emerson replied. "Rough handling might damage the collar."

The baroness burst into a roar of laughter. "It is the truth, what they say about Emerson the most distinguished. They have of you me warned, that you would scold—"

"For heaven's sake, madam, speak German," Emerson interrupted, his scowl deepening.

The lady continued in that language. "Yes, yes, everyone speaks of Professor Emerson; they have told me you would scold me for my poor little antiquities. M. de Morgan is not so unkind as you."

She proceeded to introduce the other guests. If she had deliberately selected a group designed to vex Emerson, she could hardly have done better—de Morgan, Kalenischeff (in faultless evening dress, complete with ribbon and monocle), Brother David, and three of what Emerson called "confounded tourists," from the other dahabeeyahs. The only memorable remark made by any of the tourists the entire evening came from one of the English ladies, who remarked in a languid drawl, "But the ruins are so dilapidated! Why doesn't someone repair them?"

The one person I expected to see was not present, and during a lull in the ensuing conversation I inquired of the baroness, "Where is Ramses?"

"Locked in one of the guest chambers," was the reply. "Oh, do not concern yourself, Frau Emerson; he is happily engaged with a papyrus. But it was necessary for me to confine him. Already he has fallen overboard and been bitten by a lion—"

"Lion?" Emerson turned, with a cry, from the granite statue of Isis he had been examining.

"My lion cub," the baroness explained. "I bought the adorable little creature from a dealer in Cairo."

"Ah," I said, enlightened. "Ramses was no doubt attempting to free the animal. Did he succeed?"

"Fortunately we were able to recapture it," the baroness replied.

I was sorry to hear that. Ramses would undoubtedly try again.

The baroness reassured my snarling husband. The bite had not been deep and medical attention had been promptly applied. It was tacitly agreed that we would leave Ramses where he was until it was time to take him home. Emerson did not insist. He had other things on his mind.

These were, I hardly need say, the illicit antiquities collected by the baroness. He kept reverting to the subject despite the efforts of the others to keep the conversation on a light social plane, and after we had dined he finally succeeded in delivering his lecture. Striding up and down the salon, waving his arms, he shouted anathemas while the baroness grinned and rolled her eyes.

"If tourists would stop buying from these dealers, they would have to go out of business," he cried. "The looting of tombs and cemeteries would stop. Look at this." He pointed an accusing finger at the mummy case. "Who knows what vital evidence the tomb robber lost when he removed this mummy from its resting place?"

The baroness gave me a conspiratorial smile. "But he is magnificent, the professor. Such passion! I congratulate you, my dear."

"I fear I must add my reproaches to those of the professor." The statement was so unexpected it halted Emerson's lecture and turned all eyes toward the speaker. David continued, in the same soft voice, "Carrying human remains about as if they were cordwood is a deplorable custom. As a man of the cloth, I cannot condone it."

"But this poor corpse was a pagan," said Kalenischeff, smiling cynically. "I thought you men of the cloth were only concerned about Christian remains."

"Pagan or Christian, all men are the children of God," was the reply. All the ladies present—except myself—let out sighs of admiration, and David went on, "Of course, if I believed the remains were those of a fellow-Christian, however misled by false dogma, I would be forced to expostulate more forcibly. I could not permit—"

"I thought he was a Christian," the baroness interrupted. "The dealer from whom I bought him said so."

A general outcry arose. The baroness shrugged. "What is the difference? They are all the same, dry bones and flesh—the cast-off garments of the soul."

This shrewd hit—it was shrewd, I admit—was wasted on David, whose German was obviously poor. He looked puzzled, and de Morgan said soothingly, in the tongue of Shakespeare, "No, there is no question of such a thing. I fear the dealer deceived you, Baroness."

"*Verdammter* pig-dog," said the baroness calmly. "How can you be sure, monsieur?"

De Morgan started to reply, but Emerson beat him to it. "By the style and decoration of the mummy case. The hieroglyphic inscriptions identify the owner as a man named Thermoutharin. He was clearly a worshiper of the old gods; the scenes in gilt relief show Anubis and Isis, Osiris and Thoth, performing the ceremony of embalming the dead."

"It is of the Ptolemaic period," said de Morgan.

"No, no, later. The first or second century A.D."

De Morgan's lean cheekbones flushed with annoyance at Emerson's dogmatic tone, but he was too much of a gentleman to debate the point. It was young David Cabot who peppered my husband with questions—the meaning of this sign or that, the significance of the inscriptions, and so on. I was surprised at his interest, but I saw nothing sinister in it—then.

Before long the baroness became bored with a conversation of which she was not the subject. "*Ach!*" she exclaimed, clapping her hands. "So much fuss over an ugly mummy! If you feel so strongly, Professor, you may have it. I give it as a gift. Unless Brother David wants to take it, to bury it with Christian rites."

"Not I," David said. "The professor has convinced me; it is pagan."

"Nor I," said Emerson. "I have enough damned— that is, er . . . Give it to the Museum, Baroness."

"I will consider doing so," said the lady, "if it will win your approval, Professor."

I could have told her that her elephantine flirtatiousness would have no effect on Emerson. Tiring finally of a game in which she was the only player, she invited her guests to view her new pet, which was kept in a cage on the deck. Emerson and I declined; and when the others had gone, I turned to my unhappy spouse. "You have done your duty like an English gentleman, Emerson. I am ready to leave whenever you are."

"I never wanted to come in the first place, Peabody, as you know. As I suspected, my martyrdom was in vain. The confounded woman has no demotic papyri."

"I know. But perhaps your appeals on behalf of antiquities will affect not only the baroness but the other tourists who were present."

Emerson snorted. "Don't be naive, Peabody. Let us go, eh? If I remain any longer in this storehouse of disaster, I will choke."

"Very well, my dear. As always, I bow to your wishes."

"Bah," said Emerson. "Where do you suppose that dreadful female has stowed our poor child?"

It was not difficult to locate Ramses. One of the baroness's servants stood on guard before the door. He salaamed deeply when he saw us and produced the key.

Darkness had fallen, but the room was well lighted by two hanging lamps. Their beams fell upon a table well supplied with food and drink, and upon another table that held a papyrus scroll, partially unrolled. There was no sign of Ramses.

"Curse it," Emerson said furiously. "I'll wager she neglected to nail the porthole shut." He pulled aside the drapery that concealed the aforementioned orifice, and fell back with a cry. Hanging from the wall, like a stuffed hunting trophy, was a small headless body culminating in shabby brown buttoned boots. The legs were quite limp.

Accustomed as I was to finding Ramses in a variety of peculiar positions, this one was sufficiently unusual to induce a momentary constriction of the chest that kept me mute. Before I could recover myself, a far-off, strangely muffled but familiar voice remarked, "Good evening, Mama. Good evening, Papa. Will you be so good as to pull me in?"

He had stuck, in actuality, somewhere around the midsection, owing to the fact that the pockets of his little suit were filled with rocks. "It was a singular miscalculation on my part," Ramses remarked somewhat breathlessly, as Emerson set him on his feet. "I counted on de fact, which I have often had occasion to establish t'rough experiment, dat where de head and shoulders can pass, de rest of de body can follow. I had forgotten about de rocks, which are interesting specimens of de geological history of—"

"Why did you not pull yourself back into the room?" I inquired curiously, as Emerson, still pale with alarm, ran agitated hands over the child's frame.

"De problem lies in my unfortunate lack of inches," Ramses explained. "My arms were not long enough to obtain sufficient purchase on de side of de vessel."

He would have gone on at some length had I not interrupted him. "And the papyrus?" I asked.

Ramses gave it a disparaging glance. "An undistinguished example of a twentiet'-dynasty mortuary text. De lady has no demotic papyri, Mama."

We found the rest of the party still on deck. The ladies crouched before the cage in which the lion cub prowled restlessly, growling and snapping. I kept firm hold of Ramses' arm while we made our excuses and thanked our hostess. At least I thanked her; Emerson only snorted.

Brother David announced his intention of riding back with us. "I must arise at dawn," he intoned. "This has been a delightful interlude, but my Master calls."

The baroness extended her hand and the young man bent over it with graceful respect. "Humph," said Emerson, as we left him to complete his farewells. "I presume the interval has been lucrative as well as delightful. He wouldn't be ready to leave if he had not accomplished what he came for."

"What was dat?" Ramses asked interestedly.

"Money, of course. Donations to the church. That is Brother David's role, I fancy—seducing susceptible ladies."

"Emerson, please," I exclaimed.

"Not literally," Emerson admitted. "At least I don't suppose so."

"What is de literal meaning of dat word?" Ramses inquired. "De dictionary is particularly obscure on dat point."

Emerson changed the subject.

After we had mounted, Emerson set off at a great pace in an effort to avoid David's company, but the young man was not to be got rid of so easily. Before the pair trotted beyond earshot I heard him say, "Pray explain to me, Professor, how a man of your superior intelligence can be so indifferent to that one great question which must supersede all other intellectual inquiries. . . ."

Ramses and I followed at a gentler pace. He seemed deep in thought, and after a time I asked, "Where did the lion cub bite you?"

"He did not bite me. His toot' scratched my hand when I pulled him from de cage."

"That was not a sensible thing to do, Ramses."

"Dat," said Ramses, "was not de issue, Mama."

"I am not referring to your ill-advised attempt to free the animal from captivity. It appears to be a very young lion. Its chances of survival in a region where there are no others of its kind would be slim."

Ramses was silent for a moment. Then he said thoughtfully, "I confess dat objection had not occurred to me. T'ank you for bringing it to my attention."

"You are welcome," I replied, congratulating myself on having headed Ramses off in the neatest possible manner. He scarcely ever disobeyed a direct command, but on those few occasions when he had done so, he had appealed to moral considerations as an excuse for failing to comply. I suspected the well-being of an animal would seem to him a sufficient excuse. By pointing out that he would only be worsening the unfortunate lion's condition I had, as I believed, forestalled a second attempt at liberation.

How true it is that there are none so blind as those who will not see!

The night was utterly silent; the contentious missionary and his would-be prey had drawn far ahead. Sand muffled the hoofbeats of our steeds. We might have been a pair of ancient Egyptian dead seeking the paradise of Amenti, for I was absorbed in self-congratulation and Ramses was abnormally silent. Glancing at him, I was struck by an odd little chill, for the profile outlined against the paler background of the sandy waste was alarmingly like that of his namesake—beaky nose, prominent chin, lowering brow. At least it resembled the mummy of his namesake; one presumes that centuries of desiccation have not improved the looks of the pharaoh.

When we reached the house David bade us good night and rode off toward the village. It did not improve Emerson's spirits to find the house dark and apparently deserted. John was there, however. We found him in his own room reading the Bible, and Emerson's language, when he beheld that sacred Book, was absolutely disgraceful.

Next morning John was most apologetic about his lapse. "I know I ought to 'ave 'ad your beds made up and the kettle on the boil," he said. "It won't 'appen again, madam. Duty to one's superior is wot a man must do in this world, so long as it don't conflict with one's duty to—"

"Yes, yes, John, that is quite all right," I said, seeing Emerson's countenance redden. "I shall want you to help me with photography this morning, so hurry and clear away the breakfast things. Ramses, you must—what on earth is the matter with you? I believe your chin is in your porridge. Take it out at once."

Ramses wiped his chin. I looked at him suspiciously, but before I could pursue my inquiries Emerson threw down his napkin and rose, kicking his chair out of the way as is his impetuous habit.

"We are late," he announced. "That is what happens when one allows social stupidities to interfere with work. Come along, Peabody."

So the day began. Emerson had moved the men to a site farther north and west, where the irregular terrain suggested the presence of another cemetery. So it proved to be. The graves were quite unlike those of the Roman cemetery. These were simple interments; the bodies were enclosed only in coarse linen shrouds bound in crisscross fashion with red-and-white striped cords. The grave goods included a few crude stelae with incised crosses and other Christian insignia, proving what we had suspected from the nature of the burials themselves—that they were those of Copts. They were very old Copts, and I hoped this consideration would prevent the priest from protesting. He had left us strictly alone, but I feared he might object to our excavating a Christian cemetery. Emerson of course pooh-poohed this possibility; we would handle the bodies with the reverence we accorded all human remains and even rebury them if the priest desired. First, however, he wanted to study them, and if any superstitious ignoramus objected, he could take himself and his superstitions to Perdition or Gehenna.

Emerson wanted photographs of the graves before we removed the contents. That was my task that morning, and with John's help I carried the camera, tripod, plates and other impedimenta to the site. We had to wait until the sun was high enough to illumine the sunken pits, and as we stood in enforced idleness I asked, "Did you enjoy yourself on your day out, John?"

"Oh yes, madam. There was another service in the evening. Sister Charity sang divinely that touching 'ymn, 'Washed in the blood of the Lamb.'"

"And was it a good dinner?"

"Oh yes, madam. Sister Charity is a good cook."

I recognized one of the symptoms of extreme infatuation—the need to repeat the name of the beloved at frequent intervals. "I hope you are not thinking of being converted, John. You know Professor Emerson won't stand for it."

The old John would have burst into protestations of undying loyalty. The new, corrupted John looked grave. "I would give me life's blood for the professor, madam. The day he caught me trying to steal 'is watch in front of the British Museum he saved me from a life of sin and vice. I will never forget his kindness in punching me in the jaw and ordering me to accompany him to Kent, when any other gentleman would 'ave 'ad me taken in charge."

His lips quivered as he spoke. I gave him a friendly pat on the arm. "You certainly could not have continued your career as a pickpocket much longer, John. Considering your conspicuous size and your— if you will forgive me for mentioning it—your growing clumsiness, you were bound to be caught."

"Growing is the word, madam. You wouldn't

believe what a small, agile nipper I was when I took up the trade. But that is all in the past, thank 'eaven."

"And Professor Emerson."

"And the professor. Yet, madam, though I revere him and would, as I mentioned, shed the last drop of blood in me body for him, or you, or Master Ramses, I cannot endanger me soul for any mortal creature. A man's conscience is—"

"Rubbish," I said. "If you must quote, John, quote Scripture. It has a literary quality, at least, that Brother Ezekiel's pronouncements lack."

John removed his hat and scratched his head. "It does 'ave that, madam. Sometimes I wish as 'ow it didn't 'ave so much. But I'm determined to fight me way through the Good Book, madam, no matter 'ow long it takes."

"How far have you got?"

"Leviticus," said John with a deep sigh. "Genesis and Exodus wasn't so bad, they tore right along most of the time. But Leviticus will be my downfall, madam."

"Skip over it," I suggested sympathetically.

"Oh no, madam, I can't do that."

A wordless shout from my husband, some little distance away, recalled me to my duties, and I indicated to John that we would begin photographing. Scarcely had I inserted the plate in the camera, however, when I realized Emerson's hail had been designed to draw my attention to an approaching rider. High blue-and-white striped robe ballooning out in the wind, he rode directly to me and fell off the donkey. Gasping theatrically, he handed me a note and then collapsed facedown in the sand.

Since the donkey had been doing all the work, I ignored this demonstration. While John bent over the fallen man with expressions of concern I opened the note.

The writer was obviously another frustrated thespian. There was no salutation or signature, but the passionate and scarcely legible scrawl could only have been penned by one person of my acquaintance. "Come to me at once," it read. "Disaster, ruin, destruction!"

With my toe I nudged the fallen messenger, who seemed to have fallen into a refreshing sleep. "Have you come from the German lady?" I asked.

The man rolled over and sat up, none the worse for wear. He nodded vigorously. "She sends for you, Sitt Hakim, and for Emerson Effendi."

"What has happened? Is the lady injured?"

The messenger was scarcely more coherent than the message. I was still endeavoring to get some sense out of him when Emerson came up. I handed him the note and explained the situation. "We had better go, Emerson."

"Not I," said Emerson.

"It isn't necessary for both of us to respond," I agreed. "Do you take charge of the photography while I—"

"Curse it, Peabody," Emerson cried. "Will you let this absurd woman interrupt our work again?"

It ended in both of us going. Emerson claimed he dared not let me out of his sight, but in fact he was as bored with our pitiful excavation as I was.

And of course one owes a duty to one's fellow man—and woman.

As we rode across the desert, my spirits rose—not, as evil-minded persons have suggested, at the prospect of interfering in matters which were not my concern, but at the imminence of the exquisite Dahshoor pyramids. My spirits were bound to them by an almost physical thread; the nearer I came the gladder I felt, the farther I went the more that tenuous thread was stretched, almost to the point of pain.

The baroness's dahabeeyah was the only one at the dock. We were led at once to the lady, who was reclining on a couch on deck, under an awning. She was wearing a most peculiar garment, part negligee, part tea gown, shell-pink in color and covered with frills. Sitting beside her was M. de Morgan, holding her hand—or rather, having his hand held by her.

"*Ah, mon cher collègue,*" he said with obvious relief. "At last you have come."

"We only received the message a short time ago," I said. "What has happened?"

"Murder, slaughter, invasion!" shrieked the baroness, throwing herself about on the couch.

"Robbery," said de Morgan succinctly. "Someone broke into the salon last night and stole several of the baroness's antiquities."

I glanced at Emerson. Hands on hips, he studied the baroness and her protector with impartial disgust. "Is that all?" he said. "Come, Peabody, let us get back to work."

"No, no, you must help me," the baroness exclaimed. "I call for you—the great solvers of mysteries, the great archaeologists. You must protect me. Someone wishes to murder me—assault me—"

"Come, come, Baroness, control yourself," I said. "Why was not the robbery discovered earlier? It is almost midday."

"But that is when I rise," the baroness explained guilelessly. "My servants woke me when they found out what had happened. They are lazy swine-dogs, those servants; they should have been cleaning the salon at sunrise."

"When the mistress is slack, the servants will be lazy," I said. "It is most unfortunate. Several of the possible suspects have already left the scene."

De Morgan let out a French expletive. "*Mais, chère madame*, you cannot be referring to the people of quality whose dahabeeyahs were moored here? Such people are not thieves."

I could not help smiling at this credulous statement, but I said only, "One never knows, does one? First let us have a look at the scene of the crime."

"It has not been disturbed," said the baroness, scrambling eagerly up from the couch. "I ordered that it be left just as it was until the great solvers of mysteries came."

It was easy to see how the thieves had entered. The wide windows in the bow stood open and the cushions of the couch had been crushed by several pairs of feet. Unfortunately the marks were amorphous in the extreme, and as I examined them with my pocket lens I found myself wishing, for once, that Egypt enjoyed our damp English climate. Dry sand does not leave footprints.

I turned to my husband. "You can say what is missing, Emerson. I fancy you studied the antiquities even more closely than I."

"It should be obvious," said Emerson morosely. "What was last night the most conspicuous article in the room?"

The grand piano was the answer, but that was not what Emerson meant. "The mummy case," I replied. "Yes, I saw at once it was no longer present. What else, Emerson?"

"A lapis scarab and a statuette of Isis nursing the infant Horus."

"That is all?"

"That is all. They were," Emerson added feelingly, "the finest objects in the collection."

Further examination of the room provided nothing of interest, so we proceeded to question the servants. The baroness began shrieking accusations and, as might have been expected, every face looked guilty as Cain.

I silenced the woman with a few well-chosen words and directed Emerson to question the men, which he did with his usual efficiency. One and all denied complicity. One and all had slept through the night; and when the dragoman suggested that djinns must have been responsible, the others quickly agreed.

De Morgan glanced at the sun, now high overhead. "I must return to my excavations, madame. I advise you to call in the local authorities. They will deal with your servants."

A howl of anguish broke out from the huddled group of men. They knew only too well how local authorities dealt with suspects. With a reassuring gesture I turned to the baroness. "I forbid it," I cried.

"You forbid it?" De Morgan lifted his eyebrows.

"And so do I," Emerson said, stepping to my side. "You know as well as I do, de Morgan, that the favorite method of interrogation hereabouts consists of beating the suspects on the soles of their feet until they confess. They are presumed guilty until proven innocent. However," he added, scowling at de Morgan, "that assumption may not seem unreasonable to a citizen of the French Republic, with its antiquated Napoleonic Code."

De Morgan flung up his arms. "I wash my hands of the whole affair! Already I have wasted half a day. Do as you wish."

"I fully intend to," Emerson replied. *"Bonjour, monsieur."*

After de Morgan had stamped off, cursing quietly in his own tongue, Emerson addressed the baroness. "You understand, madam," he said, squaring his splendid shoulders, "that if you call the police, Mrs. Emerson and I will not assist you."

The baroness was more moved by the shoulders than by the threat. Eyes slightly glazed, she stood staring at my husband's stalwart form until I nudged her with my indispensable parasol. "What?" she mumbled, starting. "The police—who wants them? What is missing, after all? Nothing I cannot easily replace."

"I congratulate you on your good sense," said Emerson. "There is no need for you to concern yourself further at this time; if you would care to retire—"

"But no, you do not understand!" The appalling woman actually seized him by the arm and thrust her face into his. "The stolen objects are unimportant.

But what of me? I am afraid for my life, for my virtue—"

"I really don't think you need worry about that," I said.

"You will protect me—a poor helpless *Mädchen?*" the baroness insisted. Her fingers stroked Emerson's biceps. Emerson's biceps are quite remarkable, but I allow no one except myself to admire them in that fashion.

"I will protect you, Baroness," I said firmly. "That is our customary arrangement when my husband and I are engaged in detectival pursuits. He pursues, I protect the ladies."

"Yes, quite right," said Emerson, shifting uneasily from one foot to the other. "I will leave you with Mrs. Emerson, madam, and I will—I will go and—I will inquire—"

The baroness released her hold and Emerson beat a hasty retreat. "You are in no danger," I said. "Unless you have information you have not disclosed."

"No." The baroness grinned knowingly at me. "He is a very handsome man, your husband. *Mucho macho*, as the Spanish say."

"Do they really?"

"But I do not waste time on a hopeless cause," the baroness continued. "I see that he is tied firmly to the apron strings of his good English *Frau*. I shall leave Dahshoor tomorrow."

"What of Brother David?" I asked maliciously. "He is not tied to a woman's apron strings—unless Miss Charity has captured his heart."

"That pale, washed-out child?" The baroness

snorted. "No, no, she adores him, but he is indifferent to her. She has nothing to offer him. Make no mistake, Frau Emerson, the beautiful young man is only saintly in his face and figure. He has, as the French say, an eye *pour le main chance*."

The baroness's French and Spanish were as fractured as her English, but I fancied she was not as ignorant of human nature as she was of languages. She went on with mounting indignation, "I have sent for him today, to come to my rescue, and does he come? No, he does not. And a large donation I have made to his church."

So Emerson's surmise had been correct! I said, "You do Brother David an injustice, Baroness. Here he is now."

She turned. "*Herr Gott*," she exclaimed. "He has brought the ugly *Pfarrer* with him."

"It is the other way around, I fancy."

"I escape," the baroness said loudly. "I run away. Tell them I can see no one." But in stepping forward she tripped on her flounces and fell in a disheveled heap upon the couch. Brother Ezekiel pounced on her before she could rise. Fumbling in the pile of agitated ruffles, he pulled out a hand, which he seized firmly in his big hairy fists.

"Dear sister, I rejoice that you are not harmed. Let us bow our heads and thank God for this merciful escape. Heavenly Father, let the weight of your wrath fall on the villains who have perpetrated this deed; mash 'em flat to the dust, O Lord, lay 'em low as you did the Amalekites and the Jebusites and the . . ."

The polysyllabic catalog rolled on. "Good

morning, Brother David," I said. "I am glad you are here; I can leave the baroness to you."

"You can indeed," David assured me, his mild blue eyes beaming. "The tender and womanly compassion that is so peculiarly your own does you credit, Mrs. Emerson, but there is no need for you to remain."

The baroness lay quite still. I could see her face; her eyes were closed and she appeared to be asleep, though how she could have slept through Brother Ezekiel's voice I cannot imagine. ". . . and the kings of Midian, namely Evi and Rekem and Zur and Hur . . ."

I found Emerson surrounded by the servants and the members of the crew. He was haranguing them in Arabic, to which they listened with fascinated attention. Arabs do love a skilled orator. Seeing me, he concluded his speech. "You know me, my brothers; you know I do not lie, and that I protect all honest men. Think well on what I have said."

"What did you say?" I inquired as we walked away, followed by the respectful farewells of the audience: "Allah preserve thee; the mercy and blessing of Allah be with thee."

"Oh, the usual thing, Peabody. I don't believe any of the men were directly involved in the robbery, but they must have been bribed to remain silent. An object the size of that mummy case could not have been removed from the salon without waking someone."

"Bribed—or intimidated? I sense the sinister shadow of the Master Criminal, Emerson. How far his evil web must stretch!"

"I warn you, Peabody, I will not be responsible if you go on talking of webs and shadows and Master Criminals. This is a case of sordid, commonplace thievery. It can have no connection—"

"Like a giant spider weaving his tangled strands into a net that snares rich and poor, guilty and innocent—"

Emerson leaped onto his donkey and urged it into a trot.

We had left the cultivation far behind before his countenance regained its customary placidity. I refrained from further discussion, knowing that sooner or later he would acknowledge the accuracy of my analysis. Sure enough, it was not long before he remarked musingly, "All the same, the case has one or two curious features. Why should thieves go to so much trouble to make off with an ordinary Romano-Egyptian mummy case? It was that of a commoner; there could be no expectation of finding jewelry or valuable amulets among the wrappings."

"What of the other objects that were taken?" I asked.

"That is what makes the situation even more curious, Peabody. Two other things were taken—the scarab and the statuette. They were the most valuable objects in the collection. The statuette was particularly fine, late Eighteenth Dynasty, if I am not mistaken. One might suppose that the thief was an expert in his unsavory trade, since he knew the valuable from the valueless. Yet there were other items, small and easily portable, that might have fetched a decent price, and the thieves left them in order to expend enormous effort on removing a worthless mummy case."

"You have forgotten to mention one item that was taken," I said. "Or perhaps you did not observe it was missing."

"What are you talking about, Peabody? I missed nothing."

"Yes, Emerson, you did."

"No, Peabody, I did not."

"The lion cub, Emerson. The cage was empty."

Emerson's hands released their grip on the reins. His donkey came to a halt. I reined up beside him.

"Empty," he repeated stupidly.

"The door had been closed and the cage pushed aside, but I observed it closely and I can assure you—"

"Oh, good Gad!" Emerson looked at me in consternation. "Peabody! Your own innocent child . . . You don't suspect . . . Ramses could not possibly have carried off that heavy mummy case. Besides, he has better taste than to steal something like that."

"I have long since given up trying to anticipate what Ramses can and cannot do," I replied, with considerable heat. "Your second point has some merit; but Ramses' motives are as obscure as his capabilities are remarkable. I never know what the devil the child has in mind."

"Language, Peabody, language."

I took a grip on myself. "You are right. Thank you for reminding me, Emerson."

"You are quite welcome, Peabody."

He took up his reins and we went on in pensive

silence. Then Emerson said uneasily, "Where do you suppose he has put it?"

"What, the mummy case?"

"No, curse it. The lion cub."

"We will soon find out."

"You don't believe he was involved in the other theft, do you, Amelia?" Emerson's voice was piteous.

"No, of course not. I know the identity of the thief. As soon as I have dealt with Ramses I will take him into custody."

SEVEN

The lion cub was in Ramses' room. Ramses was
sitting on the floor teasing it with a nasty-looking
bit of raw meat when we burst in. He looked up with
a frown and said reproachfully, "You did not knock,
Mama and Papa. You know dat my privacy is important to me."

"What would you have done if we had knocked?"
Emerson asked.

"I would have put de lion under de bed," said
Ramses.

"But how could you possibly suppose—" Emerson
began. I joggled him with my elbow. "Emerson, you
are letting Ramses get you off the track again. He
always does it and you always succumb. Ramses."

"Yes, Mama?" The cub rolled itself into a furry
ball around his fist.

"I told you not to . . ." But there I was forced to
stop to reconsider. I had not told Ramses he must
not steal the baroness's lion. He waited politely for
me to finish, and I said weakly, "I told you not to
wander off alone."

"But I did not, Mama. Selim went wit' me. He

carried de lion cub. My donkey would not let me take it up wit' me."

I had seen Selim that morning, but now that I thought about it I realized he had been careful to let me see only his back. No doubt his face and hands bore evidence of the cub's reluctance to be carried.

I squatted down on the floor to examine the animal more closely. It certainly appeared to be in good health and spirits. In a purely investigative manner, to check the condition of its fur, I tickled the back of its head.

"I am training it to hunt for itself," Ramses explained, dragging the loathsome morsel across the cub's rounded stomach. Apparently it had had enough to eat, for it ignored the meat and began licking my fingers.

"What are you going to do with it?" Emerson inquired, sitting down on the floor. The cub transferred its attentions to his fingers, and he chuckled. "It's an engaging little creature."

"All small creatures are engaging," I replied coldly. The cub climbed onto my lap and nuzzled into my skirt. "But one day this small creature will be big enough to swallow you in two bites, Ramses. No, lion, I am not your mother. There is nothing for you there. You had better find it some milk, Ramses."

"Yes, Mama, I will. T'ank you, Mama, I had not t'ought of dat."

"And don't try your tricks with me, Ramses. I am not susceptible to charming young animals of any species. I am really disappointed in you. I had hoped you possessed a greater sense of responsibility. You have taken this helpless creature . . ." The cub, frustrated in its quest for sustenance, sank its sharp little teeth into the upper portion of my leg, and I broke off with a yelp. Emerson removed it and began playing with it while I continued, ". . . this helpless creature into your charge, and you are incapable of giving it the care it requires. I fondly hope you do not entertain any notion that you can persuade your father and me to take it home with us."

"Oh no, Mama," said Ramses, wide-eyed. Emerson trailed the meat across the floor and chortled when the cub pounced on it.

"I am glad you realize that. We cannot always be bringing animals back from Egypt. The cat Bastet . . . Good heavens, what about the cat? She won't tolerate this infantile intruder for a moment."

"She likes it," said Ramses.

The cat Bastet lay atop the packing case Ramses used as a cupboard. Paws folded beneath her smooth breast, she watched the antics of the cub with what appeared to be an expression of benevolent interest.

"Well, well," said Emerson, getting to his feet. "We will think of something, Ramses."

"I have already t'ought, Papa. I am going to give it to Aunt Evelyn and Uncle Walter. Dere is ample space for a menagerie at Chalfont, conducted on de latest scientific principles, and wit' a veterinarian in constant attendance—"

"That is the most appalling suggestion I have ever heard," I exclaimed. "Ramses, I am thoroughly disaffected with you. Consider yourself confined to your room until further notice. No—that won't do.

You must repair some small part of the havoc you have wrought. Go immediately and fetch Selim."

Ramses ran for the door. I sank into a chair. It was the first time—though certainly not the last—that I began to have serious doubts as to my capability of carrying out the task I had so unthinkingly assumed. I have dealt with murderers, thieves and brigands of all kinds; but I suspected Ramses might be too much even for me.

These doubts soon passed, naturally, as I attacked the immediate problems with my habitual efficiency. After lecturing Selim and painting iodine on his scratches—his face resembled that of a Red Indian ready for the warpath when I finished—I set one of the men to building a cage, another to the task of constructing a heavy wooden screen for Ramses' window, and a third to the village to purchase a goat of the proper gender and lactiferous condition. Emerson protested the decimation of his work force, but not with his usual vehemence; and when I escorted Ramses into the parlor and sat him down on a footstool, Emerson took a chair next to mine with an expression of unusual gravity on his face.

I confess my own heart was lightened when Ramses declared, with a wholly convincing show of candor, that he knew nothing of the theft of the baroness's antiquities.

"I would not take dat rubbishy mummy case," he exclaimed. "I am deeply hurt, Mama, dat you should t'ink me capable of such ignorance."

I exchanged glances with Emerson. The relieved twinkle in his fine blue eyes brought a reluctant answering smile to my lips. "You observe he is not offended that we questioned his honesty, only his intelligence," I said.

"Stealing is wrong," said Ramses virtuously. "It says so in de Scripture."

"Accept my apologies for doubting you, my son," said Emerson. "You know, you might have pointed out that you lacked the strength to handle the object in question, even with Selim's help."

"Oh, dat would not have been a sufficient defense, Papa. Dere are met'ods of dealing wit' dat difficulty." And his face took on such a look of portentous calculation, I felt a shudder run through me.

Emerson said hastily, "Never mind, Ramses. Did you observe any suspicious activities at the dahabeeyah last night? Other than your own, that is."

Ramses had nothing useful to offer on this subject. His visit to the baroness's boat had taken place shortly after midnight, and he was reasonably certain that at that time the break-in had not taken place. The watchman had been sound asleep and snoring. Upon being questioned further, Ramses admitted that one of the crewmen had awakened. "I had de misfortune of treading upon his hand." A finger to the lips and a coin dropped into the abused hand had kept the grinning witness quiet.

"And I know which one of the men it was," growled Emerson. "He was laughing behind his hand the whole time I was questioning him about burglars. Curse it, Ramses. . . ."

"I am very hungry, Mama," Ramses remarked. "May I go and see if de cook has luncheon ready?"

I acquiesced, for I wished to talk to Emerson alone. "It appears that the break-in took place after midnight," I began.

"A logical conclusion, Peabody. But, if you will forgive my mentioning it, the fact is not particularly useful."

"I never said it was, Emerson."

Emerson leaned back and crossed his legs. "I suppose you have fixed on Hamid as the burglar?"

"Are not the circumstances suspicious, Emerson? Hamid was on the scene when Abd el Atti met his death. . . . Oh, you need not wriggle your eyebrows at me in that supercilious fashion, you know what I mean—we can't prove he was in the shop that night, but he was in Cairo, and he was involved in some shady negotiation with Abd el Atti. A few days later he turns up here, with some specious excuse about looking for work—and the baroness is robbed."

"Weak," said Emerson judiciously. "Very weak, Peabody. But knowing you, I am surprised you have not already put your suspect under arrest."

"I have had time to reconsider my first impulse, Emerson. What good would it do to apprehend the man? As yet we have no physical evidence connecting him to either crime, and naturally he will deny everything. The most sensible course is to ignore him, and watch his every movement. Sooner or later he will do something criminal, and we will catch him in the act."

"Watch him, Peabody? Follow him, you mean? If you think I am going to spend the night squatting behind a palm tree watching Hamid snore, you are sadly mistaken."

"That is a difficulty. You need your sleep, Emerson, and so do I."

"Sleep," said Emerson, "is not the only nocturnal activity of which I do not mean to be deprived."

"We might take it in turn," I mused. "In a turban and robe I could pass for a man—"

"The activity to which I referred requires that both of us be present, Peabody."

"My dear Emerson—"

"My darling Peabody—"

But at that point we were interrupted by Ramses, returning from the kitchen with the roasted chicken that had been prepared for us, and I had to mention several excellent reasons why it should be fed to us instead of to the lion.

II

Emerson's objections to our keeping a watch on Hamid, though frivolous, had merit. I therefore considered alternatives. The most obvious alternative was John, and when we returned to the dig after luncheon I was pleased to observe that he had carried out his responsibilities with skill and dedication. I had given him some instruction in the use of the camera; although we would have to wait until the plates were developed to be sure he had carried out the procedure correctly, his description of the method he had followed seemed correct. I took several more photographs to be on the safe side, and then our most skilled workmen were set to work clearing the graves. As the fragile and pitiful remains were carried carefully to the house I congratulated myself on our luck in having found such an admirable place. Never before, on any expedition, had I had enough storage space. Thanks to the old monks, I could now classify our finds in a proper methodical manner—pottery in one room, Roman mummies in another, and so on.

Hamid was working even more lethargically than usual. Naturally he would be tired if he had helped transport a weighty object the night before. Where the devil had he put the thing? I wondered. The mummy case was over seven feet long. Hamid was a stranger in the village, he had no house of his own. But there were hiding places aplenty in the desert—abandoned tombs, sunken pits, and the sand itself. Or the mummy case might have been loaded onto a small boat and carried away by water. There were many answers to the question of *where* it might have been hidden, but none to the most difficult question: Why take it in the first place?

Finally I reached a decision. "John," I said. "I have a task for you—one requiring unusual intelligence and devotion."

The young man drew himself up to his full height. "Anything, madam."

"Thank you, John. I felt sure I could count on you. I suspect one of our workers is a vicious criminal. During the day he will be under my watchful eye, but at night I cannot watch him. I want you to be my eyes. Find out where he is living. Take up a position nearby. If he leaves during the night, follow him. Do not let your presence be known, only observe what he does and report back to me. Can you do this?"

John scratched his head. "Well, madam, I will certainly try. But I see certain difficulties."

"Such as?"

"Won't he see me if I am standing outside 'is 'ouse when he comes out?"

"Don't be absurd, John. He will not see you because you will be in hiding."

"Where, madam?"

"Where? Well—er—there must be a tree or a wall or something of that sort nearby. Use your imagination, John."

"Yes, madam," John said doubtfully.

"What other difficulties do you anticipate?"

"Supposing someone sees me behind the tree and asks what I'm doing there?"

"If you are sufficiently well hidden, you will not be seen. Good heavens, John, have you no resources?"

"I don't think so, madam. But I will do me best, which is all a man can do. Which of the chaps is it?"

I started to point, then thought better of it. "That one. Third from the end—no, curse it, second. . . . He keeps changing position."

"You don't mean Brother 'amid, madam?"

"*Brother* Hamid? Yes, John, I believe I do mean Brother Hamid. He is really a convert, then?"

"Yes, madam, and I know where he lives, for he sleeps in a storeroom behind the mission house.

But, madam, I'm sure you are mistaken about 'im being a criminal. Brother Ezekiel has quite taken to 'im, and Brother Ezekiel could not take to a criminal, madam."

"Brother Ezekiel is no more immune than other men to the blandishments of a hypocrite." John gave me a blank stare, so I elaborated. "Godly persons are more vulnerable than most to the machinations of the ungodly."

"I don't understand all them long words, madam, but I think I take your meaning," John replied. "Brother Ezekiel is too trusting."

"That is a quality of saints, John," I said. "Martyrdom is often the result of excessive gullibility."

Whether John comprehended this I cannot say, but he appeared to be convinced. No doubt he had also realized that spying on Hamid would bring him closer to Charity. Squaring his shoulders, he exclaimed, "I will do just what you say, madam. Shall I 'ave a disguise, do you think?"

"That is an excellent suggestion, John. I am happy to see that you are entering into the spirit of the thing. I will borrow a robe and turban from Abdullah; he is the only one of the men who is anything near your height."

John went off to assist Emerson and I remained where I was, keeping a close but unobtrusive watch over Hamid. After a while Abdullah came up to me. "What is the man doing, Sitt, that you watch him so closely?" he asked.

"What man, Abdullah? You are mistaken. I am not watching him."

"Oh." Delicately Abdullah scratched his bearded

chin. "I was in error. I thought your keen eyes were fixed upon the foreigner—the man from Manawat."

"No, not at all. . . . What do you know about him, Abdullah?"

The *reis* replied promptly, "He has not worked with his hands, Sitt Hakim. They are sore and bleeding from the pick."

"How does he get on with the other men?"

"He has no friends among them. Those of the village who remain faithful to the priest are angry with the ones who have gone over to the Americans. But he does not even talk to the other new 'Brotestants.' Shall I dismiss him, Sitt? There are others who would like the work."

"No, don't do that. Only keep a close watch on him." I lowered my voice. "I have reason to think Hamid is a criminal, Abdullah; perhaps a murderer."

"Oh, Sitt." Abdullah clasped his hands. "Not again, honored Sitt! We come to excavate, to work; I beg you, Sitt, do not do it again."

"What do you mean, Abdullah?"

"I feared it would happen," the *reis* muttered, passing a shaking hand over his lofty brow. "A village of unbelievers, hateful to Allah; a curse on the very house where we dwell—"

"But we have lifted the curse, Abdullah."

"No, Sitt, no. The restless spirits of the dead are still there. Daoud saw one of them only last night."

I had been expecting something of the sort—or if I had not expected it, I was not surprised that it had occurred. As Emerson says, most men are superstitious, but Egyptians have more reason to believe in ghosts than do men of other nations. Is it any wonder the descendants of the pharaohs feel the presence of gods who were worshiped for over three thousand years? Add to them the pantheons of Christianity and Islam, and you have a formidable phalanx of mixed demons.

I was about to explain this to Abdullah when we were interrupted by a hail from Emerson. "Peabody! Oh, Peeebody! Come here, will you?"

"I will talk with you later," I said to Abdullah. "Don't yield to fear, my friend; you know the Father of Curses is a match for any evil spirit."

"Hmmm," said Abdullah.

We had moved the scene of our operations again that afternoon. As Emerson put it (rather unfortunately, in my opinion) we had enough moldy Christian bones to last us. What we were doing, in archaeological terms, was making a series of trial trenches across the area in order to establish the general nature of the remains. Critical persons, unacquainted with the methods of the profession, have described this as poking around in the hope of finding something interesting, but of course that is not the case.

I found Emerson standing atop a ridge of rock staring down at something below. John was with him. "Ah, Peabody," said my husband. "Just have a look at this, will you?"

Taking the hand he offered, I stepped up onto the ridge. At first glance there was nothing to justify his interest. Half buried in the sand, half exposed by the picks of the workers, was a wrapped mummy. The intricacy of the bandaging indicated that it was another Ptolemaic or Roman mummy, of which we already had a sufficiency.

"Oh dear," I said sympathetically. "Another cursed Roman cemetery."

"I do not think so. We are still on the edge of the Christian cemetery; two other burials of that nature have turned up."

John cleared his throat. "Sir. I have been wanting to speak to you about that. These 'ere pore Christians—"

"Not now, John," Emerson said irritably.

"But, sir, it ain't right to dig them up as if they was 'eathens. If we was in England—"

"We are not in England," Emerson replied. "Well, Peabody?"

"It is curious," I agreed. "One would expect such a carefully wrapped mummy to possess a coffin or a sarcophagus."

"Precisely, my dear Peabody."

"Was that how it was found?"

"You see it," Emerson replied, "just as the men found it—a scant two feet below the surface."

"These intrusions do sometimes occur, Emerson. Do you want me to take a photograph?"

Emerson stroked his chin and then replied, "I think not, Peabody. I will make a note of its location and we will see what turns up as the work progresses."

"Sir," John said. "These 'ere Christians—"

"Hold your tongue, John, and hand me that brush."

"It is almost time for tea, Emerson," I said. "Will you come?"

"Bah," said Emerson.

Taking this for acquiescence, I made my way back to the house. Ramses was not in his room. The lion cub ran to greet me when I opened the door, and as I tickled it under its chin I noticed it had eaten Ramses' house slippers and reduced his nightshirt to shreds. Restoring it to the cage, over its piteous objections, I returned to the parlor and put the kettle on.

We took tea alfresco, as the Italians say, arranging tables and chairs in a space cleared for that purpose before the house. The bits of sand that occasionally sprinkled tea and bread were a small inconvenience to pay for the fresh air and splendid view.

When Emerson joined me he was grumbling as usual. "How often have I told you, Amelia, that this ritual is absurd? Afternoon tea is all very well at home, but to interrupt one's work when in the field . . ." He seized the cup I handed him, drained it in a gulp, and returned it to me. "Petrie does not stop for tea. I won't do it, I tell you. This is the last time."

He said the same thing every day. I refilled his cup and said what I said every day, namely that an interval of refreshment increased efficiency, and that it was necessary to replenish the moisture lost from the body during the heat of the afternoon.

"Where is Ramses?" Emerson asked.

"He is late," I replied. "As to precisely where he may be, I cannot answer, thanks to your refusal to let me supervise his activities. You spoil the boy, Emerson. How many children of his age have their own archaeological excavations?"

"He wants to surprise us, Peabody. It would be cruel to thwart his innocent pleasures. . . . Ah, here he is. How very tidy you are this evening, Ramses."

Not only was he tidy, he was clean. His hair curled into tight ringlets when damp. Drops of water still sparkled in the sable coils. I was so pleased at this demonstration of conformity—for bathing was not something Ramses often engaged in of his own free will—that I did not scold him for being late or even object to the presence of the lion. Ramses secured its lead to a stone stub and began devouring bread and butter.

It was a pleasant domestic interlude; and I confess I shared Emerson's sentiments when he let out an exclamation of annoyance. "Curse it, we are going to be interrupted again. Doesn't that Frenchman do anything except pay social calls?"

The approaching figure was indeed that of de Morgan, mounted on his beautiful steed. "Ramses," I began.

"Yes, Mama. I t'ink dat de lion has had sufficient fresh air for de present." There was only time for him to thrust it into the house and close the door before de Morgan was with us.

After greetings had been exchanged and de Morgan had accepted a cup of tea, he asked how our work was going.

"Splendidly," I replied. "We have completed a survey of the area and are proceeding with trial excavations. Cemeteries of the Roman and Christian periods have been discovered."

"My commiseration, dear friends," de Morgan exclaimed. "But perhaps you will come upon something more interesting in time."

"Commiseration is not needed, monsieur," I replied. "We dote on Roman cemeteries."

"Then you will no doubt be pleased to receive another Roman mummy," said de Morgan, twirling his mustache.

"What the devil do you mean?" Emerson demanded.

"That is the reason for my visit," de Morgan replied, a Machiavellian smile curving his lips. "The stolen mummy case has been discovered. The thieves abandoned it a few kilometers from my camp, where it was found this afternoon."

"How very strange," I said.

"No, it is easy to understand," said de Morgan patronizingly. "These thieves are ignorant people. They committed an error, taking the mummy case; having discovered its worthlessness and tiring of its weight, they simply abandoned it."

Emerson shot the Frenchman a look of blistering contempt. I said, "No doubt the baroness is glad to have her relic back."

"She will have nothing to do with it." De Morgan shook his head. "*Les femmes*, they are always illogical. . . . That is, madame, I do not refer to you, you understand—"

"I should hope not, monsieur."

" 'Take it away,' she cries, waving her arms. 'Give

it to Herr Professor Emerson, who has scolded me. I want nothing more to do with it, it has brought me terror and distress.' So," de Morgan concluded, "my men will fetch it to you later."

"Thank you very much," said Emerson between clenched teeth.

"Not at all." De Morgan patted the damp curls of Ramses, who was crouched at his feet like a puppy. "And how is your study of mummies progressing, *mon petit*?"

"I have given it up for de present," said Ramses. "I find I lack de proper instruments for such research. Accurate measurements of cranial capacity and bone development are necessary if one is to reach meaningful conclusions regarding de racial and physical—"

De Morgan interrupted with a hearty laugh. "Never mind, *petit chou*; if you are bored with your papa's excavations you may visit me. Tomorrow I begin a new tunnel which will surely lead me to the burial chamber."

Emerson's countenance writhed. Catching my eye, he said in a muffled voice, "Excuse me, Amelia. I must—I must—"

And, leaping from his chair, he vanished around the corner of the house.

"I take my leave of you, madame," said de Morgan, rising. "I came only to tell you that the stolen property has been recovered and to give you the baroness's farewells. She sails at dawn."

"Good," I exclaimed. "That is—I am glad she is recovered enough to continue her journey."

"I thought you might feel that way," said de Morgan with a smile. "You know that her little pet escaped after all?"

"Did it?"

For the past several minutes a muffled undercurrent of thumps and growls had issued from the house. De Morgan's smile broadened. "Yes, it did. Possibly the thieves opened the cage by mistake. Ah, well; it is a small matter."

"Quite," I said, as a howl of feline frustration arose and claws attacked the inside of the door.

After de Morgan had left, grinning like a Gallic idiot, I went in search of Emerson. I found him methodically kicking the foundations of the house, and led him back to the dig.

The rest of the day went quietly, and Emerson's temper gradually subsided under the soothing influence of professional activity. After dinner he sat down to write up his journal of the day's work, assisted by Ramses, while John and I went to the darkroom and developed the plates we had taken that day. Some had turned out quite well. Others were very blurred. John tried to take the credit for the good ones, but I soon set him straight on that, and pointed out where he had gone astray in focusing the camera.

We returned to the sitting room. The cat Bastet was sitting on top of Emerson's papers. Emerson absently lifted her up whenever he added a finished sheet to the pile. The lion cub was chewing on Emerson's bootlace. As I entered, the front door opened and Ramses appeared. He had got into the habit of spending the evening with Abdullah and the other men from Aziyeh, in order to practice his Arabic, as he claimed. I had reservations about this, but felt sure Abdullah would prevent the men from adding too extensively to Ramses' collection of colloquialisms. I was pleased that he got on well with them. Abdullah *said* they enjoyed his company. I suppose he could hardly say anything else.

"Time for bed, Ramses," I said.

"Yes, Mama." He unwound the cub's leash from the legs of the table and those of his father. "I will walk de lion and den retire."

"You don't believe you can train that creature as you would a dog, do you?" I asked, in mingled amusement and exasperation.

"De experiment has never been tried, to my knowledge, Mama. I consider it wort' a try."

"Oh, very well. Put the lion in its cage before you get into bed. Make sure the shutter is tightly fastened—"

"Yes, Mama. Mama?"

"What is it, Ramses?"

He stood holding the leash, his grave dark eyes fixed on my face. "I would like to say, Mama, dat I am fully cognizant of your support and forbearance regarding de lion. I will endeavor to discover some way of proving my gratitude."

"Please don't," I exclaimed. "I appreciate your remarks, Ramses, but you can best express your gratitude by being a good little boy and obeying your mama's orders."

"Yes, Mama. Good night, Mama. Good night, John. Good night, de cat Bastet. Good night, Papa."

"Good night, my dearest boy," Emerson replied. "Sleep well."

After Ramses had gone and John had carried the tray of pottery shards to the storeroom, Emerson put down his pen and looked reproachfully at me. "Amelia, that was a very manly and loving apology you received from Ramses."

"It did not sound like an apology to me," I replied. "And when Ramses offers to do something for me, my blood runs cold in anticipation."

Emerson threw down his pen. "Curse it, Amelia, I don't understand you. Heaven knows you are an excellent mother—"

"I try to be, Emerson."

"You are, my dear, you are. Ramses does you credit. But can't you be more—more—"

"More what, Emerson?"

"More affectionate? You are always snapping at the boy."

"I am not a demonstrative person, Emerson."

"I have reason to know better," said Emerson, giving me a meaningful look.

"That is a different matter altogether. Naturally I am fond of Ramses, but I will never be one of those doting mamas who allow maternal affection to blind them to the flaws of character and behavior demonstrated by a child."

John returned at this point in the discussion. "Madam," he exclaimed, "there is a great 'uge mummy case in the courtyard. What shall I do with it?"

"It must be the baroness's mummy case," I said. "I suppose M. de Morgan's men simply dropped it and left. How vexatious! What shall we do with it, Emerson?"

"Throw the cursed thing out," Emerson replied, returning to his writing.

"We will put it with the others," I said. "Come along, John, I will unlock the storeroom."

The moon had not yet risen, but the varnished surface of the mummy case glimmered darkly in the brilliant starlight. I unlocked the door and John hoisted the coffin into his arms, as effortlessly as if it had been an empty paper shell. I was reminded of that Italian mountebank Belzoni, a former circus strongman who had turned to archaeology. He had been one of the first to excavate in Egypt, but his methods could hardly be called scientific, for among other sins he had employed gunpowder to blast his way into closed pyramids.

The storeroom was full of coffins and we had to shift several of them to find a place for the newcomer. It would have been more practical, perhaps, to open another room, but I always like to keep objects of the same type together. When the thing had been stowed away, John said, "Would you be wanting me to go to spy on Brother 'amid now, madam?"

I gave him the disguise I had procured for him. Abdullah's spare robe barely reached his shins, and the boots showing under the hem of the garment looked rather peculiar. John offered to remove them, but I decided against it. His feet were not hardened like those of the Egyptians, and if he trod on something sharp and painful he might let out a cry that would alert Hamid to his presence. I wound the turban around his head and then stood back to study the effect.

It was not convincing. However, we had done the best we could. I sent John on his way and returned to Emerson. He was curious as to why John had retired so early, but I was able to distract him without difficulty.

It seemed as if I had slept for only a few hours (which was in fact the case) when I was awakened by a furious pounding at the door. For once I was not impeded by a mosquito netting. At that season, in the desert, the noxious insects do not present a problem. Springing from the bed, I seized my parasol and assumed a posture of defense. Then I recognized the voice that was calling my name.

Emerson was swearing and flailing around in the bed when I flung the door open. The first streaks of dawn warmed the sky, but the courtyard was still deep in shadow. Yet there was no mistaking the large form that confronted me. Even if I had not recognized John's voice, I would have recognized his shape. That shape was, however, oddly distorted, and after a moment I realized that he held a smaller, slighter body closely clasped in his arms.

"Who the devil have you got there?" I asked, forgetting my usual adherence to proper language in my surprise.

"Sister Charity, madam," said John.

"Will you please ask him to let me down, ma'am?" the girl asked faintly. "I am not injured, but Brother John insists—"

"Don't move, either of you," I interrupted. "This

is a most unprecedented situation, and before I can assess it properly I must have light." A vehement curse from the direction of the nuptial couch reminded me of something I had momentarily overlooked and I added quickly, "Emerson, pray remain recumbent and wrapped in the blanket. There is a lady present."

"Curse it, curse it, curse it," Emerson cried passionately. "Amelia—"

"Yes, my dear, I have the matter well in hand," I replied soothingly. "Just a moment till I light the lamp. . . . There. Now we will see what is going on."

First I made certain Emerson was not in a state that would cause embarrassment to him or to anyone else. Only his head protruded from the sheet he had wrapped around himself. The expression on his face did his handsome features no justice.

John's turban had come unwound and hung down his back. His once snowy robe was ripped half off; the tattered remnants were blackened by what I first took to be dried blood. A closer examination proved that the stains were those of smoke and charring. His face was equally smudged, but the broad smile on his lips and the steady beam of his blue eyes assured me he had taken no hurt.

The girl was also disheveled but unmarked by fire. Her mousy brown hair tumbled over her shoulders and her face was flushed with excitement and embarrassment as she struggled to free herself from the brawny arms that clasped her. Her feet were bare. She wore a garment of voluminous cut and dismal color, dark blue or black, that covered her from the base of her throat to her ankles. It had long tight sleeves. A nightcap dangled from her neck by its strings.

"Please, ma'am, tell him to put me down," she gasped.

"All in due time," I assured her. "Now, John, you may tell me what has happened."

"There was a fire, madam."

"I deduced as much, John. Where was the fire?"

It is expedient to summarize John's statement, which had to be extracted from him sentence by sentence. He had been hiding among the palms near the chapel when he had seen a tongue of flame rise from behind that edifice. His cries had aroused the men, and with their assistance he had succeeded in quenching the conflagration before it did much damage. No help had come from the village; indeed the place had remained suspiciously dark and silent, though the shouts of the missionaries must have been heard. A search of the area revealed no sign of the arsonist. The fire had been deliberately set, getting its start in a pile of dry branches and palm fronds heaped against the foundation of the little church. Once the flames were extinguished, John had seized the girl and carried her off.

"What the devil for?" cried Emerson, from the bed.

"To bring her to Mrs. Emerson, of course," John replied, his eyes widening.

Emerson subsided with a curse. "Of course. Everyone brings everything to Mrs. Emerson. Lions, mummy cases, miscellaneous young ladies—"

"And quite right, too," I said. "Pay no attention

to Professor Emerson, my dear Miss Charity. He would welcome you with the kindness that is his most conspicuous characteristic were he not a trifle out of sorts because—"

"I beg you will not explain, Amelia," said my husband in tones of freezing disapproval. "Er—hem. I am not objecting to the presence of Miss Charity, but to the invasion that will inevitably follow. Would it be too much to ask, Amelia, that the young person be removed so that I may assume my trousers? A man is at a decided disadvantage when he receives irate brothers and indignant lovers wrapped in a sheet."

My dear Emerson was himself again, and I was happy to accede to this reasonable request. "Certainly, my dear," I replied. "John, take the young lady to your room."

The girl shrieked and resumed her struggles. "It is the only room fit for habitation that is presently available," I explained, somewhat irritated at this excessive display of sensibility. "Wait a moment until I find my slippers and I will accompany you. Curse it, where are they?"

"Madam!" John exclaimed.

"You will excuse my language," I said, kneeling to look under the bed. "Ah, here they are. Just as I suspected—Ramses has let the lion in the room, after I strictly forbade it."

"Lion?" Charity gasped. "Did you say . . ."

"You see how they are chewed. I told that child . . . Dear me, I believe the girl has fainted. Just as well. Take her along, John, I will follow."

The ensuing hour was a period of unprecedented

confusion, but I recall it without chagrin; I rise to my true powers in periods of confusion. Ramses had been awakened by the noise. He and the cat and the lion followed us to John's room, spouting questions (in the case of Ramses) and attacking the tatters of John's robe (in the case of the lion). I ordered all three back to Ramses' room, and after John had placed the girl on his cot, directed him to withdraw to the same location. The only one who refused to obey was the cat Bastet. Squatting on the floor by the bed, she watched interestedly as I sought to restore Charity to her senses.

As soon as she recovered she insisted, almost hysterically, upon leaving the room. Apparently the very idea of being in a young man's bedchamber in her nightgown was indelicate. I had ascertained that she was unharmed, so I gave in to her foolish insistence, and when we reached the parlor she became calmer.

The expected invasion had not yet occurred, but I felt sure Emerson was right; the outraged brother would come in search of his sister, and Brother David would undoubtedly be with him, though Emerson's designation of the latter as Charity's lover was only another example of Emerson's failure to comprehend the subtler currents of the human heart. I decided I had better take advantage of this opportunity to talk with the girl alone, and I got straight to the point.

"You must not be angry with John, Miss Charity. His action was precipitate and thoughtless, but his motives were of the best. His only concern was for your safety."

"I see that now." The girl brushed the waving locks from her face. "But it was a terrifying experience—the shouting, and the flames—then to be seized like that, without warning. . . . I have never—it is the first time a man . . ."

"I daresay. You have missed a great many things, Miss Charity. Most ill-advised, in my opinion. But never mind that. Don't you like John?"

"He is very kind," the girl said slowly. "But very, very *large*."

"But that can be an advantage, don't you think?" Charity stared at me in bewilderment, and I went on, "No, you would not know. But let me assure you, as a respectable married woman, that the combination of physical strength and moral sensibility, combined with tenderness of heart, is exactly what is wanted in a husband. The combination is rare, I confess, but when one encounters it—"

"Tactful as always, Amelia," said a voice from the doorway.

"Ah, there you are, Emerson. I was just explaining to Miss Charity—"

"I heard you." Emerson came into the room, buttoning his shirt. "Your tactics rather resemble those of a battering ram, my dear. Why don't you make the tea and leave the poor girl alone?"

"The tea is ready. But, Emerson—"

"Please, Amelia. I believe I hear the approach of the invasion I mentioned, and if I don't have my tea before I face it . . ."

The girl had shrunk down into her chair, her arms clutching her body and her face averted, though Emerson politely refrained from looking at her.

When the strident accents of Brother Ezekiel were heard she looked as if she were trying to squeeze her body into the framework of the chair.

Emerson hastily gulped his tea, and I went to the door to see whom the visitor was addressing. As I might have expected, it was Ramses.

"I told you to stay in your room," I said.

"You told me to go to my room, but you did not say to stay dere. Seeing dis person approaching, I felt it would be advisable for someone to meet him in order to—"

"Talks a blue streak, don't he?" Brother Ezekiel slid clumsily off his donkey and fixed Ramses with a critical stare. "Sonny, don't you know children should be seen and not heard?"

"No, I don't," Ramses replied. "Dat is to say, sir, I have heard dat sentiment expressed more dan once, but it is no more dan an opinion and it is not based on sound t'eories of—"

"That will do, Ramses," I said, with a sigh. "Brother Ezekiel, will you come in? Your sister is here, safe and sound."

"So you say." Brother Ezekiel pushed past me. "Well, she's here, at any rate. Charity, where's your penknife?"

The girl rose. Head bowed, she murmured from under the hair that veiled her face, "Under my pillow, brother. There was such confusion I forgot—"

"Didn't I tell you never to take a step without that weapon?" Brother Ezekiel thundered.

"I am guilty, brother."

"Yes, you are. And you'll be punished."

"A moment, sir." Emerson spoke in the purring

rumble that often deceived persons unfamiliar with his temperament into believing he was in an affable mood. "I don't believe we have been formally introduced."

"It ain't my fault if we wasn't," Ezekiel replied. "At least this here unfortunate event gives me a chance to talk to you, Professor. I know who you are and you know me; let's skip the formalities, I don't hold with 'em." He sat down.

"Have a chair," Emerson said.

"I already have one. I could fancy a cup of tea, if you ain't got coffee."

"By all means." Emerson offered him a cup. I resignedly awaited the explosion I knew was coming. The longer Emerson's appearance of mildness continued, the louder the eventual explosion would be.

"Do I understand," Emerson continued blandly, "that Miss Charity goes about armed with a knife? Let me assure you, Mr. Jones, that such precautions are not necessary. This is a peaceful country, and I doubt that she is capable of using such a weapon."

"She'd be able to use it on herself," Brother Ezekiel retorted. "And that's what she was supposed to do before she let a male critter lay hands on her."

"Good Gad," I cried. "This is not ancient Rome, sir."

I expected the allusion would be lost on Ezekiel, but to my surprise he replied, "They was heathens, but that Lucretia female knew the value of a woman's purity. Well, in this case no harm done. I come to fetch her home, but long as I'm here I may as well tell you what's on my mind."

"By all means unburden yourself," Emerson said earnestly. "I doubt that the organ you mention can stand any undue weight."

"What? It's about the Christian cemetery you've been digging up. You'll have to stop it, Professor. They were heretics, but they was laid to rest in the Lord."

I braced myself for the explosion. It did not come. Emerson's eyebrows rose. "Heretics?" he repeated.

"Monophysites," said Brother Ezekiel.

I had believed Emerson's eyebrows could rise no higher, but I was wrong. Mistaking the cause of his surprise, Brother Ezekiel enlightened him.

"Our Lord and Saviour, Professor, has a double nature—the human and the divine are mingled in him. 'Twas all laid down by the Council of Chalcedon, anno Domini 451. That's doctrine, and there's no getting around it. These Copts wouldn't accept it, though. They followed Eutyches, who insisted on the absorption of the human part of Christ by the divine into one composite nature. Hence, sir, the term Monophysite."

"I am familiar with the term and its meaning," Emerson said.

"Oh? Well, but that ain't the issue. They may of been heretics, but they was Christians, of a sort, and I demand you leave their graves alone."

The twinkle of amusement in Emerson's eyes was replaced by a fiery glow, and I decided to intervene. "Your sister is on the verge of fainting, Brother Ezekiel. If you don't take steps to relieve her, I shall. Charity—sit down!"

Charity sat down. Brother Ezekiel stood up. "Come along, girl, a handmaiden of the Lord has no business swooning. I've said my say, now I'll go."

"Not just yet," said Emerson. "I haven't had my say. Mr. Jones—"

"Brother Ezekiel, sir."

Emerson shook his head. "Really, you cannot expect me to employ that absurd affectation. You are not my brother. You are, however, a fellow human being, and I feel it my duty to warn you. You have aroused considerable resentment in the village; last night's fire may not be the last demonstration of that resentment."

Brother Ezekiel raised his eyes to heaven. "If the glorious crown of the martyr is to be mine, O Lord, make me worthy!"

"If it weren't such an entertaining idiot it would make me angry," Emerson muttered as if to himself. "See here, sir; you are doing everything possible to increase the justifiable annoyance of the local priest, whose flock you are stealing away—"

"I seek to save them from the fires of hell," Ezekiel explained. "They are all damned—"

Emerson's voice rose to a roar. "They may be damned, but you will be dead! It would not be the first time Protestant missions have been attacked. Court danger as you will, but you have no right to risk your innocent converts and your sister."

"God's will be done," Ezekiel said.

"No doubt," Emerson agreed. "Oh, get out of here, you little maniac, before I throw you out. Miss Charity, if at any time you need our help, we are here, at your command. Send word by John or any other messenger."

Then I realized that in his own peculiar way Ezekiel had exhibited a variety of self-control comparable to that of my husband. Emerson's final insult cracked the missionary's calm facade. A thunderous scowl darkened his brow. But before he could express in words the outrage that filled him, another sound was heard—the sound of a low, menacing growl. I thought Ramses might have let the lion cub out, and looked around. But the source of the growl was Bastet, who had appeared out of nowhere in that unnerving way of hers. Crouched on the table near Emerson, she lashed her tail and rumbled low in her throat, sensing the anger that filled the room and prepared to defend her master.

Charity let out a thin cry. "Take it away—oh, please, take it away."

"You must conquer this weakness, Charity," said Brother David, shaking his head. "There is nothing more harmless than an amiable domestic cat. . . ." He put out a hand to Bastet. She spat at him. He stepped hastily back. "An amiable domestic cat," he repeated, less confidently.

Charity retreated, step by stumbling step, her wide eyes fixed on the cat's sharp white snarl. "You know I would do anything to please you, brother. I have tried. But I cannot—I cannot—"

Observing her pallor and the perspiration that bedewed her brow, I realized her terror was as genuine as it was unusual. No wonder the mere mention of the lion had caused her to lose consciousness!

I glanced at Ramses, who was sitting quietly in a corner. I had fully expected a comment—or, more likely, a long-winded speech—from him before this. No doubt he knew I would order him out of the room if he ventured to speak. "Take the cat away, Ramses," I said.

"But, Mama—"

"Never mind, we're leaving," snapped Ezekiel. The look he gave Bastet showed that he found Charity's fear as hard to comprehend as Brother David's affection for such creatures. Then he turned to Emerson. "Don't concern yourself about my sister, Professor, she's been taught right; she knows a woman's place. I remind you, sir, of First Corinthians, fourteen, Verses thirty-four and thirty-five: 'Let your women keep silence . . . for it is not permitted unto them to speak. . . . And if they will learn any thing, let them ask their husbands at home.' You'd best apply that in your own household, Professor, before you start interfering with them that knows better."

When he and his entourage had gone, Emerson burst into a great roar of laughter. "Henpeckery!" he shouted cheerfully. "The old charge of henpeckery. Will I never live it down?"

I stood on tiptoe and threw my arms about his neck. "Emerson," I said, "have I had occasion in the recent past to mention that my feelings for you are of the warmest nature?"

My husband returned my embrace. "You mentioned it in passing a few hours ago, but if you would care to enlarge upon the subject . . ."

But after an all-too-brief interval he gently put me aside. "All the same, Peabody," he said seriously, "we cannot let those fools rush headlong to destruction without trying to stop them."

"Are matters that serious, do you think?"

"I fear so." He added, with a refreshing touch of malice, "You have been too busy playing detective to notice what has been going on. Already there is a visible division among our workers; the converts are shunned by their fellows, and Abdullah has reported several cases of fisticuffs. I really believe that wretched preacher wants to achieve martyrdom."

"Surely there is no danger of that, Emerson. Not in this day and age."

"Let us hope not. What the devil, we have wasted too much time on the creature. The men will be on the dig. I must go."

With a hasty embrace he departed, and I sat down to have another cup of tea. Scarcely had I taken a seat, however, before a cry of outraged fury reached my ears. I recognized the beloved voice and hastened to rush to his side, fearing I know not what—some fresh outrage from Brother Ezekiel, perhaps.

The pastor had gone, and Emerson was nowhere in sight. The volume of his complaints led me to him, on the far side of the house. I do not believe I had inspected that region since the day of our arrival, when I had made a circuit of the walls to see where repairs were needed. On that occasion the walls had been intact, if aged. Now a gaping hole confronted my astonished eyes. Emerson was stamping up and down waving his arms and shouting at Abdullah, who listened with an air of injured dignity. Seeing me, Emerson turned his reproaches on a new object.

"What kind of housekeeping do you call this, Peabody?"

I pointed out the injustice of the charge in a few brisk but well-chosen words. Emerson mopped his brow. "Pardon my language, Peabody. It has been a trying morning. And now this!"

"What is it?" I asked.

"It is a hole, Peabody. A hole in the wall of one of our storage rooms."

"Oh, Emerson, I can see that! How did it come there?"

"I do not know, Peabody. Perhaps Ramses has stolen an elephant and attempted to confine it in the room."

I ignored this misplaced attempt at humor. "The wall is old, and some of the mortar has fallen out. Perhaps it simply collapsed."

"Don't talk like an idiot, Peabody!" Emerson shouted.

"Don't shout at me, Emerson!"

Abdullah's head had been moving back and forth like someone watching a tennis match. Now he remarked, not quite sotto voce, "It is good to see them so friendly together. But of course it was the spirit of the old priest, trying to get back into his house from which the Father of Curses expelled him."

"Abdullah, you know that is nonsense," I said.

"Quite right," Emerson agreed. "When I expel a spirit, he stays expelled."

Abdullah grinned. Emerson wiped his forehead with his sleeve and said in a resigned voice, "Let's see what the damage is. Which of the storerooms is this, Amelia? I cannot quite get my bearings."

I counted windows. "This is the room where I keep the mummy cases, Emerson. The ones from the Roman cemetery."

Emerson struck himself heavily on the brow. "There is some strange fatality in this," he muttered. "Abdullah, go to the dig and get the men started. Come around to the door, Peabody, and we will see what is—or is not—inside."

We did as he suggested. The coffins had been jumbled about, but I noticed that none of the bricks had fallen inside—which cast a doubt on my theory of a spontaneous fall. I had not really believed it, of course. The bricks had been removed one by one until a sufficiently large opening was made. It would not have been difficult to do. The mortar was old and crumbling.

". . . five, six, seven," Emerson counted. "They are all here, Amelia."

I cleared my throat. "Emerson . . ."

"Oh, curse it," Emerson exclaimed. "Don't tell me—you put the baroness's mummy case in this room."

"It seemed the logical place, Emerson."

"Then there ought to be eight mummy cases here."

"My reckoning agrees with yours, Emerson."

"One is missing."

"It seems a reasonable conclusion."

Emerson's fingers clawed at his chin. "Fetch John," he said.

I turned to obey; this was not the time to cavil at

an unnecessarily peremptory tone. From one of the doors along the line of cells a head protruded. "May I come out, Mama?" Ramses inquired.

"You may as well. Find John."

"He is here, Mama."

The pair soon joined us and Emerson, with John's help, began removing the mummy cases from the storeroom. When they were lined up in a grisly row, Emerson looked them over.

"These are the coffins we found, Peabody," he announced. "It must be the one belonging to the baroness that has been stolen—again."

"Wrong, Emerson. That"—I pointed—"is the mummy case John and I put in this room last night. I remember the patch of missing varnish on the foot, and also the relative location, which I noted when you removed them."

"Wrong, Peabody. I know each and every one of these mummy cases. I could as easily be mistaken as to the identity of my own mother."

"Since you haven't seen the dear old lady for fifteen years, you might easily make such a mistake."

"Never mind my mother," Emerson retorted. "I can't imagine why we brought her into this. If you don't believe me, Peabody, we will check my notes. I made careful descriptions of the coffins, as I always do."

"No, no, my dear Emerson, I need no such verification; your memory is always accurate. But I am equally certain that this"—again I pointed—"is the mummy case brought to us last night."

"De conclusion is obvious, surely," piped Ramses. "De mummy case brought here last night, purportedly de one stolen from de lady, was not in fact de one stolen from—"

"I assure you, Ramses, that possibility had not escaped either of us," I replied with some asperity.

"De inevitable corollary," Ramses went on, "is dat—"

"Pray be silent for a moment, Ramses," Emerson begged, clutching his ambrosial locks with both hands. "Let me think. What with mummy cases whizzing in and out of my life like express trains . . . There were originally seven mummy cases in this room."

I murmured an encouraging "Quite right, Emerson," and fixed Ramses with a look that stilled the words hovering on his lips.

"Seven," Emerson repeated painfully. "Last night another mummy case was placed in this room. Eight. You didn't happen to notice, Peabody, how many—"

"I am afraid not, Emerson. It was dark and we were in a hurry."

"The baroness's mummy case was stolen," Emerson continued. "A mummy case believed to be that mummy case was handed over to us. You are certain that this"—he pointed—"was the mummy case in question. We must assume, then, that the mummy case we received was not the mummy case belonging to the baroness, but another mummy case, derived God knows whence."

"But we know whence," cried Ramses, unable to contain himself any longer. "Papa is correct; we have here de original mummy case discovered by our men. De one returned to us was our own. A t'ief must have removed it from dis room earlier."

"A what?" I asked.

"A robber," said Ramses.

"Who replaced the bricks after he had stolen the mummy case from us. Yes," Emerson agreed. "It could have been done. The thief then carried the stolen mummy case out into the desert, where he abandoned it. That incompetent idiot de Morgan, who would not recognize his own mummy case if it walked up and bade him *'Bonjour,'* assumed that the one found by his men was the one belonging to the baroness. Apparently that is what the thief did— but why the devil should he do it?"

This time I was determined that Ramses should not get ahead of me. "In the hope, which proved justified, that the search for the baroness's mummy case would be abandoned."

"Humph," said Emerson. "My question was purely rhetorical, Peabody. Had you not interrupted, I would have proposed that very solution. May I request that you all remain silent and allow me to work out this problem step by step in logical fashion?"

"Certainly, my dear Emerson."

"Certainly, Papa."

"Certainly, sir." John added in a bewildered voice, "I don't 'ave the faintest notion of what anyone is talking about, sir."

Emerson cleared his throat pontifically. "Very well. We will begin with the hypothesis that the thief stole one of our mummy cases in order to substitute it for the one belonging to the baroness. He went to the considerable trouble of replacing the bricks in the wall so the theft would not be noticed. Why then did he demolish the wall last night?"

He fixed Ramses with such an awful look that the child closed his mouth with an audible snap. Emerson continued, "Not to return the stolen mummy case. There are only seven here, the same number we had originally. Two possibilities suggest themselves. Either the thief wished to recover some object he had concealed in the storeroom on the occasion when he removed our mummy case, or he wished to draw our attention to his activities."

He paused. Those of us in the audience remained respectfully silent. A look of childish pleasure spread over Emerson's face. "If any of you have alternative hypotheses to suggest, you may speak," he said graciously.

My abominable child beat me to the punch again. "Perhaps some second party, oder dan de original t'ief, wished to expose de villain's act of pilferage."

Emerson shook his head vehemently. "I refuse to introduce another unknown villain, Ramses. One is enough."

"I favor the first of your hypotheses, Emerson," I said. "It was necessary to find a hiding place for the baroness's mummy case. What better place than among others of the same? I believe the thief put her mummy case in the storage room and took one of ours. Last night he broke in again and removed the first mummy case."

"I have a feeling," said Emerson conversationally, "that if I hear the words 'mummy case' again, a blood vessel will burst in my brain. Peabody, your theory is perfectly reasonable, except for one small point. There is no reason why anyone with an ounce of sense would steal the baroness's mum—property in the first place, much less go through these fantastic convolutions with it."

We stared bemusedly at one another. John scratched his head. Finally Ramses said thoughtfully, "I can t'ink of several possibilities, Papa. But it is a capital mistake to t'eorize wit' insufficient data."

"Well put, Ramses," Emerson said approvingly.

"De statement is not original, Papa."

"Never mind. Let us forsake theories and take action. Peabody, I have come around to your way of thinking. Hamid is the only suspicious character hereabouts. Let us question Hamid."

But Hamid was not on the dig. He had not reported for work that morning, and all the men denied having seen him.

"What did I tell you?" I cried. "He has flown. Does not that prove his guilt?"

"It proves nothing except that he is not here," Emerson replied waspishly. "Perhaps he has accomplished his purpose, whatever the devil that might have been, and has departed. So much the better. I can get on with my work in peace."

"But, Emerson—"

Emerson rounded on me and wagged his finger under my nose. "Work, Peabody—work! Is the word familiar to you? I know you find our activities tedious; I know you yearn for pyramids and sneer at cemeteries—"

"Emerson, I never said—"

"You thought it. I saw you thinking it."

"I was not alone if I did."

Emerson threw his arm around my shoulders, careless of the men working nearby. A low murmur of amusement rose from them. "Right as always, Peabody. I find our present excavations boring too. I am taking out my bad humor on you."

"Couldn't we start work on the pyramids here, Emerson? They are poor things, but our own."

"You know my methods, Peabody. One thing at a time. I will not be distracted from duty by the siren call of—er—pyramids."

III

For the next few days it appeared that Emerson's hopes regarding Hamid were justified. There were no further attacks on the missionaries or on our property, and one evening, when I inadvertently used the phrase "mummy case," Emerson scarcely flinched. I let him enjoy his illusory sense of tranquillity, but I knew, with that intuitive intelligence upon which I have often been commended, that the peace could not last—that the calm was only a thin surface over a seething caldron of passions that must eventually erupt.

Our decision to allow Ramses his own excavation had been a success. He was gone all day, taking his noon meal with him, and always returned in time for tea. One evening he was late, however, and I was about to send someone out to look for him when I caught a glimpse of a small form scuttling with an odd crablike motion along the shaded cloister. He was carrying something, wrapped in his shirt. I knew the cloth enclosing the bundle was his shirt because he was not wearing the garment.

"Ramses!" I called.

Ramses ducked into his room, but promptly reappeared.

"How many times have I told you not to remove any of your outer garments without sufficient cause?" I inquired.

"Very many times, Mama."

"What have you got there?"

"Some t'ings I found when I was excavating, Mama."

"May I see them?"

"I would radder you did not, Mama, at present."

I was about to insist when Emerson, who had joined me, said softly, "A moment, Peabody."

He drew me aside. "Ramses wants to keep his discoveries for a surprise," he explained. "You wouldn't want to disappoint the dear little chap, would you?"

This was not a question I could answer fully, under the circumstances, so I remained silent. A fond smile spread across Emerson's face. "He has been collecting potsherds and his favorite bones, I expect. You must exclaim over them and admire them, Amelia, when we are invited to view the display."

"Naturally I will do my duty, Emerson. When did you ever know me to fail?" I turned back to Ramses, who stood waiting outside his room, and dismissed him with a gesture. He went in at once and closed the door.

Whatever the nature of Ramses' discoveries, they could not have been poorer than our own. We had found a small family burial ground dating from the Fourth or Fifth Dynasty, but the humble little tombs contained no funeral goods worthy of preserving, and the ground in that part of the site was so damp the bones were of the consistency of thick mud. Even now I cannot recall that period without a pall of ennui settling over me.

Fortunately this miserable state of uneventfulness was not to last long. The first intimation of a new outbreak of violence was innocent enough—or so it seemed at the time. We were sitting in the parlor after our simple supper, Emerson and I. He was writing up his notes and I was fitting together my eleventh Roman amphora—a form of vessel I have never admired. Ramses was in his room, engaged in some mysterious endeavor; John was in his room trying to finish Leviticus. The lion club played at my feet, finishing off my house slippers. Since it had already eaten one, I decided it might as well have the other. Bastet lay on the table next to Emerson's papers, her eyes slitted and her rare purr echoing in the quiet room.

"I believe I must make a trip to Cairo soon," I remarked.

Emerson threw his pen down. "I knew this was coming. Peabody, I absolutely forbid you to prowl the bazaars looking for murderers. Everything is peaceful just now and I won't have you—"

"Emerson, I cannot imagine where you get such ideas. I need to shop, that is all. We have not a pair of house slippers among us, and my store of bismuth is getting low. All these people seem to suffer from stomach complaints."

"If you didn't deal it out so lavishly, you would not be running out of it."

Our amiable discussion was developing nicely

when we were interrupted from a hail without. Since the breaking in at the storeroom, Abdullah had taken it upon himself to set a guard on the house. He or one of his sons slept near the door every night. I was touched by this gesture, all the more so because I knew Abdullah was not completely convinced that Emerson had got rid of all the evil spirits.

Hearing him call out, we both went to the door. Two forms were approaching. In the light of the torch Abdullah held high I soon recognized friends. "It is the reverend and Mr. Wilberforce," I exclaimed. "What a surprise!"

"I am only surprised they haven't come before," Emerson grumbled. "It has been three or four days since we had callers; I was beginning to entertain the fond delusion we might be allowed to get on with our work in peace."

The presence of our visitors was soon explained. "We moored this morning at Dahshoor," the Reverend Sayce declared, "and spent the afternoon with de Morgan. Since we must be on our way again in the morning, we decided to ride over and call on you tonight."

"How very kind of you," I said, elbowing Emerson in the ribs to keep him from contradicting the statement. "Welcome to our humble quarters."

"Not so humble," said the American, with an approving glance at the cozy scene. "You have the true womanly knack, Mrs. Amelia, of making any abode seem homelike. I congratulate—good heavens!" He leaped backward, just in time to prevent the lion cub from seizing his foot. He was wearing elegant tassled gaiters, and I could hardly blame the young creature for being interested in this new form of fashion.

I seized the lion and tied its lead to a table leg. Mr. Wilberforce took a chair as far from it as possible, and the reverend said, "Can that be the lion belonging to the baroness? We heard it had been lost."

"Ramses found it," I explained. I do not believe in telling falsehoods unless it is absolutely necessary. The statement was true. There was no reason to explain *where* Ramses had found the lion.

The conversation turned to de Morgan's discoveries, and Emerson sat chewing his lip in silent aggravation. "There is no doubt," said the Reverend Sayce, "that the southern brick pyramid was built by King Amenemhet the Third of the Twelfth Dynasty. De Morgan has found a number of fine private tombs of that period. He has added volumes to our knowledge of the Middle Kingdom."

"How nice," I said.

Conversation languished thereafter. Not even the reverend had the courage to ask Emerson how his work was progressing. Finally Mr. Wilberforce said, "To tell the truth, my friends, we had a particular reason for calling. We have been a trifle concerned for your safety."

Emerson looked offended. "Good Gad, Wilberforce, what do you mean? I am perfectly capable of protecting myself and my family."

"But a number of alarming events have occurred in your neighborhood," Wilberforce said. "We heard of the burglary of the baroness's dahabeeyah.

The day before we left Cairo we met Mr. David Cabot, who told us of the attack on the mission."

"Hardly an attack," Emerson said. "Some malcontent had set a fire behind the chapel; but even if that edifice had been totally destroyed, which was unlikely, no harm would have come to anyone."

"Still, it is an ominous sign," Sayce said. "And Mr. Cabot admitted there is growing animosity among the villagers."

"Have you met Brother Ezekiel?" Emerson inquired.

Wilberforce laughed. "I take your point, Professor. If I were inclined toward arson, his is the first establishment I would set a match to."

"It is not a joking matter, Wilberforce," the reverend said gravely. "I have no sympathy for the creed or the practices of the Brothers of Jerusalem, but I would not like to see any of them injured. Besides, they give all Christian missionaries a bad name with their tactless behavior."

"I think you overestimate the danger, gentlemen," Emerson replied. "I am keeping an eye on the situation, and I can assure you no one will dare make a hostile move while I am on the scene." His large white teeth snapped together as he concluded. Sayce shook his head but said no more.

Shortly thereafter the two gentlemen rose to depart, claiming they must make an early start. Not until they were at the door, hats in hand, did Sayce clear his throat and remark, "There is one other little matter I meant to discuss with you, Mrs. Emerson. It almost slipped my mind; such a trivial thing. . . . That bit of papyrus you showed me—do you still have it?"

"Yes," I said.

"Might I prevail upon you to part with it? I have been considering the part of the text I managed to translate, and I believe it may hold some small interest to a student of biblical history."

"To be honest, I would not be able to put my hand on it just at the moment," I admitted. "I have not had occasion to look at it since we left Cairo."

"But you do have it?" The reverend's tone was oddly intense.

"Yes, to be sure. It is somewhere about."

"I would not want to trouble you—"

"Then don't," said Emerson, who had been watching the little man curiously. "You don't expect Mrs. Emerson to turn out all her boxes and bags at this hour of the night, I suppose."

"Certainly not. I only thought—"

"Look in again on your way upriver," Emerson said, like a genial host suggesting a call, "when you are in the neighborhood. We will try to locate the scrap and then consider your request."

And with this the reverend had to be content, though he did not look pleased.

We stood in the door watching our visitors ride away. Stars spangled the heavens in glorious abandon and the desert lay silver under the moon. Emerson's arm stole around my waist. "Peabody."

"Yes, my dear Emerson?"

"I am a selfish brute, Peabody."

"My dear Emerson!"

Emerson drew me inside and closed the door. "Though thwarted in your heart's desire, you defend me nobly. When you told de Morgan the other day that you doted on Roman mummies, I could hardly contain my emotion."

"It is kind of you to say so, Emerson. And now, if you will excuse me, I had better finish my amphora."

"Damn the amphora," Emerson cried. "No more Roman pots or mummies, Peabody. Tomorrow we begin on our pyramids. To be sure, they are not much in the way of pyramids, but they will be an improvement over what we have been doing."

"Emerson, do you mean it?"

"It is only your due, my dear Peabody. Spite and selfishness alone kept me from beginning on them long ago. You deserve pyramids, and pyramids you will have!"

Emotion choked me. I could only sigh and gaze at him with the wholehearted admiration his affectionate gesture deserved. His eyes sparkling like sapphires, Emerson put out his hand and extinguished the lamp.

EIGHT

Emerson's demonstrations of marital affection are of so tempestuous a nature that as a rule we succumb quickly to slumber when they are concluded. On this occasion, however, I found myself unaccountably wakeful long after my spouse's placid breathing testified to the depths of his repose. Starlight glimmered at the open window, and the cool night breeze caressed my face. Far off in the stilly night the lonely howl of a jackal rose like the lament of a wandering spirit.

But hark—closer at hand though scarcely louder—another sound! I sat up, pushing my hair back from my face. It came again; a soft scraping, a scarcely audible thud—and then—oh heavens!—a cacophony of screams scarcely human in their intensity. They were not human. They were the cries of a lion.

I sprang from bed. Despite my agitation a sense of triumph filled me. For once a nocturnal disturbance had found me awake and ready; for once no cursed netting interfered with my prompt response to the call of danger. I snatched my parasol and ran to the door. Emerson was awake and swearing. "Your trousers, Emerson," I shouted. "Pray do not forget your trousers."

Since there was only one lion on the premises, it was not difficult for me to deduce whence the sound came. Ramses' room was next to ours. On this occasion I did not knock.

The room was dark. The light from the window was cut off by a writhing form that filled the entire aperture. Without delaying an instant, I began beating it with my parasol. Unfortunately the blows fell upon the wrong end of the intruder, whose head and shoulders were already out of the window. Stimulated, no doubt, by the thrashing, it redoubled its efforts and made good its escape. I would have followed, but at that moment an excruciating pain shot through my left ankle and I lost my balance, falling heavily to the floor.

The household was now aroused. Shouts and cries of alarm came from all directions. Emerson was the first to arrive on the scene. Rushing headlong into the room, he tripped over my recumbent form and crushed the breath out of me.

Next to appear was John, a lamp in one hand and a stout stick in the other. I would have commended him for thinking of the lamp if I had had the breath to speak, for by its light he was able to recognize us just in time to arrest the blow of the cudgel which he had aimed at Emerson's anatomy. The lion cub continued to gnaw at my foot. It had identified me, I believe, after the first impulsive attack, and was now merely playing, but its teeth were extremely sharp.

Emerson struggled to his feet. "Ramses!" he shouted. "Ramses, where are you?"

It struck me then that I had not heard from Ramses, which was unusual. His cot was a mass of tumbled blankets, but the boy himself was nowhere to be seen.

"Ra-a-amses!" Emerson shrieked, his face purpling.

"I am under de cot," said a faint voice.

Sure enough, he was. Emerson yanked him out and unrolled the sheet in which he had been wrapped so tightly that it had the effect of a straitjacket. Crooning endearments, he pressed the boy to his breast. "Speak to me, Ramses. Are you hurt? What has been done to you? Ramses, my son . . ."

Having heard Ramses speak, I had no apprehension concerning his safety. I therefore returned the lion to its cage before saying calmly, "Emerson, he cannot talk because you are squeezing the breath out of him. Release your grip, I beg you."

"T'ank you, Mama," said Ramses breathlessly. "Between de sheet, which I only now succeeded in getting off from over my mout', and Papa's embrace, which t'ough it is appreciated for de sentiment dat prompted it, neverdeless—"

"Good Gad, Ramses," I exclaimed. "For once will you give over your rhetorical orotundities and get to the point? What happened?"

"I can only guess as to de origin of de difficulty, since I was soundly sleeping," said Ramses. "But I presume a person removed de screen and entered by way of de window. I did not awaken until he—or she, for I was not able to determine de gender of de intruder—was wrapping me in de sheet. In my attempt to free myself I fell off de cot and somehow, I cannot tell how, found myself beneat' dat object of furniture."

Being somewhat short of breath, he had to pause at this point, and I demanded, "How did the lion cub get out of its cage?"

Ramses looked at the cage. In the manner of all small creatures the cub had rolled itself into a furry ball and dropped off to sleep.

"Apparently I neglected to close de door of de cage," said Ramses.

"And very fortunate it was, too," said Emerson. "I shudder to think what would have happened if the noble beast had not warned us you were in danger."

"It could have roused us just as effectively *in* the cage as *out* of it," I said. "The only person it seems to have attacked is me; and if it had not done so I might have succeeded in apprehending the burglar."

Father and son looked at me, and then at one another. "These women!" they seemed to remark, in silent unanimity. "They are always complaining about something."

II

Next morning at breakfast I reminded Emerson of his promise to give me a pyramid. He looked at me reproachfully. "I do not need to be reminded,

Amelia. An Emerson never breaks his word. But we can't begin today. I need to do a preliminary survey of the surrounding area and close down our excavations at the cemetery."

"Oh, quite, my dear Emerson. But please don't bring me any more bones. The last lot was frightfully brittle. I set them in a stiff jelly to remove the salt, but I am running short of suitable containers."

"We have not the proper facilities to deal with bones," Emerson admitted. "To expose them without being able to preserve them would be a violation of my principles of excavation."

"Brother Ezekiel will be pleased you have given up the cemetery," I said, helping Emerson to marmalade.

"I only hope he won't think I was influenced by his outrageous demands." Emerson looked sheepish. "I went on with the cemeteries longer than I ought to have done only because he told me to stop."

"Since it will be several days before we can begin on the pyramids, I may as well make my trip to Cairo at once."

"Go away, now?" Emerson cried. "After the murderous attack on our son last night?"

"I must go, Emerson. The lion has eaten every pair of slippers we own. There is no question of leaving Ramses unprotected; I can go and come in the same day. Besides, I don't believe an assault on Ramses was intended. The intruder was after something—was, in short, a burglar, not a murderer."

"After something? In Ramses' room?"

"He may have mistaken the window. Or used it

as a means of reaching the storage rooms, which are windowless, or the parlor, whose outer door was guarded by Abdullah."

"And a fine help Abdullah was," Emerson grunted. "He must have been dead asleep or he would not have been so late in arriving on the scene. Well, well, if you are determined to go, you will go—but I entertain some doubts as to your real motive. Slippers, indeed! Don't deny it, Amelia—you are still on the trail of your imaginary Master Criminal."

"We had better devote some attention to criminals, master or otherwise; they are giving us *their* full attention. How many more of these burglarious episodes must we endure?"

Emerson shrugged. "Do as you like, Amelia. You will in any case. Only try not to be assaulted, kidnapped, or murdered, if you can possibly do so."

Somewhat to my surprise, Ramses refused to accompany me. (The invitation was proffered by his father, not by me.)

"So long as you are going, Mama," he said, "will you bring me back a Coptic dictionary?"

"I don't know that there is such a thing, Ramses."

"Herr Steindorff has just published a *Koptische Grammatik mit Chrestomathie, Wörterverzeichnis und Literatur*. Should that work be unobtainable, dere is de elementary Coptic grammar and glossary in Arabic of Al-Bakurah al-shakiyyah, or de *Vocabularium Coptico-Latinum* of Gustav Parthey—"

"I will see what I can do," I said, unable to bear any more multilingual titles.

"T'ank you, Mama."

"What do you want with a Coptic dictionary?" Emerson asked.

"Dere are a few words on de fragment of papyrus Mama found dat continue to elude me."

"Good heavens, the Coptic papyrus," I exclaimed. "I keep forgetting about it. Mr. Sayce was asking about it only last night—"

"He shan't have it," Emerson declared.

"Don't be spiteful, Emerson. I wonder what I did with the other scrap I found the night Abd el Atti was killed."

"Anodder fragment, Mama?" Ramses asked.

"It appeared to be from the same manuscript, but it was much smaller."

Ramses' face became taut with excitement. "I would like to have it, Mama."

"I don't remember where I put it, Ramses."

"But, Mama—"

"If you are a good little boy and do everything your Papa tells you, Mama will give you your treat when she returns."

III

I regretted my promise to Ramses, for I had a great deal to do, and finding a given book in the shops devoted to that trade is a time-consuming process. Instead of being neatly arranged on shelves, the merchandise is piled in stacks; and since the book-dealers are scholarly gentlemen whose shops are frequented by the learned world of Cairo, I was tempted to linger and talk. I managed to find one of the volumes Ramses had requested. Then I left the Sharia 'el Halwagi and went to the bazaar of the shoemakers, where I purchased a dozen pair of slippers, two each for myself, Ramses and Emerson, and six for the lion. I hoped, by the time he had finished these, he would have done cutting his teeth.

Then, and only then, did I go to the Khan el Khaleel.

Abd el Atti's shop was closed and shuttered. No one answered, even when I went to the back door and hammered on it. Somewhat disheartened, I turned away. I had the address of Mr. Aslimi's shop on the Muski and I was about to go in that direction when another idea occurred to me. I went on past the fountain and under an ancient arch, farther into the bazaar.

Kriticas was the best-known antiquities dealer in Cairo, a rival of Abd el Atti's and an old friend. He greeted me with mingled pleasure and reproach. "I understand you are looking for demotic papyri, Mrs. Emerson. Why did you not come to me?"

"I would have done, Mr. Kriticas, had I not been distracted by the death of Abd el Atti, of which I am sure you have heard."

"Ah, yes." Kriticas' noble Greek brow furrowed. "A sad tragedy, to be sure. Now I happen to have an excellent specimen of a Twenty-Sixth Dynasty papyrus. . . ."

I examined the merchandise, drank the coffee he pressed upon me, and inquired after his family before saying casually, "I see that Abd el Atti's shop is closed. Who is the new owner—his son, or that charming old lady his wife?"

Kriticas had a characteristic silent laugh; his whole body shook, but not a sound came from his bearded lips. "You have met the lady?"

"Yes. She appears to be a very determined woman."

"Yes, one might say that. She has no legal claim, of course. She has been acting on behalf of her son, Hassan. He is a bad hat, as you English say; a user of drugs, often in trouble with the police. But you know how these mothers are; the worse a son, the more they dote on him."

"Hmmm," I said.

"Her cause was hopeless from the start," Kriticas went on. "Abd el Atti disinherited Hassan several years ago. No doubt he is in fresh trouble of some kind; he has not been seen for several weeks."

The idea that popped into my mind was so obvious I wondered I had not thought of it before. "I think I may have seen him," I said. "Is he of medium height, with scanty eyebrows and a missing front tooth?"

"He and a hundred thousand other Egyptians," said Kriticas, with his silent laugh. "Now, Mrs. Emerson, this papyrus is particularly fine. I have a buyer for it, but if you want it . . ."

I bought the papyrus, after considerable bargaining. The transaction put Kriticas in a good humor and lowered his guard; and that was when I struck! "Is this papyrus one of the spoils of the Master, by any chance?"

I used the *siim issaagha* word. Kriticas' eyelids flickered. "I beg your pardon, Mrs. Emerson?"

"You know the argot as well as I," I said. "Never mind, Mr. Kriticas. You have your own reasons for remaining silent, but remember, Emerson and I are your friends. If you ever need our help you have only to ask."

The dignified Greek pursed his lips. "Did you say the same to Abd el Atti?" he asked.

IV

I took luncheon at Shepheard's. Emerson would have considered this a waste of time, but Emerson would have been mistaken. The hotel is the center of social life in Cairo, and I hoped to hear news about a number of individuals in whose activities I was interested. This proved to be the case. Mr. Baehler caught sight of me and—upon observing I was alone—joined me for an aperitif, and filled me in on the gossip. After he had gone I was taking coffee on the terrace when I caught sight of a familiar face. He pretended not to see me, but I rose and waved my parasol. "Prince Kalenischeff! Your highness!"

He affected great surprise at seeing me and was persuaded to take a seat at my table. "I thought you never left the side of your distinguished husband," he said.

"I am equally surprised to see you, your highness. I trust nothing is amiss at Dahshoor?"

This sample of the inanity of our conversation will suffice, I believe. I let him talk, waiting for the opportunity to insinuate a subtle but significant question. I did not notice that he was gradually oozing closer and closer until something touched my foot.

"I was in the Khan el Khaleel this morning," I said, moving my foot away.

"What a coincidence. So was I," said Kalenischeff. "It is a pity we did not meet earlier. I might have had the pleasure of offering you luncheon."

This time it was not a foot but a hand that, under cover of the tablecloth, made contact with one of my extremities. Again I moved away; again the chair of Prince Kalenischeff inched closer. "I have a charming little *pied-à-terre* here in Cairo," he went on, leering at me through his monocle. "Since we are too late for luncheon—what about tea?"

Hand and foot together intruded upon my person.

I will go to considerable lengths in my quest for truth and justice, but there are limits. I had left my useful chatelaine and its tools at home, but my trusty parasol was at my side. Raising it, I brought the steel tip down on the prince's foot.

Kalenischeff's monocle dropped from his eye and his mouth opened wide, but he did not scream aloud. I rose. "Good day, your highness. I will miss my train if I stay any longer."

All in all it had been a most productive day. I could hardly wait to tell Emerson of my discoveries.

(The encounter with Kalenischeff would have to be edited, or Emerson would rush off to Dahshoor and commit various violent indignities upon the prince's person.) The most important discovery was that the man we knew as Hamid was really Abd el Atti's renegade son. But was Hamid guilty of the dastardly sin of patricide? At first the idea pleased me, but the more I thought about it, the more my enthusiasm cooled. I could visualize a quarrel—angry words—blows struck in the heat of passion. But I could not visualize Hamid, who was not notably muscular, making the perverse and terrible effort of hanging his father's huge body from the roof of the shop. In fact, this was one of the more curious aspects of the case. Why would anyone, muscular or not, make that effort? The most superficial examination would show that Abd el Atti had not committed suicide.

I amused myself during the train journey speculating on these matters. The sun had not yet set when I reached the house. I expected Emerson would be on the dig. Conceive of my surprise, therefore, to find him in the parlor with Ramses on his knee. A thrill of apprehensive inquiry pervaded my being, but the news I brought could not be contained.

"Emerson," I cried. "I have discovered who Hamid really is."

"Was," said Emerson.

"I beg your pardon?"

"Was. Ramses has just discovered his remains, torn and dismembered by jackals."

V

I was bitterly chagrined. Now we would never be able to question Hamid. I sat down and stripped off my gloves. "I begin to wonder about you, Ramses," I said. "How did you come to make such a discovery?"

"It was de cat Bastet, in fact," said Ramses calmly. "I have been training her to fetch for me. She is particularly interested in bones, which is not surprising, considering dat she is a carnivore; and I consider it a testimonial to my met'ods as well as to de intelligence of de cat Bastet dat she has been able to overcome her instinctive—"

"Say no more, dear boy," Emerson exclaimed. "Amelia, how can you ask Ramses to discuss a subject that has struck him dumb with horror?"

"I am not at all horrified," said Ramses, squirming in his father's affectionate grasp. "A student of physiology must develop a detached attitude toward specimens dat are de object of his research. I have been endeavoring to explain dis to Papa but to no avail."

Emerson's arms relaxed and Ramses slipped out of his hold. "I saw at once, from de freshness of de specimen, dat despite de desiccation dat is de inevitable consequence of dis climate, it was dat of an individual who had recently met his demise. De cat Bastet led me to de place where de odder parts of de—"

"Enough, Ramses," I said. "Emerson, where are the—er—remains?"

"I had them fetched back here."

"That was an error. I would like to have examined them in situ."

"You would not like to have examined them at all," said Emerson. "The word 'remains' is apt, Amelia."

"I examined dem carefully, Mama," Ramses said consolingly. "De body was unclot'ed. It had been dead for several days. Dere were no marks upon it except for extensive bruising around de neck. A rope tied tightly about dat part of de anatomy may have accounted for some of de contusions, but it is my opinion dat manual strangulation was de cause of deat'."

"Very good, Ramses," I said. "What steps have you taken, Emerson?"

"I have sent for the local chief of police."

"Good. If you will excuse me, I will go and change my clothes."

As I left I heard Ramses say, "May I remark, Papa, dat alt'ough your consideration for my sensitivities was quite unnecessary, I am not wit'out a proper appreciation of de sentiment dat prompted it."

VI

The mudir was of no use whatever, but since I had not expected he would be, I was not put out. Viewing the remains—and I must confess that the word was, as Emerson had suggested, decidedly apropos—he stroked his silky beard and murmured, "*Alhamdullilah.* What will these unbelievers do next?"

"We are hoping, effendi, that you will tell us

what this unbeliever did last," said Emerson courteously.

"It appears, O Father of Curses, that he hanged himself."

"And then walked out into the desert to bury himself?"

"The Father of Curses jests with his servant," said the mudir gravely. "A friend must have performed that office for him. Only the friend did not do a thorough job of it."

"Nonsense," I exclaimed. "The man was murdered."

"That is another possibility. If the sitt desires, I will question the other unbelievers."

He was obviously puzzled by our interest in the affair. It was nothing to him if unbelievers chose to murder one another and he could not understand why the death of a peasant, who was not even one of our servants, should concern us. Since I had no desire to see the villagers lined up and beaten in the local version of police interrogation, I declined his offer. Nor was I tempted to explain that Hamid was no Copt, nor a local resident. The story would only have confused the solemn old gentleman even more.

So we bade him farewell and watched him ride away, followed by his entourage of ragged, barefoot constables. I was about to return to the house when Emerson, leaning with folded arms against the door, said, "We may as well wait here, Amelia. The next delegation should be arriving at any moment."

"Whom are you expecting?"

"Jones—whom else? He will have heard the news

by now. I dismissed the men, since it is almost sunset, and there was no getting any work out of them once they learned what had happened."

Sure enough, it was not long before a familiar procession appeared in the distance. The two men rode side by side. It was not until they had drawn closer that I saw the third donkey and its rider. "Good heavens," I exclaimed. "He has brought Miss Charity. Emerson, you don't suppose that dreadful man expects her to—to—"

"Lay out the remains? Even Brother Ezekiel would hardly go so far as that, I fancy. He likes to have the girl tagging at his heels like an obedient hound."

Brother David urged his mount to a gallop and was soon before us. "Is it true?" he asked in agitated tones. "Is Brother Hamid . . ."

"Dead," Emerson said cheerfully. "Quite dead. Very dead indeed. Unquestionably dead and . . ." The others had come up by then and he broke off. Charity had heard, however; her small calloused hands gripped the reins so tightly, her knuckles whitened. No other sign of emotion was apparent, for her face, as usual, was shadowed by the brim of her bonnet.

Ezekiel dismounted. "We have come to take our poor brother back for burial," he announced. "And to call down the wrath of the Lord on his murderer."

"I suppose you could fancy a cup of tea," I said.

Ezekiel hesitated. "It will lubricate your vocal cords," Emerson said hospitably. "And strengthen the volume of your anathemas."

Smiling to myself, I led the way into the parlor.

Emerson might complain all he liked about my detective interests, but he was not immune to the fever. Here was a chance to find out from the missionaries what they knew about their "convert."

I had intended to spare John the embarrassment of appearing, after his unorthodox behavior following the fire, but the presence of Charity sent out invisible tentacles that wrapped round his heart and drew him inexorably to her. Shortly he appeared, wreathed in blushes, to ask if he might serve us. To send him away would have been to wound him, so I acquiesced and resigned myself to watching him fall over the furniture and spill the tea, for he never took his eyes off the object of his affections.

The discussion turned at once to Hamid's death. "Poor fellow," David said mournfully. "You did him an injustice, Brother, when you said he had run away."

"I did," Ezekiel acknowledged. Then he looked around at the rest of us as if expecting admiration for his admission of fallibility. Presumably he got enough of it from Brother David to satisfy him, for he went on in the same rotund, self-satisfied voice. "He was a true vessel of grace."

"A fine man," Brother David said.

"He will be greatly missed."

"One of the elect."

"I never liked him."

The interruption of the litany by this critical remark was almost as surprising as its source; the words issued from under Charity's black bonnet. Her brother turned a look of outraged astonishment upon her and she went on defiantly. "He was too obsequious, too fawning. And sometimes, when you were not looking at him, he would smile to himself in a sneering way."

"Charity, Charity," Brother David said gently. "You are forgetting your name."

The girl's slight, dark-robed form turned toward him as a flower seeks the sun. She clasped her hands. "You are right, Brother David. Forgive me."

"Only God can do that, my dear."

Emerson, who had been watching the exchange with undisguised amusement, now tired of the diversion. "When did you see the fellow last?" he asked.

All agreed that Hamid had not been seen since the night of the fire. He had taken his evening meal with the other converts before retiring to his humble pallet. Brother David claimed to have caught a glimpse of him during the confusion later, but Brother Ezekiel insisted Hamid had been conspicuous by his absence among those attempting to put out the flames. When he failed to appear the following morning, it was discovered that his scanty possessions were also gone. "We assumed he had gone back to his village," David said. "Sometimes our converts are . . . Sometimes they do not—er—"

"Yes, quite," said Emerson. "Your naïveté amazes me, gentlemen. Leaving aside the question of conversion, to introduce into your home a complete stranger, without credentials or local references . . ."

"We are all brothers in the Lord," Ezekiel proclaimed.

"That is your opinion," Emerson retorted. "In this case Miss Charity appears to have had better sense than either of you men. Your 'brother' was not a Copt but a Muslim; he did not come from a neighboring village but from the underworld of Cairo; he was a liar, most probably a thief, and very possibly a murderer."

Had Emerson consulted me beforehand, I would have advised against betraying this information—which, the reader will note, he implied he had discovered. However, the blunt announcement had the result of enabling me to study its effect on the missionaries. Since it is my practice to suspect everyone, without exception, I had naturally wondered whether one of them had murdered Hamid—for reasons which were at that time irrelevant to the inquiry. But their astonishment appeared genuine. Brother David's expression was one of polite incredulity. Brother Ezekiel was thunderstruck. His heavy jaw dropped and for a few seconds he could only sputter unintelligibly. "What—where—how did you—"

"There is no doubt about it," Emerson said. "He was a thorough rascal, and he took you in very nicely."

"You accuse the poor chap of being a thief," said Brother David. "Since he is no longer here to defend himself, I must do it for him. Do you accuse him of robbing you?"

"He stole nothing from us. That is . . ." A shade of vexation crossed Emerson's face. I knew he was thinking of the peripatetic mummy cases. He decided not to attempt to explain this. Instead he said, "He was responsible for the theft of the baroness's antiquities."

"How do you know that, sir?" Brother Ezekiel demanded.

"Mrs. Emerson and I have our methods," Emerson replied.

"But at least one of the missing objects was recovered," Ezekiel said.

"That was an error. The mummy—" Emerson's voice caught, but he got the word out. "The mummy case was not the one belonging to the baroness. It is still unaccounted for. But we are on the track of it; it won't be long before we locate it."

Brother David rose to his full height. "Forgive me, Professor, but I cannot listen to accusations against the dead. Our servants must have arrived by now; if you will show me where our unfortunate brother lies, we will take him away with us."

"Certainly. I will also lend you a sack in which to carry him."

The sun was setting in fiery splendor when the funeral procession made its way toward the village, in somber outline against the darkening blue of the eastern sky. We had been bidden to attend the obsequies of "our dear brother" on the following morning, an invitation to which Emerson replied with sincere astonishment. "Sir, you must be out of your mind to suggest such a thing."

John had lit the lamps when we returned to the parlor. Ramses was there too. He had been eavesdropping, for he said at once, "Papa, I would like to attend de funeral."

"Why on earth would you want to do that?" Emerson asked.

"Dere is a variety of folktale dat claims dat de murderer is drawn to de funeral services of his victim. I suspect dat is pure legend, but a truly scientific mind does not dismiss a t'eory simply because it—"

"Ramses, I am surprised at you," Emerson said. "Scientific inquiry is one thing, but there is a form of morbid curiosity—to which, I regret to say, certain adult persons who ought to know better are also prone . . ."

Here he stopped, having got himself into a hopeless grammatical tangle. I said icily, "Yes, Emerson? Do go on."

"Bah," said Emerson. "Er—I was about to suggest an alternative form of amusement. Instead of attending the obsequies we might go to Dahshoor and harass—I mean, visit—de Morgan."

"An excellent idea, Emerson," I said. "But there is no reason why we cannot do both. The funeral is early in the morning, and after that we can ride to Dahshoor."

Somewhat to my surprise Emerson agreed to this proposal. Ramses was also kind enough to consent. Later, after Ramses had been sent to bed and John had retired to his room—he had finally finished Leviticus and was now deep in the even greater intricacies of Numbers—I said to my husband, "I commend you on your self-control, Emerson. You didn't once lose your temper with Brother Ezekiel."

"He isn't worth my anger." Emerson pushed his

notebook aside. "In fact, I find the creature quite entertaining. He is the most absurd person I have encountered recently."

"Do you think he murdered Hamid?"

Emerson stared. "Why the devil should he?"

"Emerson, you are always worrying about motive. You ought to know by now that is not the way to solve a case." Emerson continued to gape at me. I continued, "I can think of several reasons why Brother Ezekiel might exterminate Hamid. The man may have made unwelcome advances to Miss Charity—Ezekiel is such a prude he would interpret a polite greeting as an unwelcome advance. Or Ezekiel may have discovered that Hamid was not sincere in his conversion."

"Peabody—" Emerson began in an ominous tone.

"I have made a few notes on the case." I opened my own notebook. "We know now that Hamid was the disinherited son of Abd el Atti and that he was a member of the criminal ring of antiquities thieves. I agree with you that a falling-out among thieves is the most likely explanation of his murder. These secret societies are devilish things. If Hamid had betrayed his oath—sworn in secret ceremonies and sealed in his own blood—"

"Peabody, you never cease to astonish me. When do you find time to read such trash?"

Recognizing this as a rhetorical question, I did not answer it. "Drug takers are notoriously unreliable; the Master Criminal may have concluded Hamid was dangerous, and ordered him executed."

"I believe this is our first Master Criminal, is it

not? I don't care for them, Peabody. The noble amateur villain is much more to my taste."

"Or—which is, in my opinion, more likely—Hamid decided to set up in business for himself, thus robbing the ring of the profits to which they believed themselves entitled. The Master Criminal is unquestionably the most likely suspect."

"Oh, quite." Emerson folded his arms. "I suppose you have deduced the identity of this mysterious—one might almost say apocryphal—figure?"

"Hardly apocryphal, Emerson. We can now be certain that more than one evildoer is involved, for Hamid was not the person who entered Ramses' room last night. He had been dead for several days, probably since the night of the fire."

"Humph," said Emerson. "I grant you a gang, Peabody—though that is stretching the evidence. But a Master Criminal?"

"A gang must have a leader, Emerson. Naturally I have given some thought as to who he may be." I turned over a page of my notebook. "Now pray don't interrupt me again. This is a complex problem and you will confuse me."

"I wouldn't do that for the world," said Emerson.

"The Master Criminal is obviously not what he seems."

"Brilliant, Peabody."

"Please, Emerson. What I mean to say is that he—or she—for one must not denigrate the natural talents of the so-called weaker sex. . . . Where was I?"

"I have no idea, Peabody."

"The Master Criminal undoubtedly has another persona. He or she may be in outward appearance the most respectable of individuals. A missionary— a Russian nobleman—a German baroness—an archaeologist. . . ."

"Humph," said Emerson. "I assure you, Peabody, I am not your Master Criminal. I claim an alibi. You know where I am at night."

"I never suspected you, Emerson."

"I am relieved to hear it, Peabody."

"Let us take the suspects in order. First, Brother Ezekiel. What do we know of him before he appeared at Mazghunah this year? I don't doubt that the Brothers of the Holy Jerusalem are a legitimate sect, but they seem only too ready to accept plausible scoundrels into their ranks. The entire mission staff may be involved—Brother David as the liaison between Ezekiel and the Cairo underworld, and Miss Charity as a decoy. Her presence adds a look of innocence to the group."

Emerson's interest was growing, but he tried to hide it. "There it is again, Peabody—your weakness for young persons of pleasant appearance. Miss Charity herself may be the Master Criminal. There certainly is no less likely suspect."

"Oh, I don't deny she may be criminally involved, Emerson. She is almost too good to be true—a caricature of a pious young American lady. Or Brother David may be the head of the gang, with Ezekiel as his dupe or his confederate. However, I consider Prince Kalenischeff to be just as suspicious. His reputation is none of the best. His title is questionable, his source of income unknown. And Slavs, in my opinion, are very unstable persons."

"And Germans, Peabody?"

"Bismarck, Emerson—I remind you of Bismarck. And the Kaiser has been extremely rude to his grandmama."

"A palpable hit, Peabody." Emerson rubbed his chin thoughtfully. "I confess the idea of the baroness being a Master Criminal delights me. However, she is probably in Luxor by now. A successful leader of criminals should supervise her henchmen more closely."

"Ah, but she is not at Luxor," I cried triumphantly. "I spent the afternoon at Shepheard's, catching up on the news. The baroness's dahabeeyah went aground at Minieh, two days after she left Dahshoor. She returned to Cairo by train and is now staying at that new hotel near the pyramids—Mena House. Giza is only two hours from Dahshoor by donkey, less by train."

"The theft of her antiquities was a blind, then, to remove suspicion from her?"

"Possible but not probable; she was not under suspicion at that time—at least not by us. I consider it more likely that the theft was an act of rebellion by Hamid. If, that is, the baroness is the Master Criminal."

"And who is your archaeologist suspect? Surely not our distinguished neighbor."

"What better disguise could a Master Criminal adopt? An archaeologist has the most legitimate of excuses for excavation, and the best possible means of learning of new discoveries. As inspector general, M. de Morgan can control all other excavators, heading them away from sites that promise to yield valuable objects. He worked at Dahshoor, where there are Twelfth Dynasty tombs, last spring; and last summer we first heard of the Twelfth Dynasty pectoral appearing on the market."

Emerson's face took on a far-off look; his brilliant blue eyes softened. Then he shook his head. "No, Peabody. We must not be led astray by wishful thinking. There must be some other way of getting de Morgan to give us Dahshoor besides putting him in prison. Your suggestion of a criminal archaeologist has intriguing aspects, however. And de Morgan is not the only excavator of my acquaintance who has displayed weakness of character."

"I do not for a moment believe that Mr. Petrie is the Master Criminal, Emerson."

"Humph," said Emerson.

Though we discussed suspects a while longer, we could add nothing to the list I had made. Emerson's suggestions—the Reverend Sayce, Chauncy Murch, the Protestant missionary at Luxor, and M. Maspero, distinguished former head of the Antiquities Department—were too ridiculous to be considered. As I pointed out to him, theories are one thing, wild improvisation is quite another. I hoped that the morrow's projected visit to Dahshoor would enable us to learn more. Kalenischeff was still there, purportedly assisting de Morgan, and I promised myself another interview with that gentleman.

It was rather late before we got to sleep, and although my famous instinct brought me instantly alert at the sound of a soft scratching at the window, I was not quite as wide-awake as I ought to have been. I was about to strike with my parasol at the dark bulk looming at the open window when I recognized the voice repeating my name.

"Abdullah?" I replied. "Is it you?"

"Come out, Sitt Hakim. Something is happening."

It took only a moment to throw on my robe. Finding my slippers took a little longer; I had been forced to hide them to keep Ramses from feeding them to the lion, and in the muzziness of lingering sleep I could not recall where I had put them. At last I joined Abdullah outside the house.

"Look there," he said, pointing.

Far to the northeast a bright pillar of flame soared heavenward. There was something so uncanny about the scene—the utter stillness of the night, unbroken even by the lament of jackals— the vast empty waste, cold under the moon—that I stood motionless for a moment. The distant flame might have been the sacrificial fire of some diabolic cult.

I reminded myself that this was the nineteenth century A.D., not ancient Egypt, and my usual good sense reasserted itself. At least the mission was not under attack; the fire was somewhere in the desert. "Quickly," I exclaimed. "We must locate the spot before the flames die down."

"Should we not waken the Father of Curses?" Abdullah asked nervously.

"It will take too long. Hurry, Abdullah."

The site of the blaze was not as distant as it had appeared, but the flames had died to a sullen glow before we reached it. As we stood gazing at the molten remains Abdullah hunched his shoulders and shot a quick glance behind him. I sympathized with his feelings. The ambience was eerie in the extreme, and the smoldering embers were gruesomely suggestive of the contours of a human form.

The sound of heavy breathing and running footsteps made us both start. Abdullah knew Emerson's habits as well as I; he prudently got behind me, and I was able to prevent Emerson from hurling himself at the throat of—as he believed—my abductor. When the situation was explained, Emerson shook himself like a large dog. "I wish you wouldn't do this to me, Peabody," he complained. "When I reached out for you and found you gone I feared the worst."

He had paused only long enough to assume his trousers. His broad chest heaved with the speed of his running and his tumbled locks curled about his brow. With an effort I conquered my emotions and recounted the cause of my departure.

"Hmmm," said Emerson, studying the dying coals. "They have an ominous shape, do they not?"

"Less so now than before. But it cannot have been a human body, Emerson. Flesh and bone would not be so completely consumed."

"Quite right, Peabody." Emerson knelt and reached out a hand. "Ouch," he exclaimed, putting his fingers to his mouth.

"Be careful, my dear Emerson."

"Immediate action is imperative, Peabody. The object is almost entirely reduced to ash. A few more moments . . ." He succeeded in snatching up a small fragment, scarcely two inches across. It crumbled even more as he tossed it from hand to hand, but he had seen enough.

"I fancy we have found the missing mummy case, Peabody."

"Are you certain?"

"There are traces of brown varnish here. I suppose it could be one of ours—"

"No one has approached our house tonight," Abdullah assured him.

"Then it must be the one belonging to the baroness," I said.

"Not necessarily," Emerson said morosely. "There must be four or five thousand of the cursed things that have not yet passed through our hands."

"Pray do not yield to despair, Emerson," I advised. "Or to levity—if that was your intention. I have no doubt this is the mummy case we have been seeking. What a pity there is so little left of it."

"It is not surprising it should burn so readily, since it was composed of varnish and papier-mâché, both highly flammable."

"But, Emerson, why would a thief go to so much trouble to obtain this article, only to destroy it?"

He had no answer. We gazed at one another in silent surmise, while the sun rose slowly in the east.

I was pleased with the appearance of our little party when we set out for the funeral service. John's scrubbed cheeks shone like polished apples, and Ramses had an air of deceptive innocence in his little Eton jacket and short trousers. Emerson snorted when I suggested he put on a cravat, but Emerson can never appear less than magnificent; and I fancy I looked my usual respectable self, though the fact that we planned to proceed directly from the village to Dahshoor necessitated a less formal costume than I would ordinarily have assumed when attending religious services.

Emerson flatly refused to enter the chapel. We left him sitting on his favorite block of stone, back ramrod-straight, hands on knees in the very pose of an Egyptian pharaoh enthroned.

The service was less prolonged than I expected, possibly because Brother Ezekiel's command of Arabic was not extensive, and possibly because his new-founded doubts as to Hamid's character curtailed the fervor of his eulogy. A few lugubrious hymns were sung—John and Ramses joined in, to disastrous effect—and then half a dozen stalwart converts shouldered the rough wooden coffin and the company straggled out after them.

A considerable crowd had assembled outside the chapel. At first I thought they had come to watch, or even protest, the ceremonies of the intruders. Then I saw that all were laughing or smiling, and I realized that they were gathered around my husband, who was chatting with all the graciousness of his ancient model holding court. Emerson has, I regret to say, an extensive store of Arabic jokes, many of them extremely vulgar, which he keeps for masculine company. Catching sight of me, he broke off in the middle of a word and rose to his feet.

Trailed by the spectators, we followed the coffin through the grove of palm trees to the edge of the cultivation. I assumed Brother Ezekiel had marked the spot for a cemetery, but there was no symbol of that purpose except for the grimly significant hole in the ground. No fence enclosed the area, no religious symbol marked it. It was a desolate and forbidding final resting place; only too appropriate, I feared, for the wretched man whose bones were to lie there.

His Bible open in his hands, Brother Ezekiel stood at the head of the grave with David beside him and Charity the customary two paces to the rear. John began edging toward her. I poked him with my parasol and shook my head, frowning. Ordinarily I am sympathetic to romantic feelings, but this was not the time or the place.

The somber message of Isaiah sounded even more dismal in Ezekiel's guttural Arabic. "All flesh is grass, and all the goodliness thereof is as the flower of the field. The grass withereth, the flower fadeth: because the spirit of the Lord bloweth upon it."

Ezekiel did not proceed to the comfort of the following verses, with their assurance of immortality in the grace of God. Instead he closed the Book with a slam and began to speak extemporaneously.

I was anxious to be on our way, so I paid little attention to his words until I felt the muscles of Emerson's arm stiffen under my hand. Then I realized that Ezekiel's eulogy had turned into a tirade, stumbling but passionate—a bitter denunciation of the Coptic Church, its beliefs and its local representative.

A murmur of anger arose, like the first wind of a storm through dry grasses. David turned to look with surprise and alarm at his associate. Emerson cleared his throat loudly. "I would like to say a few words," he called out.

His voice stilled the mutter of the crowd and Brother Ezekiel broke off. Before he could draw breath, Emerson launched into a flowery speech. He was not hypocrite enough to praise Hamid, of whom he said only that he had worked for us, so that we felt the need to acknowledge his passing. He went on to quote the Koran and the Bible on the sin of murder, and proclaimed his intention of bringing the killer to justice. Then he dismissed the audience with the blessing of God, Allah, Jehovah, Christ and Mohammed—which pretty well covered all possibilities.

The listeners slowly dispersed, with the exception of the few who had been designated as grave diggers. They began shoveling sand into the pit and Emerson confronted the angry preacher. "Are you out of your mind?" he demanded. "Are you trying to start a small war here?"

"I spoke the truth as I saw it," Ezekiel said.

Emerson dismissed him with a look of scorn. "Try to contain your friend's candor," he said to David, "or you will find yourself burning with your church."

Without waiting for a reply, he strode away. I

had to run to catch him up. "Where are you going, Emerson? We left the donkeys at the chapel."

"To see the priest. Word of the affair has already reached him, I fear, but we will do what we can to mitigate its effect."

The priest refused to see us. According to the hard-faced disciple who responded to our call, he was absorbed in prayer and could not be disturbed. We turned reluctantly away. "I don't like this, Peabody," Emerson said gravely.

"You don't believe we are in danger, Emerson?"

"We? Danger?" Emerson laughed. "He would hardly venture to threaten us, my dear Peabody. But the lunatics at the mission are another story, and Ezekiel seems bent on starting trouble."

"The priest was courteous enough to me the other day. At least," I added, thinking ruefully of my ruined chapeau, "he meant to be courteous."

"Ah, but that was before we began entertaining his rival to tea and encouraging our servant to patronize the other establishment. Never mind, Peabody, there is no cause for alarm at present; I will call on the priest another day."

John returned to the house and Ramses, Emerson and I set out for Dahshoor. As we rode along the edge of the fields, the first of the Dahshoor monuments we encountered was the Black Pyramid. Ramses, who had been silent up to that time, began to chatter about Egyptian verb forms, and Emerson, whose strength lay in excavation rather than in philology, was at something of an embarrassment. We drew near the base of the pyramid and he stopped, with an exclamation of surprise. "What the devil, Peabody—someone has been digging here."

"Well, of course, Emerson."

"I am not referring to de Morgan's incompetent probing, Peabody. These are fresh excavations."

I saw nothing unusual, but Emerson's expert eye cannot be gainsaid. I acknowledged as much, adding casually, "Perhaps some of the villagers from Menyat Dahshoor are doing a little illicit digging."

"Practically under de Morgan's eye? Well, but he would not notice if they carried the pyramid itself away."

"He is a very forceful individual," said Ramses in his piping voice. "All de Arabs are afraid of him."

Emerson, who had been studying the tumbled terrain with a thoughtful frown, replied to his son, "They are afraid of the mudir and his bullwhip, Ramses. English gentlemen do not employ such threats—nor are they necessary. You must win the respect of your subordinates by treating them with absolute fairness. Of course it helps to have an inherently dominant personality and a character both strong and just, commanding and yet tolerant. . . ."

We found the workers sprawled in the shade taking their midday rest. De Morgan was not there. We were informed that he was at the southern stone pyramid, with his guest, who had expressed an interest in seeing that structure. So we turned our steeds in that direction, and found de Morgan at luncheon. At the sight of the table, which was covered with a linen cloth and furnished with china and crystal wineglasses, Emerson let out a sound of disgust. I paid no heed; the near proximity of the noble monument in all its glory induced a rapture that overcame all else.

Emerson immediately began berating de Morgan for taking so much time from his work. "You leave the men unsupervised," he declared. "They have every opportunity to make off with their finds."

"But, *mon vieux*," said de Morgan, twirling his mustache, "you are also away from the scene of your labors, *non*?"

"We were attending a funeral," Emerson said. "I presume you heard of the mysterious death of one of our men?"

"I confess," de Morgan said superciliously, "that I take little interest in the affairs of the natives."

"He was not one of the local people," I said. "We have reason to believe he was a criminal of the deepest dye—a member of the gang of antiquities thieves."

"Criminals? Thieves?" De Morgan smiled. "You insist upon your interesting fictions, madame."

"Hardly fictions, monsieur. We have learned that the murdered man was in reality the son of Abd el Atti." I turned abruptly to Prince Kalenischeff. "You knew him, did you not?"

But the sinister Russian was not to be caught so easily. His arched brows lifted infinitesimally. "Abd el Atti? The name is familiar, but . . . Was he by chance an antiquities dealer?"

"Was, your highness; your use of the past tense is correct. Abd el Atti is no more."

"Ah yes, it comes back to me now. I believe I heard of his death when I was last in Cairo."

"He was murdered!"

"Indeed?" The prince fixed his monocle more firmly in his eyesocket. "I fear I share M. de Morgan's disinterest in the affairs of the natives."

I realized it would be more difficult than I had thought to trick Kalenischeff into a damaging admission. He was an accomplished liar. Also, I found myself increasingly distracted as the conversation went on. I soon realized what the problem was. Once again detective fever warred with my passion for archaeology. It was not hard to keep the latter within reasonable bounds when the distraction consisted of decadent Roman mummies and scraps of pottery; but in the shadow of a pyramid—not any pyramid, but one of the most majestic giants in all of Egypt—other interests were subdued, as the brilliance of the sun dims the light of a lamp. My breathing became quick and shallow, my face burned. When finally de Morgan patted his lips daintily with his napkin and offered us coffee I said, as casually as I could, "Thank you, monsieur, but I believe I will go into the pyramid instead."

"Into the pyramid?" De Morgan paused in the act of rising, his eyes wide with astonishment. "Madame, you cannot be serious."

"Mrs. Emerson never jokes about pyramids," said my husband.

"Certainly not," I agreed.

"But, madame . . . The passages are dark, dirty, hot. . . ."

"They are open, I believe? Perring and Vyse explored them over sixty years ago."

"Yes, certainly, but . . . There are bats, madame."

"Bats do not bodder my mudder," said Ramses.

"Pardon?" said de Morgan, quite at a loss.

"Bats do not bother me," I translated. "Nor do any of the other difficulties you mentioned."

"If you are determined, madame, I will of course send one of my men along with a torch," de Morgan said doubtfully. "Professor—you do not object?"

Emerson folded his arms and leaned back in his chair. "I never object to any of Mrs. Emerson's schemes. It would be a waste of time and energy."

De Morgan said, "Humph," in almost Emerson's tone. "Very well, madame, if you insist. You may take your son with you as guide," he added, with a sidelong glance at Ramses. "He is quite familiar with the interior of that particular pyramid."

Emerson swallowed the wrong way and burst into a fit of coughing. I looked at Ramses, who looked back at me with a face as enigmatic as that of the great Sphinx. "You have explored the Bent Pyramid, Ramses?" I asked, in a very quiet voice.

"But of a certainty, madame," said de Morgan. "My men were some time searching for the little . . . fellow. Fortunately one of them saw him enter, otherwise we might not have found him in time to save him."

"As I endeavored to explain, monsieur, I was not in need of rescue," said Ramses. "I could have retraced my steps at any time, and had every intention of doing so once my research was completed."

I felt certain this statement was correct. Ramses had an uncanny sense of direction and as many lives as a cat is reputed to have—though by now, I imagined, he had used up several of them.

I said, "I should have known. One day when you

returned home and took a bath without being told to do so—"

"De odor of bat droppings is extremely pervasive," Ramses said.

"Did I not forbid you to explore the interiors of pyramids?"

"No, Mama, I am certain you never uttered dat specific prohibition. Had you done so, I would of course—"

"Never mind. Since you know the way, you may as well come with me."

We left the others at table and sought the entrance, with one of de Morgan's men in attendance. I was extremely vexed with Ramses. I could not punish him for disobeying me, since it had not occurred to me to forbid him to explore pyramids. That omission at least could be remedied, though I felt sure Ramses would immediately find some other activity I had not thought of prohibiting.

"Ramses," I said. "You are not to go into any more pyramids, do you understand?"

"Unless it is wit' you and Papa?" Ramses suggested.

"Well—yes, I suppose I must make that exception, since it applies to the present situation."

The entrance to the interior of the pyramid was on the north side, thirty-nine feet from the ground. Thanks to the unusual slope, the climb was not as difficult as it appeared; at close range the seemingly smooth facing was seen to have innumerable cracks and breaks that provided holds for fingers and toes. Ramses went up like a monkey.

At the opening the guide lit his torch and preceded me into a narrow, low-roofed corridor that descended at a moderate gradient. The air became increasingly close and hot as we went on, down, down, ever down, into breathless darkness. I remembered from my reading that the corridor was almost two hundred and fifty feet long. It seemed longer. Finally it leveled out; then we found ourselves in a narrow but lofty vestibule whose ceiling was shrouded in shadows—and in bats. They set up an agitated squeaking, and began to stir uneasily; it was necessary for me to reassure them before they settled down again.

I was familiar with the general plan of the place from my reading, but Ramses had to point out the exit from this vestibule, which was more than twenty feet above the floor, in the southern wall of the chamber. Another room, with a fine corbeled ceiling—another passage . . . It was absolutely delightful, and I was enjoying myself immensely when the guide started to whine. The torch was burning low for lack of air; he was choking; he had sprained his ankle on the rubble littering the floor; and so on. I ignored his request that we turn back, but I was a trifle short of breath myself, so I suggested we sit down and rest for a while.

We were in one of the upper corridors near a great portcullis stone, which had been designed to block the passage and prevent robbers from reaching the burial chamber. For some reason it had never been lowered into place, and it provided a convenient back rest.

As we sat there, the full wonder and mystery of the place overshadowed me. We were not the first to penetrate that mystery; several modern archaeologists had entered the pyramid, and three thousand years before that, a group of hardy robbers had braved the physical dangers and the curses of the dead to rob the pharaoh of his treasures. When those intrepid but unscientific explorers, Perring and Vyse, explored the passages in 1839, they found only scraps of wood and baskets, and a few mummified bats, inside a wooden box. There was no sarcophagus and no royal mummy. Since Pharaoh Snefru, to whom the pyramid belonged, had another tomb, he may never have rested here; but something of value must have occupied the now-empty chambers or the ancient thieves would not have broken into them, with baskets to carry away their loot.

As I mused in blissful enjoyment, with the perspiration dripping from my nose and chin, there occurred the most uncanny event of that entire season. The stifling air was suddenly stirred by a breeze, which rose in an instant to a gusty wind. It felt cold against our sweating bodies. The torch flickered wildly and went out. Darkness closed in upon us—a darkness filled with movement. The guide let out a howl that echoed gruesomely.

I ordered him to be quiet. "Good Gad, Ramses," I said excitedly. "I have read of this phenomenon, but I never thought I would be fortunate enough to experience it myself."

"I believe Perring and Vyse mention it," said the high, piping voice of my annoyingly well-informed son, close beside me. "It is indeed a curious phenomenon, Mama, leading one to de suspicion dat dere are passageways and exits to de exterior as yet undiscovered."

"I had reached that conclusion myself, Ramses."

"It was in de investigation of dat t'eory I was engaged when M. de Morgan's men interrupted me. One of dem had de effrontery to shake me, Mama. I spoke to M. de Morgan about it, but he only laughed and said—"

"I don't want to know what he said, Ramses."

The wind subsided as suddenly as it had begun. In the silence I could hear our guide's teeth chattering. "Sitt," he moaned, "oh, Sitt, we must go at once. The djinns are awake and looking for us. We will die here in the darkness and our souls will be eaten."

"We could continue de search for de unknown opening, Mama," said Ramses.

To say that I was tempted is like saying a starving man is a trifle peckish. Common sense prevailed, however. The search Ramses proposed would be the work of days, possibly weeks, and it could not be carried out without advance preparation. I had lost all track of time, as I am inclined to do when I am enjoying myself, but I suspected we had been gone longer than we ought to have been. I was therefore forced to refuse Ramses' request; and after I had relit the torch (a supply of matches, in a waterproof tin box, is part of my supplies), we retraced our steps.

Ramses must have sensed the pain that filled my heart, for as I was crawling up the last long passageway he said, "It is too bad Papa was not able to obtain de firman for Dahshoor, Mama."

"No one is perfect, Ramses, not even your papa.

Had he allowed ME to deal with M. de Morgan . . .
But that is over and done with."

"Yes, Mama. But you would like to have dis site,
would you not?"

"It would be futile for me to deny it, Ramses.
But never forget that your papa is the greatest living Egyptologist, even if he is somewhat lacking in
tact."

Emerson kept a discreet distance from us as we rode
back to Mazghunah. As Ramses had noted, the smell
of bat droppings is extremely pervasive and unpleasant. I knew it was Emerson's sense of smell, not his
affections, that dictated the removal. After a while
he called out, "Did you have a pleasant time, Peabody?"

"Yes, thank you, my dear Emerson. Very pleasant."

Emerson touched his donkey and the animal
sidled nearer. "You know I would have got you
Dahshoor if I could, Peabody."

"I know that, Emerson."

There was a stiff breeze blowing from the south.
Emerson's nose wrinkled and he let his donkey fall
behind. "Don't you want to know what I learned
from the sinister Russian while you were gadding
about inside the pyramid?" he called.

"I would like to know, Papa," cried Ramses, turning his donkey. Emerson hastily covered his face
with his sleeve. "Later, Ramses, later. Why don't you
ride with your mama?"

Emerson's hints of Russian revelations were only intended to pique my curiosity, as he finally admitted. But after we had dined and Ramses had gone to his room, Emerson seated himself at the table, folded his hands, and regarded me seriously.

"We must talk, Peabody. The time has come for us to face a painful truth. I have reason to believe that we are involved with a sinister criminal conspiracy."

"Emerson," I exclaimed. "You astonish me!"

My husband shot me a sour glance. "Sarcasm does not become you any more than it does me, Peabody. Until recently your wild theories were no more than that. The repeated invasions of our premises, however, indicate that for some reason as yet unknown we are the objects of active malice. Even more significant is the fact that someone has been digging near the Black Pyramid. And," he added, frowning, "if you use the words 'Master Criminal' . . ."

"We may as well call him that in lieu of a less distinctive pseudonym, Emerson."

"Humph," said Emerson.

"Then you agree that our burglaries were committed by the gang of antiquities thieves?"

"Wait." Emerson raised a magisterial hand. "For once, Peabody, let us work out this problem step by step, in strictly logical fashion, instead of leaping across an abyss of speculation onto an unstable stepping-stone of theory."

I took up my mending. Emerson's shirts always

need to have buttons sewn on. "Proceed, my dear Emerson."

"Point number one: illicit digging at Dahshoor. You may recall my mentioning that one of the objects to come on the market recently was a Twelfth Dynasty pectoral, with a royal cartouche. Dahshoor has three Twelfth Dynasty pyramids, the Black Pyramid being one of them. There are other royal tombs of that period in Egypt; but, given the evidence of recent excavation, I think there is a strong presumption that the pectoral came from that site."

"I agree, Emerson. And the thieves have not finished, so there may be other tombs—"

"Point number two," Emerson said loudly. "Abd el Atti's association with the Master . . . with the gang. His death, the presence of his renegade son here at Mazghunah, the latter's murder, support this connection. Do you agree?"

"Since it was I who first put forth that theory, I do agree."

"Humph," said Emerson. "But from here on, Peabody, we are adrift in a sea of conjecture. What possible interest could these villains have in an innocent party like ours? Their aim cannot be to silence us; neither of us saw anything that would identify the murderer of Abd el Atti—"

"We may have observed a clue without recognizing its significance."

"The fact remains, Peabody, that no attacks have been made on our persons. It seems clear that these people are looking for something we have in our possession—or that they believe we have in our possession."

"I believe you have hit it, Emerson," I exclaimed. "We know we have nothing of value; the mummy portrait was attractive, but not worth a great deal, and the papyrus fragments are completely worthless. Do you suppose something else was missing from the shop—sold, hidden away, or stolen by a third party—and that the gang attributes its loss to us?"

"It is a plausible theory," Emerson admitted. "I have a fairly clear memory of the objects that were scattered around the shop that night. It is a pity you did not get into the back room on your first visit; we might then compare inventories."

"I didn't but Ramses did. Shall we ask him?"

"I hate to involve the lad in this dirty business, Amelia. I waited until he had retired before discussing it."

"Emerson, you underestimate Ramses. In the past weeks he has been taken in custody by the police, half-stifled in a sheet, and buried in the sand; he has stolen a lion and examined a body in an unpleasant state of disrepair, without turning a hair."

Emerson demurred no longer. Detective fever burned as bright in his manly chest as it did in my bosom. I felt sure Ramses was not in bed, and the slit of light under his door proved me correct.

Emerson knocked. After a moment the door opened and Ramses' tousled head appeared. He was in his nightgown, but his lamp was alight and there was a heap of papers on the table that served as his desk. The Coptic grammar was open.

Emerson explained his idea. Ramses nodded. "I believe I can supply de information, Papa. Shall we retire to de parlor?"

At my suggestion Ramses put on his dressing gown and one of his slippers. The other was nowhere to be found, and I was glad I had kept one pair in reserve. After Emerson had detached the lion cub from his bootlace we retired to the parlor, with Bastet following. Emerson took up his pen. Ramses closed his eyes and began.

"A heart scarab of blue faience, with a prayer to Osiris; a tray of mixed beads, cylindrical; a piece of linen approximately ten centimeters by forty, wit' a hieratic docket reading 'Year twenty, day four of the inundation. . . .'"

I picked up my mending. We had obviously underestimated Ramses' powers of visual recall.

His voice droned on. "Fragments of a coffin of de Roman period, consisting of de foot and portions of de upper back; anodder coffin, Twenty-First Dynasty, belonging to Isebaket, priestess of Hathor. . . ."

It was a good twenty minutes later before he stopped talking and opened his eyes. "Dat is all I can recall, Papa."

"Very good, my boy. You are certain there were no pieces of jewelry, aside from cheap beads?"

"Small objects of value would be in de locked cupboards, Papa. I did not attempt to open dem, since Mama had forbidden me to touch anyt'ing."

"And because such an act would have been illegal, immoral, and unprincipled," I suggested.

"Yes, Mama."

"It is a pity you didn't, though," Emerson remarked.

"Can you remember what items from Ramses' list were missing?" I asked. "Not that it would necessarily prove anything; Abd el Atti might have sold them during the afternoon."

"True." Emerson looked at the list.

"I don't remember seeing any mummy cases," I said.

Emerson threw the list across the room. The cat Bastet pounced on it and batted it back and forth. "I do not want to talk about mummy cases, Peabody!"

"Yet dey continue to intrude, do dey not?" Ramses said. "I believe we must consider de mummy case of de baroness as vital to de solution. Until we can explain dat, we are at sea."

"I agree, Ramses," I said. "And I have an idea."

Ramses slid down off his chair and went to retrieve the list from Bastet. Emerson looked off into space. Neither asked me to explain my idea; so I proceeded.

"We have concluded, have we not, that someone has found treasure at Dahshoor and hopes to find more."

Emerson shook his head. "A possibility only, Peabody."

"But when you have eliminated de impossible, whatever remains, however improbable, must be de trut'," said Ramses, returning to his chair.

"Very good, Ramses," exclaimed his father. "How pithy you are becoming."

"It is not original, Papa."

"Never mind," I said impatiently. "Gold and jewels are sufficient causes of violence, as the history of mankind unhappily demonstrates; but a commonplace mummy case is not. But what, I ask, is a mummy case?" I paused for effect. My husband and son regarded me in stony silence. "It is a container," I cried. "Normally it contains a human body, but what if this mummy case were used as a hiding place for small, stolen antiquities? The baroness would have taken it away with her, out of the country, and it is most unlikely that the authorities would have inspected it. She purchased her antiquities openly and no doubt has the proper papers."

"That explanation had of course occurred to me," said Emerson, stroking his chin. "But why did the thieves steal the mummy case back from her if they meant her to smuggle their stolen goods out of the country?"

"Because we were interested in it," I explained. "Don't you see, Emerson? The baroness is a woman of volatile and impetuous character and she was trying to make an impression on you. She offered the mummy case to you upon one occasion; though she spoke half in jest, there was a chance she might have gone through with the plan. The thieves had to retrieve it. They extracted the stolen goods and destroyed the mummy case, having no more use for it."

"I perceive several difficulties wit' dat explanation, Mama," said Ramses.

"Hush, Ramses." Emerson pondered. "If that

idea is correct, Peabody, the baroness cannot be the Master Criminal."

"I suppose you are right, Emerson."

"Cheer up, Peabody, it is only an idea. We may yet think of something that proves the baroness guilty." Emerson grinned at me.

"The baroness was only one of our suspects," I replied. "Several of the others were present that evening, when the baroness offered you the mummy case. Or one of the servants—if he was in the pay of the Master Criminal he could have warned his superior that the hiding place was no longer safe."

"But who is that unknown superior? (If you have no objection, Peabody, I prefer that term to 'Master Criminal,' which smacks too strongly of the type of sensational literature to which I object.) Our deductions may be valid so far as they go, but we are still in the dark as to the identity of the person who is behind all this."

"We will catch him, Emerson," I said reassuringly. "We have never failed yet."

Emerson did not reply. Ramses sat swinging his feet—one bare, one enclosed in a red morocco slipper—and looking pensive. After an interval Emerson said, "We may as well give it up for the time being. Off to bed, my boy; it is very late. I regret having kept you from your rest."

"Dere is no need to apologize, Papa. I found de discussion most stimulating. Good night, Mama. Good night, Papa. Come along, de cat Bastet."

We replied in kind—Emerson and I in words, Bastet by falling in behind Ramses as he walked to the door. Just before it closed behind him I heard him say musingly, "What is a mummy case? A most provocative question. . . . What indeed is a mummy case? A mummy case is . . . A mummy case . . ."

I began to agree with Emerson, that I would rather not hear those words again.

NINE

The following day saw the moment I had awaited so long—the beginning of work on our pyramids (or, to be precise, our pyramid, Emerson having selected the northernmost of the two). Dare I confess the truth? I believe I do dare. Though a measurable improvement over Roman mummies and Christian bones, the pitiful excuse for a pyramid I saw before me held little charm. Too late, alas, I knew I should not have yielded to the temptation to explore the Bent Pyramid, well-nigh irresistible as that temptation had been.

Nor was Emerson his usual cheerful self. Something was troubling him—my affectionate perception told me that—but it was not until that evening, when we set to work recording the activities of the day, that he deigned to confide in me.

We worked in silence for some time, at opposite ends of the long table, with the lamp shedding a pool of brightness between us. From time to time I glanced at Emerson, but always found him writing busily. All at once my labors were interrupted by a loud "Curse it!" and the whiz of a missile through the air. The pen hit the wall with a spattering of ink, and fell to the floor.

I looked up. Emerson's elbows were on the table. His hands clutched his hair. "What is wrong, Emerson?" I asked.

"I cannot concentrate, Peabody. Something is nagging at my mind. I felt sure you would sense my distraction, but every time I looked at you you were busy writing, and I did not want to interrupt."

"But I felt the same," I cried eagerly. "Our mental communication is truly remarkable, Emerson. I have noticed it often. What is troubling you?"

"Do you remember the intrusive mummy we found a few days after the robbery of the dahabeeyah?"

I had to think for a few moments before the memory returned. "I believe I do. On the edge of the Christian cemetery, was it not?"

"Yes. I wondered at the time. . . ." Emerson leaped to his feet. "Do you recall where you put it?"

"Certainly. Nothing is stored away in *my* expedition house without my having a distinct . . . Emerson! I believe I know what you are thinking."

We collided in the doorway. "Just a moment," I said breathlessly. "Let us not be precipitate. Fetch a light and I will call John; we will need to move a few objects to reach the mummy."

With John's assistance we removed the mummy from its shelf and carried it back to the parlor. Emerson cleared the table by the simple expedient of sweeping his papers onto the floor, and the mummy was placed on its surface.

"Now," said Emerson. "Look at it, Peabody."

There was nothing out of the ordinary about the mummy, except for the arrangement of the wrappings. Instead of being wound haphazardly around the body, the strips of linen were arranged in complex patterns of intersecting lozenges. It was this technique, among other factors, that had enabled Emerson to date it. So ornate were some of the designs I had sometimes wondered whether there were pattern books to which the embalmers might refer. Some mummies of that period had cartonnage masks. Others had painted panels with a portrait of the deceased laid over the bandaged head. In the case of our mummy there was neither mask nor portrait panel, only a shapeless expanse of bandages.

"It has been removed," said Emerson, as I ran an inquiring hand over this part of the mummy.

"I believe you are right, Emerson. There are streaks of glue, or some other adhesive, remaining, and the bandages seem to have been disturbed."

"And," Emerson concluded, "here it is."

Over the featureless head he laid the portrait panel he had rescued from Abd el Atti's shop.

John gasped. The painting, which was remarkably lifelike, animated the whole anonymous bundle and changed its character. A woman lay before us, swathed in grave clothes. Her great liquid dark eyes seemed to return our curious stares with an expression of gentle inquiry; the curved lips smiled at our consternation.

"Two pieces of the puzzle," said Emerson. "All we need now is a coffin."

"It is destroyed—burned," I said certainly. "This is the baroness's mummy, Emerson."

"I believe so, Peabody. As I watched the coffin burn the other night, I was struck by the fact that it was so quickly consumed, with little remaining except ashes. Certainly these mummified bodies, saturated with bitumen, burn readily, but there ought to have been some sign of its presence—a scrap of bone or the remains of an amulet. John—"

The young man jumped. His eyes were fixed in horrified fascination on the mummy. "Sir," he stuttered.

"You put the mummy case in the storeroom. Did you notice any difference in the weight, compared to the ones you had handled before?"

"It was not so heavy as the others," John said.

"Why the devil didn't you say so?" I demanded.

"Now, Peabody, don't scold the boy. He is not accustomed to handling mummy cases; one cannot expect him to realize that the fact was significant."

"True. I apologize, John."

"Oh, madam—" John broke off with a gulp. His eyes widened till the whites showed around the pupils. Emerson had picked up a knife and poised it over the breast of the mummy. "Oh, sir—oh, my goodness—sir—"

"I don't want to disturb the pattern of the bandaging," Emerson explained. "The fabric closest to the body is probably set in a solid mass anyway." The muscles on his forearms stood out as he forced the knife through the layers of linen.

John yelped and covered his eyes with his hands.

"Hmmm," said Emerson, cutting delicately. "Here's one—a *djed* pillar in blue faience. The heart scarab should be nearby. . . . Yes, and a rather good specimen too. Green feldspar."

"He is looking for amulets," I told John. "Magical objects, you know. Quantities of them were wrapped in with the bandages. The *djed* pillar indicated stability, the heart scarab insured that the heart—the seat of the intelligence—would not be taken away by demons. These two amulets are almost always found in the chest area—"

"Don't tell me about it, madam," John begged, pressing his hands tightly over his eyes.

Emerson threw down the knife. "There is no need to dismember the specimen further. Doubtless we would find more amulets and ornaments—the lady appears to have been moderately well-to-do—but the point has been made, I believe."

I nodded. "The mummy and its accoutrements are as unremarkable as the coffin. How very vexing! Come, come, John, Professor Emerson is finished; don't stand there like a model posing for a statue of horror."

John uncovered his eyes, but kept them resolutely turned away from the mummy. "I beg pardon, sir and madam. It was just—she looks so real, lying there like that."

Now there seemed to be a look of mild reproach in the luminous dark eyes. I picked up a coverlet from the sofa and tossed it over the mutilated body. John let out a sigh of relief. "Thank you, madam. May I take her back to the storeroom now?"

"'It,' not 'she,'" Emerson said shortly. "You will never make an archaeologist, John, if you allow such bathetic thoughts to intrude."

"Thank you, sir, but I don't want to be an archaeologist. Not that it isn't useful work, sir, I don't say that; but I don't think I 'ave the temperament for it."

"I am afraid you are right, John. It is a pity you cannot emulate ME. These are only specimens; they have no identity; one must regard them with calm dispassion and not allow sentimentality to affect one." He had stretched out his hand to remove the portrait panel. For a moment his fingers hovered. Then he said, "Fasten it on, Amelia, or it will fall and be broken when the mummy is moved."

It would have been simpler to return the panel to the padded box I had prepared for it, but I did not make that suggestion. I placed the padding carefully over the portrait and bound it in place with strips of cloth. Wrapping the coverlet around the mummy, John lifted it in his arms.

Lamp in hand, I accompanied him as he carried it back to the storeroom. If I may say so, the subject was worthy of one of our finest painters—the somber shadows of the ruined cloister, the single bright circle of lamplight, and the mighty form of the young man pacing in measured strides with the white-wrapped form held to his breast. I was not unsympathetic with John's mood, but I did hope he was not about to transfer his affections from Charity to the mummy. Charity had not encouraged him, but there can be no more unresponsive recipient of love than a woman who has been dead for seventeen hundred years, give or take a century.

After I had locked the door I thanked John and told him he could now retire. He said hesitantly, "If it would not be an inconvenience, madam—could I sit with you and the professor for a while?"

"Certainly, John; you know you are always welcome. But I thought you were occupied with Leviticus."

"Numbers, madam; I had got as far as Numbers. I don't think madam, I will ever get past Numbers."

"Don't lose heart; you can succeed at anything if you try." To be honest, my encouragement was a trifle abstracted. John's romantic and religious problems had begun to bore me, and I had more pressing matters on my mind.

As we passed Ramses' door I saw the too-familiar slit of light beneath it. I was surprised he had not popped his head out to ask what we were doing, for he was usually as curious as a magpie. I tapped on the door. "Lights out, Ramses. It is past your bedtime."

"I am working on somet'ing, Mama. May I have a half-hour's grace, please?"

"What are you working on?"

There was a pause. "The Coptic manuscript, Mama," he said at last.

"You will ruin your eyes studying that faded script by lamplight. Oh, very well; half an hour, no more."

"T'ank you, Mama. Good night, Mama. Good night, John."

"Good night, Master Ramses."

"I wonder how he knew you were with me," I said musingly.

When we returned to the parlor Emerson was gathering his scattered papers. "What a mess," he grumbled. "Give me a hand, will you, John?"

John hastened to oblige. The papers having been restored to the table, he asked eagerly, "Is there anything I can do for you, sir?"

"No, thank you; I will have to sort them myself. Go back to your Bible, John—and much good may it do you."

John gave me a look of appeal and I said, "John wants to sit with us awhile, Emerson. Proceed, John. Sit."

John sat. He sat on the edge of the chair, hands on his knees and eyes fixed on Emerson. It was impossible to work with that silent monument present; I was not surprised when after a time Emerson put down his pen and commented, "You appear to be at loose ends, John. You have about you a certain air of indecision. Is something troubling you?"

I knew John would not confide in him. The poor lad had been subjected to many derisive comments on the subject of religion, and although Emerson had been—for Emerson—fairly considerate about John's romantic yearnings, his generally sardonic look and manner was not of the sort that would inspire a young lover to pour out the (usually insipid) sentiments that fill his heart. Emerson's attachment to me is romantic, but it is never insipid.

John scratched his head. "Well, sir . . ."

"The young lady, I suppose. Give it up, John. You will never make headway there; she has given her heart to Brothers David and Ezekiel, and to Jesus—not necessarily in that order."

"Emerson, you are being rude," I said.

"I am never rude," Emerson said indignantly. "I am consoling John and assisting him to a better understanding. If he wishes to persist in his absurd attachment I won't stand in his way. Have I stood in his way? Have I prevented his wandering off to the mission half the evenings in the week? What do you do there, John?"

"Well, sir, we talk, sir. It is what Brother Ezekiel calls the hour of social intercourse."

Emerson's mouth widened into a grin. I coughed in a pointed manner, catching my eye, he refrained from comment, and John went on, "Brother Ezekiel speaks of his boyhood days. His mother, sir, must have been a regular saint. He can't tell how many switches she wore out on him—beating the devils out, you know, sir. I tell them about what's going on here—"

"You gossip about us?" Emerson demanded in awful tones.

"Oh, no, sir, I would never gossip about you and Mrs. Emerson. Only the little things that happen, and Master Ramses' adventures, like . . . Brother David explains Scripture and helps me with my reading."

"And what does Charity talk about?" I asked.

"She don't talk, madam, she sits and sews—shirts for the children and for Brother Ezekiel."

"It sounds very dull," said Emerson.

"Well no, sir, I won't say dull; but it ain't exactly lively, if you understand me."

"Aha!" Emerson burst out laughing. "Amelia, I believe I detect the first crack in the devotional facade. There may be hope for the lad yet. John, you had better spend your evenings with Abdullah and the men, improving your Arabic. Their conversation is a good deal more lively."

"No, sir, I can't do that. To tell the truth, sir, I'm worried about the reverends. There ain't so many converts as there was. One of the children threw a stone at Sister Charity t'other day. And there's been other things."

"Humph." Emerson stroked his chin. "You confirm my own fears, John. Something will have to be done about it. Well, my lad, I'm glad you unburdened yourself. Off to bed with you now; Mrs. Emerson and I will deal with the matter."

After John had gone, Emerson said complacently, "I knew he had something on his mind. You see, Amelia, a little tact, a little sympathy are all that is needed to win the confidence of an unassuming lad like John."

"Humph," I said. "What are you going to do, Emerson?"

"Steps must be taken," said Emerson, firmly but vaguely. "I do wish people would work out their own problems and not expect me to rescue them. No more, Amelia; I have work to do."

His pen began driving across the page. I picked up my pen; but instead of the scale drawing of the pottery fragments I was making, a vision intruded between my sight and the page—that of a painted woman's face with liquid dark eyes and a faint, enigmatic smile.

How could I concentrate on pots or even pyramids when an unsolved crime demanded my attention? The very perplexity of the problem held an unholy fascination; for I felt sure all the scraps of fact fit into a pattern, if I could only make it out. Mummy and mummy case, portrait panel and Twelfth Dynasty pectoral, murder, burglary, arson. . . . All parts of a single underlying plot.

Before me on the table lay the lists Emerson had made of the contents of Abd el Atti's shop. I put out a cautious hand. Emerson did not look up. I drew the lists to me.

It came, not as a dazzling burst of mental illumination, but as a tiny pinhole of light. Slowly it widened, meeting another crack of understanding here, connecting with something else there. . . .

The scratch of Emerson's pen stopped. I looked up to find him watching me. "At it again, Amelia?"

"I think I have it, Emerson. The clue is here." I held up the lists.

"One of the clues, Peabody."

"You have a new theory, Emerson?"

"More than a theory, my dear. I know who murdered Hamid and Abd el Atti."

"So do I, Emerson."

Emerson smiled. "I expected you would say that, Peabody. Well, well; shall we enter into another of those amiable competitions—sealed envelopes, to be opened after we have apprehended the killer?"

"My dear Emerson, there is no need of that. I would never doubt your word. A simple statement to the effect that you knew all along will suffice—accompanied, of course, by an explanation of how you arrived at the answer."

Emerson reflected, but the advantages of the arrangement were so obvious that he did not reflect long. A humorous twinkle brightened his blue eyes as he nodded agreement. "I can hardly do less than return the compliment. Your hand on it, my dear Peabody!"

II

I spoke no more and no less than the truth when I told Emerson I had discovered the identity of the murderer; however, in the privacy of these pages I will admit that a few of the details still eluded me. I was pondering how best to acquire the necessary information when an event occurred that gave me the chance I needed. I refer to the discovery of the entrance to our pyramid.

So bright was the flame of detective fever that that statement, which would ordinarily be adorned by several exclamation marks, is presented as a simple fact. I was not entirely unmoved, never believe that; the sight of the dark hole gaping in the ground roused a brief spurt of enthusiasm and only Emerson's strong arm, plucking me back, prevented me from entering at once.

After a brief examination he emerged covered with dust and gasping for breath. "It is in wretched condition, Peabody. Some of the stones lining the passageways have collapsed. They will have to be shored up before any of us goes farther in."

His eyes moved over the group of workmen, all of whom were as excited as he. One man bounced up and down on his toes, waving his arms. Mohammed was short and fat, with small, pudgy hands; but those hands had a delicacy of touch unequaled by any others in the group. He was a carpenter by trade, when he was not employed by us—the best possible man for the task that awaited us—and he knew it.

Emerson grinned companionably at him. "Be careful, Mohammed. There are some planks remaining from the construction of the donkey shed, I believe; start with those. I will go to the village and find more."

"You could send one of the men," I remarked, as we walked away, leaving Abdullah shouting orders.

"So I could," said Emerson agreeably.

"I will go with you."

"I rather thought you might, Peabody."

"And afterwards, a call on M. de Morgan?"

"We are as one, Peabody. A final roundup of our suspects, eh?"

"Suspects, Emerson? You said you knew the answer."

"Ah, but this is a complex matter, Peabody—a criminal conspiracy, no less. Several people may be involved."

"Quite true, Emerson."

Emerson grinned and gave me an affectionate pat on the back. "I also intend to have a word with the missionaries. I promised John I would. . . . Just a moment, Peabody. Where is Ramses?"

He was, as Emerson had feared, in the thick of the group clustered around the entrance to the pyramid. Emerson took him aside. "You heard me warn Mohammed to be careful?"

"Yes, Papa. I was only—"

Emerson took him by the collar. "Mohammed is our most skilled carpenter," he said, emphasizing each word with a gentle shake. "The task will be dangerous, even for him. You are not under any circumstances to attempt to assist him or go one step into that or any other passageway. Is that clear, my boy?"

"Yes, Papa."

Emerson released his grip. "Will you come with us, Ramses?"

"No, Papa, I think not. I will just go and do a little digging. I will take Selim, of course."

"Don't go far."

"Oh, no, Papa."

I had not been in the village for several days. Outwardly it looked normal enough—the group of women gathered around the well filling the huge jars they carried with such apparent ease atop their heads, the men lounging in the shade, the stray dogs sprawled in the dust of the path. But the greetings were strangely subdued, and none of the children accosted us with their perennial and pitiful demands for baksheesh.

Emerson went straight to the house of the priest. At first it appeared we would be refused entrance. The guard—one of the "deacons," as Emerson called them—insisted the priest was still praying. Then the door opened.

"You fail in courtesy to guests, my son," said the deep voice of the priest. "Bid them enter and honor my house."

When we had seated ourselves on the divan the priest asked how he could serve us. Emerson explained our need of wooden planks, and the priest nodded. "They shall be found. I hope your walls have not fallen down—your roof given way—your peace disturbed, in that ill-omened place?"

"It is the pyramid that has fallen down," Emerson replied. "We have had troubles at the monastery, to be sure, but they were not caused by demons; they were the work of evil men."

The priest shook his head sympathetically. I almost expected him to click his tongue.

"You did not know of these things?" Emerson persisted. "The breaking into my house, the attack on my son?"

"It is unfortunate," the priest said.

"'Unfortunate' is not the word. A man murdered, a fire at the mission—it seems, Father, that there have been too many 'unfortunate' happenings."

Even in the shadows where he sat I saw the flash of the priest's eyes. "Since the coming of the men of God. We had no trouble before they came."

"They did not set the fire," Emerson said. "They did not break into my house."

"You think my people did these things? I tell you, it is the men of God who are responsible. They must go. They cannot stay here."

"I know there has been provocation, Father,"

Emerson said. "I beg you—I warn you—do not let yourself be provoked."

"Do you take me for a fool?" the priest asked bitterly. "We are no more than slaves in this country, tolerated only so long as we do nothing. If I lifted my hand against the men of God, I and all my people would die."

"That is true," I said.

The priest rose. "You come here and accuse me of violence and crime. I tell you again—look to the men of God for answers to your questions. Find out for yourself what kind of men they are. They must leave this place. Tell them."

We could not have been more firmly dismissed. Emerson bowed in silence, and I felt a certain . . . well, perhaps embarrassment is the proper word. For the first time I could see the priest's point of view. The strangers had moved into his town, told his people they were wrong, threatened his spiritual authority, and he had no recourse, for the strangers were protected by the government. A way of life centuries old was passing; and he was helpless to prevent it.

We walked away from the priest's house. Emerson said, "Perhaps we can persuade Brother Ezekiel to set up headquarters elsewhere."

"It will require superhuman tact to persuade him, Emerson. The slightest hint that he may be in danger will only make him more determined to stay."

"Tact, or a direct order from the Almighty." Emerson's face brightened. "I wonder . . ."

"Put it out of your head, Emerson. Your simple parlor magic may work with our people, but I do not believe you can deceive Brother Ezekiel into taking your voice for that of Another."

The mission was a scene of utter tranquillity. School was in session. The drone of voices came through the open windows like the buzz of bees on a lazy summer afternoon. The shadows of palm and tamarisk lay cool upon the ground; and in a shady corner a sewing class was in progress. The little girls sat with their bare feet modestly tucked under their somber robes and their shining black heads bent over their work. Perched on the block that had served Emerson as a seat, Charity was reading aloud from the Arabic translation of the New Testament. Her gown was of the same dark print she always wore, and perspiration sparkled on her face, but for once she was without the hideous bonnet. Her pronunciation was poor; but her voice was soft and sweet, and the beautiful old story took on added charm because she read it with such feeling. " 'And Jesus said "Let the little children come to me; for the Kingdom of Heaven is theirs." ' "

I felt as if I were seeing the other side of the argument the priest had presented so eloquently. Brother Ezekiel was the most irritating man in the world and, in my opinion, wholly unfit for the profession he had embraced; but the missionaries were performing a worthwhile task, particularly with the ignorant and ignored little girls. Coptic women were no better off than their Muslim sisters. If the missionaries did nothing else, they might be the salvation of the women of Egypt.

I think even Emerson was moved, though one would not have known it from his expression. Few people see Emerson's softer side; in fact, some people deny that he has one.

It was not the time for sentiment, however. I repressed my emotions and Emerson said in a low voice, "We are in luck. Here's our chance to talk to the girl alone."

I cleared my throat loudly. There was a serpent in the little Paradise after all; the harmless sound made Charity start violently and look around with fear writ large upon her face. I stepped out from the shadow of the trees. "It is only I, Miss Charity. And Professor Emerson with me. Resume your seat, I beg, and let us have a little chat."

She sank down upon the stone from which she had risen in her alarm. "You may go home now girls," I said. "Class is over."

One of the youngsters began the old cry of baksheesh, but cut it off after glancing at Charity. I took a seat beside the girl. "I apologize for startling you," I said.

Emerson made an impatient gesture. "We are wasting time, Peabody. Heaven knows how soon we will be interrupted. What are you afraid of, child?"

He knelt beside her. I expected she would flinch away, but something in the stern face so near her own seemed to give her courage. She even smiled faintly. "I was absorbed in that wonderful story, Professor. I was not expecting anyone—"

"Bah!" Emerson exclaimed. "Doesn't your creed tell you that lying is a sin, Miss Charity?"

"It was the truth, sir."

"A half-truth at best. This village is no longer safe, child. Can't you persuade your brother to go elsewhere?"

The girl lifted her head. "You see what we are doing here, sir. Can we admit defeat—can we abandon these helpless infidels?"

I caught the eye of one of the infidels, who was peeking at us from behind a tree trunk. She gave me a wide impudent grin. I shook my head, smiling.

Emerson shook his head, frowning. "You are in danger, and I believe you know it. Is there no way . . . What is it, Peabody?"

"Someone is watching from the window of the house," I reported. "I saw the curtain move. Yes, curse it—the door is opening; he is coming."

"Curse it," Emerson repeated. "Don't get up, Miss Charity; listen to me. There may come a time when you need our help. Send to us, at any hour of the day or night."

Charity did not reply. Brother Ezekiel was almost upon us.

"Well, if it isn't the professor and his worthy helpmeet," he said. "What are you setting there for, Charity? Why don't you invite them to come in?"

Charity rose like a puppet pulled by strings. "I am neglectful," she said. "Forgive me, brother."

"Not at all," said Emerson, though the apology had not been intended for him. "We were just—er—passing by."

"You will come into my house," Brother Ezekiel said solemnly. "We will break bread together. Charity, summon Brother David."

"Yes, brother." She glided off, hands clasped, head bowed, and we followed her brother into the house.

I had always thought the expression "painfully clean" a figure of speech. The small parlor into which we were ushered made me wince, it was so bare, so blazingly whitewashed, so agonizingly spare of comfort. A few straight chairs, a table upon which were several candles and a Greek New Testament; no rug on the floor nor cloth on the table nor picture on the wall, not even one of the hideous religious chromos I had seen in homes of other religious persons. The Brethren of the Holy Jerusalem appeared to take the Bible literally, including the injunction against graven images. The only attractive piece of furniture in the room was a bookcase; I was drawn to it as a person coming in from the cold is drawn to a fire. Most of the books were ponderous theological tomes in several languages, or collections of sermons.

We were soon joined by Brother David. I had not seen him for some time, and the change in him made me stare. His black suit hung loosely on his frame; the glowing marble of his skin had a sickly cast, and his eyes were sunk in their sockets. My inquiries after his health were sincere. He smiled unconvincingly. "Indeed, I am quite well, Mrs. Emerson. Only a little tired. I am not accustomed to the—to the heat."

I exchanged an expressive look with Emerson. We were now well into the winter season, and the climate was superb—cool enough after sunset to make a wrap necessary and pleasantly warm during the day.

Brother Ezekiel appeared to be in an unusually

affable mood. Rubbing his hands, he declared, "Charity is getting the food ready. You'll have a bite with us."

"We cannot stay," I said. "We found the entrance to the pyramid this morning and our men are at work shoring up parts of the passageway that have collapsed. We ought to be there."

I had unconsciously turned to Brother David as I made this explanation; it was his colleague who replied, and his words explained some of his good humor. "Yes, we heard you had stopped digging at the cemetery. I'm glad you took my words to heart, friends. You committed a grievous error, but your hearts were not of adamant; you did right in the end."

Emerson's eyes flashed, but he can control his temper when it serves his purpose. "Er—yes. Mr. Jones, we came to talk to you about a serious matter. There have been a number of distressing incidents, not only here but in our house."

"You are referring to the death of poor Brother Hamid?" David asked.

"In the past ten days," said Emerson, "there has been a murder, three burglaries, a fire here at the mission and another mysterious fire in the desert. I understand Miss Charity was also attacked."

"Some naughty child—" Brother David began.

"It was no child who broke into my son's room."

"Are you implying that these incidents are connected?" Brother David asked doubtfully. "How can that be? The criminal acts committed against you—and the baroness—have nothing to do with us. Our own small difficulties are of the sort we have come to expect; the hearts of those who wander in darkness are of flint, but eventually our gentle persuasion will—"

Emerson cut him off with a loud "Bah!" He went on, "I warned you before. I warn you again. The dangers that threaten us all may not be entirely of your making, but you are not improving matters by your intemperate behavior. Leave off attacking the priest, or find another place in which to employ your gentle persuasion."

Brother Ezekiel only smiled smugly and emitted a string of pompous references to truth, duty, salvation and the glorious crown of the martyr. The final item cast a deeper gloom over Brother David's morose countenance, but he remained silent.

Emerson turned to me. "We are wasting our time, Amelia. Let us go."

"I bear no malice," Brother Ezekiel assured him. "The meek shall inherit the earth, and I stand ready at all times to pour the refreshing water of salvation on the spirit of the haughty. You have only to ask and it will be given unto you, for there is no way to the Father but through me. Come to me at any hour, Brother Emerson."

Fortunately Emerson was at the door when he heard this affectionate epithet, and I was able to propel him out with a hard shove.

We had not gone far when we heard footsteps, and turned to see Brother David running toward us.

"Do you really think we are in danger?" he panted.

Emerson's eyebrows rose. "What the devil do you suppose I came here for if not to warn you of that? It was not for the pleasure of Jones's company, I assure you."

"But surely you overestimate the peril," the young man persisted. "Brother Ezekiel's zeal sometimes overcomes his sense of caution. The saints of the Lord do not know fear—"

"But we weaker vessels do," Emerson said drily. "Don't be ashamed to admit it, Mr. Cabot."

"I am concerned," David admitted. "But I tell you, Professor, the incidents you mentioned cannot be the result of our labors here."

"What is your theory?" Emerson asked, watching him keenly.

David flung out his hands in a despairing gesture. "It can only be that, by an unhappy accident, we have stumbled into the midst of some sinister conspiracy."

"An interesting idea," said Emerson.

"But what can we do?"

"Leave," Emerson said tersely.

"That is impossible. Brother Ezekiel would never consent—"

"Then let him stay and roast," said Emerson impatiently. "Take the young woman and go. That idea does not appeal to you? Think it over. If common sense triumphs over your devotion to your leader, we will assist you in any way possible. But the decision must be yours."

"Yes, of course," David said unhappily. He stood twisting his hands, the very picture of guilt and indecision.

We walked back to the fountain, where we had left the donkeys. As we rode away Emerson said,

"An interesting encounter, Peabody. Cabot knows more than he is telling. Would you care to hazard a guess as to the nature of the guilty secret that lies hidden in his heart?"

"Nonsense, Emerson. It is not guilt but terror that affects him. He is suffering all the torments of cowardice—afraid to go and afraid to stay. I am sadly disappointed in the young man. What a pity that his manly face and figure do not indicate his real character."

"So that is the way your theories tend, is it?"

"I will say no more at the present time," I replied. "Let us assume, however, just for the sake of argument, that the missionaries are innocent but stupid. Your attempt at persuasion has failed, as I knew it would; do you intend to take any further steps to save them?"

"I suppose I might talk to Murch or another of the Protestant missionaries, and endeavor to find the home base of the Brothers of Jerusalem. Ezekiel's superiors ought to know what is going on here. But I have a feeling, Peabody, that other events are about to transpire that will make such a step unnecessary."

I felt the same. But neither of us knew how imminent were those events, or how dreadful would be their consequences, not only to the missionaries but to ourselves and those we held dear.

III

Though in one sense our visit had not borne fruit, it had not been entirely without value insofar as our criminal investigations were concerned. I had confirmed one of my suspicions. I wondered if Emerson's thoughts tended along the same line. He looked rather pleased with himself, so I was afraid they did.

We were not so lucky with our second group of suspects. De Morgan was not in camp, and his men were sprawled in the shade, resting and smoking. Emerson's roar made them scramble to their feet. The foreman came running to greet us. He hung his head when Emerson began lecturing him, but said that the effendi had given them leave to stop work; it was the time of the midday rest period. The effendi had gone to visit the lady on the dahabeeyah.

"What lady?" I asked.

"You know her, Sitt. The German lady who was here before. She has returned. It is said," the headman added naively, "that she wishes to give the effendi much money for his work. Will you go there also, to get money from the lady?"

"No," Emerson said hastily.

"No," I agreed. "When will M. de Morgan return?"

"Only Allah knows, Sitt. Will you wait for him?"

"Shall we, Emerson?" I asked.

"Hmmm." Emerson rubbed his chin. "I think I will just have a quick look around. You might wait in the tent, Amelia."

"But, Emerson, I also want to—"

"You might wait in the tent of M. de Morgan, Peabody."

"Oh. Oh, yes. That is an excellent idea, Emerson." It seemed like an excellent idea then, but it did not prove to be so, except in a negative sense. I discovered that M. de Morgan was a tidy man, which I had already suspected, and that his notes were not well organized, which I had also suspected. However, there was nothing in the notes, or in the packing cases that served as storage cupboards, that should not have been there. I had never considered de Morgan a serious suspect, of course.

I felt a little uncomfortable searching the place, but told myself that all is fair in love, war and detective work. I then put my head in the next tent, which was presumably occupied by Prince Kalenischeff, but it was even more barren of clues. In fact, it was bare. There was no sign of his personal possessions.

I found Emerson squatting by one of M. de Morgan's tunnels peering into the depths and lecturing the foreman. "Look at this, Peabody," he cried. "He has hopelessly disturbed the stratification. How the devil the man expects—"

"If you have finished, we had better return," I said.

"That wall is almost certainly of the Old Kingdom, and he has cut straight through without . . . What? Oh yes. Let us be off."

The head man's dour expression lightened. He had been deprived of most of his rest period; he saw hopes of enjoying a part of it, at least.

"Where is the other gentleman?" I asked.

"The One with the Glass Eye? He is gone, Sitt. He sails with the lady tomorrow."

"Aha," said Emerson.

"Aha," I repeated.

We mounted our donkeys. "Thank goodness that is over," Emerson said. "I have learned what I needed to know and can wind this business up in short order."

"What did you learn from the foreman, Emerson?"

"What did you find in the tent, Peabody?"

"Slow down, if you please. I cannot talk or think while bouncing up and down on a donkey."

Emerson obliged. "Well? Fair is fair, Peabody."

"Oh, certainly, Emerson. But I have nothing to contribute. Only the fact that Kalenischeff has left, which I deduced from the absence of his luggage."

"Nothing suspicious among de Morgan's gear?"

"Not a thing."

Disappointment lengthened Emerson's face. "Ah, well, I feared it was too good to be true. He is making little headway with his excavations. No sign of the burial chamber, and the nearby private tombs have all been robbed—stripped of everything, even the mummies."

"I never really suspected him, Emerson."

"Neither did I, Peabody."

IV

When we reached Mazghunah we found that work had stopped. The passage was in such poor condition it could not be dug out. Mohammed had narrowly escaped being buried alive when the shattered walls gave way; and, after he had examined the situation, Emerson commended Abdullah on his good sense in halting further attempts.

"I feared from the start this would eventuate," he told me. "We will have to clear the entire area and get at the chambers of the substructure from above. The superstructure has entirely disappeared, except for that small mass of brickwork on the north side. Apparently the subterranean passageways have collapsed; you saw how the ground above has sunk in."

"I am sure you are right, Emerson."

"My heartfelt apologies, Peabody. I know how you love crawling on your hands and knees through dark, stifling tunnels; but in this case . . ."

"My dear Emerson, it is not your fault that the pyramid is in disrepair. We must not risk our men on a hopeless task."

My cheerful tone did not deceive my husband, but I kept the smile fixed on my face until he had left me. Only then did I allow my countenance to reflect the disappointment that filled my heart. I had resigned myself to a sunken pit in place of a towering pyramid, but I had hoped for a substructure. In some pyramids the burial chamber and the passages leading to it were built into the pyramid itself. The internal chambers of others were dug wholly or in part into the rock of the plateau on which the pyramid stood. Ours was one of the latter type, but now my dreams of exploring its mysterious interior were over.

Ramses heard the tragic news with his customary appearance of equanimity, remarking only, "I surmised as much when de wall fell on Mohammed." I had begun to believe he might have inherited my enthusiasm for pyramids, but this phlegmatic reaction cast grave doubts on such a hypothesis. He did not join us when we returned to work after a hasty luncheon.

Early in the afternoon the men came on a portion of wall over forty inches thick. Deducing that this was part of the enclosure wall of the pyramid, and that its outline defined the extent of the pyramid foundations, Emerson set the crew to work tracing its four sides. I could see it would take several weeks to clear the entire enclosure, for the loose sand kept trickling back into the trenches almost as fast as it was dug out.

Ramses went to his room immediately after supper, while Emerson and I turned to the clerical and recording chores that are a necessary if boring part of any archaeological expedition. The next day was payday; with John's assistance Emerson began totaling the men's wages, which varied according to the hours each had put in, the type of work, and the rewards given for objects found. Our evenings had been so lively, with burglaries and detective investigations, that to pass one quietly was an anticlimax. I found myself yawning over my work and was about to suggest we retire early when I heard voices outside.

One was the voice of our loyal Abdullah, raised in peremptory challenge. The other was softer; I could not make out the words it spoke. After a moment Abdullah knocked at the door.

"A man brought this, Sitt," he said, handing me a folded paper.

"What man?"

Abdullah shrugged. "One of the infidels."

"Thank you, my friend."

Abdullah bowed and withdrew.

"Well, Peabody, what is it?" Emerson asked, adding a finished page to the stack of pay sheets.

"It appears to be a note. It is addressed to me. I don't recognize the writing, but I think I can guess—"

"Stop guessing and open it," Emerson said impatiently.

I shook off the strange apprehension that had seized me. Never before had I had so strong a sensation of evil—of some monstrous shadow waiting in the darkness with fangs bared. And all from a folded sheet of paper!

Something in my expression as I read alerted the others. Emerson threw down his pen and rose. John sat staring, mute and expectant.

"It is from Charity," I said. "Your warning was not in vain after all, Emerson. She asks for our help."

"When?"

"Now. This very night."

John leaped to his feet. "Wot 'as 'appened?" he cried, wringing his hands. "Where is she? Is she in danger?"

"Now, John, calm yourself. She is in no immediate danger. She asks us to meet her . . ." I checked myself. John's staring eyes and pallid cheeks testified to the depth of his concern. I did not want him running to the mission to rescue his lady; he had already displayed an unfortunate propensity for unnecessary rescues. I said, "Go to your room, John."

"You can't talk to him as if he were Ramses," said Emerson. "Speaking of Ramses—"

"Yes, quite. I follow you, Emerson. John, I assure you there is no need for alarm. We will meet the young lady and listen to her story. If in our opinion there is the slightest cause for concern as to her safety, we will fetch her here."

"You'll come at once and tell me what 'as 'appened, madam," John implored.

"Of course. Run along now."

John departed, with dragging steps and backward looks. I handed Emerson the note.

"Midnight," Emerson muttered. "Why do all persons in distress pick on midnight? It is a damned inconvenient hour, too early to get some sleep beforehand and too late to—"

"Sssh. I don't want anyone to overhear. Especially Ramses."

"She does not appear to have any sense of imminent peril," Emerson said, reading on. "But she is obviously distressed. What do you suppose, is this 'terrible thing' she has discovered?"

"I have an idea, I think."

"Oh yes, so do I. I only wondered whether she had discovered what I already know."

It lacked an hour till the time of the assignation. We employed it in putting Ramses to bed. He was in an aggravating mood, inventing one distraction after another in order to detain us. "I have deciphered de Coptic, Mama," was his final effort. "Do you want to know what it says?"

"Not now, Ramses. Tomorrow."

"It is very interesting, Mama. Dere is a mention on de smaller fragment of de son of—"

" 'The Son of God' is one of the appellations of Jesus," I explained. "Your religious training has been sadly neglected, Ramses. It is an omission I mean to remedy for, whatever are your dear papa's opinions on the subject, an English gentleman should be familiar with the rudiments, at least, of Anglican doctrine. Hop into bed, now."

"Yes, Mama. De gospel according to Saint Thomas—"

"That is just what I mean, Ramses. There is no gospel of Saint Thomas. Matthew, Mark, Luke and John. . . . There is a pretty little prayer that begins with the names of the Evangelists; I will teach it to you. But not now. Good night, my son."

"Good night, Mama," Ramses said resignedly.

The remaining time passed very slowly. I was intensely curious to hear what Charity would say. Finally Emerson decided we should leave. Abdullah had fallen asleep, but he woke instantly when we opened the door. Emerson explained we were going for a stroll and would be back before long.

"I wonder why she chose such a remote spot," he said, as we set out across the moonlit sands.

"She could hardly arrange to meet us in the village, Emerson. And she knows we have been working at the pyramid."

My heart beat fast as we approached the sunken area. The trenches of our excavations cast dark shadows against the pale ground. At first there was no sign of a living form. Then something moved. I caught Emerson's arm. "It is she! I would know that shape anywhere, especially that horrid bonnet."

For an instant she stood motionless as a black paper silhouette, slender and featureless. One arm lifted. The dark form glided silently away.

"She is beckoning us to follow," I exclaimed.

"So I see."

"Where the devil is she going?"

"No doubt she will explain when we catch her up."

Emerson increased his pace. I had to trot to keep up with him, yet the distance between us and the slender form ahead never grew less.

"Curse it," Emerson said. "This is ridiculous, Amelia. Is she going to run all the way to Dahshoor? I will give her a hail."

"No, don't do that! Even a low voice carries a long distance here; a shout would waken everyone for a mile around."

"Well, damnation, we have been walking for a mile."

"Hardly that, Emerson."

We went on for a time in silence. I began to share Emerson's annoyance, and yet there was something uncanny about that silent pursuit across the quiet sand. Ever retreating yet ever beckoning us onward, the figure ahead seemed not a living woman but a symbol of mysterious fate.

"Can she have mistaken us for someone else?" I panted.

"Impossible. The night is bright as day and we are, if I may say so, quite distinctive in appearance. Especially you, in those bloomers."

"They are not bloomers. They are Turkish trousers."

"And you are clashing like a German brass band."

"One never knows . . . when one will need . . ."

"Save your breath, Peabody. Ah—there—she is turning east toward the cultivation."

One lone palm, a giant of its kind, had invaded the rim of the waterless desert. The slim shadow vanished into its shade. Emerson broke into a trot and I into a run.

She was there. She awaited us. Her head turned.

Then from out of the very ground, or so it seemed, three ghostly forms emerged. Barely visible against the darkness, they moved with the speed and ferocity of the afreets they resembled. My hand went to my belt—too late! They were upon us. I heard Emerson's shout and the smack of his fist on flesh. Rough hands seized me; I was flung to the ground.

TEN

So sweet, submissive Charity was in reality the Master Criminal mistress of vicious thugs! I proceeded no further with my reflections on the case, for other considerations supervened: for one, a large foot planted in the small of my back holding me prostrate while rough hands stuffed a gag into my mouth and rapidly enclosed my body with cords. Even more distracting than physical discomfort was my apprehension concerning Emerson. No longer did the sounds of complaint and struggle reach my ears. The miscreants must have rendered him unconscious—or worse. . . . But no; I could not, I would not, entertain that ghastly thought.

One of the villains picked me up and tossed me over his shoulder. The muscular arm holding my lower limbs warned me of the futility of attempting to escape; I bent all my efforts instead to twisting my neck far enough to get a glimpse of Emerson. As my captor set out across the sands, I was finally rewarded in this endeavor, but what I saw was far from reassuring. Close behind came a pair of bare feet and a ragged robe. I could see no more of the second villain than that, owing to my unconventional posture, but behind the feet a lax, limp hand trailed through the sand. They were carrying him. Surely that must mean my dear Emerson yet lived. I clung to that thought while endeavoring to discern some sign of animation, however faint, in the member.

I could look no more. The discomfort of strained neck muscles forced me to relax. This brought my face in close proximity with the dirty robe covering my captor's body, and I was conscious of a strange odor, even more unpleasant than that of unwashed flesh. I knew that smell. It was the unmistakable stench of bat droppings.

I could see only a small expanse of the desert floor, but I am not a trained archaeologist for nothing; the nature of the debris that, before long, cluttered the surface told me of my location. We were approaching the Black Pyramid. My kidnapper came to a stop before a gaping hole in the ground. If I had not been incapable of speech I would have cried, "Good Gad," or something equally indicative of surprise; for that hole had not been in existence earlier. I did not like the look of it. I resumed my struggles. The wretch replied by dropping me onto the ground. Emerson lay beside me. His eyes were closed, but he looked quite peaceful. Most marvelous of all was the rise and fall of his massive breast. He lived! Thank heaven, he lived!

But for how long? This unpleasant question inevitably arose, and ensuing events made the answer seem highly doubtful. The man who had been carrying me seized me by the collar and started into the hole, dragging me after him.

It was not a grave pit, then, but a structure considerably more extensive. A wild surmise rose and strengthened as we went on into the darkness. I deduced the presence of a flight of steps leading downward, from the impression they made upon my helpless form. At the bottom of the stairs my captor paused to light a candle; then we went on, more rapidly than before, and in the same manner. In justice to the fellow who transported me in such an uncomfortable manner I must admit he had little choice; the ceiling of the passage was so low he had to bend double, and it would have been impossible for him to carry me.

The thieves had discovered the entrance to the interior chambers of the pyramid, which de Morgan had sought in vain. A thrill of archaeological fervor overcame my mental and physical distress. It soon faded, however, for even a lover of pyramids cannot enjoy being in one when she is in the position I then occupied—my collar choking me, the stones of the floor bruising my lower back. Another discomfort soon took precedence. The floor of the passageway was thick with sand and disintegrated bat manure. This rose in a cloud as we proceeded, and being so low to the floor, I found it increasingly hard to breathe.

The candle held by my kidnapper gave little light to my own surroundings. A twinkling starry point behind indicated the presence of the others. Were they still transporting my unconscious spouse, or had they flung his corpse into an empty tomb!

Decayed bat droppings are not precisely poisonous, but they cannot be breathed in too long without ill effect. My head began to swim. I was barely aware of being raised and dragged, or carried, up a wooden ladder. This occurred several times, and I verily believe that but for these intervals I would have been overcome by the effluvium of the excretions of the flying mammals. I had lost all sense of direction, despite my efforts to make a mental map of the path we followed. The passageways formed a veritable maze, designed to confuse tomb robbers as to the location of the king's burial chamber. It succeeded in confusing me, at any rate, but in my defense it must be said that my position was not conducive to clear thinking.

Finally the villain came to a stop. My eyes were streaming with tears from the irritation of the dusty dung. The man bent over me. I did not want him to think I was weeping from fear or weakness, so I blinked the tears away and frowned—that being the only expression of disapprobation available to me at that time. An unpleasant smile spread over his face, which shone like greased mahogany in the dim light. He held the candle in one hand. In the other hand was a long knife, polished to razor sharpness. The light ran in glimmering streaks along the blade.

Two quick slashes, and a sharp shove. . . . I toppled—tried to cry out—fell, helpless and blind, into impenetrable darkness.

An individual who has been kidnapped, bound

and gagged, suffocated and tossed into a seemingly bottomless pit in the heart of an unexplored pyramid—that individual is a fool if she is not afraid. I am not a fool. I was terrified. In the Stygian blackness the pit seemed a chasm into infinite depths where the monsters of the abyss lay waiting to devour the bodies and souls of the dead. One part of my frozen brain knew better, of course, but that part was well aware that the bottom of the pit was undoubtedly floored with stone, against which my bones would be broken to splinters.

I now believe the tales of those who claim to have relived their entire lives in the space of a few seconds, for those thoughts and others that do not merit description flashed through my mind in the moments that elapsed before I reached the bottom of the pit. To my astonishment I found it was covered with water. Under the water was mud and under the mud was stone. The presence of the water and the mud broke my fall, though it was hard enough to bruise me and knock the breath clean out of me. Not until I made instinctive swimming motions did I realize that my limbs had been freed. Swimming was unnecessary; the water and underlying slime were scarcely three feet deep. After I had gained my feet my first act was to pluck the gag from my mouth. It was saturated with water and tasted foul, but it had prevented me from swallowing the revolting liquid.

Scarcely had I gained an upright position when I was thrown back into the water by the impact of a heavy object that narrowly missed me and sent a fountain of spray high in the air. Without an instant's hesitation I dropped to my hands and knees and began feeling about. My groping hands encountered a substance that felt like the fur of a drowned animal, slippery with slime and water, but I knew the feel of it, wet or dry, muddy or slimy; and thanking heaven for Emerson's thick, healthy head of hair, I twisted both hands in it and dragged his head up from under the water. The angelic choir will sound no sweeter to me than the sputtering and cursing that told me Emerson was alive and conscious. Presumably the water on his face had brought him around.

His first act, after spitting out the mud that had filled his mouth, was to aim a blow at my jaw. I had expected this, and was able to avoid it, while announcing my identity in the lowest possible voice.

"Peabody!" Emerson gurgled. "Is it you? Thank God! But where the devil are we?"

"Inside the Black Pyramid, Emerson. Or rather, under it; though overcome by bat effluvium and other physical inconveniences, I am certain the general direction of the passageway was—"

During my reply Emerson had located my face by feeling around; he put an end to the speech by placing his mouth firmly over mine. He tasted quite nasty, but I did not mind.

Eventually Emerson stopped kissing me and remarked "Well, Peabody, we are in a pretty fix. The last thing I remember is an explosion somewhere around the base of my skull. I take it you did not have the same experience; or are you merely producing one of your imaginative hypotheses when you claim we are inside the pyramid? I have never been in one that was as wet as this."

"I was gagged and bound, but not unconscious. Emerson, they have found the entrance! It is not on the north side, where de Morgan looked, but at ground level near the southwest corner. No wonder he could not find it." A critical clearing of the throat from the darkness beside me reminded me that I was wandering off the subject, so I went on, "I suspect we are in the burial chamber itself. This pyramid is quite near the cultivation, if you recall; the recent inundation must have flooded the lower sections."

"I don't understand the point of this," Emerson said, in almost his normal voice. "Why did they not murder us? You can, I presume, find the way out."

"I hope so, Emerson. But this is a very confusing pyramid—a maze, one might say. And I was not at my best. The kidnapper dragged me most of the way and my—er—my body kept bumping on the stones, and—"

"Grrr," said Emerson fiercely. "Dragged you, you say? The villain! I will have his liver for that when I catch up with him. Never mind, Peabody; I would back you against any pyramid ever built."

"Thank you, my dear Emerson," I replied with considerable emotion. "First, though, we must have a look at our surroundings."

"I don't see how we are going to manage that, Peabody. Unless you can see in the dark, like the cat Bastet."

"According to Ramses, that is a folktale. Even cats require a small amount of light in order to see, and this darkness is almost palpable. Wait, Emerson, don't go splashing about; I will strike a light."

"All this banging on the posterior has weakened my poor darling's wits," Emerson muttered to himself. "Peabody, you cannot—"

The tiny flame of the match reflected in twin images in his wide eyes. "Hold the box," I instructed. "I need both hands for the candle. There. That is better, is it not?"

Standing in muddy water up to his hips, a purpling bruise disfiguring his brow and another, presumably, rising on the back of his head, Emerson nevertheless managed a broad and cheerful smile. "Never again will I sneer at your beltful of tools, Peabody."

"I am happy to find that the manufacturer's claim of the waterproof quality of the tin box was not exaggerated. We must not take chances with our precious matches; close the box carefully, if you please, and put it in your shirt pocket."

Emerson did so. Then at last we had leisure to look about us.

Our poor little candle flame was almost overcome by the vast gloom of the chamber. It illuminated only our drawn faces and dank, dripping locks. At the farthest edge of the bright circle a dim-looming object could be made out, rising like an island from the watery surface. Toward this we made our way.

"It is the royal sarcophagus," said Emerson unnecessarily. "And it is open. Curse it; we are not the first to find the pharaoh's final resting place, Peabody."

"The lid must be on the—oh dear—yes, it is. I have just stubbed my toe on it."

The red granite sides of the sarcophagus were as high as Emerson's head. Seizing me by the waist, he lifted me so I could perch on the ledgelike rim; it was fully a foot thick and made a commodious if uncomfortable seat.

"Let me have the candle," he said. "I will make a circuit of the walls."

He splashed through the water to the nearer side of the chamber. The walls shone in the candlelight as smoothly as if they had been cut from a single block of stone. My heart sank at the sight of the unbroken surface, but I summoned up a firm voice as I called to Emerson, "Hold the candle higher, my dear; I fell some considerable distance before striking the water."

"No doubt it seemed farther than it was," Emerson replied, but he complied with the suggestion. He had gone around two of the walls and was midway down the third before a darker shadow was visible high above the glow of the light. Emerson held the candle above his head.

He stood still as a statue, which in the dim light he rather resembled. His wet garments molded his muscular body and the candlelight brought the muscles and tendons of his upraised arm into shaded outline. The sight was one that will remain printed on my brain—the solemn grandeur of his pose, the funereal gloom of the surroundings—and the knowledge that the opening of the shaft which was our only hope of escape was far out of reach. Emerson is six feet tall; I am five feet and a bit. The hole was a good sixteen feet from the floor.

Emerson knew the truth as well as I. It was several moments before he lowered his arm and returned to my side. "I make it sixteen feet," he said calmly.

"It is nearer seventeen, surely."

"Five feet one inch and six feet—add the length of your arms—"

"And subtract the distance from the top of my head to my shoulders. . . ." In spite of the gravity of the situation I burst out laughing, the calculations sounded so absurd.

Emerson joined in, the echoes of his hearty mirth rebounding ghostily around the chamber. "We may as well try it, Peabody."

We had neglected to deduct the distance from the top of his head to his shoulders. When I stood upon the latter, my fingertips were a good three feet below the lip of the opening. I reported this to Emerson. "Humph," he said thoughtfully. "Supposing you stood on top of my head?"

"That would only give us another twelve or thirteen inches, Emerson. Not nearly enough."

His hands closed over my ankles. "I will lift you at arms' length, Peabody. Can you keep your knees rigid and maintain your balance by leaning toward the wall?"

"Certainly, my dear. When I was a child my highest ambition was to be an acrobat in a fair. Are you sure you can do it?"

"You are a mere feather, my dear Peabody. And if you can be an acrobat, I can aspire to the position of circus strongman. Who knows, if we ever tire of archaeology we can turn to another profession."

"Slowly, please, my dear."

"But of course, Peabody."

I believe I have had occasion to mention Emerson's impressive muscular development, but never before had I realized the full extent of his strength. A gasp escaped my lips when I felt nothing but empty air under the soles of my boots, but my initial trepidation was quickly succeeded by a thrill of pure excitement. I heard Emerson's breath catch and fancied I could almost hear his muscles crack. Slowly I rose higher. It was like flying—one of the most interesting experiences I have ever had.

I was afraid to tilt my head back in order to look up; the slightest movement might have destroyed the precarious balance Emerson and I were maintaining between us. When the upward movement finally ceased, there was nothing under my outstretched hands but the same cold, smooth stone. Emerson let out an inquiring grunt. I looked up.

"Three inches, Emerson. Can you—"

"Ugh," Emerson said decidedly.

"Lower me, then. We shall have to think of something else."

Going down was considerably less pleasant than going up. It was not only the consciousness of failure that weakened my knees, it was the ominous quivering of the arms that supported me. When my feet once more found secure footing on the brawny shoulders of my heroic spouse I leaned against the wall and let out a deep breath. It was as well I did so, for one of Emerson's hands lost its grip and I feared we were both going to topple over backwards.

"Sorry, Peabody," he said, taking a firmer hold. "Cramp."

"Small wonder, my dear Emerson. Don't bother to lower me, I will just let myself down bit by bit."

Somehow he found strength enough to laugh. "I will play Saint Christopher and carry you back to the sarcophagus. Sit on my shoulders."

After he had returned me to my seat he hoisted himself up beside me. We sat side by side, our feet dangling till Emerson got his breath back. "Have you still got the matchbox, Emerson?" I asked.

"You may be sure I have, Peabody. That little tin box is more precious to us now than gold."

"Let me have it, then, and I will button it into my shirt pocket. Then, if you agree, I will blow out the candle. I only have the one, you see."

He nodded, his face somber. The dark closed in upon us, but I did not mind; Emerson's arm was around me and my head rested on his shoulder. For some time we did not speak. Then a sepulchral voice remarked, "We will die in one another's arms, Peabody."

He seemed to find this thought consoling. "Nonsense, my dear Emerson," I said briskly. "Do not abandon hope. We have not yet begun to fight, as one of our heroes said."

"I believe it was an American hero who said it, Peabody."

"Irrelevant, my dear Emerson. It is the spirit of pluck I mean to conjure up."

"But when I die, Peabody, I would like the condition I mentioned to prevail."

"And I, my dearest Emerson. But I have no intention of dying for a long time. Let us turn our brains to the problem and see if we can't think of a way out."

"There is always the possibility of rescue," Emerson said.

"You need not attempt to raise my spirits by false hopes, Emerson. To be sure, I did wonder why our kidnappers would carry us here instead of murdering us outright; but they knew our chance of escape was almost nil. They won't come back. As for rescue from anyone else—to the best of my knowledge, no archaeologist has succeeded in locating the entrance. The villains will have filled in the hole they dug; do you suppose de Morgan can find it? He has no reason to look, for even after our disappearance is discovered, no one will think of searching for us here."

"De Morgan is certainly the least likely person to find an entrance to a pyramid," Emerson agreed. He added, "Peabody, I adore you and I meant it when I said I would not be averse to dying in your arms, but you do have a habit of running on and on, which is particularly trying at a time like this."

My dear Emerson was trying to cheer me with that teasing comment; I gave him an affectionate squeeze to show I understood. "Be that as it may," I said, "we had better not depend on outside help. What we need is something to stand on. A mere three inches shall not defeat us, Emerson."

"We can't move the sarcophagus. It must weigh half a ton."

"More, I fancy. And the cover is probably several hundred pounds in weight. But there may be other objects in the chamber, hidden under the mud. An alabaster canopic chest or cosmetic box—anything made of stone. Wooden objects would be rotted by time and immersion."

"We will have a look," Emerson agreed. "But first let us ascertain whether there are any other possibilities."

"Another entrance, for instance? That is certainly something we must investigate. A pity the ceiling is so high. It will be hard to see a crack or crevice, with only a candle for light."

"At any rate, we know there is no opening at floor level. Had that been the case, the water would have drained out."

Silence followed, as we bent our mind to the problem. Then Emerson chuckled. "This will do Petrie one in the eye," he said vulgarly. "He ran into something of the same sort at Hawara, if you remember. You know how he brags endlessly of how he cleared the chamber of the pyramid by sloshing around underwater and shoving things onto a hoe with his bare toes."

"He found a number of fine objects," I said. "That alabaster altar of Princess Ptahneferu—"

"Something of that nature would make an admirable box on which to stand."

"Alabaster dishes and bowls. . . . Only think, Emerson, what we might find here."

"Don't let archaeological fever get the better of you, Peabody. Even if . . . Even *when* we get out of here, we will not have the right to excavate. It is de Morgan's pyramid, not ours."

"He can't object if we make a few discoveries

while seeking a means of escape. That is our main purpose, is it not—escape!"

"Oh, certainly," Emerson agreed.

"I fear the writing implements attached to my belt have been rendered useless by the water. My pocket rule is functional, however; we will have to make mental notes of the location of anything we might find. That should not be difficult."

"You are a remarkable woman, Peabody. Few individuals, male or female, could think about antiquities while engaged in a struggle for survival."

"Your approbation pleases me more than I can say, Emerson. May I return the compliment?"

"Thank you, my dear Peabody. We will return to that subject later in—let us hope—more salubrious surroundings. Now, before you light the candle, let us be sure we have our strategy clearly in mind."

I was about to reply when I saw something that made me wonder if my brain was not beginning to weaken. It was only the faintest suggestion of light; but in that dank darkness, so thick it seemed to press against one's staring eyeballs, even a natural phenomenon carries sinister suggestions. The pale glow strengthened. It came from high in the wall—from the opening of the corridor. I pinched Emerson.

"Look," I hissed.

"I see it," he replied in equally subdued tones. "Quick, Peabody, down into the water."

He slid off the sarcophagus. With his assistance I followed suit. "Is it the villains returning, do you think?" I breathed.

"It can be no one else. Get behind the sarcophagus, Peabody. Keep out of sight and don't make a sound."

I heard the soft susurration of the water as he waded slowly away from me. There was no need for him to explain; my dear Emerson and I understand one another without words. The criminals had returned to make sure we were deceased, or to taunt us in our agony; if they saw no trace of us, they might be moved to descend, in order to search for our bodies. There was a slight hope of escape in that, if they lowered a rope or a rope ladder, and Emerson could seize it. I crouched low behind the shelter of the great stone box, braced and ready for whatever action suggested itself.

The opening was now a glowing yellow. Something showed silhouetted against the light. I could not see Emerson, but I knew he was pressed against the wall, under the shaft. My fingers closed around the handle of my knife.

Then occurred the most astonishing event of that astonishing evening. A voice spoke—a voice I knew, pronouncing a name only one individual in all the world employs for me. So great was my wonderment that I stood erect, banging my head painfully on the rim of the sarcophagus; and in that same instant, as I reeled and tried to collect my wits, the light went out, a voice shouted in alarm and horror, and something splashed heavily into the water not far away.

My initial impulse was to rush into action. But reason prevailed, as I hope it always does with me. I knew from the sounds of splashing, cursing and heavy breathing that Emerson was doing all he could to locate the fallen object; my intervention would only impede his search. My first act, therefore, was to strike a match and light the candle which I anchored carefully in a pool of its own grease on the wide rim of the sarcophagus. Then and only then did I look to see whether Emerson's quest had been successful.

He had risen from the water. In his arms was a muddy, dripping object. It moved; it was living. I groped for appropriate words.

"Ramses," I said. "I thought I told you you were never to go into any more pyramids."

ELEVEN

"Y ou said I might go in if you and Papa were wit'
me," said Ramses.

"So I did. Your reasoning is Jesuitical, Ramses; I
see we will have to have a talk about it one day.
However . . ." I stopped. Had Ramses emphasized,
ever so slightly, the preposition "in"? As I explained
earlier, the chambers and passages of pyramids are
sometimes internal, sometimes subterranean. Surely
not even Ramses' diabolically devious mind would
be capable of a distinction so Machiavellian. . . . I
promised myself I must explore that suspicion at a
more appropriate time.

"However," I resumed, "I appreciate your motives,
Ramses, and—Emerson, will you please put the boy
down and stop babbling?"

Emerson interrupted his mumbled endearments.
"I cannot put him down, Peabody. His mouth would
be underwater."

"That is true. Fetch him here, then. He can sit on
the sarcophagus."

I kept a precautionary hand on the candle when
Ramses was set down beside it. He was a dreadful

spectacle. A coating of dark mud covered him from head to foot. But I had seen him looking worse, and the bright eyes that peered at me from the mask of slime were alert and steady.

"As I was saying, Ramses, I appreciate your motives in coming to our rescue, as I suppose you intended. But I must point out that jumping into the pit with us was not helpful."

"I did not jump, Mama, I slipped. I brought a rope, t'inking dere would be some point of attachment in de passageway by means of which I might be able to—"

"I follow your reasoning, Ramses. But if the rope is, as I suppose, down here with you, it cannot be of great assistance."

"Dat was an unfortunate mishap," Ramses admitted.

"My boy, my boy," Emerson said mournfully. "I had consoled myself with the expectation that you would carry on the name of Emerson to glory and scientific achievement. Now we will all perish in one another's—"

"Please, Emerson," I said. "We have already discussed that. I don't suppose it occurred to you, Ramses, to fetch help instead of rushing in where angels fear to tread?"

"I was in some haste and concerned for your safety," said Ramses, swinging his feet and dripping. "However, I did leave a message."

"With whom?" Emerson asked hopefully.

"Well, you see, de circumstances were confusing," Ramses said calmly. "I had followed you when you slipped out of de house—I debated wit' myself for some little time before doing so, but could not recall, Mama, dat you had specifically forbidden me to follow you and Papa when you slipped out of de—"

"Good Gad," I said helplessly.

"Pray don't interrupt the boy, Peabody," Emerson said. "His narrative may yet contain information of practical interest to us in our present situation. Skip over your struggles with your conscience, Ramses, if you please; you may take it that for now there will be no recriminations."

"T'ank you, Papa. I was not far away, in conceal- ment, when de men struck you and captured Mama. I could not go for help at dat time since it was expedient dat I discover where dey were taking you. Nor could I abandon you after you were dragged into de substructure of de pyramid, for I feared dey might dispatch you fort'wit'. Dere was only time for me to snatch up a coil of rope from de equipment dey had brought wit' dem, and scribble a brief mes- sage, before I followed."

"The message, Ramses," I said between my teeth. "Where did you leave the message?"

"I tied it to de collar of de cat Bastet."

"To de collar of de—"

"She had accompanied me, of course. I could hardly leave it lying on de ground, Mama," Ramses added in an injured tone—my comment, though brief, had admittedly held a note of criticism. "Even if it was not found by de villains, its chances of be- ing discovered by someone would have been slight in de extreme."

"Do you mean," Emerson demanded, "that you

have been inside the pyramid all this time? How did you elude the criminals when they returned?"

"And why did it take you so long to reach this place?" I added.

Ramses settled himself more comfortably. "Bot' questions will be answered if you will allow me to proceed wit' de narrative in an orderly fashion. I heard splashes, and surmised dat dey had t'rown you into de burial chamber. I also heard Papa cry out, which relieved my anxiety as to his survival. When de man came back I had to hide in one of de side passages. Dese passages are not all in good condition, as you may perhaps have observed. De route used by de criminals has been shored up by timbers, but some of de side passages are less secure. De one I selected, *faute de mieux*, I might add, collapsed. I was some time extricating myself."

"Good heavens," Emerson gasped. "My dear child—"

"You have not heard de worst, Papa. Upon reaching de main passage again I decided to return to de outside world and summon assistance. You may imagine my consternation when I discovered dat de way was blocked—deliberately, I believe, by the removal of the timbers that had supported de stones lining de passage. Dere was not'ing for it but return to you, but it took some little time owing to de state of perturbation dat afflicted me and de fact dat, because of dis emotional disability, I had forgotten dat, in emulation of Mama's admirable custom, I always carry wit' me a box of matches and a candle, among odder useful equipment. But I fear I lost dem when I fell into de water."

For once Ramses had succeeded in finishing a statement without being interrupted. It was less diffuse than usual, though it might certainly have profited by judicious editing. However, my silence was the result of considerable emotion. It appeared we were doomed, unless the message tied to the cat's collar was found before she chewed it off or lost it. Among other emotions—I confess it without shame—was maternal pride. Ramses had displayed the qualities I might have expected from a descendant of the Emersons and the Peabodys. I might even have told him so had not Emerson begun showering him with profuse compliments. Ramses' smug look as he sat there swinging his legs convinced me he had quite enough commendation.

"You have done well, Ramses, but it is necessary to do better," I said. "We must get out of this chamber."

"Why?" Emerson inquired. "If the passage is blocked, we can't get out of the pyramid."

"For one thing, it is very damp here. Without a flannel belt, which you refuse to wear, there is the danger of catarrh."

"The danger of having one of the passageways fall in on us strikes me as more life-threatening, Peabody. We will be safer here, while we await rescue."

"We may wait a long time, Emerson. The cat Bastet will eventually return to the house, no doubt, but Ramses' note may be lost before then."

"And also," Ramses added, "if we wish to apprehend de miscreants, we cannot wait. Dey are planning to leave at dawn. I heard dem say so."

"But if the passage is blocked—"

"Dere is anodder way out, Papa."

"I beg your pardon, Ramses?"

"It leads to a vestibule beside de pyramid containing several subsidiary tombs of members of de royal family. It was de means by which I originally entered dis pyramid. And," Ramses added hastily, "if Mama will allow me to postpone de explanation of dat circumstance until a more propitious moment, we would be better employed in ascertaining whedder dat entrance is still open."

"Quite right, my boy." Emerson squared his shoulders and flexed his biceps. "Our first problem, then, is to find some object on which to stand. Your mama and I were about to begin that search when you—er—joined us."

"No, Emerson," I said. "We must first find the rope Ramses so carelessly let fall."

"But, Peabody—"

"Think, Emerson. We lacked, initially, three feet of height. Here is an object over three feet long." I indicated Ramses, who returned my gaze with an owlish stare.

"Ha!" Emerson cried. The echoes repeated the syllable in an eerie imitation of laughter. "Correct as always, my dear Peabody."

Ramses' offer of diving to look for the rope was unanimously refused. It did not take Emerson long to locate it. The rope, tied in a coil, had fallen straight down from the opening and sunk to the bottom of the mud, from which Emerson finally drew it. We could not dry it, but we rinsed off the worst of the slime, which would render it slippery and dangerous to climb. Then we once more formed our human ladder, with Ramses at the top. The procedure was almost laughably easy now. Ramses swarmed up our bodies with the agility of a monkey. Once his hands had closed over the rim of the hole, I was able to assist him by pushing on the most conveniently located portion of his anatomy, and he was soon in the passage.

It was then necessary for us to wait while Ramses lit the candle and attempted to locate some protruding stub of stone around which the rope could be tied; for it was clearly impossible for him to support my weight. This was the part of the business that worried me most. Given the decaying condition of the interior stonework, there was a danger that the wall might give way if excessive strain were put upon any of the stone that lined it. Unlike the larger pyramids of Dahshoor, this last structure was not built of stone throughout, but of brick faced with stone. The shapelessness of the exterior demonstrated what could happen when the facing stones were removed.

I could hear the boy moving cautiously along the passage and was happy to note that he was taking his time in selecting a suitable support. Glad as I was to be leaving the burial chamber, I was somewhat disappointed that Emerson and I had been foiled in our hopes of exploring that room. We would never have the chance now.

Ramses finally announced that he had located a protruding stone he considered suitable. "It won't stand much strain Mama," he called. "You will have to be quick."

The section of rope that hung beside me twitched

and wriggled, for all the world like a snake. Breathing a wordless prayer to whatever Deity guides our ends I seized the rope. Emerson flung me up as high as he could manage. For one long moment I hung supported only by the frail strand between my hands. I felt the line sag ominously; then my boot found a purchase, slight but sufficient, against the wall; my left hand closed over the edge of the opening; and after a brief but exciting scramble I drew myself into (temporary) safety.

I announced my success to Ramses and Emerson, both of whom replied with suitable congratulations. "You may give me the candle now, Ramses," I said.

He dropped it, of course. After I had retrieved it, and the matches, I struck a light and turned to examine the support he had found.

It was not an encouraging sight. Several of the stones in the lower portion of the wall had buckled under the pressure of the bricks beyond. Around one of the protruding edges Ramses had looped the rope—*faute de mieux*, as he might have said, for there was nothing else that would serve. I had depended on the rope as little as possible, but Emerson would have to use it for most of his ascent, and his weight was considerably greater than mine. There was a distinct possibility that the loosened block might be pulled completely out by the strain, which would not only precipitate Emerson back into the water but would bring the wall toppling down. I seriously considered asking him to remain below until we could fetch help. The only reason I did not do so was because I knew he would become bored with waiting and try to climb the rope anyway. He is not and has never been a patient man.

"I am coming up, Peabody," he shouted.

"Just a moment, Emerson." I sat down on the floor with my back against the loosened block and my feet braced against the opposite wall. "Ramses," I said. "Proceed along the passage, around the next corner."

I fully expected another of those eternal "But, Mama"s. Instead Ramses said quietly, "Very well," and went trotting off. I waited until he was out of sight and then called to Emerson to proceed.

The ensuing moments were not among the most comfortable I have undergone. As I had feared, Emerson's tugging and jerking of the rope had a deleterious effect on the block that held it, and though I pressed against the stone with every ounce of strength I possessed, it outweighed me by some six hundred pounds. The cursed thing gave a centimeter or so every time Emerson's hands took a fresh hold on the rope, and it made an obscene groaning sound as it rubbed against the adjoining surface. The softest, gentlest touch on my hand, which was pressed against the floor, almost brought a cry to my lips—but, I hope I need not add, that cry was suppressed before it found utterance. The touch was that of sand—the crumbled substance of ancient mud brick—trickling slowly and horribly from the widening crack.

It seemed hours before I finally saw his shaggy, slime-smeared head appear at the opening. By that time the pressure of the stone against my back had raised my knees to an acute angle from the floor. I was afraid to speak aloud; it seemed as if the slightest vibration would push the block past the delicate point on which it hung balanced.

"Emerson," I whispered. "Don't delay an instant, but follow me. On hands and knees, if you please, and with the most felicitous combination of speed and delicacy of movement."

Once again I had reason to bless the unity of spirit that binds my husband and me. Without question he at once obeyed. I abandoned my strained position and with aching back and pounding heart crawled ahead of him down the passage. When we turned the corner and reached the place where Ramses was waiting, I felt it was safe to stop for a brief rest.

If this were a sensational novel instead of an autobiography, I would report that the wall collapsed just as we scrambled to safety. However, it did not. I remain convinced that the peril was imminent, despite the assurances of those who examined the spot later and insisted that the stone would have moved no farther.

But to resume. Like the preceding section, this part of the passageway was lined with blocks of limestone. It was barely four feet high. Even Ramses had to duck his head. I wiped my bleeding hands on my trousers, tucked my shirtwaist in, and tidied my hair, which had been sadly disarranged. "Lead on, Ramses," I said. "That is—are you fully recovered, Emerson?"

"I may never fully recover," said Emerson, still prone. "But I am ready to go on. First let me retrieve the rope. We may need it."

"No! We must do without the rope, Emerson. It is a miracle the wall has not collapsed. I won't let you go back there."

"A rope will not be required," said Ramses. "At least . . . I hope it will not."

With that doubtful assurance we had to be content.

There were several places in which we might have made good use of a rope, for the ancient architects had used every trick they could think of to foil grave robbers, from gaping pits in the floor to concealed entrances high in the walls. Fortunately for us, the long-dead thieves had been shrewder than the architects. I never believed I would think kindly of these ghouls who had looted the treasures buried with the pharaohs, foiling modern archaeologists in their quest for knowledge; but as I scrambled around a huge portcullis stone, through the narrow tunnel dug by the invaders of the pyramid, I blessed their greedy and ambitious souls.

I also blessed Ramses' uncanny sense of direction. The maze-like corridors and chambers turned and twisted, some ending in blind alleys, but he led us unerringly toward his goal. "I believe we can assume that these complex substructures are typical of Twelfth Dynasty pyramids," I remarked to Emerson, as we crawled along single-file. "This example resembles the one at Hawara that Petrie explored in '87."

"It seems a reasonable assumption," was the reply. "I suspect our pyramid is of the same period, so it will probably have a similar substructure. A pity we have not been able to find an inscription naming the pharaoh for whom it was built."

"We may yet find it, Emerson. I think this must be earlier than ours. It is more sturdily built—"

At this point I was struck smartly on the head by a mass of mixed mud brick and sand falling from a gap in the ceiling and had to save my breath for moving more rapidly. Emerson also quickened his pace, and we did not resume our conversation until we had gone a little distance.

It may seem strange to some that we should carry on a scholarly discussion at a time when our sole preoccupation should have been bent toward escape from deadly peril. Yet the act of crawling does not in itself engage all the critical faculties, and what better way to pass the time than in conversation? Archaeological passion burns brightly in our family, thank heaven, and I sincerely trust that my penultimate breath will be employed in speculating on the latest Egyptological theories. The ultimate breath, I hardly need say, will be reserved for the affectionate descendants who stand by my couch.

The fall of rubble that raised another lump on my aching head was not the only such peril we had to contend with. In several places the stone lining of the corridor had given way. One place was almost completely blocked, with only a narrow tunnel through at one side of the fallen stones. Ramses became very quiet at this point—he had been lecturing us about the construction of Middle Kingdom pyramids—and looked even more enigmatic than usual as we carefully widened the tunnel to permit our larger bodies to pass. I said nothing; I had determined to reserve my remarks on his mendacious behavior until after the other criminals had been dealt with.

Except for such occurrences and Ramses' falling into a pit (from which Emerson drew him up by means of my waist flannel—proving once again the usefulness of this article of dress), we had no real difficulty until we reached the end of our underground journey. A long, straight passageway led into a sizable chamber cut in the rock. It, too, had been robbed in antiquity (at least I assumed so at the time); for it contained nothing but an empty stone sarcophagus. Here at last we were able to stand upright, and Ramses directed Emerson to hold his candle up toward the roof.

One of the stones was missing. "It is de opening of de shaft from de surface," said Ramses. "De depth is not great—twelve feet eight inches, to be precise. My only concern is dat de stone I placed atop de surface opening of de shaft may be too heavy for Papa to move. It took bot' Selim and Hassan to put it dere."

I promised myself an interview with Selim and Hassan later. "What do you think, Emerson?" I asked.

Emerson's fingers rasped across his unshaven chin. "I can but try, Peabody. After all we have been through I don't mean to let a mere stone stop me."

The shaft was so narrow he could climb by bracing his back against one side and his feet against another—chimney climbing I believe the process is called. It was an awkward position from which to exert pressure on a considerable weight, and Emerson's grunts and groans testified to the effort he was putting forth. "Try sliding it to one side instead of lifting it, Emerson," I called.

"What the devil do you think I am doing?" was the reply. "It is hard to get a grip on the cursed thing. . . . Ah, there. I believe—"

His speech was interrupted by a shower of sand, some of which sprinkled my upturned face. The bulk of it, unfortunately, fell full on Emerson's head. I have seldom heard such a rich wealth of invective, even from Emerson. "You should have kept your mouth closed, my dear," I said. "— — —," said Emerson.

"I had to spread sand on de stone," Ramses explained, "in order to conceal de location of de—"

A positive avalanche of sand and pebbles put an end to this inapropos remark. Emerson continued to curse inventively as he put his back into his task; no doubt mental irritability and physical discomfort gave him additional strength. At last the downpour slowed to a trickle. "Look out below," Emerson cried grittily. "I am coming down."

He descended with a rush and a thud. The candle flame quivered in my hand as I contemplated him; sand coated every inch of his body, sticking to the perspiration and slimy water. From the stony mask of his face two red-rimmed eyes blazed blue sparks.

"Oh, my dear," I said sympathetically. "Let me bathe your eyes. This little flask of water, which I always carry with me . . ."

Emerson's tightly pressed lips parted. He spat

out a mouthful of mud and remarked, "Not now, Peabody. I feel my usually equable temper beginning to fray. You first. Let me give you a hand up."

He assisted me into the mouth of the shaft. It was not the first time in our adventures I had ascended a narrow fissure in such a fashion, but for a moment I was unable to move. A few feet above me was a square of deep-blue velvet strewn with sparkling gems. It looked so close I felt I could reach up and touch it. My shaken mind refused to recognize it for what it was—the night sky, which I had wondered if I would ever see again.

Then a querulous question from Emerson, below, reminded me of my objective, and I began my final labor. Not until I lay at full length upon the hard desert floor, with the night breeze cooling my flushed face, did I fully realize our dreadful ordeal was over.

I raised my head. Three feet away, silent in the moonlight, an amber statue sat motionless, staring at me with slitted eyes. So might the ancient goddess of love and beauty welcome a devotee after his journey through the perilous paths of the underworld.

The cat Bastet and I communed in silence. There was considerable criticism in my mind, mild curiosity in hers, to judge by the placidity of her expression. She tilted her head inquiringly. I snapped, "He will be with you in a moment."

Ramses soon emerged. His fingers and toes found purchases in the stones of the shaft I had not even seen. When I dragged him out, the cat Bastet mewed and trotted to him. She began busily licking his head, spitting irritably between licks. After Emerson had pulled himself from the shaft he shook himself like a large dog. Sand flew in all directions.

The ruined mound of the Black Pyramid rose up beside us. We were on its north side. To the west, calm in the starlight, stood the silver slopes of the Bent Pyramid, with its more conventional neighbor visible farther north. Silence and peace brooded over the scene. Eastward, where the village of Menyat Dahshoor lay amid the palm groves and tilled fields, there was not a light to be seen. It must be late; but not so late as I had feared, for the eastern sky still waited in darkness for the coming of dawn.

The cat Bastet had given up her attempt to clean Ramses. She was an intelligent animal and had no doubt realized that only prolonged immersion would have the desired effect. The same had to be said about Ramses' parents. Emerson looked like a crumbling sandstone statue, and as for myself . . . I decided not to think about it.

I reached for the cat. A ragged scrap of paper was still attached to her collar. "Half of the note is still here," I said. "It is just as well we decided not to wait to be rescued."

"Furder training would seem to be indicated," said Ramses. "I had only begun dis aspect of de program, since I had no reason to anticipate dat an emergency would—"

"We have a good three-mile walk ahead of us," Emerson interrupted. "Let us be off."

"Are you up to it, Emerson? We are closer to

Menyat Dahshoor, perhaps we ought to arouse de Morgan and request his assistance. He could supply us with donkeys and men."

"Be honest, Peabody—you are no more keen than I to go crawling to de Morgan for help."

"But, my dear, you must be tired."

Emerson thumped himself on the chest. "I have never felt better. The air is like wine, particularly after the noisome substitute for air we have been breathing. But you, my dear Peabody—perhaps you ought to go to Dahshoor. You are shivering."

"I will not leave you, Emerson. Where you go, I go."

"I expected you would say that," Emerson replied, his sandy mask cracking in a fond smile. "Excelsior, then. Ramses, put down the cat and Papa will carry you."

The assorted bruises and aches that had stiffened as we stood talking were soon forgotten. Brisk walking warmed us and the pleasures of familial intimacy were never more keenly felt. Had I not been anxious to come to grips with the villains who had attempted to exterminate us, I might have wished that stroll to be prolonged.

Our plans were soon made. They were simple: to collect our loyal men and procure a fresh supply of firearms (my pistol, being choked with mud, was unusable) before proceeding to the village to arrest the Master Criminal.

"We must catch him unawares," I said. "He is desperate and may be armed."

"He?" Emerson said. "Miss Charity is not your choice for the role?"

I had had time to revise my first hasty impression, so I replied, "We never saw the face of the elusive figure, Emerson. Any young person, male or female, could have worn Charity's dress, and that unfashionable bonnet concealed the person's features as effectively as a mask could do. Nor does the message I received incriminate her, for I have never seen her handwriting. Anyone could have written that note."

"Not anyone, Peabody."

"Correct, Emerson. If the note was a forgery, as I believe, it could only have been penned by Brother Ezekiel or Brother David."

"Which have you settled on?" Emerson asked.

We were now so close to concluding the case that further equivocation seemed futile. "Brother Ezekiel, of course," I said.

"I disagree. Brother David."

"You only choose him because you dislike his manners."

"People who live in glass houses, Peabody. You have a weakness for pretty young men with smooth tongues. Whereas Brother Ezekiel—"

"All the clues point to him, Emerson."

"Quite the contrary, Peabody. They point to Brother David."

"Would you care to explicate, Emerson?"

"Not just at present, Peabody. There are one or two minor questions to be resolved. What about you?"

"I am also undecided about a few exceedingly unimportant details, Emerson."

So the discussion ended. Ramses' attempt to

offer his views was rejected by mutual consent, and we went on in silence. It was fortunate that we did. Sounds carry some distance in the desert, and we were close to the house when Emerson, who had been casting increasingly anxious glances about, came to a sudden stop.

"Ramses," he said softly, "did you leave a light in your room?"

"No, Papa."

"Nor did we. Look."

Two squares of yellow broke the darkness of the house. Emerson took my arm and pulled me to the ground. Ramses slipped from his shoulders and crouched beside us.

"John may have discovered Ramses' absence and be looking for him," I suggested.

"In utter silence? And where is Abdullah? I have an uneasy feeling about this, Peabody."

"I think I see Abdullah—there, to the left of the door. He seems to be asleep."

I half rose, for a better look. Emerson held me down.

Around the corner of the wall, from the direction of the ruined church, came a dark and ghostly shape. Flitting from shadow to deeper shadow, it passed the sleeping form of Abdullah and vanished into the house.

I reminded myself that bare feet on sand make no sound, and that most of the villagers wore dark robes. If Abdullah had seen the form, he would have been certain that the spirit of one of the murdered monks had returned.

On hands and knees we crept forward. The

huddled form was indeed that of our loyal *reis;* he did not stir, even when Emerson shook him gently. It was with a sense of infinite relief that I heard Emerson say, "Drugged. Hashish, from the smell of it. He'll be none the worse in the morning."

In the same whisper I said, "Do we assume our other men are in the same condition?"

"Or worse," was the grim reply. "Give me your pistol, Peabody."

"You dare not fire it, Emerson. The mud—"

"I know. I can only bluff. Will you stay here?"

"No, Emerson, I will not."

"Then Ramses must be the lookout." Turning to the boy he went on, "You understand, Ramses, that if your mama and I do not succeed in overpowering the intruders, you will have to go for help."

"But, Papa—"

My nerves were a trifle strained. I seized Ramses by his thin shoulders and shook him till his teeth rattled. "You heard your papa. Wait fifteen minutes. If we have not summoned you by then, set out for Dahshoor as fast as you can go. And if you say one word, Mama will slap you."

Ramses scuttled off into concealment without so much as a "Yes, Mama." Like me, he is a literal-minded person.

"Really, Peabody, must you be so brusque?" Emerson inquired. "The lad has performed prodigies of devotion and skill tonight; some slight show of appreciation—"

"Will be rendered at the proper time and in the proper manner. Ramses knows I am not emotional. He does not expect it. Now, Emerson, let us not waste any more time. What the devil can they be doing in Ramses' room?"

Whatever it was, they were still at it when we reached the courtyard. The door of Ramses' room stood open, and we could hear voices. Obviously they did not fear interruption. Our men must be prisoners, as Emerson had suggested. And John— what had they done with poor John?

We moved noiselessly, close to the wall, until we stood behind the door, which opened out into the courtyard. Concealed behind it, Emerson applied his eye to the crack. I followed suit, on a lower level.

We could see one end of the room—the table that served Ramses as a desk, the screened window, the cage containing the lion cub, and the lower part of the bed, which had been overturned. Blankets and sheets lay in a tumbled heap. There were two men visible, both wearing the dark-blue turbans customary in the village. No, they did not fear interruption; not only had they left the door wide open but they were making a considerable amount of noise. The sounds of voices uttering expletives indicative of frustration and anger were interspersed with the crashes of the objects they overturned in their search and by the frantic yelps and growls of the lion. One of the men kicked the cage in passing. I ground my teeth. Nothing angers me so much as cruelty to an animal.

My hand closed over the handle of my parasol. We had no other weapon; our pistols were in our bedchamber, which was also occupied by the uninvited visitors. Fortunately I had left the parasol in the parlor the night before. I stood on tiptoe and applied my mouth to Emerson's ear. "There are only two of them," I breathed. "Now, Emerson?"

"Now."

I am sure our attack would have been a complete success had not Emerson got in my way. There was a little confusion in the doorway, as both of us tried to enter at once. By the time I regained my feet, and my parasol, I was distressed to note that one of the men was pointing a pistol at us.

His features were vaguely familiar. I thought I had seen him among the "deacons" who served the priest. The other man was a complete stranger, and when he spoke I recognized the Cairene accent.

"You are hard to kill, O Father of Curses. Shall we see if a bullet can do what burial alive could not?"

As if in response the little lion gave a piercing wail. The other villain gave the cage a vicious kick.

Then a voice replied to what I had believed to be a rhetorical question. It came from the end of the room we had not been able to see and it spoke the purest classical Arabic-Egyptian. "There will be no killing unless Emerson leaves us no choice. And do not kick the cage. Did not the Prophet cut off his sleeve rather than disturb his sleeping cat?"

The speaker stepped forward into the illumination cast by the lamp on the table. Dark turban, black robe, black beard—and the features of Father Girgis of the church of Sitt Miriam.

In my astonishment I almost let my parasol fall from my hand. "You? You are the Master Criminal?"

He laughed and replied, in English as unaccented

as his Arabic had been, "A melodramatic term, Mrs. Emerson. I am only the chairman of a business organization with whose operations you and your family have been interfering."

Hands raised, eyes watchful, Emerson said calmly, "You speak excellent English. Is that, by any chance, your nationality?"

The "priest" smiled. "I speak most of the European languages with equal facility. Speculate, Professor—speculate! You are a determined pair of busybodies. If you had kept out of my way, you would not be in danger."

"I suppose tossing us into a pyramid and sealing the entrance was not dangerous," I said tartly.

"I would have taken steps to ensure your release once we had left the region, Mrs. Emerson. Murder is not my business."

"What of the priest of Dronkeh? I am sure the Patriarch in Cairo has no idea that his local representative has been replaced. What have you done with the poor man?"

A flash of white teeth broke the blackness of that extraordinary beard. "The dear old gentleman is an honored prisoner. He is learning first-hand of the worldly pleasures he has abjured. I assure you, the only dangers he faces are spiritual."

"And Hamid?"

A spark glimmered darkly in the deep-set eyes. "I would have executed the traitor, yes. But I did not. Another's vengeance reached him before mine."

"You don't expect me to believe that, I hope?"

"Amelia," said my husband, "there is surely no profit in annoying this—er—this gentleman."

"It doesn't matter, Professor. I don't care whether Mrs. Emerson believes me or not. I am here on business. I was looking for a certain item. . . ."

"That?" I raised my parasol to point, and both the Copts (or pseudo-Copts) jumped. Their leader swore at them. Then he answered my question.

"I am not such a fool as to waste my time over a fragment of Coptic manuscript, Mrs. Emerson. No. I came for this."

He drew the box from the breast of his robe and removed the lid.

Lamplight caressed the gleaming gold and the soft glow of turquoise, the royal blue of lapis lazuli, the red-orange of carnelian. I caught my breath. "The Twelfth Dynasty pectoral!"

"Another Twelfth Dynasty pectoral," the priest corrected. "With its necklace of gold and carnelian beads, and a set of matching bracelets. The parure of a princess of the Middle Kingdom, hidden so well under the floor of her tomb that it escaped the tomb robbers who looted her mummy. It is the second such cache we have found at Dahshoor, Mrs. Emerson, and were it not for that interfering brat your son, we would perhaps have found others. He has been digging around all the Dahshoor pyramids for the past weeks. One of my men was watching when he found the princess's tomb and removed these ornaments, but we refrained from repossessing them because we hoped he would abandon his pursuits and leave us to go on with our work in peace. That hope has not been realized. You spoil the child, Mrs. Emerson; how many boys of that age are allowed to excavate on their own?"

I was about to reply when I saw something that made my blood run cold. It was a face, pressed against the barred window, and set in a hideous grimace. I might not have recognized it, had it not been for the nasal appendage that protruded into the space between two bars. Ramses!

The priest went on. "Such, however, are the unavoidable vicissitudes of my profession. Now I must beg you to excuse me. I must notify the men who are searching your room that the objects I wanted have been found. This, then, is farewell. I trust we may not meet again."

He strode toward the door.

His men watched him go. Emerson's back was to the window. I was the only one who saw the framework of wooden bars shiver and give way. Silently it swung out—and then I knew how Ramses had come and gone by night without being observed. I was helpless. I could not order him away without calling attention to his presence. I could only avert my eyes and plan the indignities I hoped to perpetrate upon his person.

Neither Emerson nor I had replied to that last taunt, though I knew the same thought was in both our minds: "We will meet again, never fear; for I will make it my business to hunt you down and put an end to your nefarious activities." Emerson always has to have the last word, however. The priest was at the door when my husband shouted, "Are you leaving us to be slaughtered by your henchmen? I might have known you would leave the dirty work to others; but our blood will be on your head, you villain!"

"My dear Professor, not a drop of your blood will be shed if you accept the inevitable. My men have orders to bind and—" Turning, the priest broke off with a gasp.

Ramses fell into the room. He picked himself up off the floor and started forward. "Give it back to me," he said, in a growl that was terrifyingly like that of his father.

The priest laughed contemptuously. "Imp of Satan! Seize him, Mustafa."

With a malevolent grin the man he addressed threw out a careless arm. The blow caught Ramses across the midsection and lifted him clean off his feet. His body hit the wall with a horrible crash; he fell in a heap and lay motionless.

I heard Emerson's roar, and the crack of a pistol. I saw nothing. Inky blackness engulfed me, like a cloud of thick smoke shot with bursts of flame. A great rushing filled my ears, like the thunder of an avalanche. . . .

After an immeasurable interval I became aware of hands clasping me and a voice calling my name. "Peabody! Peabody, for God's sake . . ."

The mists before my eyes cleared. I was still on my feet, parasol in hand, and Emerson was shaking me.

Ramses sat bolt upright, his back against the wall, his hands braced on the floor, his legs sticking straight out. His mouth hung open; his eyes were popping.

"You are alive," I said.

Ramses nodded. For once in his life he seemed incapable of speech.

On Emerson's face I saw the same expression of incredulous horror. Yet there was no reason for alarm; one villain lay facedown on the floor, his arms over his head. The second huddled in a corner, babbling incoherently. The priest was gone.

"You seem to have the situation well in hand, Emerson," I said, wondering why my voice sounded so hoarse. "My congratulations."

"I didn't do it," Emerson said. "You did."

"What are you saying, Emerson?"

Emerson released me and staggered back. He dropped heavily onto the tumbled blankets. "There is blood on your parasol, Peabody."

I realized that I was holding the instrument poised, as if to strike. There was certainly some viscous substance on the steel-dark tip. A drop formed and fell as I stared.

"Berserk," Emerson went on, shaking his head dazedly. "That is the term. . . . A berserker rage. I have heard it described. One could almost believe in the old legends, that the one possessed is impervious to blows, weapons, bullets. . . . The maternal instinct, roused to fury—the tigress defending her cub. . . ."

I cleared my throat. "Emerson, I cannot imagine what you are talking about. Tear one of the sheets into strips, and we will tie up the criminals before going out to rescue our men."

The rescue proved to be unnecessary. While we were binding the two thugs (who were in a peculiar

state of trembling paralysis and gave us no trouble),
our men from Aziyeh rushed into the house in an
agitated and vociferous body. They had been unaware of danger until one of them awoke to find
himself held at gunpoint by "a cursed Christian," as
Ali naively expressed it. Emerson hastened to clear
the name of the Copts. The expression "Master
Criminal" confused Ali at first; after further expla-
nations he proceeded with his narrative.

"When I saw the gun I cried out and woke the
others. The man told us not to move, Sitt Hakim, so
we did not; it was a Mauser repeating rifle, you understand. Yet we would have come if we had known
you were in danger; indeed, we were about to rush
the villain, risking our lives in your service, when out
of the night a man appeared, waving his arms and
crying out. . . ."

I knew it must have been the priest from Ali's
description. "He had a long black beard, Sitt, and
a cross hanging at his waist. There was blood all
down his face and he was screaming in a high voice,
like a frightened woman."

Emerson shot me a glance from under his brows,
which I chose to ignore. "Go on, Ali."

Ali put a finger under his turban and scratched
his head. "They ran away, Sitt, both of them. We
were so surprised we could not think what to do.
We talked for a while and Daoud said we should
stay where we were, in case the man with the gun
was hiding, watching us—"

Daoud squirmed and started to protest. I reassured him, and Ali finished his story. "Mohammed
and I said, no, we must find you and make sure you

were safe. So we came. Our honored father is very drunk on hashish, Sitt."

Abdullah looked so happy it seemed a shame to rouse him. So we carried him in and put him to bed, with Ali to watch over him. I ordered another of the men to go with Ramses to put his room in order.

Ramses lingered. To his meager breast he still clutched the box containing the pectoral. "Do you wish to talk to me, Mama?"

"I will have a great many things to say to you later, Ramses. Now go and do as I order."

"One question," said Emerson, absently scratching his now excessive beard. "What the devil induced you to climb in that window, Ramses? I thought I told you to go for help."

"De criminal was about to steal my pectoral," Ramses replied. "It is MINE. I found it."

"But, my dear boy, it was horribly dangerous," Emerson exclaimed. "You cannot go about demanding your rightful property from thieves; they are not amenable to such appeals."

"It was not dangerous," Ramses said serenely. "I knew you and Mama would not allow de men to harm me."

Emerson cleared his throat noisily and passed his sleeve across his eyes. Ramses and I exchanged a long, steady look. "Go to bed, Ramses," I said.

"Yes, Mama. Good night, Mama. Good night, Papa."

"Good night, my dear boy."

Beneath his muscular exterior Emerson is a very sentimental person. I tactfully looked elsewhere while he wiped his eyes and got his face under control. Then he said, "Peabody, that was the most magnificent testimonial any child ever gave his parents. Could you not have responded more warmly?"

"Never mind, Emerson. Ramses and I understand one another perfectly."

"Humph," said Emerson. "Well, my dear, what next?"

"John," I said. "He must certainly be next."

"John? John! Good Gad, my dear, you are right. Where is the poor fellow?"

Emerson sprang to his feet. I waved him back into his chair, for despite his extraordinary stamina he was showing signs of fatigue. "There is only one place he can be, Emerson. But before we go in search of him I insist upon a bath and a change of clothing. There is no further danger in delay; if harm was intended, it must already have befallen him. Let us pray that the killer of Hamid and Abd el Atti has spared the lad."

Emerson's eyes narrowed. His concern for his unhappy servant was wholly sincere, but for the moment another matter had taken precedence. "Aha," he said. "So you believed that villain when he disclaimed responsibility for the murders?"

"Why should he lie? We had caught him red-handed. No, Emerson, the priest—or, if you prefer, the Master Criminal—is unquestionably a villain of the deepest dye and I am certain he has several murders on his conscience (if he possesses such an organ, which is doubtful); but he did not kill Abd el Atti and Hamid."

"Amelia."

"Yes, Emerson?"

"Did you suspect the priest? Be honest."

"No, Emerson, I did not. Did you?"

"No, Peabody, I did not."

"But I was not altogether wrong," I continued. "The person I suspected of being the Master Criminal is the murderer. It is a meaningless distinction, actually."

"Curse it, Peabody, you never give up, do you? Hurry with your bath, then, and we will go to the mission and apprehend Brother David."

"Brother Ezekiel," I said, and left the room before Emerson could reply.

TWELVE

The sun was well above the horizon before we were ready to set forth on our errand of justice and—I hoped—mercy. The morning air was clear and fresh; the eastern sky flaunted the exquisite golden glow of a desert sunrise. Yet we walked with dragging steps, oblivious for once to the marvels of nature. I did not anticipate danger, but the interview promised to be a painful one, and I was filled with apprehension for poor John.

He had gone to the mission, of course. I could not blame him for disobeying my express command; when we failed to return he must have feared for us as well as for his beloved. Since I had not told him where we were to meet the girl, he would search for her in the most obvious place.

Arriving, he had found . . . what? What scene of horror or massacre had met his astonished eyes, and made it necessary for the killer to add another crime to his list? That John had failed to return made it certain he had been prevented from returning; but was it murder or kidnapping that had prevented him? Whatever had happened had happened hours before. If John was no more, we could only avenge him. If he was held prisoner, we would be in time to save him.

One of my first acts, even before bathing and changing into fresh attire, had been to dispatch a message to de Morgan. I mentioned this to Emerson, hoping to cheer him, for his expression as he tramped along was gloomy in the extreme.

He only grunted. "De Morgan has no evidence on which to arrest Kalenischeff, Peabody. Even if the rascal has stolen antiquities, he is under the protection of the baroness. It would take a direct order from Cromer to interfere with such a distinguished visitor."

"Kalenischeff must be one of the gang, Emerson. It is too much of a coincidence that he should be leaving Dahshoor at the same time as the Master Criminal."

"Oh, I agree. His job was to act as spotter. If de Morgan found anything of interest, Kalenischeff would notify his leader. But we will never prove it, Peabody, nor even convince de Morgan that he was taken in."

"It appears that this is one of those cases where everyone is guilty," I said.

"You exaggerate, Peabody. The baroness was duped; de Morgan is innocent of everything except congenital stupidity; and of the three at the mission, only one is guilty."

"Ah, do you think so? What about two out of three?"

The challenge roused Emerson from his depression. "Which two—or which one?"

"I did not say two were guilty. I only present it as a possibility."

"Are you sticking to your guns, then? Ezekiel?"

"Er—yes."

"It was at Brother David that Bastet spat, Peabody."

I was sorry he had noticed that. I had had some difficulty fitting it into my theory and had finally decided to ignore it altogether. "The incident was meaningless, Emerson. Bastet was in a bad mood—"

"And why was she in a bad mood, Peabody? Her keen sense of smell had recognized the spoor of the man who had been in Abd el Atti's shop—"

"You are becoming as fanciful as Ramses where that cat is concerned, Emerson. Oh, I don't doubt that was what the child intended when he returned to the shop and found out that Abd el Atti had been murdered; he is only a little boy, and does not understand that animals can't be trained to do what he wants. But if you are naive enough to suppose that Bastet tracked the murderer through the extensive and odorous byways of Cairo and that, many days thereafter, recalled the scent of the individual who threw a boot or some other missile at her—"

"Humph," said Emerson.

It did sound absurd, when put into words. But I wondered. Brother David had not been the only stranger present that day.

The village ought to have been teeming with activity, for the working day in such places begins at dawn. Not a soul was to be seen. Even the dogs had slunk into hiding. Not until we reached the well did a timid voice call out to us. Then I realized that behind every window were watching eyes, and that the doors stood a trifle ajar. One of them opened cautiously and a head appeared. It was that of the shy little *sheikh el beled*. We stopped and waited, and finally he summoned up courage to emerge.

"The peace of God be upon you," he said.

"And upon you," Emerson said automatically. Then he added, "Curse it, I have no time for this sort of thing. What the devil has happened here?"

"I do not know, effendi," the mayor said. "Will you protect us? There was much shouting and shooting in the night—"

"Oh, heavens," I exclaimed. "Poor John!"

"He is just making a good story of it," Emerson said in English; but he looked grave. "Shooting, your honor?"

"One shot," the mayor admitted. "One, at least. . . . And when we woke this morning, the priest was gone and all his friends with him; and the sacred vessels are gone too. They were very old and very precious to us. Has he taken them to Cairo to be repaired, perhaps? Why did he tell no one he was going?"

"He is half right," said Emerson. "I don't doubt that the sacred vessels are on their way to Cairo by now."

"I ought to have anticipated this," I said in some chagrin. "To be honest, Emerson, I did not notice the vessels when I attended the service."

This exchange had been in English. The little man looked timidly from me to Emerson. Emerson patted him on the back. "Be of good cheer, my friend," he said in Arabic. "Go back to your house and wait. It will be explained to you later."

We went on through the deathly silence. "I have the direct forebodings, Emerson," I murmured.

"I expected you would, Peabody."

"If we have brought that boy to his death, I will never forgive myself."

"It was my idea to bring him, Peabody." That was all Emerson said, but his haggard look expressed the depth of his remorse.

"Oh no, my dear. I agreed; it was as much my fault as yours."

"Well, let us not borrow trouble, Peabody," Emerson said, squaring his shoulders and exhibiting the dauntless spirit I expected.

We reached the open space before the mission. The small neat buildings looked peaceful enough, but the same brooding silence hung over the place.

"Let us hurry," I said. "I can bear the suspense no longer."

"Wait." Emerson drew me into concealment among the trees. "Whatever awaits us in that ominous place, there is one thing we know we will find—a raving madman. Our theories agree on that, at least?"

I nodded. "Then it behooves us to behave with extreme circumspection," Emerson said. "We don't want to push the fellow into a rash act."

"You are correct as always, Emerson. But I cannot wait much longer."

"You won't have to." Emerson's voice dropped to a thrilling whisper. "By heaven, there he is—as unconcerned as if he were not a murderer twice over. Amazing how normal he looks; but that is often true of madmen."

He spoke of Brother David. The young man did not appear mad, but neither was he unconcerned. He stood just outside the door of the house looking nervously from side to side. After a long, suspicious survey of the scene, he summoned the courage to proceed. Emerson waited until he had got halfway across the clearing; then, with a roar, he bounded out of concealment.

When I reached them, Brother David was flat on his back and Emerson was sitting on his chest. "I have him safe," my husband cried. "There is nothing to be afraid of, Peabody. What have you done with my servant, you rascal?"

I said, "He can't answer, Emerson; you are squeezing the breath out of him. Get off him, why don't you."

Emerson shifted his weight. David took a long shuddering breath. "Professor?" he gasped. "Is it you?"

"Who the devil did you think it was?"

"That fiendish priest, or one of his adherents—we are beset with enemies, Professor. Thank God you are here. I was just going to try to reach you, to ask for your help."

"Ha," said Emerson skeptically. "What have you done with John?"

"Brother John? Why, nothing. Has he disappeared?"

No theatrical person could have counterfeited the bewilderment on the young man's face, but Emerson is notoriously hard to convince, once he has set his mind on something. "Of course he has disappeared! He is here—you have kidnapped him, or worse. . . . What of the shots in the night, you wretch?" Seizing David by his collar, he shook him like a mastiff worrying a rat.

"For heaven's sake, stop asking him questions and then preventing him from answering," I exclaimed.

Emerson let go of the young man's collar. David's head hit the sand with a thud and his eyes rolled up in his head. "What was it you asked? . . . I am not quite myself. . . . Shots in the night. Oh, yes—Brother Ezekiel was forced to fire his revolver at a would-be thief. He fired high, of course, only to frighten the fellow off."

"Brother Ezekiel." Emerson fingered his chin and glanced at me. "Hmmm. Where is Brother Ezekiel? He is usually the first on the scene."

"He is at prayer, in his study. He is asking the Almighty to defend his saints against the enemies that surround them."

Still astride his victim, Emerson studied him intently while he continued to stroke the dimple in his chin. "You were right, Amelia," he said at last. "I concede defeat. This helpless weakling is not a murderer."

Rising, he lifted David to his feet. "Mr. Cabot, your leader is a dangerous maniac. For his own sake, as well as the sake of others, he must be put under restraint. Follow me."

The moment he released his hold, David scuttled away. The door of the church opened and banged shut. A pale face peered out from one of the windows.

"Leave him be, Emerson," I said in disgust. "If you were mistaken about the creature, so was I. He will only be in our way. Let us smoke the murderer from his lair. I only hope we are not too late."

The advantage of surprise now being lost, we proceeded without further ado to the house. The front door stood open as David had left it. There was no one in the parlor; it was as barren and cheerless as before. The Greek Testament was no longer on the table.

"Which do you suppose is his study?" Emerson asked, contemplating the pair of doors at the back of the room.

"There is only one way to find out." Carefully I turned the knob of the right-hand door. The small chamber within was obviously Charity's bedroom. The bonnet, and a gown of the familiar dark calico, hung from pegs on the wall. There was nothing else in the room except a cot as narrow and probably as hard as a plank. A single thin coverlet was thrown back, as if the sleeper had risen in haste.

I closed the door. "That one," I said, indicating the other door.

We had spoken softly, but some sound of our presence ought, by then, have reached the ears of a listener. I began to wonder if the house were inhabited after all. Or were the occupants of that silent room lying dead in their gore?

I drew my pistol. "Stand back, Emerson."

"Certainly not, Peabody. You are going about it the wrong way." He knocked gently at the door.

To my astonishment a voice promptly replied. "I told you, Brother David, to leave me be. I am speaking with my Father."

Emerson rolled his eyes expressively. "It is not Brother David. It is I—Emerson."

"Professor?" There was a pause. "Come in."

Emerson opened the door.

Prepared as I was for any ghastly sight—priding myself as I do on my aplomb under all circumstances—even I was struck dumb by the sight that confronted me. My eyes went first to John, who sat on the edge of the bed. A bloody bandage encircled his brow, but his eyes were open—staring wildly, in fact—and he did not appear seriously injured. I breathed a sincere but necessarily brief prayer of thanksgiving.

One of the two chairs was occupied by Charity. She appeared to be in a trance; her white face was utterly expressionless and she did not look up when the door opened. Brother Ezekiel sat at the table, an open book before him and a pistol in his hand. It was pointed at John.

"Come in, brother and sister," he said calmly. "You are just in time. I have been wrestling with the demons that possess this unfortunate young man. There wasn't any swine to cast 'em into, you see. I figure the only way to get rid of 'em is to shoot him, but first he must acknowledge his Saviour. I wouldn't want his soul to burn in hell."

"That is most considerate of you," said Emerson, with equal coolness. "Why don't I fetch a goat—or a dog? You can cast the demons into it."

"Afraid that won't do," said Ezekiel, shaking his

head. "See, Professor, you have got a few demons in you too. I'll have to deal with 'em before I let you out of here or they might lead you astray."

"Mr. Jones—"

"That's not the way to talk to me, my son. Call me by my right name. For I am the Annointed One, whose coming to redeem Israel was foretold by the prophets."

"Good Gad," I said involuntarily.

Emerson grimaced at me, and Ezekiel said, "She's got more demons than any of 'em. Come in, sister, and acknowledge your Lord and Saviour."

My pistol was in my hand, hidden by the voluminous folds of my trousers, but I never thought of using it. How long had the madness been festering in his poor warped brain? He had maintained a semblance of normalcy till now.

Emerson edged into the room. "That's far enough," said Ezekiel. "Now you, sister. Come in."

I could not think what to do. The room was so small the madman was bound to hit someone if he pulled the trigger, and he might pull it if he were physically attacked. It seemed equally dangerous and fruitless to reason with him. Then something moved at the open window. Was it rescue—reinforcements? No. It was David, wild-eyed and pale with fright. We could not count on assistance from him.

Emerson saw him too, and with the brilliance that always marks his actions, seized the only possible advantage from his presence. "Look there, at the window," he cried. As Ezekiel turned, Emerson leaped.

The gun went off. The bullet struck harmlessly

into the ceiling. David shrieked and vanished. John jumped to his feet and promptly sat down again as his knees gave way. Charity slid fainting from her chair. Emerson tossed me the gun and enveloped Brother Ezekiel in a tight embrace. Footsteps sounded in the outer room. "*Nom du nom du nom,*" de Morgan ejaculated. "What has transpired here?"

Behind the Frenchman was my son Ramses.

"It was de Coptic manuscript after all," Ramses said, some time later. Ezekiel was under guard and his victims had been attended to; we were once more in our own home and John, though pale and shaken, had insisted on making tea.

"*Quel manuscrit coptique?*" de Morgan demanded. "I understand nothing of this—nothing! It is of a madness unexampled. Master Criminals, manuscripts, raving missionaries. . . ."

I explained about the Coptic manuscript. "I knew all along it must be involved," I said. "But I could not think what to make of it. The trouble was—"

"That two different groups of criminals were at work," said Emerson. "The first was the gang of antiquities thieves. They had discovered a cache of royal jewelry at Dahshoor and were searching for more. Their leader took the place of the village priest at Dronkeh in order to supervise their illicit digging—"

"But the thieves fell out, as such persons are wont to do," I went on. "Hamid, who was a minor member of the gang, was not content with his share of the profits. He saw an opportunity to rob the thieves and sell some of his finds himself. He persuaded his father to market them. And among these objects—"

"Was the mummy case purchased by the baroness," Emerson interrupted.

"No, no, my dear. There were *two* mummy cases. From that fact arose much of the confusion. Both are now destroyed, but I fancy they were twin coffins, made at the same time by the same craftsman. Belonging, I do not doubt, to a husband and wife who wished to express their mutual affection by eventually occupying identical—"

"Never mind that, Amelia," Emerson growled. "The point is that they were made of the same materials—waste linen and old papyrus, dampened and molded into shape before being painted. Such cartonnage coffins are common; fragments of Greek manuscripts have been found in some. We should have realized that our papyrus scraps came from such a source."

"My dear Emerson, you do yourself an injustice," I said. "Our papyrus was Coptic, not Greek; Christian, not pagan. The baroness's mummy case obviously belonged to a worshipper of the old gods. It was early Roman in date, and Christianity did not become the official religion of the Empire until 330 A.D., under Constantine the Great. Yet the Coptic Church was established in the first century, and Egyptian Christians survived, though subjected to cruel persecution, until—"

"Until they got the chance to persecute everyone else," said Emerson.

"I beg you will refrain from expressing your unorthodox religious opinions just now, Emerson. I am endeavoring to explain that Christian writings of the first and second centuries did exist, and that it would be natural for a pagan to consider them waste paper, fit to be used in the construction of a coffin."

"Granted, granted," de Morgan said, before Emerson could pursue his argument. "I will grant anything you like, madame, if you will only get on with your story. This business of the twin coffins—"

"It is really very simple," I said, with a kindly smile. "Abd el Atti gained possession of the two mummy cases; they came, of course, from the same tomb. One, belonging to the wife, may have been damaged to begin with. Abd el Atti realized the papyrus used in its construction contained Coptic writing. Being a shrewd old rascal, he understood the nature of his find—"

"And looked for a customer who would appreciate its value," Emerson broke in. "Unluckily for him, the clergyman he approached was a religious fanatic. Ezekiel Jones was no mean scholar. His crude manners and speech caused us to underestimate him, but there were, in fact, a number of indications of his intellectual ability, including his knowledge of Greek. He translated the manuscript Abd el Atti sold him, and the startling revelations in the text drove him over the brink into madness. He determined to destroy the blasphemous manuscript. But it was incomplete. He visited Abd el Atti on the night of the murder. . . ."

Emerson's breath gave out, and I took up the story. "He went there in search of the rest of the manuscript. No doubt he had harassed and threatened Abd el Atti; the old man was in deadly fear— not, as I had supposed, of his criminal associates, but of the unbeliever who was behaving so strangely. On that last night Abd el Atti admitted to Ezekiel that there had been two coffins, one of which had been sold to the baroness. He also told Ezekiel I had a fragment from the first coffin. Ezekiel went berserk. He strangled the old man then and there—"

"And hanged him from the roofbeam," Emerson said grimly. "There was always a suggestion of ritual murder in that, for why go to the trouble of hanging a man who is already dead? I took it for some ceremony of the gang Abd el Atti had betrayed; but did not Judas, the greatest of traitors, hang himself, and was not David's treacherous and beloved son Absalom found hanging from a tree? In Ezekiel's darkening mind it was the proper treatment for a blasphemer."

"Ezekiel broke into our room at Shepheard's hoping to retrieve the fragment," I went on. "He had removed the remaining pieces of the first mummy case from Abd el Atti's shop the night of the murder. He was not interested in the mummy; along with other items it was knocked over and the painted panel fastened to it was dislodged from the wrappings. That was the painting Emerson—"

"Ahem," said Emerson loudly. "So much for the first coffin and mummy. The second, that of Ther-

moutharin, was in the salon of the baroness's dahabeeyah. Ezekiel knew his holy mission would not
be complete until he had obtained and destroyed it.
There was a strong possibility that it contained the
remainder of the blasphemous manuscript."

"That clumsy fellow broke into the baroness's
cabin and single-handedly carried off the mummy
case?" de Morgan asked incredulously.

Emerson beat me to the draw, as the American
idiom has it. "No, that was Hamid, with the help of a
few confederates. He knew how desperately Ezekiel
wanted the mummy case. He discarded the mummy
itself, since it was worthless—and heavy—but he removed the painted portrait in an effort to render
the mummy anonymous. I don't know what has become of that painting. Perhaps Hamid sold it to a
passing tourist. The portrait we had, that of—er—
Mrs. Thermoutharin, appeared to fit the mummy of
her husband, because they were the same size."

It was my turn to speak. "Hamid probably took
the other objects he had stolen from the baroness
directly to his leader as proof of his loyalty; but the
leader, who is no fool, was bound to wonder what
he had done with the mummy case and why he had
stolen it in the first place. Hamid could invent some
lie to explain the latter question—he had been mistaken about its value, he had believed it contained
valuable jewels—that sort of thing. But he had to
account for its disappearance. His tricks with the
mummy cases coming and going were designed to
confuse his leader as well as us."

"It was clever of him to conceal his prize among
others of the same sort," Emerson said grudgingly.

"The old 'Purloined Letter' device. He put it in our storeroom and carried one of our coffins into the desert. Later, after Ezekiel had agreed to buy it, he removed it from the storeroom. Ezekiel had no intention of paying him; he had no more money, but he had his murderous hands. The rope around Hamid's neck was a symbolic gesture. Ezekiel could hardly hang the man from the roofbeam of his own house."

"He was still clinging to the rags of sanity then," I remarked.

"You are mixing your metaphors, Peabody, I believe. His hold on reality was weakening every day. But he had sense enough to know he could not hide the mummy case indefinitely. He destroyed it by fire a few days later. That was his real aim, after all—to destroy the manuscript. That," Emerson added nonchalantly, "was one of the vital clues. The Master Criminal—curse it, I mean the leader of the gang— would have no reason to steal an antiquity only to destroy it."

De Morgan could contain himself no longer. "But what was it?" he cried. "What was this terrible manuscript that drove a man to murder?"

There was a brief pause, fraught with drama. Then Emerson turned to Ramses, who had been an interested spectator. "Very well, my boy; not even your mama can deny that you have a right to speak. What was in the manuscript?"

Ramses cleared his throat. "You understand dat I can only t'eorize, since de fragments remaining are only a small fraction of de whole. However—"

"Ramses," I said gently.

"Yes, Mama, I will be brief. I t'ink dat de manuscript is a copy of a lost gospel, written by Didymus Thomas, one of de apostles. Dat much could be surmised from de first fragment. It is de second fragment, found by Mama later, dat may provide an explanation for de madness of Brudder Ezekiel."

"Ramses," said Emerson.

"Yes, Papa. It contained t'ree words. Dey are: 'de son of Jesus.'"

"*Nom de Dieu,*" de Morgan gasped.

"You are quick, monsieur," I said. "You see the significance of those words."

"They may not mean what we think," de Morgan muttered, passing a trembling hand across his brow. "They cannot mean what we think."

"But we may reasonably conclude from the actions of Brother Ezekiel that the lost gospel contained matter he would consider blasphemous and heretical—matter that must never come to light. It is not unheard of even for supposedly sane scholars to suppress data that does not agree with their pet theories. Imagine the effect of such information on a man whose brain was already reeling; who suffered from incipient megalomania."

"You must be right," said de Morgan. "There is no other explanation that fits the facts. *Mais, quel mélodrame!* You are a true heroine, madame; the murderer seized, the thieves routed. . . . I congratulate you from my heart."

I stretched out a hand to Emerson. "Congratulate us both, monsieur. We work together."

"Admirable," said the Frenchman politely. "Well, I must return to work. I only hope the thieves have left me something to discover. What a coup it would be if I could find such a cache!"

"I wish you luck," I said politely. Emerson said nothing.

"Yes, a veritable coup." De Morgan sighed. "My picture would be in the *Illustrated London News*," he explained, rather pathetically. "I have always wanted to be in the *Illustrated London News*. Schliemann has been in the *Illustrated London News*. Petrie has been in the *Illustrated London News*. Why not de Morgan?"

"Why not indeed?" I said. Emerson said nothing.

De Morgan rose and picked up his hat. "Oh, but madame, there is one little thing you have not explained. Your escape from the pyramid was truly marvelous. Accept my felicitations on that escape, by the way; I do not believe I expressed them earlier. But I do not understand why the Master—the leader of the gang—should put you there in the first place. It was the evil Hamid and the insane Ezekiel who were responsible for the other attacks on you, searching for the mummy case and the papyrus. Was the Master—the leader of the gang—also looking for the papyrus?"

Ramses stopped swinging his feet and became very still. Emerson cleared his throat. De Morgan looked inquiringly at him. "A slight touch of catarrh," Emerson explained. "Hem."

De Morgan stood waiting. "It seems," I said, "that the leader—the Master Criminal—was under the impression we had some other valuables."

"Ah." De Morgan nodded. "Even Master Criminals are sometimes wrong. They suspect everyone, the rascals. *Au revoir, madame. Adieu, professeur.* Come soon to visit me, *mon petit* Ramses."

After the Frenchman had gone out I turned a critical eye on my son. "You must give it back, Ramses."

"Yes, Mama. I suppose I must. T'ank you for allowing me to arrange de matter wit' de least possible embarrassment to myself."

"And to me," Emerson muttered.

"I will go and talk to him immediately," said Ramses.

He suited the action to the word.

De Morgan had mounted his horse. He smiled at the small figure trotting toward him and waited. Ramses caught hold of the stirrup and began to speak.

De Morgan's smile faded. He interrupted Ramses with a comment that was clearly audible even at that distance, and reached out for him. Ramses skipped back and went on talking. After a time a curious change came over the Frenchman's face. He listened a while longer; then he dismounted, and squatted down so that his face was close to Ramses'. An earnest and seemingly amicable dialogue ensued. It went on so long that Emerson, standing beside me, began to mutter. "What are they talking about? If he threatens Ramses—"

"He has every right to beat him to a jelly," I said.

Yet when the conversation ended, de Morgan appeared more puzzled than angry. He mounted. Ramses saluted him courteously and started back toward the house. Instead of riding off, de Morgan sat staring after Ramses. His hand moved in a quick furtive gesture. Had I not known better, I would have sworn the cultured, educated director of the Antiquities Department had made the sign of the evil eye—the protection against diabolic spirits.

II

What was in the lost gospel of Didymus Thomas? We will never know the answer, although Emerson often engages in ribald and unseemly speculation. "Does he describe the trick the disciples played on the Romans, to make them believe a man had risen from the dead? Was Jesus married and the father of children? And what exactly was his relationship with Mary Magdalen?"

Brother Ezekiel, the only living person who actually read part of the lost gospel, will never tell us what it contained. He is a raving lunatic; and I have heard that he wanders the corridors of his home near Boston, Massachusetts, dressed in a simple homespun robe, blessing his attendants. He calls himself the Messiah. He is tended by his devoted sister and his sorrowing disciple, and I suppose that one day—if it has not already occurred—Charity and Brother David will be wed. They have in common not only their devotion to a madman but their invincible stupidity. Some persons cannot be rescued, even by me.

John was sure his heart was broken. He went about for weeks with his large brown hand pressed

to the precise center of his breast, where he errone-
ously believed that organ was located. However,
one of the housemaids is a charming girl, with
mouse-brown hair and a dimple in her cheek, and I
begin to detect signs of convalescence.

We left Egypt in March and returned to England to greet our newest nephew. Mother and infant survived the ordeal in excellent condition. We
had uncovered the substructure of our pyramid
before we left, and although no remarkable discoveries were made I became quite attached to the
place. I was able to abandon it with equanimity, however, since de Morgan had offered us the firman for
Dahshoor the following year. He was not very gracious about it, but that was of small concern to me.
That half-submerged chamber in the heart of the
Black Pyramid—I felt sure that under the dark
water something fascinating awaited us.

It was not until after we had returned to England
that we learned of de Morgan's remarkable discovery of the jewels of the princesses, near the pyramid of Senusret III. It was featured in the *Illustrated
London News*, with a flattering engraving of de Morgan, mustache and all, holding up the crown of Princess Khnumit before the audience he had invited
to admire his discovery. I could not but agree with
Emerson when he flung the paper aside with a critical "These Frenchmen will do anything to get in
the newspaper."

One of the necklaces on the mummy of the princess bore striking resemblance to the one Ramses
had found. I remembered the long conversation

between Ramses and de Morgan; the sudden concession of the Frenchman to our wishes; and I wondered. . . .

The lion seems to have settled in very nicely at Chalfont. Walter has suggested we bring back a young female next time.